RENDER UNTO THE VALLEY

ALSO BY ROSE SENEHI

THE WIND IN THE WOODS

IN THE SHADOWS OF CHIMNEY ROCK

PELICAN WATCH

WINDFALL

SHADOWS IN THE GRASS

RENDER UNTO THE VALLEY

Rose Senehi

KM

Published by

K.I.M. PUBLISHING, LLC
Post Office Box 132
Chimney Rock, NC 28720-0132

Cover design by Debra Long Hampton

Published in the United States of America.

PUBLISHER'S NOTE

This is a work of fiction. Though there are numerous elements of historical and geographical accuracy in this portrait of Fairview, NC, and its environs, the names, places, characters and incidents either are the product of the author's imagination or are used factitiously, and any resemblance to actual persons, living or dead, is entirely coincidental.

PUBLISHER'S CATALOGING-IN-PUBLICATION DATA

Senehi, Rose.
   Render unto the valley / Rose Senehi
      p. cm.
   ISBN 978-0-615-49995-6 (trade pbk. : alk.paper)
   1. Hickory Nut Gorge—North Carolina—Fairview
   —Fiction. 2. Appalachian Region—Southern Fiction.
   3. Habitat (Ecology)—Fiction. I. Title.
      PS3619.E659R6 2012

   Library of Congress Control Number: 2011910366

First Printing: March 2012

For Bruce Whitaker who has kept the history of Fairview

The Charlotte Highway portion of Route 74 snakes through eight hairpin curves on its steep descent from the Hickory Nut Gorge and spills gracefully from the gap onto the lush bottomlands of Fairview on its journey to Asheville, North Carolina.

Farmers and settlers have toiled since the 1700s to make their mark on this valley, but in actuality, this valley has made its mark on them. From the privileged few who brought along their wealth, to the hardy settlers who came to escape religious persecution, the seductive beauty of this valley not only captured their imagination, but also instilled in them an indelible sense of place that would remain for generations.

CHAPTER ONE

February, 1985

Icy air streamed through her nostrils and doused her hopes. The fire hadn't lasted the night. Sunlight ricocheted off the fresh blanket of snow outside and cast a weird pattern of shadows on the crackled ceiling, unleashing the dread she had fought for the twelve years of her life. She drew her knees up to her chest, buried her face under the warmth of the covers and willed the feeling away. She couldn't let every blemish on the old house drag her into a mood, or she wouldn't get the kids through the day with any kind of order.

Her sister's bony elbow stabbed her in the back. She had to get Amy and Travis out hunting for firewood soon, or she'd never get the place warmed up enough to give them their Saturday night baths. A mountain of split logs leaned against the stone hearth, but they used up the last of the kindling yesterday when they came home from school. If only Grandpa would stop handing her mother money for gas, she might stay home and keep the fire going instead of gadding all over the countryside.

Grandpa gave her mother money for heating oil in the fall, and Karen had to bite her tongue every time Granny got a whiff of her smoky clothes and questioned her about the furnace.

"Karen, don't let the kids go on at the mouth with your grandma about our burnin' wood," her mother had yelled to her last Saturday when she dropped them off. Her mother looked all beautiful and carefree with her long black hair and bangs glistening in the sunlight as she slipped an arm around her new boyfriend's shoulder. With the beads around her neck, she looked just like Cher.

Karen wondered if her mother's boyfriend, Wally, was still in the back bedroom. They'd made a lot of noise when they came in last night, and the reek of corn whiskey lingered in the air long after her mother peeked in their room.

Karen didn't mind him as much as some of the others since he kept his hands off her. But he smacked Travis a couple of times for staring at him, and she didn't like the way he kept asking Amy to sit on his lap. They all knew she was way too old for that sort of thing.

She turned and nudged Amy's shoulder, gently. "Come on, you and Travis gotta help me gather kindlin'." Karen didn't want to tell Amy right now, but she was hell-bent on the three of them stacking enough in the back room to last the rest of the winter. With all the wood her mother's last boyfriend lugged in, she was sure they weren't going to get any oil. Last week, the boy who sat behind her got the whole class giggling when he pinched his nose and said she stank like a soggy piece of charred wood. From now on she would get up in the night and get the wood stove going good, so she wouldn't have to get it started again in the morning.

She sat up and threw back the covers.

"You're mean," squealed Amy, who was hugging her kitten.

Karen pried Missy from her sister's arms and placed it on the floor, then watched the poor little critter limp across the room on three legs. Of all the hateful things Travis ever did, cutting off Missy's leg was the meanest.

The two girls dressed in a hurry, and while Amy went to shake Travis awake, Karen hung her English composition marked with a big "A" on the wall where her mother would see it. Pages torn from magazines papered every square inch. Madonna and Billy Joel smiled mindlessly past her, pinned haphazardly over pictures of Glen Campbell and the Carpenters that her mother had plastered on the walls back when she was a kid.

That's where she and her brother got their names, Travis being Glen Campbell's middle name. She loved to hear her mother tell how, two days after she was born, she saw Karen Carpenter on TV singing, *I Won't Last a Day Without You.* "I was only fifteen at the time, honey, but that's how I felt about you."

None of them wanted to face the consequences of waking Wally and making him cross, so they crept quietly down the stairs. As usual, Travis ate his cereal in silence. Karen marveled at how sweet he looked. Sandy blond hair, big blue eyes, and just about the most appealing features she'd ever seen in a boy of nine. He got good marks in school along with commendations for good behavior, so nobody but she and Amy knew what he was really like.

Amy didn't cry when they found her puppy hanging limply from the tree behind the house, but she refused to kiss Travis goodnight after that. Karen wouldn't let Amy say anything to their mother because she knew she'd go and tell one of her boyfriends and sooner or later there'd be talk. She just never let Travis out of her sight.

The narrow-planked oak floor creaked as they pulled on boots and slipped into their jackets—every last one of them navy blue so they could be handed down. Karen pulled the hat Granny had knitted for Amy snug on her sister's head, making her mass of red ringlets balloon out from the edges, then she shepherded them out through the kitchen and into the small room they used for storage. It was the original log cabin Grandpa's people had lived in, with one whole wall a stone fireplace and hearth, and the others neatly nailed over with wide hand-planed planks.

The blinding snow stabbed her in the eyes. Row upon row of long narrow blue shadows cast by the stand of hickory trees knifed across the white blanket. With all the leaves gone and the way the snow cloaked the earth, she could make out all the dark craggy ins and outs of the mountain towering overhead.

Sunlight bounced off the raging stream with its jagged icy edges. Icicles glistened from the barren bushes near enough to get splashed. With the rocks hidden under the snow, it would be tricky gathering tree limbs from the steep part of the mountain. She'd take everyone to the meadow below.

Karen walked ahead onto the virgin layer of snow and pretended she was the regal mistress of a mysterious, pure and perfect world. Travis trudged dutifully behind dragging the sled, with Amy chasing helter-skelter after animal tracks. Karen looked back at the trampled snow and noticed mud oozing from their footprints and quickly looked away. It bothered her to see how easily something could be sullied.

With the air so still, the three were rosy-cheeked and sweaty by the time they reached the meadow.

"Look, Karen, it's frozen," Amy shouted as she ran out on the pond.

"Get off that! You want to drown? You know the ice gets thin in the center."

They worked for more than an hour gathering fallen limbs, breaking them down and packing them tightly onto the sled. Karen used one of the ropes to tie up the first load and fretted about what to do with Amy and Travis. If she let them come with her to unload, she'd have a devil of a time getting them back down. They'd pitch a fit and wake their mother who would let them come in no matter how she pleaded. At the Cane Creek Church last Sunday, Preacher Ryan talked about how not forgiving was a sin, but it was still hard not to resent the way her mother messed things up every time she had them working at something.

Amy and Travis were doing pretty good and into the rhythm of gathering. "You two keep getting firewood, and stack it right here. I'll take this load up and be back with a couple of cookies.

Travis, don't let Amy wander off. You hear me?"

"Yeah, I hear ya."

It took longer to stack the kindling than she intended, but still she tiptoed inside for the cookies. If her mother and Wally were up and heard her, they'd yell down for her to make them breakfast.

She started to close the cupboard door, and thought she heard something outside. She stopped and listened. Nothing. Probably just a jay. Suddenly a horrid shadow shot across her consciousness. She ran out of the kitchen, through the storeroom and down the path, barely keeping from slipping and tripping on the rocks and gnarled tree roots as she flew. She strained her eyes to see the clearing ahead, and her heart thumped at the eerie sight of the deserted landscape.

A shrill cry from a bird punctured the silence. As she got closer to the pond she could see the snow was disturbed and Amy's hat lay balled up in a clump next to a crack in the ice.

An arm rose silently from out of the pond, then slowly disappeared.

Terror clawed her brain. She searched frantically for the rope she'd left lying on the ground and quickly tied one end to a tree and held on as she crept out onto the ice. Now, close to the shattered crack, she could feel the ice billowing up and down. *Do you want to drown? The ice is thin in the middle.*

She quickly tied the rope around her waist and gave herself just enough slack to reach the water. She lay down on her belly and shimmied to the spot. A bloated navy blue jacket slowly emerged on the surface of the water. She lunged for it, dug in her fingernails and pulled Travis over the edge. His blue face made her gasp.

She dragged him to where the ice was solid, then pumped on his chest, crying and shrieking Amy's name and staring at the still water until her eyeballs ached.

Water spewed from Travis's mouth. He choked. She grabbed him up in her arms and rocked him as she threw her head back and cried out in anguish for Amy. Suddenly a hand on her shoulder startled her and she almost dropped Travis. Amy stood next to her, calm and dreamy like.

"Oh my God! Amy! What happened?!"

The corners of Amy's lips turned up slightly, "Nothin'. The ice broke and he fell in."

"Why in God's name didn't you holler for help?!"

Amy looked off in the distance with a pout on her face. "I guess now we're just gonna have to take him back home."

CHAPTER TWO

April 2010

HOW MANY TIMES can you reinvent yourself? She got away with it once, but when her husband Joel died, so did Karen Godwell, leaving no one but the steely mountain girl she buried inside her the day she walked into the freshman dorm at North Carolina's Salem College. The murky dread she thought was gone had started to creep back in. But this time it was different. It had more guilt in it than shame.

Karen drifted onto the bus and studied the passengers. They looked different—foreign, yet intrinsic to the exhilarating city swirling around them like an eddy. She gripped a handrail overhead and yearned for the swaying rhythm to carry her to the same comforting zone she knew when Granny rocked her by the fireplace.

The bus stopped in front of New York's Metropolitan Museum, and the crowd streamed out in their colorful spring garb like a school of koi. Her dark suit was a blot on the swarm.

Horns blared from every direction and she looked around. A

young man in cuffed jeans and a tight-fitting black tee shirt straight out of *West Side Story* was piling out of a beat-up white van and backing up traffic. The girl behind the wheel watched nervously in the rearview mirror as he wrestled out band instruments. Karen smiled at the street performer's determination and wished him luck. She remembered what it was like to need money.

He yanked out a guitar case with one hand and a drum stand with the other and the case unlatched. He let go of the stand in a desperate attempt to catch the guitar before it hit the pavement. Karen ran out in the path of an oncoming bus and snatched it up.

Why did I do that? she asked herself as she handed the stand to him, ignoring the crowd of bystanders. She hated the way she was always making herself useful, as if she had to earn her place. A gust of wind swirled her long chestnut hair around her face as she tossed a brisk wave to the grateful young man and dashed up the first flight of stairs to the museum.

She would go straight to the American Wing to see how her Appalachian crafts exhibit was shaping up. It was going to be tough facing everyone for the first time since the funeral, but she spotted her favorite guard at the door and her apprehension faded a little.

"Good to see you back, Ma'am." He swung open the door.

She wanted to hug him. How many hurting people had the tall dignified man's tender voice soothed? Yes. This was where she belonged, she told herself, and she had to hang onto it until she got a grip on herself.

Invisible ears listened to her spike heels tap out the rhythm of her self-confident gait across the marble-cloaked Great Hall. She threaded her way through the deserted museum to the American Wing and slipped through the door to the temporary wall hiding the unfinished exhibit.

Someone from the set-up crew was already straddling a ladder and hanging a sign. She waved and he nodded, then she slowly reviewed the exhibit she had put together with the curator of Asheville's Folk Art Center before Joel's condition had turned critical. This was the first time the center had loaned out such a big chunk of their traditional Southern Appalachian crafts. Small by Met standards, she had been pleased when someone told her the exhibit was getting a fair amount of buzz.

Clicking of heels sounded from behind.

Her assistant had heard she was in the building and rushed down from her office on the third floor. Carrie Castilano bounced along like she was comfortable in her own skin. In her late twenties, she was short and plump and wore her hair in a cropped pixy cut that matched her personality. Karen liked her a lot. Carrie had whispered into her black veil at the cemetery: *You're only thirty-five, Karen. You've got your whole life ahead of you. Think of little Hali.*

Karen was convinced that only God could have dropped this refreshingly genuine person in her lap. With the intense competition for the prized curator spots, the world-famous institution was a hothouse of ruthlessly ambitious and brilliantly talented individuals willing to stop at nothing to get to the top of the heap. And Karen was working for the master of the craft.

"It looks great, Carrie." Karen gave her a hug. "You really came through for me."

"I just followed the plan." Carrie went over to a weather-beaten gate. The slats were made of five crudely carved wooden figures that a long time ago must have represented a mountain family. "This piece was so fantastic I put it where people will spot it the moment they walk in." She cocked her head and raised an eyebrow. "It can stay there, can't it?"

Karen smiled to herself. *Carrie gets it.* The gate spoke of mountain folk art more than anything in the collection. A farmer needed a gate, but not just any gate would do. She pictured him lovingly carving it in his isolated log cabin in front of the evening fire while the whole family stood by like a somber Greek chorus. The crude figures probably didn't look a whole lot like the family members, but enough for them to know which one they were.

Karen put an arm around Carrie. "Sure it can stay. I don't want to lose an argument on my first day back."

A question had been on Karen's mind for the past week, and now was as good a time as any to ask. "Are you going to take that job at the Folk Art Center in Asheville?" *Oh, God. If only Joel had made it, I would have taken it myself,* she had cried out in her head when Carrie told her about it. She would have had to go from a hefty six-figure salary to somewhere in the low fifties, but it would have been worth it to see Joel happy. Now, it was a perfect fit for Carrie, since she didn't have the temperament to slug it out for a curator position at the Met.

"I'm going to pass it up. I was tempted… but I can't move away from my mother right now. She's not doing well."

Karen's throat tightened. That morning she had awakened with a desperation she hadn't felt since the day after her mother stuffed all their things into a pillow case, and then dumped the three of them off at Granny's. From the smug look on the boyfriend's face as he and her mom drove away, she knew she'd never see her again. Her mother had to be hitting fifty. Was *she* doing well? Or even alive? If she was, did she ever think of her? *I won't last a day without you,* played in her head.

Karen became aware of Carrie's concerned stare as she brushed away a tear. She had promised herself she would be utterly unemotional today; and now, not yet ten o'clock, she was already coming apart.

They moved along. "It looks good," Karen said as she stopped to admire a hand-carved rocking chair. A quilt was artfully draped across it. She fought off an urge to pick it up and wrap it around herself and spend the rest of the morning rocking away the hurt.

"Have you seen Earl yet?" Carrie asked.

Earl had been Karen's boss since before she landed her position as curator of special exhibitions for the American Wing.

"Not yet."

"He's been in a bad mood lately over the Bernie Madoff scam."

Just what she needed to hear, thought Karen. Joel's money was in the same rat hole. Thank God, news of the Ponzi scheme hadn't surfaced until after Joel was too ill to care about anything but staying alive. Now that the dividends had dried up, she had to sell the co-op and find something smaller and farther uptown.

18

She gazed at the exhibit, but saw only blurred images somewhere off in the distance. One bad thing after another seemed to be coming at her, prophesizing doom. She felt suddenly unnerved. It was as if, one at a time, all the layers she'd sheathed herself in were being stripped away, down to that scrappy mountain girl with dirt in her nails and a twang in her voice.

"Are you all right Karen?" Carrie was staring at her, brows furrowed.

"I'm fine." Karen was embarrassed her attention had to be refocused by her assistant again, and she moved on to another part of the exhibit. After nearly an hour checking things out, she asked Carrie to finish up so she could pay her boss the respect of a visit before going to her office and getting buried under six weeks of backlog.

The sign on the door read *Earl Williams, Director, The American Wing.* Karen Godwell was definitely dead. Before Joel got sick, there wasn't a night she didn't go to sleep thinking she would kill for his job. Now she felt nothing.

She knocked and went in. As usual, his antique mahogany desktop lay barren except for the ubiquitous Post-its meticulously lined up in rows. Facing his desk was the high-back chair he dragged out every time he expected a donor. It was upholstered in green brocade because he believed colors had psychological powers, with green meaning *go* and red *stop.* Assuming yellow meant caution, once she had gotten her own office, she hadn't been able to resist playing with his head a little. She had the walls painted bright mustard and brought in red chairs.

"I see you're expecting someone," she said.

The phone rang before he could respond. She sat down on the edge of the chair, gingerly, as if she didn't deserve the honor since she wasn't there to hand a hefty check to the museum. She smiled inwardly as Earl casually straightened the silk hanky in his pocket, making sure his diligently cultivated *GQ* image remained intact. His thick shock of white hair was combed straight back from his handsome eternally tanned face. He was at the top of his form.

The donors' chair proving uncomfortable, she got up and went over to an item that caught her eye as she entered. What had to be a priceless Gilbert Stuart painting was propped up on an easel. The beautiful woman in a delicate, white lace dress took her breath away. Ever since she wrote her Master's thesis on how Early American dynasties dominated the art of the era, she had a keen interest in the personalities depicted in the paintings of the time. Besides dozens of portraits of George Washington, Stuart did over a thousand of notable colonists, and she was dying to know just who this elegant lady was.

Finished with his call, Earl came to stand beside her.

"Where did you get it?" she asked.

"It's from the Whettle collection."

"She's beautiful."

"Yes, she is." He turned to her with a raised eyebrow. "But she's a fake."

"You mean this is *not* a Stuart?"

"The folks from research are coming to get it this afternoon. They'll carbon date it and go at it with their whole arsenal, but I'm sure in the end they're going to agree with me that it was forged sometime in the early 1800s. It's a shame. It's been in the Whettle family since 1838, and they assumed she was one of their ancestors."

His hands became animated, yet he was careful not to touch the painting. "It's a wonderful likeness of a Stuart portrait... the glowing colors... look at the vivid pinks... the bold white splashes. The artist was good..." He turned to Karen and shook his finger. "...but not good enough to fool this trained eye." He leaned close enough to the painting to almost touch it with his nose. "Notice how the brushwork doesn't quite capture Stuart's controlled spontaneity. He always used flamboyant layers of quick light strokes. These are a *little* too timid. A *little* too studied. Unfortunately, they stop short of Stuart's brilliance." He shook his head. "She's gorgeous... but undoubtedly a fake."

Karen left impressed with another of her boss's masterful appraisals. You could only be that good if you lived for art... had the love of it running through your veins. She needed that today.

Anything that would make sense of her coming back.

A passion for protecting and sharing the beauty created by the hand of man permeated the halls of the museum, and she knew Earl had what it would take to eventually move into its top position—genius coupled with unbridled ambition. An empty feeling overcame her, and the thought of eventually moving into his spot as the head of the American Wing when he got there suddenly held none of the excitement that had driven her for the past fifteen years.

She reached the back hallway and yanked open the glass door with more force than necessary, annoyed with the outrage that washed over her when she found out the beautiful woman in the painting was a phony. Probably the daughter of some farmer or tradesman all dressed up to look like an aristocrat.

Thank God, she was finally alone. She stopped and leaned back against the cold marble. What was she doing here? Joel was supposed to beat the colon cancer, and they were going to restore the old creek house Granny gave them. He'd finally be starting on the novel he had wanted to write since college. She thumped her head against the wall and stared up at the ceiling. God, why didn't I go along with his dream while we had a chance? Maybe he wouldn't have gotten sick if I had.

This question would always haunt her. Only she knew that something other than her career had kept her from going back home, an ugly something she'd trained herself never to think about. She wanted to jump out of her skin. She failed the kindest man she'd ever known.

Someone turned the corner up ahead, and she forced a smile. Then two more people stopped to express their condolences before she escaped to her office. She quickly shuffled through a fistful of phone messages her receptionist handed her, stopping at one from Amy. Her breathing quickened. Her sister would only call her at work if something were wrong. She punched in the numbers and pictured herself on a crowded evening flight to Charlotte. The mountains tugged at her like some dreadful unfinished business.

"Valley View Kennel."

"Amy, it's me."

"What did I tell ya, girl. That brother of ours has gotten up to no good again."

Thank God, that's all. Karen slowly let out the breath she'd been holding and fell back in her chair. "What is it this time?"

"He's gone and put Granny in a nursing home in Asheville."

Something clutched at Karen's gut. An image of Granny being torn from her beloved farm gave her an icy shiver.

"Karen, are you still there?" asked Amy.

Karen muttered a response.

"And gettin' her out ain't gonna be easy. You got no idea the kind of shit Travis has pulled. I've been too busy with all the puppies comin' on in the kennel to visit Granny much... in fact, I hadn't seen her since I went over and told her about Joel. I was fixin' to, but I couldn't stand to set eyes on that brother of ours."

Why did her sister have to go on like that! "Amy, for God's sake, spit it out!"

"Well... when I couldn't get hold of her last week, I drove to the homeplace and there was Travis... as big as life, sittin' on the porch chewin' on a toothpick with that shit-eatin' grin on his face. When I started to go in, he blocked my way. I told him I was there to see Granny and to get his filthy hands off me. He said it was his house now, and if I wanted to see Granny I had to go on down to the nursing home."

"What sort of explanation did he give?"

"Well, we all know Granny's been slippin,' but I wouldn't exactly call her a vegetable like he did. I marched right over to Cousin Bruce. He spent the better part of Friday checking out what Travis said, and sure 'nough, Granny's in a nursing home in Asheville, Travis has her power of attorney and the farm's been put in his name. All six hundred acres."

"That's impossible."

"That's what I said, but Bruce was over here this morning with a copy of the deed he had someone at the Register of Deeds run off. Bruce says there's nothing much we can do 'cept take him to court."

Thank God, Granny had given her the old creek house they

had lived in when they were kids, thought Karen. "Have you seen Granny yet?"

"Yeah… and once I got a look at the place, I tried to take her home, but they wouldn't hear of it. Got downright nasty. Threatened to call the police when I tried to wheel her out. They say Travis is the only one who can do that, and only after her doctor releases her. Lord, I do hope no one ever puts me away in that kind of place. It ain't that easy gettin' out."

"Amy, don't get yourself all worked up over this. I promise you we're going to turn this around." I'm going to turn this around if it kills me, was what she really meant. Granny's farm wasn't some six-room co-op that changed hands every three years. It was six hundred acres saturated with five generations of blood, sweat and tears.

Family stories she'd heard time and time again echoed in her ears. All the characters who endured gut-wrenching hardships to hold onto the land for over two hundred years suddenly came alive. She hardly heard a word.

"Granny was fixin' to give us two hundred acres each and put some kind of easement on the property so no one could ever chop it up for a bunch of houses. She was downright adamant about that. She'd never give everything to Travis outright."

While Amy carried on about how much she and Eddie were counting on getting the land, Karen's thoughts locked onto the woman in the painting who'd gotten away with her charade for over two hundred years. She gasped as if she'd been running so hard she had to stop dead in her tracks and suck air in her lungs or they would burst. The only thing that running away from the past had gotten her was failing Joel… and now Granny. The job at the Folk Art Center shot into her head and stuck.

"Stop worrying, Amy. I'm coming home."

CHAPTER THREE

HALI'S SHORT CANDY-STRIPED skirt swished around her pink Capri tights as she waltzed across her room to the doorway and leaned into the hall. "Mom, can I please ask Mamie over to help me finish packing?" Hearing no response, she got a running start down the hall and catapulted into a cartwheel. She landed on her feet in front of her mother who was packing some books in the living room, unfazed by the stunt.

Hali caught her breath. "Well, Mom, can I?" A gauzy pink scarf held her hair in a ponytail, lopsided as if she'd done it herself. Masses of red ringlets circled her flushed freckled face. At ten, her baby fat was waning and her features a veiled image of what she would look like when she grew up. "Come on, Mom. Can I?"

Karen glanced up from a book she held in her hand, weighing if she should keep it or give it to Goodwill. "Why don't you put some slippers on those bare feet?"

"Mom, I figure if we're going to be hillbillies, I might as well get used to it."

"Ha, ha. Now go back to your room and finish packing."

Hali flung herself onto the couch bottom-first and slapped an arm over the back.

Karen opted for Goodwill and tossed the book in the box. "I mean it, Hali. Get up and get going."

"Why can't I just go get my Mamie?"

Hali always called Monique Segal her Mamie, their French nickname for grandmother. She was only in her fifties, but she'd never been married and seized upon Hali as the granddaughter she'd never had. She lived in the co-op next door and, with Joel's mother and brother Marty, made up their New York family.

"We're putting enough on Monique, asking her to handle the movers. We've got to have every last thing packed before we take off tomorrow. Now get in there and put what's left in boxes, and I'll come and help you label everything when you're done."

"First, can I have another piece of your retirement cake?"

Karen looked at her watch. "Honey, it's almost four. You can have another piece after dinner." She shot her a glance, "And I'm not retired."

"Yeah, I forgot. You're re-cycled."

Hali suddenly jumped off the couch and raced back to her room. Shortly, the notes of *Turkey in the Straw* echoed down the hall. Karen took a peek and saw Hali wearing a straw hat and fiddling on her violin with a big grin. This stunt finally succeeded in making her laugh. She shouted loud enough to be heard, "I don't know if North Carolina's ready for you, babe."

Karen had been packing nights for two weeks and nothing was left but things she'd put out on purpose. Boxes were stacked almost to the ceiling and the rugs were rolled up. Carefully wrapped paintings and prints leaned against a wall.

She strolled into the kitchen. The disconnected refrigerator with its door propped open looked unflatteringly naked without all the magnets and drawings. She flipped up the lid of the pizza box and the sight of two slices floating on oil-stained cardboard gave her an unsettling feeling she quickly fought off. She had to stop thinking of herself and Hali as two souls adrift and focus on getting to the mountains and taking care of Granny.

Over the past weeks she had gotten nowhere over the phone

with the nursing home. She'd been speaking almost daily with her second cousin, Bruce Whitfield, who assured her Granny was all right, but kept insisting she get a lawyer and go after her brother. It all seemed so easy to Bruce, but he didn't know the whole story. As long as Granny was safe, the lawyer could wait until she had a chance to sit down and talk with Travis.

She slapped the pizza box shut and shoved it into a plastic trash bag together with the empty coffee cups and condiment packets left over from two days of takeout. Tonight she and Hali would go to Mama Rosa's on the corner and sit down to a decent meal.

There wasn't much left of the cake from her party at the museum. She trimmed off all the edges Hali had picked at, cut what was left into four neat pieces and lifted them onto a paper plate. Before tossing the box in the trash, she peeked down the hall to make sure Hali wasn't looking, then popped a chunk of discarded cake into her mouth.

Finished in the kitchen, she went over to the couch, picked up Hali's calico cat, Bonnie, and sank down, confident their last night in the co-op was going to go smoothly since she didn't think she had anything left to cry with. She pressed her eyes tight at the thought of the way she had fallen apart the night she packed Joel's clothes. Hali had to run and get Monique who gave her a shot of vodka and put her to bed.

Bonnie stood up and stretched, then spotting something, leapt to the floor and batted it around. Karen reached over and snatched up the dust ball and noticed a small item buried inside. She rubbed it clean and saw it was the quarter-carat diamond earring she'd misplaced years ago when she'd been up all night helping Joel finish his first major article for *Sports Illustrated*.

So much came back to her in stabbing waves. The barren walls had witnessed so much happiness. Years ago when they were waiting for the truck to deliver their furniture, Joel had looked so proud to be bringing in enough money to buy the place. He had slowly led her up against the wall in the kitchen, lifted her skirt and pressed against her. She could almost feel his hand running along her thigh.

A knock at the door startled her. She jumped up and opened it as far as the chain would allow, letting in the familiar smell of ethnic foods that permeated the building. Monique Segal stood looking just the way Karen knew she would always picture her—stylish and elegant. She still had the slim figure and bearing of a woman in her thirties. A bright purple silk scarf was wrapped around her slender neck and pinned in place with a jewel-studded antique brooch.

Karen unlatched the chain and swung the door open singing out, "Hali, Mamie's here."

Monique handed a box to Karen as Hali ran down the hall. "There's some pastries for you to take to the jungle."

Karen rolled her eyes, forgivingly.

Hali ran up and wrapped her arms around Monique, then tugged at her. "Come help me finish packing."

Karen listened to the soft laughter coming from Hali's room and wondered if she were making a mistake. Hali seemed to be handling Joel's passing so well. Was this the right time to take her away from all she'd ever known or loved? Karen meandered down the hall, leaned against the door frame and watched Monique lovingly tuck Hali's stuffed animals into a box.

Monique had been Joel's friend first. She worked as a buyer at Macy's, and one day when she told him how she was sent as a child to live with a Jewish family in Maine while her mother fought in the French Resistance, he encouraged her to tell her story in a book. It turned into a history of women who fought in the French Resistance and was published with great praise.

But in the end, it was she and Monique who bonded the tightest. From the moment they discovered they both had lost their mothers in childhood, they were drawn to each other like two survivors grasping for a life raft.

Monique looked up and pointed to the twin beds Karen and Hali had been sleeping in ever since Joel was taken to the hospital. "Tomorrow, just leave everything. I'll take the sheets up and wash them."

Karen sank down on a bed. "We're really going to miss you. I hope you won't forget us."

Monique sat down next to her, pulled out a lace hanky and wiped her eyes. "You need me to tell you this, after seven years?"

Karen patted her leg. "We'll let you know when the movers will be coming. The realtor wants everything out and the place painted as soon as possible, but I don't want the furniture to arrive in North Carolina before we've got the house ready."

Hali sat down next to them, draped herself on Monique's shoulder, and they all fell deep in thought.

"I wish you didn't have to sell this place," said Monique.

"We don't have a choice."

"That bastard Madoff! To think you two have to go live in a jungle with money troubles."

Hali threw an arm in the air with a flourish. "Don't worry, Mamie, we can always set up a still."

"Still? What are you talking about?"

Karen shook her head. "Ignore her, Monique."

THE NEXT MORNING on Route 17, a tractor trailer roaring by their SUV failed to waken Hali, but produced a mournful yowl from Bonnie. Her carrier sat on one of the stacks of boxes that filled the vehicle. They were bringing two inflatable mattresses and enough clothes, linens and kitchenware to last until the movers showed up.

Hali woke up groggy as the SUV turned off Interstate 81 in Maryland just over the Pennsylvania state line. She didn't say much during the lunch at McDonalds, and after munching a couple of Monique's pastries and texting a few of her friends she seemed content to just watch the scenery go by before dozing off again.

As the SUV approached Winchester, VA., Karen didn't want to miss this chance to show Hali the lush green Shenandoah Valley below. She glanced over to see how soundly she was sleeping. *Poor darling. She's just like Joel.* He always passed out after every major assignment, too. Hali looked so peaceful she decided not to wake her, but it troubled Karen that Hali had barely shed a tear other than at the cemetery when she had to be carried away by her uncle. When she had mentioned her concerns to Monique, the sadness in her friend's eyes told her Hali had done her crying in her Mamie's arms.

It occurred to her, as the road carried them deeper into the Blue Ridge Mountains and farther from New York, that her relationship with her daughter had to be rebuilt around just the two of them. Joel had been irrepressibly playful, and from the moment they first met, she always had to be careful to laugh in all the right places. But, by the time Hali was six, he had met his match, and it was like a pint-sized Lucille Ball meets Jim Carrey, with her ending up as the object of the dynamic duo's incessant teasing—a niche she was comfortable with.

And then there was Monique. The intimacy she and Hali had developed, traipsing all over New York together weekends while Karen was stuck at the museum, was going to be a tough one to duplicate, but she was counting on this new job to give her the time she needed to do it. With Joel and Monique gone, her wonderful harbor of community had dissolved. After years of artfully balancing work and family, she was back where she never wanted to be again, solely responsible for the well-being of the entire family.

Sticking to her new role was a challenge. When she went for the interview at the Folk Art Center, the director held back from hiring her because she refused to start until Hali finished the semester. But he finally agreed to wait when their curator promised to do some commuting, and he got Earl's glowing recommendation. She never doubted Earl would come through for her, because that was his style—never make an enemy unless it buys you something—and he knew there was nothing he could do to keep her.

During that trip, she'd only spent enough time at the creek house to meet with a contractor and order a heat pump and a new roof. She'd never purchased anything for the co-op in New York except furniture and wall hangings, but if they were going to live there, these things needed to be done.

All in all, she was surprised at what good shape the place was in. Mostly because Granny always had one of her hired hands living there with his family and things got taken care of.

Other than driving past the homeplace and not being able to go in, the toughest part of the trip had been visiting Granny in Asheville. She had just lain there, motionless; and when they came in to change her diaper, her skeletal appearance dashed any hopes of bringing her home.

The nurse's gentle handling convinced Karen that the place wasn't as bad as Amy had made it out to be, but she still needed to straighten things out with her brother so she could talk with Granny's doctor and get some answers.

Almost to Roanoke, she pulled into the first motel she spotted off Route 81, and with the help of the girl who checked them in, found a restaurant.

There was something about the place, or maybe it was the breathtaking scenery that had whizzed by her for the past seven hours, that made Karen feel strangely alive. The place had a welcoming lived-in ambience that was helped along by lighthearted laughter and the murmur of pleasant conversations.

"Ladies, I'll give you a minute to decide what you want and I'll be right back," the waitress told them. She had an easy, friendly way about her. Karen picked up on her mountain accent. Slight, but it was there all right.

The woman's slow mellow tone brought so much back. Karen reached across the table, took Hali's hands in hers and batted back tears. "Mama's taking you home, baby."

Seeing a veil of worry spread across Hali's face, she added, "Don't worry. I'm crying because I'm happy, honey. I know this whole thing's crazy. Packing up... leaving a job most people would kill for... and... wait 'til you see the house." She rolled her eyes. "Honey, you have to promise me you won't tell Monique how rustic it is."

Hali picked up a breadstick, twirled it in the air and thought for a moment. She raised her eyebrow with a twinkle, "I think she already knows. When we were packing, she said, *Why such a fuss about clothes you're going to wash on rocks in the river?*"

Karen laughed, and Hali broke into a grin.

The nice lady came back with a basket of warm Italian bread

and took their order. They fell silent until Karen felt it was her turn to joke around. "I should tell you what's not to worry about, tripping on the chickens on your way to the outhouse."

Hali slowly shook her head. "Don't try so hard, Mom. You can't take Dad's place."

The food arrived and Karen dug in, not daring to look up.

Hali reached over and patted her hand. "I love you, Mom. But, face it, you're not funny."

Karen looked up at Hali's unruffled expression and smiled, relieved that her daughter had the sense to nip her attempt as a sidekick in the bud.

Hali folded her hands in her lap. The way her shoulders slumped made her look fragile. "Mom, I don't think what you're doing is all that nutty. I'm glad we left New York. Every night I kept listening for Daddy to come down the hall and kiss me goodnight. One day on the playground I was sure I saw him on the street and I ran along the fence until I caught up with him; but... it wasn't Daddy."

Karen didn't tell her she suspected something like that had happened when the school called and said they found her crying against the chain-link fence and had to pry her hands free.

They didn't talk much after that, each wrapped in her own thoughts. Karen left what she figured must have been a bigger tip than the waitress was used to from the enthusiastic way she urged them to come back again as they walked out the door.

When they pulled into the motel parking lot, they put some food and fresh water in Bonnie's carrier. Hali begged to have the cage door left open so the cat could get out and walk around in the SUV a little. Karen reluctantly agreed and they went into the motel.

Someone new was behind the counter. Had to be the night shift since she gave them such a perky greeting. Once they found their room, Karen flicked on the TV for Hali, then went in to take a shower.

Stepping out of the tub, she caught a glimpse of her figure in the mirror and let the towel slip to the floor. All the exercising, all the hundreds of incredibly irresistible pastries she waved away, all the fasting if she put on so much as a half-pound... all for naught. She did it for Joel. He said she was the most beautiful woman he'd ever seen, and she had wanted to keep him thinking that for as long as she could. She slipped into her pajamas and gave herself another glance. *To hell with it. Tomorrow morning, for the first time in twenty years, I'm going to eat a stack of pancakes.*

When she entered the room, the TV was off and Hali was pulling her pajamas out of her backpack. "I'm tired, Mom. I'm gonna get ready for bed."

While Hali was in the bathroom, Karen checked her BlackBerry for the first time that day and couldn't decide whether she was relieved or disappointed that there wasn't a single message. Hali came out wearing an oversized tee shirt bearing a picture of Beethoven with *da da da daaa* printed underneath, and jumped into bed.

Karen sat down beside her and started to tuck her in. Suddenly a grin surfaced and she said, "I may not be funny but I can still tickle," and went at her with her fingers.

Hali rolled into a ball, laughing, "*Stop! Stop!*"

Karen gently patted Hali's head, then twirled one of her curls around her finger the way she used to do with Amy's hair when she was a kid. She kissed Hali on the forehead and looked into her green eyes. "Baby, I want you to know that you can come to me and cry whenever you want. I can take it."

Hali tucked a shock of her mother's hair behind her ear. "Mom, Daddy told me to take care of you... so... you can come to me and cry whenever *you* want. I can take it, too."

Karen gave her a hug, turned off the lights and went over to the window. She could see the glow from the cars on the interstate. It was easy to tell the big semis...all lit up so you could read the signs on their sides. Another stratagem dreamed up by some marketing maven. Can't even escape them in the dark.

This was the first time she and Hali had talked about Joel as if they had accepted his passing as a fact of life, and she had a sneaky suspicion that the whole conversation had been orchestrated by her daughter. Evidently, she wasn't the only one who wanted to restructure their relationship.

The endless trail of red lights snaking along the interstate toward North Carolina made her think about the days ahead. What was Travis like now that he was in his thirties? She hadn't seen much of him since she left for college. Just the time she took Joel home to meet everyone. Back then, Joel sensed something was wrong with Travis, and she wanted to tell him everything; but as time went on, she came to the conclusion it was just as well she hadn't.

CHAPTER FOUR

I F THE DOOR hadn't been locked, they would have sworn
Bonnie had escaped. Instead, she had burrowed under the
boxes, and they only knew she was there from her angry yowl.
With the food untouched and the litter box unused, she was
going to be one unhappy cat by the time they reached Fairview, a
good four hours away.

A strum of a banjo played in Karen's head as they cruised
south along Interstate 77. Noticing the sign for Galax, Karen
tossed her head toward the exit. "Honey, someday I want to take
you there to pick some galax leaves. They're a beautiful dark
green and stay fresh for weeks."

Hali leaned forward and studied her mother's face. "Next
you'll be telling me you're going to take me square dancing."

Karen threw her a grinning glance. "Heck. Why not?" She
swayed with the SUV as it sailed around a camping trailer. "I bet
they're still holding them at The Big House." The way Hali was
frowning, Karen saw she didn't understand. "It's what they call
Sherrill's Inn up on the mountain overlooking the Hickory Nut
Gap. A mile or so from our place. It's a big ole drover's inn

where folks taking their livestock to market in Charlotte used to stay overnight before entering the gorge. Cousin Bruce told me they still hold square dances there for folks in the gap."

Hali pulled out her cell phone and started texting her pals, disappointing Karen. Her daughter was totally indifferent to one of the most beautiful sections of the Blue Ridge Mountains, only a glance away. That fact alone convinced her this move was a good idea.

When they hit Interstate 40 that crosses the state of North Carolina east to west, an unexpected sensation washed over Karen. A yearning to be back home. The last time she made the trip was twelve years ago with Joel right after they were married, and she had dreaded every mile. She had feared the minute Granny would open her mouth and spew out her mountain-speak she'd be found out, and Joel would know she was nothing but a hillbilly mountain girl pretending to be someone else.

In fact, she wouldn't have gone at all except out of respect for Granny. It had been more like facing the music than a homecoming. But Joel amazed her. He loved the place. Two days, and this guy who was raised in the concrete jungle was an expert at rounding up the cattle and getting them to a new pasture. He wasn't bad at rocking on the front porch and spinning yarns, either. That hit it off with Granny, a well-known storyteller herself, and had to be what inspired her to give them the old house on the creek on Sugar Hollow Road.

Karen was sure it was to get them to move there... and it worked with Joel. She had cursed the gift every time he came up with another rationale for relocating to the mountains. *He could write anywhere, but what would she do?* Now, the irony of returning without him smarted.

Once they hit Route 9 in Black Mountain and started weaving their way on the narrow two-lane road toward the gorge, Hali put down her phone and gripped the armrest. This scenery wasn't way off in the distance; it was in her face. Granite monoliths rose up a few feet from the freckled nose pressed against the window. The thick forest with trees towering a hundred feet overhead swallowed them in its dark undergrowth.

The SUV hugged the asphalt and danced to the rhythm of the twisting and turning road until it suddenly opened to a view of an abyss four hundred feet below.

"O M G!" gasped Hali.

Karen laughed. The Shenandoah Valley had failed to get a rise out of her city kid, but the trek to the Hickory Nut Gorge grabbed her by the gut, to say nothing of Bonnie who emitted an ominous groan at every swerve.

After the steep climb, Route 9 made a twisty descent down the mountain and spilled into Bat Cave. They turned right onto Route 74 where the road flattened out, settling everyone down.

Suddenly the cat appeared on top of the boxes, making the hair on the back of Karen's neck rise. She quickly nosed the vehicle over to a driveway up ahead. "Hali, Bonnie's right behind you. Be careful, but try to get her into the carrier."

The cat was successfully put back in the cage, and they started their climb through the Hickory Nut Gorge. Karen searched her brain for all the landmarks. If only she could infuse Hali with the same sense of place she knew as a kid. The same sense of place that had captured Joel's heart. She wished she had felt this way when she brought him to meet the family instead of acting indifferent to everything around her. Maybe it was because now there was no turning back.

"Look over there, honey. See that ridge on your left. That's Grant Mountain. And Burntshirt Mountain is directly overhead on your right; but you really can't get a good look at it from this vantage point."

"Why is it called Burntshirt?"

"I don't know exactly, but Cousin Bruce used to take us hiking up there and bring along an old shirt to burn. He said if we didn't, we'd have bad luck for a year."

At her mention of her second cousin, Karen realized she needed to get to know him better. He had grown up with her mother, and could probably answer a lot of questions that Granny had always refused to talk about. Especially about whether anyone had heard from her since she left.

As she drove along, a lot of the thoughts that had tormented her as a child surfaced, but compared with the terror of watching Joel waste away, they now seemed trivial. She had always kept the question of who her father was locked in a compartment in her head she didn't dare open. Surprisingly, the thought of him didn't gnaw at her like before; yet she was curious.

Out of the corner of her eye, Karen could see Hali straining to get a look at the mountain above. This was working out pretty well, she thought as she pointed ahead. "And coming up to your left is Bearwallow Mountain."

Hali faced her with an awed expression. "Mom, have you ever considered getting yourself a little bus and starting a tour guide business? Can't you just see it? 'Karen's Caravan... *we fill in the gaps.*'"

Karen rolled her eyes. *She had to do better.* She racked her brain as the SUV climbed to the road's highest point at the Eastern Continental Divide just above Gerton. Finally, she remembered the historic marker in front of Sherrill's Inn and kept an eye out.

Hali became more engrossed in the scenery as they wove around the series of switchbacks in a steep descent from the gorge, almost as if they were spiraling into a dark hole. Massive oaks and poplars cloaked the mountain trail with occasional misty beams of light streaming through the shadows, as from a window in a vaulted cathedral ceiling. They hadn't laid eyes on another vehicle since Bat Cave, and the loneliness of the place added to its eeriness.

Karen spotted the marker in a clearing on the left just beyond a small gravel turnoff. She glanced in the rearview mirror, and seeing no one behind her, pulled in. Hali sat with an elbow on the window ledge, propping up her head with her hand, curious.

Karen slapped her on the leg. "Come on, kiddo. I want to show you something."

The air was much cooler than it had been when they stopped for gas in Statesville two hours earlier. They took a moment to shake out the stiffness from the long ride and settle into the newness of the environment. An ancient oak sat on top of a tall abutment on the edge of the road, its massive network of exposed gnarled roots clutching layers of rock. A rooster's crow pierced the silence, drawing their attention across the road where a gentle grassy pasture rose up the mountain. A large, two-story white frame house stood at its head, surrounded by a cluster of outbuildings.

Karen pointed out a marker a little way up, next to a split-rail fence that zigzagged along the road for some distance. It corralled a couple of idly grazing horses casually flicking flies with their tails. They strolled over and read the words etched on the silvery plaque. *Sherrill's Inn Established in 1834 to serve travelers crossing the Hickory Nut Gorge. In continuous service until 1909. House stands 300 yards south.*

Hali pointed to the meadow. "Look, Mom. There's some people on horseback up there."

Karen nodded, thinking the Clarkes were probably still operating their riding academy. "Do you want to take some lessons?"

"Yes, Mom. I would."

Good, thought Karen. Now we're getting somewhere.

They walked back toward the SUV that was parked next to the obvious reason for the turnoff, an information platform that was set up like a slanted table top. Karen nudged Hali. "Go on, honey, read it."

Hali glanced up, looking pleased to be the center of her mother's attention, then started to read. "On March 24, 1865, Union General George Stoneman led 6,000 cavalrymen from Tennessee into southwestern Virginia and Western North Carolina to disrupt the Confederate supply line by destroying sections of the Virginia & Tennessee R.R."

Hali's tone had started in a sing-song rhythm but was beginning to fill with genuine interest. "He struck at Boone on March 28, headed into Virginia on April 2, and returned to North Carolina a week later. Stoneman's raid ended at Asheville on April 26, the day Confederate General Joseph E. Johnson surrendered to Union General William Sherman near Durham."

"Gee, Mom. Were people around here rooting for the North or the South?"

"Both, honey. It varied from farm to farm and family to family. Cousin Bruce can tell you all about it." She nudged her again. "Keep going."

Hali quickly found her place. "Col. William J. Palmer, who called himself a Quaker Warrior, commanded one of Gen. George Stoneman's brigades and made his headquarters here at Sherrill's Inn on April 27, 1865." Hali slowly shook her head. "This place is really historic."

"Go on."

"The Sherrill family fed the officers, and one of the daughters is said to have shaken her stocking over the eggs as they cooked and declared, 'Those Yankees can eat the dust off my feet and think it's pepper.'"

Hali leaned back and looked up at her mother. "I think I like her."

Karen bent down, slipped her arms around Hali's neck and gave her a peck on the cheek. "Now can I read *my* favorite part?"

Hali nodded.

"It's from the diary of Capt. Harry Weand, 15th Pennsylvania Cavalry." Karen continued with her arms crisscrossing Hali's chest, their cheeks touching.

"Our march today was through the grandest scenery we have looked on during our term of service. We went up through the Hickory Nut Gap in the mountains, along the Broad River, up to its source. Towering above us, almost to the clouds, were the precipitous crags of the Hickory Mountains; and at High Falls the water dropped 300 feet from the summit." Her voice became a whisper. "It wasn't surprising that the usual chat of the riders was hushed as they gazed with awe on the sight."

Hali gave her mother an exaggerated wink. "Mom, this tour bus idea is looking better all the time."

Karen tousled Hali's hair. "Lesson over. Let's go, kid."

They got back on the road and, when they pulled out of the final switchback, saw the roadway ahead open to a vast green meadowland surrounded by a far-off series of smoky blue ridges. "They call this valley Lynch's Bottom after a surgeon from Asheville who did a lot in the early 1900s to restore the overused land back to fertility. Grandma's house is next to his old place."

"Is that where we're going to live?"

"No, honey. We've got the old homestead down this way." Karen made a sharp turn onto Sugar Hollow Road and crossed her fingers, hoping Bruce had gotten someone to clean up around the outside and do some mowing like she had asked.

BRUCE WHITFIELD HADN'T seen his second cousin since she brought the Yankee she captured in New York City down to meet everyone. She had been thin and girlish back then, but as she slid out of the SUV he could see all that had changed. She was strikingly beautiful like her mother and definitely possessed the self-assured manner of the Whitfield clan.

The ruffles on her white silk cowl-neck blouse fluttered in the breeze as she came toward him. Her suede strapped wedgies and tight legging jeans were jarringly out of place, and her smile appeared forced as she looked around.

Suddenly, Hali tripped over some debris and one of her silver ballet flats flew off, landing her foot in a puddle. Karen stopped, shifted her weight and stared down at the pool of water.

Getting the message she wasn't happy, Bruce quickly bent down with Hali to pick up the shoe and their eyes met. She was the image of her Aunt Amy at that age and had the same devilish twinkle in her eye. He was convinced she was taking delight in the way the place looked.

After giving both of them awkward hugs, Bruce watched Karen agitatedly inspect the scene around her. Deep ruts had been gouged across the front lawn when they dragged off the container of torn-off roof shingles, and a mountain of construction debris sat in the middle of the driveway.

He wished he hadn't promised her the place would look good when she phoned him. Actually, as he recalled, he didn't promise her at all. She just *told* him to have it looking neat... and something about getting the lawn cut. At least the new windows looked fresh.

Karen paced in stiff hesitant steps for a few moments before going into the house, as if she were weighing whether to turn around and go back. Bruce wanted to follow right after her, but felt obligated to help Hali who was struggling with the cat carrier. He couldn't help gawking at the getup she had on before grabbing it up. The gauzy pink skirt and striped tights made her look like she was fitted up for ballet class.

"If my mother is your second cousin, what am I?" she asked him.

"Ten, going on twenty." He took the carrier and headed for the house. "I wouldn't let your cat outside for a while, if I were you."

"Are you going to try to scare me with bear stories?"

"Nah. It's the timber rattlers you want to watch out for."

Entering the house, he was surprised to see Karen pushing a broom in that outfit. "You two are tired from the trip. We can get your stuff out of the car, and tonight you can sleep over at my house." He bit his tongue so as not to throw in that they could also put on some decent shoes.

Karen didn't look up. She kept sweeping, putting enough into every stroke to wear out the finish. "No thanks, Bruce. This is my place and I'm going to sleep in it. The power's on, the toilet flushes... we'll be fine."

Just then the contractor pulled in with a dump truck and two workers. Relief surged on Karen's face, and she got downright giddy when they made quick work of picking up the mess on the lawn before pitching in and helping unload the SUV.

Surprised at the turnaround, Bruce shook his head as he watched her write out a check for the contractor. If she could make such a big to-do about a bit of trash on the front lawn, how was she going to handle the mess with his aunt's property? He was beginning to worry that the wily mountain gal he remembered had turned into a tight ass Yankee.

CHAPTER FIVE

HALI KNEW SOMETHING big was going down when all morning her mother kept drawing in long breaths and then slowly letting them out. Twice, when she had asked her something, she acted as if she hadn't heard, just like her best friend said *her* mother always did.

"Buckle up, honey. We've got to get going." Karen put her foot on the gas and sped out of the muddy rut. She was dressed nicely, but not as nicely as in the city.

They hadn't had a chance to chat much since they arrived, other than at night when they slid between the sheets and talked in the dark before falling off to sleep. Hali was seeing a side of her mother she never knew existed. "Remember," she had told her, "black snakes and rattlers don't want to mess with you. If they hear you coming they'll take right off, but a copperhead will hold its ground. Heck, they'll even chase you if you get them mad enough. So be careful where you step and don't reach down into the brush."

The way her mother went at the house, Hali knew enough to keep out of the way and spent most of her time outside exploring. After the first day, she didn't bother putting Bonnie on a leash since the cat barely ventured more than a few feet away. The sense of freedom felt odd. In the city, her mother never let her out of her sight, and now, the only time she seemed interested in her whereabouts was when she had a meal ready. However, she did pull herself away from her feverish cleaning once to show her how to make a waterfall by building a rock wall across the creek.

As bizarre as everything seemed, the whole adventure was intriguing. Her mother's childhood had always been a mystery, but now, all of a sudden there was a Cousin Bruce who looked at her as if she were from Mars, and this morning she was finally going to meet the mysterious aunt who everyone swore she resembled.

Every time her mother kicked open the screen door and tossed a bucket of dirty water onto the lawn she wondered who this lady really was. The only cleaning she had ever seen her do was loading the dishwasher and straightening up the kitchen in her high heels after meals. All the hard work had been done by their housekeeper.

For the past two days, there had been something about the way her mother scrubbed all the floors on her hands and knees that made it seem like a rite she alone had to do to make the place officially theirs. Last night her mother looked out of place as she went around in her silk pajamas and fuzzy pom-pom slippers writing neat notes on bright pink paper squares and sticking them onto the wooden plank walls where she wanted an electrical outlet. The only time Hali had seen her so driven was on the sick days she had to go to work with her. But, as strange as the past few days had been, this was a big improvement over the sight of her lying silently in bed, staring up at the ceiling with tears streaming down her face.

They drove for a while on asphalt, then hardscrabble, then on asphalt again. Hali began to understand that in the mountains you were either going up and around or down and around.

Her mother glanced over at her. "Baby, I probably won't be picking you up until late in the afternoon. Please help your Aunt

Amy out with her animals as much as you can. Remember, she doesn't have kids and isn't used to having them around."

Hali knew her mother was preoccupied with something important and didn't dare create any kind of fuss, even though she could picture herself being chased around by a big old pig. "Sure, Mom."

They passed a few farms chiseled out of the mountains before coming to a section of deep woods, then turned onto a narrow gravel lane. Her mother drove slow enough to give a scattered flock of chickens time to get out of the way. Abandoned appliances that looked like they'd been sitting exactly where they had been unloaded years before lay on either side. Ahead, the lane opened to a clearing strewn with stacks of chicken coops and broken-down farm equipment.

On the left, was a small, surprisingly neat house surrounded by a colorful garden of fluffy hollyhocks and pink cosmos, and on the right, a parking area next to a metal building with a couple of white plastic rockers on the front porch. A long row of chainlink pens, separated in sections and teeming with dogs, sat beside the building; beyond, a corral held a smattering of goats and horses. Never before had Hali seen so many discordant things all crammed together with such an overwhelming impact of disorder.

They pulled up to the building, and a woman emerged with a welcoming smile, oblivious to the incessant barking and the piercing crow of the rooster strutting around the lot. Her aunt was tall and slender and not beautiful in the same way as her mother, but with the same self-assured manner. Her tightly curled auburn hair was tied back, and familiar ringlets circled her face. Her skin was tan and stretched taut against firm, lithe muscles.

There was a definite resemblance between the sisters but their clothes set them apart. Amy's washed-out shorts and tee made no statement other than she was plainly and simply herself. The only trace of individuality was a small gold locket around her neck.

Since her mother had been talking a lot with Amy on the

44

phone, she evidently felt comfortable giving her a quick hug before taking off. Amy told her to wait, ran in the building, brought out an envelope and handed it to her. "It's a copy of Granny's will. It might help you get everything back."

Her mother had a puzzled expression.

"It says you're to get the house," offered Amy.

Karen looked genuinely surprised. "I thought she was going to give it to you since she gave me the creek house."

"Granny asked me which piece I wanted and I told her. The east two hundred acres are mostly meadowland. Perfect for raising horses. ... so that's what she was planning to give us."

While the two sisters talked, Hali ran over to the fence. The pen at the end held a boxer. The next one over had a bunch of dachshunds frantically pawing at the chainlink and barking for attention.

Once Karen left, Amy came over and stood next to her with her hands on her hips and an inquisitive expression on her face. Hali liked the way her aunt communicated with her head and body—an unspoken language she probably developed for talking to animals. Hali looked up at her. "The boxer is kinda cute."

Amy threw her head back and tossed a hand. "She's a mess. See that fence separating her pen from the next? She keeps digging a tunnel underneath and coaxing those itty bitty dachshunds into her space."

"Maybe she's lonely."

"She's lonely all right. Wants to play with them, but she's too big and roughs them up somethin' awful. We're gonna move her next to someone her own size."

Hali pointed to a big white dog in the corral. "Why is he in there with those goats?"

"Oh, that's a Great Pyrenees. He's a guard dog. Even though he looks big and cumbersome, his bones are hollow so he's light and travels fast. His job is to keep coyotes from bothering the livestock."

Hali followed her aunt into the building and was relieved it had air-conditioning. She was used to hot summers, but not the dense humidity that permeates the mountains.

45

"Let's start in here." Amy opened one of the doors leading from the hall.

"Stop it! Stop it! Get Back! Get Back!" The shrill scream came from a large cage.

"Hold your horses. I'm gittin' you," said Amy as she reached in and brought out a parrot with a vivid red head and vibrant yellow body. "He doesn't squawk or make a racket when he's on my shoulder." She reached over to Hali with the bird perched on a finger. "See if he'll step up to you."

Hali shied away.

"He ain't gonna hurt ya." Amy ran a finger down the bird's back. "He a sun conure. Rides on my shoulder a good part of the day."

With the bird on Amy's shoulder, the two quickly fell into a routine of sending one dog at a time into their outside run while they cleaned the pen.

"This gives them a chance to walk around a little and potty," said Amy. "We do this four times a day."

They went about getting fresh water and food and clean bedding where needed. At a run with a fenced-in ceiling, a little white poodle ran up to Hali. She picked her up and asked why the run was covered with a roof.

"Oh, she's a little Houdini. That rascal will climb right up that eight foot fence and jump over the top to the other side if we let her."

Hali giggled as Amy went on about how "some of them are genuine devils, tearing up their blankets and shredding their stuffed animals." Her aunt had a contentment about her, like there was no other place in the world she'd rather be.

Once they finished passing out treats, they sent the dogs that were in the outside pens to a fenced-in play yard, then changed the water and "scooped the poop." Finished, they laundered a load of towels and blankets before going into the house for lunch.

Hali entered the living room and the frilly, feminine look of the place surprised her... except for an imposing leather recliner in the corner surrounded by stacks of books and magazines. Had to belong to her Uncle Eddie, whom she hadn't met.

Hali ambled along the tables crowded with photographs, mostly of dogs. A big orange cat that was sprawled on the back of the couch watched her every move. She picked up a black-and-white snapshot in a tarnished frame. Three kids in overalls leaned against a fence. There was something about the "take charge" stance of the tall skinny girl with braids that made Hali pretty sure it was her mother.

Amy shouted from the kitchen as she prepared a couple of sandwiches. "Now, when I'm boarding forty dogs, it takes me 'til nine to finish up, but with just twenty-four and you helpin', we should be done by five."

Hali meandered into the kitchen with the picture. "Who are these people?"

Amy didn't bother to glance at the photo as she put two plates on the table and pulled out a chair. "Them's us. Your ma's the tall one next to me and Travis."

Hali sat down and started in on her sandwich. "What's Travis like?"

Amy twisted her face in an expression of utter contempt, delighting Hali. Then her aunt pressed her tongue to the inside of her cheek and thought. Finally, she leaned forward inches from Hali's face. "Just how much has your ma told you?"

Hali's eyebrow raised in a conspiratorial arch. *"Nothing."*

Amy nodded, slowly. "That's just like her. Always glossing things over... or worse yet, sweepin' 'em under the rug. Okay, kid. We're gonna be spending the better part of the summer together, so we might as well set things straight right here and now. I promised my sister I wouldn't say a word about Travis or none of the things he's gone and done, but I'm not like her... always putting a good face on things." She raised both hands with fingers crossed. "And I was doin' this when I told her I wouldn't. So let's make a pact. I can't tell you everything, 'cause I ain't that mean, but I ain't gonna lie through my teeth either. Just don't let on that I told you anything, and promise if Travis ever comes to the door and your ma's not there, you won't let him in."

This was turning out to be a very interesting day, thought

47

Hali after she swore to secrecy and promised never to let Travis in the house. She'd always imagined her mother's family to be like her dad's, reserved and formal, even more so; but she couldn't picture her father's brother Marty ever joining with her in a conspiracy.

Amy reached over and snatched a bag of chips from the counter. "Here, have some of these." She sprinkled some on Hali's plate, totally unrepentant about breaking her promise. "Well, to start off, the reason you ain't seein' no granddaddy hangin' about, is because we don't know just *who* he might *be.* Granny says, one thing for sure, we all had different ones."

"You mean your mother got divorced?"

"Divorced?! Heck, girl. She never even got married." She reached over to a plastic napkin holder in the middle of the table, took one for herself and slid one over to Hali. "She took off when we were just kids. How'd you like to be raised in a small place like Fairview with that hangin' over your head?"

She got up, poured some coffee left from the morning and put the cup in the microwave. "Your mom never let Travis and me say a bad word about our ma, and when kids teased us about her she'd run right at them and start up a fight." Amy laughed. "She wasn't so good with the boys, but got in enough licks to make them think twice about calling our ma names." The bell rang. She took the cup from the microwave and sauntered over to the table. "I guess I really can't blame your ma for turning her back on us once that highfalutin college went and gave her that scholarship. It was her ticket outta here."

A sudden uproar in the kennel signaled they were getting another border and they both ran out.

IN SPITE OF the years since Karen had last visited the old homeplace, when she turned off Route 74 and drove onto Granny's gravel road to meet with Travis, it was as if she'd never left. Long rows of vegetables were growing in the fields along the main road down from Granny's place, and a farm stand stood to one side. She stopped and got out into the cool, sweet-smelling mountain air, then made her way through the dewy grass to the edge of a recently plowed field. She bent down and picked up a small clump of dirt and slowly crumbled the loamy dark soil in her hand.

The scent of honeysuckle somewhere off in the distance wafted by, and a calm fell over her just as it had when she worked the fields as a kid. They all said she was Granny's best hand, but she didn't deserve the credit. The interminable strain of pulling up weeds and the monotonous bending and picking let her escape to a place where she could pretend to be someone else.

She noticed a woman in an endless row of tomatoes at the far side of the next field. Bruce had said one of the Clarke clan's granddaughters and her husband were farming fourteen acres of the Clarke family land. That had to be Annie Louise. She wanted to go talk with her, but when three people toting cartons came from behind a truck parked in the aisle, she could see they were busy picking.

She wiped her hand clean on the dew-covered grass and got back in the SUV. She drove over the bridge spanning Ashworth Creek, now just a trickle since it was well past spring, then through the woodland surrounding the house. The giant poplar they used to climb still stood in the middle of the dusty circular driveway in front. All the clutter around the house her grandpa built in 1947 made it look much older.

Giant oak logs cut from land he bought on the ridge facing north across the valley had been planed on two sides. When they were stacked horizontally on their rounded end and mortar put in between, they made a flat surface with the alternating dark wood and light grey mortar giving the foot-thick walls a striped look on both the inside and out. The first floor was constructed in this fashion, including the interior walls. The second floor was stick-built.

An old Buick sat nosed up against the woods. Two small feist squirrel dogs calmly lying on the driveway signaled to Karen that Travis wasn't home. Those two mountain rat terriers weren't going to waste their time sounding an alarm if their master wasn't around to appreciate it.

Karen checked her watch. Only a half-hour early. Travis knew she was coming. Why wasn't he around? She got out and scampered up the wide cement steps. Finding the screen door unlocked and the door open, she went in.

Memories rushed at her the minute she entered. Familiar cotton throws and tattered quilts were draped over well-worn sofas and sagging easy chairs, waiting forlornly for the clan to assemble in front of an evening fire. Sixty years of mementos and photographs sat collecting dust on the chestnut mantle over the stone fireplace.

Her eyes followed the solid oak floorboards that ran the length of the house clear past the staircase in the hall and into the dining area. Scarred and scratched, they had stood up well to the thousands of paws and boots that had tread on them. The dark stillness of the room was unwelcoming, but it was the dank air wafting out of the kitchen instead of the aroma of her grandma's home cooking that disappointed her the most.

She shouted out Travis's name. Getting no response, she started toward the hall and thought she heard a noise in the corner. She looked over and saw something was on the floor covered with a blanket. She peeked under and discovered a batch of newly hatched chicks. It was just like one of Travis's field hands to pull something like this instead of going to the trouble of repairing the brooder house.

She crept through the hall past the staircase and poked her head in the dining room. The long chestnut table her grandpa had made from a tree off the property had the familiar row of condiments and hot sauces, along with a pair of pliers and a pile of screws.

Tools had been left lying everywhere. A ragged easy chair and Granny's rocker flanked the fireplace. The handmade glass-front cabinets fashioned from wormy chestnut barn siding were still crammed with the same collection of pink Depression Ware that had been there when she was a kid, only now, they looked as if a lot of Sundays had gone by without their being used.

As she inched her way to the kitchen behind the fireplace wall that split the two rooms, the general disarray caused a wave of guilt to roll over her. She remembered how lovingly the place had always been cared for, with cupboards proudly packed with enough canned vegetables, jams and jellies to get them through the winter and beyond. She was amazed Granny had willed this precious place to her, and she worried that the old woman might have feared she wouldn't want it, since she never came to visit.

She stepped back into the hall and called up to the second floor. There was no response. She began creeping up the wide staircase. The old grandfather clock still stood on the landing. A plastic laundry basket filled with odds and ends sat next to it. She ran her hand along the clock, and remembered how proud she was the first time her grandfather handed her the key and let her adjust the time.

She continued up the stairs. No matter what it took, she was going to get this house back; yet she felt conflicted. Until everything was straightened out, she couldn't act as if it were hers. She started to go back downstairs, but the urge to keep on going overtook her.

She climbed, inventing dozens of reasons why she should be doing this, even though in the back of her mind she knew exactly why and didn't want to admit it. At the same time, she asked herself if she had been sucked into some kind of crazy tailspin since Joel's death, leaving all caution to the wind.

Once at the top, she crept into Granny's bedroom. All the furniture was gone except for a bookcase full of Granny's diaries and a table holding the doll house she and Amy had played with at the creek house. The large home-made structure, filled with rustically carved furniture, looked dolefully abandoned. A scruffy miniature dog sat forgotten, its wool fur worn smooth from a child's grip. She remembered that no matter how many dolls Granny made for Amy, this was the only toy she ever played with. Karen broke away a spider web running to its torn ear, and it struck her that things had turned out just the way Amy said they would. She had always stated in a matter-of-fact manner that she would never have kids and would raise animals instead because they were nicer.

She picked up the small hand-carved figure of a man with a

winter coat and pulled his knitted scarf aside. The ugly scar on the glued-on head sent a shiver down her spine, even though she knew it was there. She remembered as if it were yesterday, getting out of bed to play in her nightgown and finding all the dolls' heads snapped off. She kept them hidden until she managed to bring some glue from school. If Granny had come over and found out, she'd have whipped Travis black and blue, but it wouldn't have done any good. Every time she asked him why he did all those mean things, he just shrugged his shoulders like it didn't matter at all.

She went over to the fireplace and picked up the picture of three beaming people she had sent Granny two Christmases ago. She swallowed hard, then looked around bewildered. Where was Granny's beloved East Lake bedroom set? It certainly hadn't been at the nursing home. *That's it.* Granny had always said she was going to give it to Amy. *That's who had it.*

On the way out, she peeked into the adjoining bedroom. Just the two iron beds she and Amy slept on with the mattresses covered with yellow sun-faded newspapers. She walked around the large stairwell and was surprised to see nothing much had changed in Travis's room except for stacks of unopened mail now crowding the dresser.

Curious, she thumbed through them, careful not to disturb anything. One from a bank addressed to both Pearl and Travis Whitfield caught her eye. She picked it up and turned it over. It was unopened. She tapped it on her hand, pondering whether to look inside. If Travis found out she'd been snooping, there'd be no way she could talk him into giving her and Amy back their share of the farm; but why would he and Granny have a joint account?

Suspicions she couldn't smother made her look more carefully through the stack. She was surprised to see several unopened envelopes from various investment houses, again addressed to Granny and Travis. She took a long thoughtful look at the pile. Damn. For once, Amy was right. Travis had been up to a lot more than she had suspected.

Hearing a commotion of barking dogs, she hastily scooped

up a fistful of envelopes and stuffed them into her shoulder bag, then quickly rearranged the pile on the dresser. She rushed down the hall to the staircase and flew down the steps. Swinging around the turn at the landing, she lost her footing and tumbled down the flight. *She had to keep her head!* How would it look to Travis to find her sprawled on the staircase? Ignoring the pain, she awkwardly fumbled for the railing, pulled herself up and tottered down the last two steps, thankful nothing felt broken.

She could see straight through the living room to the front door. No one. She hobbled to a chair in the dining room, sat down and nervously combed her fingers through her hair, trying hard to quiet her breathing. *Oh, my God!* Did any of the envelopes fall out of my purse? She started to get up to check, when the kitchen screen door squeaked open and then slammed shut. Someone shuffled over to the sink and poured a glass of water. It had to be her brother.

Travis came around to the dining room. "I see you finally found your way back home." He'd always been beautifully blond and blue-eyed, but now his six-foot, wide-shouldered frame and lean, leathery looks were startling. She was reminded of a photograph her mother had left behind. The mirror image of Travis had stood next to her with the famous Chimney Rock in the background. She had thought then how handsome the man in the picture was.

Now, she at least knew what Travis's father looked like. "I'm staying at the old place," she said as she sized up her brother, now leaning against the cabinets that ran the length of the back wall.

"Yeah. I heard." He casually folded his arms and crossed his feet at the ankles. A shadow of a sneer crawled across his face. "For how long?"

"It all depends," she answered. He was curious. A good sign. Now, maybe they could have the conversation she had wanted to have with him since she found out Granny was in a nursing home.

"I hope you don't expect to get anything out of this place?"

"What do you mean?"

"You know god dammed well what I mean."

"Travis, let's not start off this way."

He barely tossed his head toward the living room. "There's the door. Get your sorry ass out of here and don't come back."

She stared up at the handsome face. It was as if he was standing behind bullet-proof glass and she was clawing to reach him. In all the years of their growing up she'd never been able to touch his soul, and now she had a painful lump in her throat as she feared she never would.

A fever rose in her cheeks, but she wasn't going to let him see how embarrassed she was. All Bruce's warnings were turning out to be true. She should have taken his advice and engaged a lawyer weeks ago. She casually picked up her purse and started for the living room, trying hard not to limp. As she passed through the hallway, she stole a glance at the stairscase and noticed an envelope lying on the landing.

Her ears burned and a scrape on her knee stung as she climbed into the SUV and took off for Asheville.

On the drive to the Folk Art Center, she found it difficult to fight back the disappointment from her first encounter with Travis. All these past weeks, she expected to make some headway with him on their first face-to-face meeting. She'd call Bruce and have him set up an appointment with the lawyer as soon as possible.

As she pulled off the highway onto the Blue Ridge Parkway, the guilt for taking the envelopes dissolved into an unfamiliar kind of triumph, and she got an uncomfortable feeling her old boss felt the same way every time he pulled a fast one on someone at the museum.

She arrived at the Folk Art Center and someone in the upstairs gallery led her to her office. She wasn't scheduled to begin work until Monday, but wanted to have all her personal things set up beforehand so she could start off running. No one else was around and she was grateful for a tranquil afternoon browsing through the file cabinet and setting up her desk.

On her way back to Fairview, she stopped off at the hardware store, and when a couple of people she hadn't seen in years recognized her, she figured the word was out that she had come home.

When Amy insisted she stay for dinner, Karen welcomed the opportunity to see how Hali was getting on with her and Eddie. As they sat at the dinner table, Karen was glad she hadn't told Amy she was going to see Travis. The less she knew the better. "This chicken is delicious," Karen said, reaching for another leg. She noticed Hali savoring a mouthful more enthusiastically than she'd seen her do at home.

"You won't find any antibiotics in my chickens. They're raised the way nature intended."

Karen scooped some salad onto her plate, and put some on Hali's. Eddie ate as if it were his reason for being, while Amy picked at her food.

"You know," said Amy, "I read where they think hormone residue in beef is the reason so many girls are reaching puberty so fast. Heck, I didn't have more than two pimples on my chest until after I was married."

"You ain't got much more than that now," piped up Eddie.

Karen grinned. She didn't think Eddie had it in him to come up with a wisecrack that fast.

Dinner finished, Karen took it as a good sign that Hali asked if she could go play with a batch of puppies in the kennel. Amy washed and Karen wiped while Eddie relaxed in his recliner and skimmed through an automotive magazine.

The dishes done, Karen dropped heavily onto a chair at the table and Amy poured her a cup of coffee. Noticing the bruise on Karen's knee from the fall down the stairs that morning, she asked, "Where'd you get that?"

"Oh, I just bumped it on my desk."

Amy got a bowl of sugar out of the cupboard and set it in front of Karen. "I never dreamt I'd ever see you livin' in that old creek house. But once Travis went and did what he did, I figured it was gonna take more than all those big city manners to knock the fight outta ya, and you'd be back."

Karen stirred in some sugar. "I wish you had called and told me when Travis moved in with Granny. If you had, maybe we wouldn't be in this mess." She looked up and saw anger written on Amy's face; but she didn't care. She couldn't keep the bitterness bottled up any longer.

Amy's lips contorted. "With the way your husband was ailin', jus' what were you gonna do about it?"

"Oh, hell, Amy. Something! Anything would be better than letting Travis take over."

Amy put her hands on her hips and swiveled them as she talked. "You got some nerve tellin' me that. We all knew somethin' was wrong with Travis from the get-go. What kind of kid strings up puppies and cuts legs off kittens?! You and Granny never did a damn thing about it 'cept sweep everything under the carpet. Hell, you two did it so much you could have gotten the Good Housekeeping seal of approval."

"We were praying he'd grow out of it."

Amy waved an arm and paced. "All he grew outta was lettin' anyone know what he was really like. That mean bastard is nothin' but a sneaky, lyin' SOB." She stopped and swung around to face Karen. "The thing that pisses me off the most is he gets away with it. If one more person tells me how charming he is..."

"Amy, there's no use in rehashing everything. I'm sorry I said anything."

"What the hell's wrong with rehashing everything, for Christsake!? It's goddamned time we rehashed all the crap that's come down! While you were sittin' pretty in New York City, me and Granny were livin' it!"

Eddie suddenly appeared. "Calm down, Amy. You're just gettin' yourself all worked up. You don't want that little girl hearin' this stuff."

Amy shooed him off, sat down and spoke in a near whisper. "I don't know how you've got the nerve to be so high and mighty. You got that scholarship and up and left Granny and me holdin' the bag."

"I always kept tabs on what was going on."

"You kept tabs! Don't hand me that shit! When Travis got fired from his job at the automotive store, Granny had to make up the money missin' from their till or they were gonna

prosecute. We sat there and listened to that lying bastard deny everything all cool and relaxed, then they showed us the video of him doin' it! Granny near died of shame. From what they said, he'd probably been stealin' from them the whole five years he worked there. Granny fussed at him when we were goin' to the car, and the lying bag of shit acted as if he didn't do a damn thing wrong." Amy shook her head. "And after that mess blew over, what happened? Some rich hussy took him in and put him on easy street."

She got up, took a beer from the fridge and twisted off the cap as if she did it often. "You want one?"

Karen shook her head.

Amy took a long, slow swallow. "You should have been here to hear all the talk about him and that widow. He conned her out of her husband's store, then took off. They say she's half out of her head over him leavin' her." Amy leaned back against the counter and casually sipped her beer. "I don't know how he gets away with all this shit. But I swear, sooner or later, someone's gonna kill him."

"Don't talk like that, Amy."

"I hate him, Karen. And sometimes I hate you for turnin' your back on us the way you did."

Karen looked at her with a pained expression.

Amy rolled her eyes. *"Oh, geez.* I'm sorry, Karen. I just hate him so much, it… it makes me crazy." She took another long swallow, then slapped the bottle on the counter as if she had made up her mind. "I can never hate *you.* If it weren't for you, I don't know what would have happened to me the way that no 'count ma of ours brought all those nasty men home."

Her wide toothy grin appeared. "I'll never forget how every time I got real hungry and there was no food in the house, you'd whip up some flour pancakes. It's funny, but whenever I make some for Eddie, I remember those times."

Karen let out a bitter little laugh. "You have every right to hate me, Amy. I got a chance to get out of here, and I grabbed it and never looked back. The whole mess just wore me out." A melancholy smile appeared. "But I'm not going to quit this time… and I'm not going to sweep what Travis has done under the rug either. I promise you, I'm going to see to it that he doesn't get away with this if it's the last thing I do."

AMY STOOD AT THE DOOR and waved goodbye to her sister. Amy would never want Karen to know how much she envied her the sweet, easy going little girl that resembled her more than she did her mother. She had envied her Joel, too.

She had been pushing twenty-five with nobody around showing any interest, so she set her sights on Eddie. At the time, Amy was working for a veterinarian practice and Eddie for the company that delivered their supplies. She made him work two jobs like she did, and ignored his constant gripes about why they ever got married in the first place if they weren't going to have any time together.

Once they put aside enough money to build on land he got from his family, she quit her job and they went into the kennel business. As the years went by and no children arrived, Amy added the breeding of pedigree dachshunds they now shipped all over the country. The extra money helped them get by. Amy only let Eddie dabble in antiques because his getting out and looking for them was a sight better than gambling or drinking.

She and Eddie weren't exactly a love match, but it worked. It took someone like Amy, with a keen insight into human nature, to unearth whatever good qualities Eddie might have had. She rarely let him in on the business end of the kennel operation, and he only had an inkling of what was going on with her side of the family.

Although he wasn't all that bright, Eddie had enough animal cunning to overlook Amy's temper, for he knew no one else would ever take a liking to him as much as she did. Their partnership wasn't without its vexations; but like a lot of unions, they both figured the other was the best they could do.

CHAPTER SIX

IT WAS BARELY mid-morning and Asheville was already sweltering when Tom Gibbons started across the parking lot tucked behind the court house. He had just gone up against his old Law School roommate on a project the land conservancy he worked for was sworn to protect.

Tom reached his mud-splattered pick-up and ruffled his dog Sweetie's head as she rose from the back and stretched. When he pulled out of the parking space, he caught a glimpse in the rearview mirror of his old friend speeding off in a BMW.

If he'd stayed with Biddle and Biddle in DC, he'd probably be driving those kinds of wheels, too. But when the president of one of their big corporate clients asked them to help his daughter fight a developer in the mountains, he got the assignment and caught the fever. The blatant polluting of a pristine river taught him what outrage was all about, and that conflict between greed and respect for nature changed the direction of his life.

He loosened his tie enough to pull it over his head, opened his shirt at the collar and headed toward Hendersonville. He'd just won a court decision to put an injunction on a builder who was trying to divert a creek that ran through one of their properties. In the over-arching scale of things, this win wasn't that big a deal. But when he thought about all the creatures that depended on that rivulet for their very existence he filled with pride. Thousands of these small victories were being won every day, and he was part of the army that was turning the tide in favor of sustaining the natural world.

When he pulled into the conservancy's parking lot, the number of cars told him the board meeting had started. He entered through the back door with his dog trailing behind and reached his office just in time to answer the phone. It was Jack Reese from the Southern Blue Ridge Conservancy.

As Jack talked, Tom pictured him leaning way back in his high-priced ergonomic chair with his feet up on the desk and his shirt gaping open between the buttons. He was chunky to the point that he'd be looking obesity in the face in a couple of years if he didn't watch out.

In spite of always appearing as if he had just wakened from a nap, Jack was one of the most forceful, hard-driving characters in the land-saving business. He had mastered one of the most successful conservation techniques—borrow money to buy land in danger of going to developers, then hold onto it until the state or the federal government comes up with the money to buy it.

After the call, Tom fiddled with a rubber band, relieved the meeting in the conference room hadn't broken up yet. He needed a moment to catch his breath after what Jack just told him. *How could anyone shoot his wife in the face?*

Like everyone else in the building, he was on edge. When they heard the director had called an unscheduled board meeting, they knew what it meant. With the economy in the tank and contributions at a critical low level, someone was going to lose their job.

Rosemary, their public relations director, passed by his door and made a face that indicated she was worried about the outcome of the meeting. The way she dressed was always a barometer of how she felt. And today, instead of the usual jeans, she wore a simple navy sleeveless dress, appropriate for an exit interview in the event she was the one to lose her job.

The sounds of the meeting breaking up floated down the hall: scrapping of chairs on the floor, people saying goodbye. Kevin Rhodes, the conservancy's director, finally drifted into Tom's office.

"How'd the meeting go?" Tom asked.

"As well as expected. The board had no choice but to make cuts."

Tom grimaced.

"Don't worry. Nobody's going," said Kevin. "We're just cutting back hours."

"In that case, I don't know if you want to hear what I've got to say."

Kevin leaned against the door jamb with a beleaguered expression. Ever since the recession rolled over them, bad news had become all too familiar to the small staff of the Carolina Mountain Land Conservancy.

"You remember the deal Jack Reese made for the Grassy Patch Mountain tract over in Lake Lure?"

Of course Kevin would remember. Everyone in the conservation field in Western North Carolina was flabbergasted over his deal with the bankruptcy trustee for the 1600-acre tract. After being forced to pay sometimes as much as $18,000 an acre to wrestle prime scenic parcels from the hands of developers during the boom years, they grabbed up this pristine chunk of the mountains for an incredible $1,500 an acre.

"Well… Jack just told me they're not going to close on it and they want to offer the deal to us." Tom could see the news startled Kevin as much as it had him. "With this downturn they've got no choice but to reduce their exposure."

Kevin took a moment to think. "Boy. That place is a gem. You can see those granite cliffs from Lake Lure and Chimney Rock State Park."

"I've seen their environmental study," said Tom. "That site is loaded with all kinds of rare species. Hell, there's over twenty miles of pristine trout streams."

Kevin had one hand on his hip and the other scratching the

back of his head as if he were trying to keep himself from getting overly excited. "It would be a sin to let this property get away... especially at that price." Kevin was tall and slender like Tom, but while Tom was deeply tanned from traipsing all over farms and mountains checking out prospective easements under the hot Carolina sun, Kevin worked long hours in the office and never saw the light of day. A high forehead and wire-rim glasses added to his professorial appearance.

He crossed one arm and stroked his chin. "If we get it, what are the chances you can get the state to take it off our hands?"

Tom tossed his pencil on the desk and leaned back in his chair. "With their budget in the hole, they've stopped handing out letters of intent to buy anything anybody's been able to save, and there's no telling when they'll start up again."

Kevin took off his glasses, held them up as if checking for smudges, and put them back on. "This deal scares the heck out of me. Things are too dicey out there. I know we haven't seen $1,500 an acre in over five years, but if we jump into this, it could be the whale that sinks our little dinghy." He thought for a moment. "How much time do we have?"

Tom smiled. Attaboy, Kevin. He wouldn't be asking that question unless he wanted to make a push for it. "Their option is good for another sixty days."

"Who's out there right now that might buy it if we don't?"

Tom's expression was tinged with bitterness. "Some lumber company will probably grab it up and log it 'til it's a moonscape... all for a bunch of pallet wood. They're not stupid. They've seen enough recessions come and go to know someday the market's gonna come back strong. So what if they've logged the hell out of it... the folks from Florida are still gonna come up and buy, and they'll end up making three to four hundred percent profit... plus what they'll pull in for the timber."

Kevin turned to leave. "Okay, I'm in. I'll scratch around for the money. You find out what it's going to take to get our hands on the option."

Just then the phone rang. Tom's thoughts drifted to something else Jack had said as he picked up the receiver and scarcely listened. Jack had told him the Orlando police had just arrested Grassy Patch's bankrupt developer for murder. He allegedly shot his wife in the face in their mansion in the Isleworth Country Club in Orlando, Florida, the same community where Tiger Woods and Shaquille O'Neal lived. That grim bit of news was on top of rumors that emotions were running high with all the folks who had bought a lot from him at the Graystone Development that adjoined Grassy Patch.

Suddenly it sank in that the receptionist had said a woman on the phone wanted to talk with someone about her grandmother's farm in Fairview. He punched the blinking button. "Hello, this is Tom Gibbons. Can I help you?"

"Yes, please. I'm Karen Godwell, and my sister and I think our grandmother, Pearl Whitfield, has talked to you about her farm in Fairview."

Tom reached over and pulled a folder out of a stack he was about to file. He glanced at his notes and could see she was one of Pearl's granddaughters. Here we go again, he said to himself. Someone trying to close the barn door after the horses were already out. "Yes. I've been working with her, but I understand from her grandson, Travis Whitfield, that he now owns the land and at this time has no interest in a conservation easement."

"That's why I'm calling. I intend to turn this around."

With all he had on his plate, the last thing he needed was a lost cause. This woman evidently had no idea how difficult a thing like that could be. "Things are pretty much out of my hands right now. I suggest you get in touch with a lawyer."

"I'm planning to. But I still need to gather as much information as I can. Please tell me what's been done about the property so far."

Tom flipped open the file and rattled off all the studies, thinking his time would be better spent on the Grassy Patch Mountain tract.

"Can I get copies?"

"I gave everything to your brother."

"Not Granny?"

That question bothered him. He recalled his uneasiness when

Pearl became suddenly inaccessible once her grandson moved in. Twice when he tried to reach her, the grandson told him she was either resting in bed or not at home. But the man's apparent enthusiasm about seeing the project go through calmed his fears. He had said to just drop the papers off and he'd make sure Pearl took a look at them.

Tom thought for a moment and decided to step lightly. The last thing he could afford right now was to get drawn into a family feud and possibly a messy lawsuit. "No," he responded, guardedly.

"How'd you find out she wasn't going to go through with this?"

"Actually, I stopped by the house a week or so after I dropped off the papers, and Travis told me, after considering everything, she decided to hold off a while before going ahead with it."

He had questioned the situation for a couple of days afterward and intended to try again in a month, and this time to speak with Pearl. Then, when he heard she had given the entire farm to Travis after saying she would split the land among her three grandchildren, his suspicions grew.

In the end, he reasoned Travis wouldn't be living with Pearl in the first place if she didn't trust him. He was an affable sort of guy, not at all affected by his extraordinary good looks; and his keen interest in hearing about the possible tax benefits made Tom believe that someday he might consider the conservation easement himself. Then there were the two sisters, one only a few miles up the road. Surely, they made it their business to know what was going on at the house.

The compelling tone in the woman's voice made Tom wonder what she looked like. She sounded sure of herself, yet every once in a while her voice cracked like she was fighting with her emotions. Professionally, he knew he was going to be sorry if he didn't end the conversation at that point, but his Southern manners obligated him to take the time to let the lady down gently. "Have you spoken to your grandmother about this?" he asked.

"She's in a nursing home… and not responsive right now."

The comment jolted him. That was the last place he could picture the feisty old woman. At their first meeting, which lasted over two hours, she talked on and on about the farm and related every fact about the place from memory, back to naming the carpenters who built the house and barns.

He checked his notes. That wasn't but seven months ago. She was up there in age, but how could she have slipped so much in such a short time? No wonder the woman on the phone sounded so militant.

"I suggest you get an attorney who specializes in estate law," he offered.

"First, I want to get a clear picture of what my grandmother wanted done with the property, and you're the only one other than me and my sister she's confided in."

He knew he'd regret it, but he suddenly dealt himself in.

"Until four months ago, we expected her to put a conservation easement on the six hundred acres. I'll give you copies of everything in my file." Most of the things in his file, he meant. No one was getting his notes.

"Where is your office?" she asked. "I'll come pick it up."

Her ease with putting pressure on him convinced him she was the sister who lived in New York. He had met the other one, and this was definitely not her. "Where are you staying?"

"I'm living in the old homeplace on Sugar Hollow Road."

That surprised him. Pearl had been so proud to tell him her eldest granddaughter had an important position at the Metropolitan Museum. What was she doing in Fairview?

He wouldn't have time to assemble and copy what she needed today, but he was planning on working the weekend and could do it then. "I'm going to be up that way Monday and can bring it to you then. Are you going to be home… I want to say… around six?"

"Yes. Yes. We're two and a half miles up on the right next to the creek. Look for a silver SUV in the driveway."

He thought for a moment before putting the receiver back down. He was buried in work, and the Grassy Patch project looming in front of him meant even more. Sixty hours was a light week; *and now what did he go and do?* Let a persistent woman with an intriguing voice suck him into what he was pretty sure would turn into a losing battle.

Actually, what had finally gotten to him was the picture of the displaced old woman who had put her trust in him. He remembered how small and bone-thin she was, yet still with a flinty quality about her. And then when she put the plate of banana pudding in front of him, her gnarled hands looked like they didn't belong to her. They were the hands of a hard-working laborer. He remembered her catching him staring at them and quickly stuffing them into her apron pockets.

All his clients were like family. He sat in their homes and listened to their deepest yearnings and fears and marveled at the way they all had the same single overriding concern. They knew they were just temporary custodians of their cherished piece of earth, and had come to terms with the inevitable. They weren't going to live forever, and wanted to make sure, once they were gone, nothing bad would happen to it. He filled with regret. The steely, resilient mountain woman had come so close. All they had needed was her signature.

THE LAST THING Bruce wanted was to be put under a microscope by a precocious ten-year-old Yankee imp. Still, Karen had managed to talk him into taking Hali with him to the Pickens Flea Market. Bonding is what she called it. Karen was domineering just like his Grandma Nicholson. Evidently the trait had wormed its way down the line. His Grandpa would never argue with that old woman, never talk back to her, and never do a thing she said. He could still picture her chewing him out, then saying, "Henry did you hear what I said?" And him answering back, "Yes." And then her saying, "Are you gonna do as I said," and him saying, "No."

It was still dark, and the heavy air promised more rain. Good. The crowd would be light and make it that much easier to buy at a good price. When he told Karen she'd have to have the kid ready to go in the morning by six, he thought that would put an end to everything, but it didn't make one bit of difference. With that breezy attitude of hers, it wasn't hard for him to tell her to dress the kid in something regular. "Once those dealers sense someone's not from around these parts, they jack up the prices," he had told her.

He pulled off Sugar Hollow onto their driveway and could see the silhouette of the girl in the open doorway against the light coming from within. Karen appeared and waved as Hali ran down the steps in the glare of the headlights and jumped into the car. She had on a regular pair of shorts and a tee shirt, but was still wearing ballet slippers.

She snapped on her seatbelt, then reached into the basket she was carrying and pulled something out. "Here's a blueberry muffin. My mom got up early to bake them for you."

Oh, boy. Does that woman think she's got a sucker here, he said to himself.

"I picked the blueberries at Aunt Amy's." She nudged him with the muffin until he took it, reluctantly.

He bit in, then finished it off in two bites before pulling back on the road. Since they were going to be together most of the day, he decided it wouldn't hurt to be civil. "How's life treatin' you these days?" he asked.

"Good. I like going over to Aunt Amy's when Mom's at work. Ever since my dad... you know... since he was sick... I've wanted to be a doctor. But now, maybe I'll be a vet." She looked over at him. "Do you think it's a good thing for a woman to be a doctor?"

"Heck, yeah. Doctoring was always a woman's deal around these parts. It wasn't until the Civil War when you had men doctors comin' in."

The car reached the sparsely populated Fairview business district, turned onto Cane Creek Road and headed southwest to Pickens, South Carolina.

"Back in the 1800s there used to be a woman who owned the Sherrill's Inn property who doctored folks. Her name was Ann Ashworth and they called her a witch. She grew herbs and cast spells on people and would put curses on them if she got mad."

67

He gave Hali a quick glance. "She didn't have any real powers... just psychological ones." His eyes back on the road, he continued. "She'd make up formulas, and then every little thing that happened you'd chalk up to the spell. Every time she got kicked out of the church for doin' it, she'd put curses on the deacons; then when things went bad, they'd let her back in. But she wasn't what you'd call a church woman by no means."

"Mom says you're the town historian. We read one of your newspaper articles. It was way cool."

"Been doin' that since before I retired from the Post Office."

Daybreak exposed a dark gray cloudy sky, and the dim light began to unveil small farms and country homes tucked in the foothills.

"I can't imagine the way my mom says she and her brother and sister worked on her grandma's farm. It's *sooo* not like her. Is that what everyone did around here?"

"Up until 1925 you were a farmer and that's all you ever did. Nothin' else. Then the mills moved in and started hiring mountain men. Still, everyone always farmed two or three acres. They'd put up enough so essentially they could live all winter without buying nothin'. That way they kept themselves independent and didn't have to rely on what they earned at the mills. And they saved most of what they earned."

He couldn't help wondering how much of the big money Karen and her husband had been making had been put away. She had to be plowing through it from the way she was throwing money at that house. With a few patches, that roof would have been good for another ten years. And who needed all that air-conditioning in the mountains? He hoped this wouldn't end up a riches to rags story.

It took over an hour on the back roads to reach the flea market. Not yet eight and the huge grassy lot that ran along the road was almost full.

The Pickens Flea Market had to be the biggest recycling center in South Carolina. The tables groaned with thousands of items a lot of folks would have just tossed in the garbage. Instead, vendors from near and far had hauled them all to the market's twenty acres, hoping to find someone who would give them a second life… and put a few extra dollars in their pockets.

Bruce pulled into a parking space and snapped on his belly pack.

"Here," said Hali as she handed him another muffin and kept one for herself.

This time, he readily accepted the offering, then grabbed his keys and got out. Looking around at all the empty vendor spaces, he figured the ones that showed up in spite of the call for rain must need the money and would be ready to deal.

Savoring the muffin, he strolled along the nearest aisle of vendors with Hali trailing behind. He'd inherited his medium stature and stalwart build from his German and English ancestors, and his deliberate and resolute personality from five generations of mountain men. He stopped frequently, scanning the items for glassware. He already had four china cabinets full, along with every table and shelf in the house, but he always kept an eye out for a bargain he could trade up.

He'd picked up his knowledge of Depression glassware from tagging along after his two aunts to flea markets and auctions as a kid, and noticed how prices were pretty much always going up. Over the years, what had started as a game to see how much he could make on buying and trading, evolved into a collection that now represented a significant part of his assets.

He had a lot of fun along the way, traveling all across the countryside to flea markets, estate sales and out-of-the-way antique shops. Almost by osmosis, he expanded his knowledge to include the Early American pressed glass that was the forerunner of the Depression-ware made in the U.S. and Canada between 1830 and 1915.

He'd become an expert of this tableware that was mechanically formed by forcing molten glass into molds and made by a team of workers one piece at a time, often with hand shaping and fire polishing to remove the ridges the molds left. With the expense of producing pressed glass now cost-prohibitive, the industry was almost non-existent, making Bruce's weekly jaunts in search of it an endless adventure.

They meandered through aisle after aisle of vendors with Bruce noting everything, including the way Hali kept tripping on her shoes. Occasionally he picked up an item, studied it and then put it back down.

The booths consisted of one or two tables with a pickup or van pulled in behind and an occasional canopy. Some were well merchandised and centered around a theme; others held nothing more than junk picked up at garage and estate sales. Those were the booths that excited Bruce the most, even though he was careful never to show it. Usually, the vendor had no idea of the value of the items tossed haphazardly into broken-down cardboard cartons and miscellaneous totes.

There had to be between three and four hundred people pawing through boxes and examining everything from antique kitchenware and tools, to used appliances and household furnishings of every kind. Vintage linens, chickens, rabbits, knives, guns, and stacks of LIFE magazines all vied for their attention.

Bruce kept an eye on Hali and liked the way she was taking everything in, just like he used to when he was a kid. He could tell she was absorbing the energy of the place.

They worked their way up and down the aisles until they reached the covered pavilion that had to be a quarter-mile long and packed with mostly food and apparel items. Hali ran over to a table loaded with jewelry and feverishly tried on bracelets. She brandished her wrist saying, "Cousin Bruce, can I have this one."

He sauntered over and asked how much.

"Five dollars," said a disinterested middle-aged man who obviously didn't care or know squat about jewelry.

Bruce casually took the bracelet off Hali's wrist, clasped her shoulder and led her away. She looked up at him and made a face. Then she quickly rebounded and ran ahead to another booth to examine more jewelry.

A stack of shoe boxes caught his eye. Mostly hiking boots. The printed price was slashed through with twenty dollars scrawled over in red. They looked good, but at that price had to be knock-offs. It didn't matter. Anything was better than Hali breaking her neck on those slippers.

He studied Hali's feet for a moment, then went through the stack. He tapped her on the shoulder and motioned toward a stool. "Go sit over there and take off your shoes." He plucked a pair of socks from a basket. "Here. Put these on." Then he opened the box and handed her a hiking boot.

"Cousin Bruce, I don't think I like these."

"You'll love 'em. Put them on." Surprisingly, he got the right size. "Now stand up and walk around."

She took a few awkward steps, turned and looked up at him with big forlorn puppy eyes. He pulled out his wallet and tossed a twenty, plus another dollar for the socks on the counter. "Don't worry, you'll be used to them by the time we leave."

Her pleading expression turned into a mean glare. He could see she was struggling to hold her tongue. From the moment he laid eyes on her, he figured he was up against another Yankee with a superior attitude and it wouldn't be long before he hated her guts. But it was starting to look like her character was of a different stripe. *This* little girl was going to figure him out before she made a move. And it was a good thing, too. One smart remark and it was going to be the last time he had anything to do with her.

She resignedly laced up the shoes and clomped her way to the next booth where she pawed through a bin of stuffed animals. She pulled out a big fuzzy pink pig and hugged it. *"Aw... Cousin Bruce, I gotta have it."*

"How much," he asked the woman who was standing around jingling change in her apron.

"Ten dollars."

Bruce reached over and picked up a large ceramic piggy-bank he spotted in the back. He took the stuffed animal from Hali and shoved the bank in her hands, then pulled a ten dollar bill from his wallet and gave it to the woman. "She'll take this one."

CHAPTER SEVEN

THE BLUE RIDGE PARKWAY runs for 469 miles along the crest of the Southern Appalachians through Virginia and North Carolina, linking two national parks: Shenandoah and the Great Smoky Mountains. Karen pulled into the parking lot of the Folk Art Center straddling the parkway's milepost 382 and was surprised at how elated she felt as she slipped down from the SUV.

She tugged on her skirt to get out the wrinkles before making her way over to a large plaza tucked in a forest of dogwoods and redbuds. A crow was already up and calling out. She had expected to have a tough time swallowing her pride on her first day on the job, but in spite of this step down her career ladder, she couldn't wait to dig her hands into the center's historical crafts. They represented who she was and where she came from, and these days that seemed to be what she was searching for.

As she ran up the wide cement staircase leading to the modern two-story structure, the strain from years of suppressing her mountain culture evaporated. Instead, a feeling of belonging surged through her. After years of trying to fit into the world beyond the coves and hollows of Western North Carolina, she was finally home, and it felt good.

The staircase suddenly brought back an old hurt. She could hear the girl in the dorm hall imitating the *hillbilly hick* to a giggly crowd as she hid unseen in the stairway. She had slunk out of the building and tramped around the campus in the rain until nightfall, swearing she'd erase every trace of her mountain twang if it killed her. However, the dread that anyone would learn she was illegitimate, never left her to this day. Now at the top step of the Folk Art Center, she approached the glass threshold with confidence. She'd come full circle. But this time around, she was prepared.

She wondered what Joel would think. He never saw the logic of her searching for acceptance in the crazy tangle of New York's art world, while her whole history was steeped in the crafts of Southern Appalachia. She pictured his silly grin in her mind's eye and smiled back at him.

The executive director, who had been waiting on the main floor so he could greet her at the door, followed up a warm welcome with a whirlwind of introductions. On Saturday when she brought in her things, she had a chance to chat with some of the people at the U.S. Park Service's Information Center and bookstore located at the entrance, but this morning all the faces were new.

They toured the Allanstand Craft Shop filled with a dazzling display of world-class works by their guild members. Then she was paraded around to a few of the volunteers in the upstairs galleries and the rest of the staff before she finally got a chance to settle down in her office.

She glanced at the schedule she'd set up while still in New York and hoped her last meeting would end on time, so she wouldn't be late for the appointment Bruce had made with his estate attorney over the weekend.

The day was filled with meetings, and by three-thirty, she was in the main gallery upstairs going over an upcoming show with two guild members. So it wouldn't run over, she glanced at her watch to give them a signal. Luckily, the two were just as eager to get going as she was and took the hint, quickly wrapping up the session. She hated to cut out early on her first day, but today at four was the best the lawyer could do.

She raced to her office, grabbed her purse and left the building buoyed by the enthusiastic way she'd been received. Clearly, everyone was impressed with her credentials. She smiled inwardly. Being a big fish in a little pond wasn't going to be all that bad after all.

She drove to the lawyer's office located in a less than impressive commercial complex and parked head-on in front of a door stenciled with his name. The reception room was barely big enough for its two unmatched chairs. A basket of dog-eared magazines lay on the floor in the corner. She stood waiting for a receptionist when the attorney appeared in a business suit and swiftly led her into a large room with nothing but a desk, two chairs and a couple of framed certificates floating on a massive wall.

She sat down figuring this either had to be some sort of satellite office, or Cousin Bruce had shopped around for a cut-rate operation. The message he sent by buying Hali a piggy-bank hadn't gone unnoticed.

Richard Mailo was well groomed, good looking and confident. In his early forties, he had a straightforward, concise delivery as if he understood that neither of them had time to waste, yet both wanted the job done right.

"I understand from your cousin that your grandmother, who's now in a state of dementia, verbally promised you and your sister each a third of her farm in Fairview, but since, has deeded the entire parcel to your brother."

Karen nodded.

He flipped open a file on his desk. "Your cousin gave me a copy of the deed he received from the Buncombe County Register's office." He looked her straight in the eye. "I understand you want it invalidated."

"Correct," she answered. The deposition style of his questioning gave her an uncomfortable feeling.

He leaned back in his chair, fingered his pen and appeared to be mulling over his approach. "You have two things going on here. Anything verbal in real estate is almost always unenforceable. If all she did was tell you girls that she wanted to give you the property, it doesn't rise to the level of an actual deed. It just shows her intentions... what was on her mind at that very point." He looked directly at her. "So your only fallback is to prove that your brother unduly influenced her to sign... or that the notary was fraudulent."

Karen quickly pawed through her purse and pulled out some papers. "I've got something better than a verbal promise. Here's a copy of her will that states the farm is to be split between the three of us. Amy was to get the east parcel, Travis the west, and I was to get the piece in the middle with the house and barns."

"A will is not valid until someone dies. Again, all it does is prove intention. Your grandma overrode that piece of paper when she signed the deed over to your brother."

Karen put her elbows on the table, clasped her hands and thought for a moment. This was going to be a lot harder than she had imagined. "Granny always kept a diary... what if she states unequivocally in it that she planned to give us the land?"

"You've got to keep in mind your brother has an irrevocable deed... and all you'll have is intentions. Diary notations versus a hard deed. The deed overrides everything else unless you can invalidate it."

"Fine. That's exactly what I want to do. What I need to know is, how."

"The first thing we have to do is to establish whether or not the notary was fraudulent. Your brother probably took Grandma down to a bank or a paralegal. For a deed, all that has to happen is that a notary has to acknowledge her signature. No witnesses. They just look at her ID and confirm that she is who she says she is. The notary can be anybody as long as it isn't a relative or someone who can benefit from the deed. We've got to find this out."

Karen nodded that she understood. And she was beginning to understand a lot more than what the lawyer was telling her. Travis was as cunning as he was engaging when he wanted to be.

It would be nothing for him to act relaxed and businesslike as he forced Granny into the bank.

Mailo continued. "If that doesn't pan out, we'll have to prove that she was already in the state of dementia when she signed it."

"How?"

"Subpoena hard medical records from her doctor showing she was mentally incapacitated. Get testimony from a psychologist... someone who examined her right around the date she signed the deed. If you can prove she was incompetent at the time of the deed or before, you've got a good chance at turning it over. But remember, even if someone's starting to slip, they can still have lucid moments, and that will be brought up at trial."

Karen wrung her hands. "That's not going to happen. Granny hardly ever went to see a doctor; and why would my brother take her to a psychologist, if all he wanted was the deed?" It was beginning to look like the only way they were going to get the land back was prove Travis coerced Granny into signing, and that was the last option she was hoping for.

"Were you or your sister seeing her regularly?"

"I lived in New York City up until recently. My sister Amy didn't want to tell me about what was going on at the house because I was in the middle of a personal crisis." She looked away and pulled herself together before going on. "My sister and my brother have never gotten along. Once he moved in, she had to stop going over there or they were going to kill each other. She did say that when she went to tell Granny about my husband dying, she was shocked at how feeble she'd become in two short months."

Damn! She had promised herself she wouldn't get teary eyed. She quickly took out a tissue. "I've been to see my grandmother three times since I got here, and she didn't even know who I was."

He rocked in his chair and appeared to be rethinking their options. "Okay, then. See if you can find something in her diary that would prove duress... and was written at the time she signed the deed; then we might have something to work with. It has to say that she was in immediate threat of physical harm. Something like, 'He's been acting weird, gets drunk and threatens me,' won't do it. It has to be more like, 'I'm going in to sign the deed today; and if I don't, he's going to kill me.' You need a smoking gun... literally."

"When I was a kid, I used to hide out in my room when Granny was away from the house and read her diary." Karen omitted that she was looking for information about her mother. "Granny was pretty opinionated and didn't hesitate to jot down her fears and suspicions."

"Good. Where is this diary right now?"

"It's got to be at the house. She has a whole bookshelf full of them. Can we get a search warrant?"

"Not with what we've got right now. First, we have to see if the notary was valid."

She was reluctant at first, but then reached into her purse and pulled out two of the envelopes she'd picked up when she went to the house. "I found these in my brother's room." She handed them over. "There's almost two hundred thousand dollars in the bank and in stocks in both Granny's and Travis's name. Can you find out when he was put on as a co-owner?"

Mailo examined the reports and shook his head like he'd seen this done once too many times. "We're going to have to file a lawsuit before I can subpoena records. Are you willing to do that?" When she nodded, he added, "Something tells me we're going to find out she put him on shortly after he moved in."

She pulled a card from her wallet. "She's at this nursing home. They won't tell me anything and keep referring me to my brother. Can you find out what's going on there? When she was admitted? Who's paying for it? All that sort of thing."

He took the card. "The medical records might tell us if she was examined by a psychologist when they admitted her." He handed her one of his cards. "You can call me at this number. No matter which one of my three offices I'm in, my secretary will get in touch with me."

Karen glanced at her watch. Four-thirty. She quickly jotted down her address and phone numbers on a piece of paper and pushed it across the desk. "Send the bills here, and let me know what you turn up as far as the notary is concerned."

He put everything she gave him in the folder and slapped it shut. "I'll start the lawsuit, and you try to find the diary. If we can build a good case, your brother probably won't contest it, and we'll settle out of court."

She stood up and extended her hand, a little ashamed of judging him by the office's appearance. "Thank you, Mr. Mailo." As they walked to the door, she asked, "Could this ever turn into more than a civil matter?"

"You mean involving the judicial system?"

"Yes."

"Possibly."

"I don't want that to happen without my permission." She stopped and faced him. "Hopefully, I can bring my brother to his senses before things go too far."

An eyebrow shot up. "Mrs. Godwell, just how far *is* too far? I don't want to go into some of the possibilities I see here, but Grandma could have been brutalized. You told me she went downhill fast. That leads me to wonder what could have been happening at that house. It wouldn't be surprising if your brother brandished a gun in front of her before taking her into that notary." He studied her face as if he couldn't understand why she wasn't demanding more retribution from her brother, then added for good measure, "I recommend you be very careful looking for that diary."

The lawyer's comments about Granny tore at her as she headed home. A question kept swirling around in her head: had the abused turned into an abuser?

She knew Travis wasn't right way back before they even started school. She could still see him poking out her doll's eyes with a pencil. All the years they were growing up she studied him, searching for an explanation. He seemed to have been born without a sense of remorse. And it was scary how charming he could be when he wanted something. But it wasn't until after the horrible day when her mother left them alone with the drifter that she noticed how deliberately sinister his misconduct had become. She'd never known him to hurt anyone physically, but the things the lawyer had said were beginning to make her wonder.

Suddenly a horn blared and she swerved back into her own lane. She turned onto Village Road, then onto the road to Amy's. She glanced at the clock on the dash. Just a little past five. She'd pick up Hali and be home well before the man from the conservancy was supposed to show up with the papers.

She swung around the bend and the old Forester place sprang into view straight ahead. She slowed down and couldn't keep her eyes off the house as she remembered her lie. *I gave him my money from working at the stables* she had insisted when Jeb Forester's daughter questioned her about where Travis got the money to buy the used Indian bike. The lie still bothered her. Every penny she earned over at the Clarke's stables was hidden in a sock under her mattress when she told it.

It all started when the daughter barged into Granny's house and confronted Travis. He coolly told her how he went to get paid for fixing the old man's pig pen and found him slumped over in a chair in front of the fire, dead. She could still remember how it sent chills down her spine as she listened to him glibly lie that she had given him the money for the motorcycle. The shame of knowing he had no fear of her contradicting him still bore down on her.

All the times she had covered for Travis ricocheted around in her head. Had she enabled him like Amy said? Did she create this mess they were in? Her throat tightened painfully and she swallowed hard. There must have been one split second in their hideous childhood when something in her character made her take over. Irreversibly. As if she alone were responsible for him. It didn't matter that she wasn't equipped for it, and it didn't matter that he was afflicted by a strange, elusive malady. And as if all that weren't enough, there was that afternoon in the shed.

She was nothing more than a kid back then, but after all the desperate months of watching Joel fade from a strapping young man to an ashen skeletal figure, it was going to take more than regrets about what had happened with that drifter to deter her.

She had no intention of hurting Travis, but over her dead body was he going to get away with stealing their heritage.

A man sped by honking his horn. She quickly pulled back on the road and headed to Amy's. Tonight she'd start building a timeline on her computer. Yes. Establish when the deed was signed and then all the circumstances surrounding it, so she had a clear picture of what she was working with. There was a slim chance Travis put Granny in the nursing home before he got her to sign over the land. In that case, she would have been examined and possibly found incompetent by the admitting doctor.

She recalled her phone conversation with the man from the conservancy. He sounded like a nice guy. Just the kind of chump Travis could charm into thinking whatever he wanted him to. She'd seen him do it a thousand times. It was important to find out the exact day the man brought over the easement papers and compare it with the date Travis took Granny to the notary.

Horrible images shot through her brain. Amy knew what Travis was like. Why in God's name did she allow Travis to stay alone in the house with Granny.

CHAPTER EIGHT

S NAKE BOOTS ARE a land conserver's best friend, and Tom had his on as he hiked Josh Freeman's farm. He listened carefully. It was too hot for the birds to be flitting around, but the unusually dry weather was sure to drive rattlers toward water.

He could see the stream beyond trickling down to the edge of Josh's field and into his neighbor's woods. He pulled a pencil from behind his ear and added the information to the drawing on his clipboard. Good. Now, he could make a rough estimate of how much Josh and Josephine might expect from various conservation funds if their proposal got accepted.

He always did his own hands-on investigation before recommending that his clients spend money for a resource survey. Today, it didn't take a study to tell him years of timbering, grazing and wetland ditching had severely altered the farm's three hundred acres. Most of it had been so heavily invaded by nonnative plants, there'd never be enough money to eradicate them.

Spying a table rock on the edge of the property, he made his way through the tall grass, peeled off his backpack and flopped down. Rivulets of sweat streamed down his bronzed face and droplets fell from his wet dark hair as if he'd been standing in the rain. He grabbed the last bottle of water from his pack and gulped it clear down, then took out a towel and rubbed his hair dry as he watched Josh make his way toward him from across the meadow.

"See ya left Sweetie by the truck." Josh was ambling along with his thumbs hooked around his overall straps.

Tom smiled. "Too many snakes out there."

"You're right about that."

Tom stuffed the towel back in the bag. "I caught sight of your bird. Pretty sure it's a sharp-shinned hawk. They're rare around here, but I spotted its nest." Tom rose, slinging his backpack over his shoulder, and they started for the truck. He slowed his pace so Josh, who had inherited the medium height and stalwart build of the Scots-Irish mountaineer, could catch up with his long strides. "Saw a couple of ruffled grouse near the cluster of butternut trees up on the east slope."

"Just two years of not farmin' and the place is gettin' overrun with wildlife," said Josh. "The first time I ever laid eyes on a bear or bobcat on this here property was after I hit forty. Farmers in these parts had run them all off so they wouldn't get to their crops or livestock. But once everyone started movin' to the cities, they came right back in."

Josh chatted a while longer before getting around to asking, "So what do you think?"

"The folks over at Clean Water Management will probably go for the restoration of the wetlands and streams. They're gonna want to raise the water table to improve the wildlife habitat."

Josh stopped and rubbed his jaw. "It's funny. When I was just a youngun' we'd all sit around at night, and my grandpa would tell how when they come onto this place it was mostly swampland. They had to drain it before they could do much plantin'. They ditched it out and cut chestnut logs and buried them below the mud to firm up the land.

"Back then, twenty-five percent of the trees was chestnut.

They couldn't farm on it right away and had to live off animals. He'd tell about how they killed seven bears to last them through their first winter. And they were eatin' plenty of chestnuts, too."

As they neared the pickup, Tom's blue tick hound came from underneath and stretched. Tom dropped his gear on the tailgate and let Sweetie off her lead. Then, seeing the way she pranced anxiously around, he crouched down and ruffled her thin low-hung ears. "You always know when it's time to eat, don't you girl." He got her dish and poured out some food. With his truck in its fifth year of tooling all over the countryside for the conservancy, it was a virtual warehouse. Tom perched himself on its tailgate, yanked off his boots and put on his shoes while listening to Sweetie slobber down her food and Josh reminisce.

"Heck, back in 1950 I dug up one of them chestnut trees and it was still in good shape after 150 years. It took 'til around eighteen hundred for most of this here land to be drained and usable... and we had to fight it all the while to keep the water table down." He shook his head. "And now, what do we want to go and do? Undo all that and bring the water table back up again."

The men didn't say much as Tom collected Sweetie's dishes and packed up. They both knew the conservation path was the only way that made any sense for the aging mountaineer. He and his wife were too old to farm and none of their kids was interested in taking over. An easement would help lower the taxes enough so they could stay in their home, and they'd get hard cash for stream setbacks and restoration. But mostly, they would know what was going to happen, after they were gone, to the land their clan had called home for five generations.

Tom checked his watch. Past seven. He was late for his appointment with Pearl's granddaughter and better hurry. The only clean tee shirt he could find in his pack was something one of their Americorps members had given him. He quickly changed and gave Josh a reassuring pat on the back, then jumped in the truck with Sweetie in the bed and headed for the gap.

It felt so good to be sitting down, he dreaded the thought of having to get up again at the next stop. He reached for a half empty bottle of water lying on the seat. It was warm, but he gulped it down anyway. His head hit the roof a couple of times as the pickup bumped and jostled over the rutted lane to the main road.

He tried to recall the last time he had anything to eat. He glanced down at the Krispy Kreme box on the floor and fondly remembered the two lemon-filled donuts from the morning. He reached over to the glove compartment. Maybe he still had an energy bar. Paper napkins and ketchup packages fell out, along with a tube of Holly's sun-block.

He laughed to himself, bitterly. By now, he should have gotten rid of every trace of her. But, as far as he'd gotten was ceremoniously burning their engagement album in the fireplace one page at a time over a six-pack of beer. He could still see her mother the day they carted off all Holly's belongings, pointing to the exercise bike and saying, "Whose is this?" When he told her they both kicked in for it, she let out a nasty little laugh and said, "In that case, we're taking it." He still couldn't part with the few remnants Holly left behind, like the two pencils with the chewed ends in the cup on the kitchen counter and her sunglasses in the basket by the door.

It happened the night he pulled off one of the conservancy's biggest deals. It was as if he were having a nightmare when he unlocked the door to the house, turned on the light and found her sitting at the kitchen table solemnly waiting for him. The instant he laid eyes on the red dress she bought to wear to her law firm's Christmas party, he threw his head back and moaned in angst.

She had already packed a lot of things into her car, but kept the dress on as a blazing symbol of his transgression. He'd spotted her last spring laughing animatedly at a sidewalk cafe in Asheville. A chunky looking guy all suited up for trial was sitting with her. She was flicking her long blonde hair over her shoulder like she did when she was nervous. When the guy reached over and put his hand on hers, he wanted to cross the street, yank him out of his chair and punch him out.

He had pulled off one of the conservancy's biggest deals, and in the process screwed up his life. His growling stomach shifted his thoughts to food. Hopefully, it wouldn't take more than a half-hour to run through the documents with Pearl's granddaughter, and he could grab a bucket of wings on his way through Hendersonville.

His mind wandered to a conversation he'd had with Jack Reese on his cell phone earlier in the day. It was around lunch time, and he could tell Jack was talking in between bites. Boy, he had the life. Tom couldn't imagine Jack skipping a meal to survey someone's farm. He had called to tell him Southern Blue Ridge was planning to let their contract with the bankruptcy court die, and for Carolina Mountain Land Conservancy to negotiate a new one for Grassy Patch on their own.

Tom argued with Jack that the only way to make sure the property stayed safe, and to hold the price at fifteen hundred an acre, was to keep the original contract alive. If Southern Blue Ridge voided it, the trustee wouldn't necessarily have to enter into a new one with them. And if a lumber company got wind of it, they could easily offer more than fifteen hundred, and the trustee would have to take it.

Jack agreed to discuss it again with their headquarters, but wasn't holding out much hope. Welcome to the nerve-racking world of land conservation, he told himself.

He glanced in the side-view mirror. Sweetie's ears fluttered in the breeze behind him as she hung over the side. He slowed down to make the turn onto Sugar Hollow Road, and once he got up a good mile, kept an eye out for a silver SUV. Spotting it by a small mountain house next to a creek, he swung in, grabbed a big manila envelope off the dash and jumped out. He was late, but still took the time to put Sweetie on her lead. She'd follow her nose if she caught a scent and it could be hours before she came back.

Approaching the house, he could see what had to be a kitchen door next to the broad stone chimney. He decided to go around to the front so as not to disturb anyone who might be in the middle of a meal. The house, sheathed in weathered oak shingles, was old but had been built right, and stood with a straight back and solid walls on masterfully laid stone footings. The sound of crickets pierced the air as he climbed the stone steps to the covered porch. A cool breeze carried the sweet smell of newly cut hay lying in a field off in the distance.

He started to knock when the door flew open. A girl of about ten stood in the doorway. She looked him over long enough to make him feel uncomfortable. He could see the room behind her was completely empty except for a cluster of paint cans and rollers on the floor in the corner.

"Hello. Is your mother home?"

She crossed her arms firmly, tilted her head and gave him an intimidating glare. "You're late."

"I'm sorry... I..."

"Don't bother explaining it to me..." She raised an eyebrow and smirked as she threw a thumb over her shoulder. "You're going to have to tell it to my mother."

A woman he assumed was Karen Godwell appeared at the doorway at the far end of the room. She was wearing a fitted skirt that ended just above the knee and a silky sleeveless blouse. She had wrapped a dishtowel around her waist and taken off her shoes. Her long brown hair looked as if it had been hastily tied back. He suddenly felt stupid wearing the tee shirt with "Conserve water. Shower with a Friend" on it.

"It's him, Mom," said the little girl.

The woman eyed him steadily, barely smiling. "Thanks for coming Mr. Gibbons. I'm Karen Godwell and this is my daughter, Hali." The smile faded. "We waited for you for over an hour, but I had to feed my daughter so I'm in the middle of cooking dinner."

The edge on her voice bothered him. He shifted his weight and offered the envelope. "I'm sorry. I've got everything right here. I'll just drop it off and you can call me with any questions."

The little girl reached over, took the envelope and wrapped her arms firmly around it. "Have you eaten?" she asked.

He didn't take his eyes off Karen who was obviously perturbed about his being late. "No... I... haven't."

Regret instantly registered on Karen's face. "I'm so sorry. I didn't mean to run you off." She swiftly crossed the room and extended her hand. "Please join us for dinner."

His eyes darted down at the girl.

"Don't worry, we got plenty," she said.

He eyed the mistrust on the rosy-cheeked face, but the tempting aroma of meat and onions sizzling on the grill convinced him he could handle her scorn. "Thanks. I'd like that."

Karen led the way to the next room and pulled out a chair. "Here. Sit at the table."

The way she said it, gave him the impression she was used to giving orders. After she disappeared into the kitchen, he sat down and looked at Hali who was standing with her feet firmly apart, still hugging the envelope. He couldn't figure out if her expression was leaning more toward disdain or curiosity, and wondered if he had stepped into a hornet's nest by accepting the invitation. He tried softening her up with a smile, but got no reaction and felt even more foolish.

"Set another place, sweetheart," trailed from the kitchen. A few minutes later, Karen peeked in the room. "Do you want a beer?"

"Yes, please." The funny grin on her face made him think his reply sounded a bit desperate. The sound of the refrigerator door opening and a cap being popped off a bottle softened the sting from the little girl's glare.

Hali cautiously laid the envelope on the far end of the table, then went over to the corner cupboard and got out another dish. Karen returned with a cold beer in one hand and a steaming dish of corn on the cob in the other. "Come on, honey," she said to Hali, "Help me bring in the rest of the food."

They sat down and chatted casually through the meal. When Karen offered that she was now the curator of collections and exhibits at the Folk Art Center, he thought it strange she left the Met. There had to be a story behind that, as well as why there wasn't a Mister Godwell. In spite of Karen's amiable conversation, there was something about the way the little girl was acting that told him this family was in crisis, and he took care not to say anything that might be hurtful.

"Why do you want to save the mountains?" asked Hali.

Tom reached for a roll. "It's taken them millions of years to form. If all kinds of unplanned developments get smeared all over them, they'll fade into a messy background. It's like taking a beautiful woman and dressing her in rags." He broke the roll into two halves, reached over for a knifeful of butter and spread it over them. "Then there's the animals and plants. You wouldn't believe all the unique, wonderful things that live and grow only around here. If things aren't planned right, they'll be crowded out and won't have a place to live."

Hali considered what he said. "My mother took me for a walk and showed me a green salamander peeking out of a crevice. She said it was rare."

His eyes met Karen's. He was surprised she knew that. "That's right. This is one of the only places that little guy lives."

As the meal progressed, Hali started offering him food and insisting he reload his plate once it was empty. It gave him the impression he was beginning to meet with her approval. Unable to hold another bite, he pushed his chair away from the table and leaned back.

"Wait 'til you see what we've got for dessert," Hali said with a wink.

After throwing down so much food, Tom was ashamed to be so interested. He raised his eyebrows in a question.

"Blueberries," she boasted.

He reached for her hand and examined the blue stains. "And I bet these are the fingers that picked them, too."

Karen served coffee with the berries. Once they were finished, they all pitched in to clear the table. He took his plate into the kitchen and couldn't help noticing how lovingly Karen was wiping off the table when he came back in.

She noticed him staring at her and smiled. "My great grandfather made this by hand out of black walnut the year our family settled in the gap."

Her tone was saturated with the kind of pride Tom had seen displayed over and over again by mountain folk when they spoke of their beloved hand-crafted heirloom belongings, and it touched him. He looked hard at her and was puzzled. Every time she revealed her mountain roots, she contradicted her sophisticated and worldly essence. Yet, there was still something about her that recalled the tenacity that separated the tough mountaineer from the rest.

"It's been stored in my second-cousin's barn for years," she went on. "He helped me drag it out last week. Bruce Whitfield. Do you know him? He's the town historian."

"I've heard of him," he responded as he opened the envelope and spread the contents on the table. As he started in on the first study, she squeezed his arm and told him to wait.

"Give me a minute to change my clothes and get my laptop." She disappeared into an adjoining room.

When the door opened, he got a quick glimpse of two air mattresses lying on the floor.

Hali sat with her elbows on the table, nestling her chin on her fists. "Nothing gets done without the laptop," she said matter-of-factly.

Tom didn't know how to respond. The child had an eerie habit of commenting on everything as if she were some kind of oracle.

"Hali, you can go out and play if you want," Karen shouted from the other room.

Hali ignored the remark and instead leaned back in her chair and folded her arms. Finally, she said, "I know more about what's going on than she thinks."

"You do?" *I bet you do* is what he really wanted to say.

"Uh-huh. My Aunt Amy has told me a lot. Not everything... *but a lot.*" She ran a finger along a seam in the tabletop. "Do you know my father's dead?"

"No... I'm... really sorry."

"I'm glad you didn't ask about him at dinner. In fact, it's better you don't talk about him with her. It'll just make her cry."

"Thank you for telling me. I appreciate it."

"I'm glad my mom is getting all wrapped up in the trouble with her grandmother's land. It takes her mind off... you know...

my dad. It's good you came over with all those papers. I'll really appreciate it if you help her."

Tom resisted an urge to give the kid a big hug.

"Cousin Bruce says she's not going to turn things around... but he doesn't know my mother. When she says she's going to do something, it's gonna get done."

Karen returned with the laptop. She had changed into a short jersey skirt and a dressy tee, and just like Hali said she would, typed in everything he told her. Hali got bored after a while and went outdoors. Tom finished going over the resource study and various applications, then the room grew quiet. Tom braced himself for the question that had hung in the air all evening.

Finally, she asked it. "Can you tell me the exact date you gave my brother the easement papers?"

He purposely left his notes in the truck, hoping she wouldn't ask. For days, he had been chasing the thought out of his head, that by giving the papers to Travis, he inadvertently tipped him off to the restrictions that were about to be filed on the land. "My notes are in my truck. I'll go get them."

He quickly retrieved his folder and, before going back into the house, thought he better give Sweetie some water. She hadn't barked when he came out, but he was still surprised to see she wasn't in the back of the truck. Damn! If she's picked up a raccoon scent she could be gone all night.

This was turning out to be a day from hell. He ran up the steps to the porch to tell Karen he had to go look for his dog when he heard Hali talking to someone. He peeked around the corner to the side porch and did a double take. Sweetie stood with a pink tutu around her middle, wagging her tail while Hali fastened a pom-pom on the top of her domed head.

"Doesn't she look cute?" cooed Hali as Tom neared.

"Well, we better get her back in the truck before the folks from the Bolshoi discover her."

"Don't worry. *Nobody's* going to get her away from *me.*"

He studied Sweetie as the child gently stroked her neck. She wins, he said to himself. Sweetie's not going anywhere.

Tom entered the house to find Karen poised at her laptop

ready to go. He sat down heavily, as though he were on the witness stand and as guilty as sin. "Let me see now." He opened the folder and thumbed through his notes. "Here it is. I went over on January seventeenth and gave the documents to Travis Whitfield." He slowly lifted his lids and was relieved to see her typing away with no apparent concern on her face.

This was the first chance he had to really study her features. She didn't resemble her daughter in the least. She had an oval face and porcelain complexion and a cool, self-possessed way about her. But there had been a flicker of emotion in her deep blue eyes when she talked about her grandmother.

He knew he was going to kick himself for asking, but it was going to come out sooner or later so he went ahead. "When did Pearl sign the deed?"

She looked him straight in the eye and raised an eyebrow in such a way he knew she wanted to make a statement with it. "Eight days after you gave my brother the papers."

Tom felt his blood rise. One bad judgment call was all it was. He never would have left the documents if Travis hadn't been so charmingly accommodating. He had said he was sure everything was just as his grandma had wanted, and after she was feeling better, he'd personally drive her down to have them signed. Tom had taught himself to read people ever since his introduction to all the bad guys in his law school books, but nothing in Travis's demeanor raised the least suspicion.

"Can I have copies of your notes?" she asked.

"No. I never do that."

"Okay, then. Can you get me an outline... or a couple paragraphs summarizing your contacts with my grandmother... especially the date you gave the documents to my brother?"

This is it. She was dead set on taking her brother to court. He knew her lawyer would get the information from him in a deposition, but mostly he remembered the little girl's plea. "Sure. I'll get it to you in a couple of days."

"Just email them to me," she said as she jotted her address on a piece of paper.

Feeling dismissed, he said his goodbyes, collected Sweetie

and went to the truck. When he pulled out, the sun was sinking behind the mountains at the far end of the valley, cooling it down a bit.

He glanced in the rearview mirror to see Sweetie strain at her lead as Hali waved from the porch, but by the time they were back on Route 74, she resumed her usual position hanging over the side of the truck behind him. It had been another rough day in the "saving the earth one easement at a time" business, but he felt unusually content. Nothing like a full belly to make everything look a little less threatening.

He laughed out loud remembering the going-over Hali gave him. She obviously didn't like seeing her mother upset. He shook his head. He'd never understand women. He was only an hour late.

Then his smile faded as he pictured Karen. She was beautiful, but that didn't matter much to him; it was her quiet intensity that intrigued him. She was slowly drawing him into her battle with her brother and he wondered, with all he had going on, why he didn't seem to mind.

CHAPTER NINE

TRAVIS SLAMMED THE refrigerator door, and the papers sitting on top slid to the floor. It was the shit Karen's lawyer had served him with. He kicked the pile aside. He'd be long gone before they got him into court. He tossed the package of sliced cheese on the counter and opened the mayonnaise.

The damn antique dealer should have shown up over an hour ago. He could have been sitting down to a decent meal at Angelo's right now instead of rummaging around the lousy kitchen for something to eat like some no account. He spread the dressing on a piece of white bread and threw on two slices of cheese, then folded the bread over and took a huge bite.

He kept listening for the dogs. One of these days those two were going to get theirs. What good were they if they couldn't keep that bitch from coming into the house and grabbing the mail off his dresser? Damn! It wasn't like him to be so careless. If he had burned all the bank statements and stock notifications after he cleaned out the accounts, she never would have known.

He stood by the counter and gazed out the window. The weeds had grown a good two feet since he moved in. A smile spread across his face. None of this would have fallen in his lap if he hadn't sold the store in Morganton and walked out on the widow when he did. Her taking a liking to him was his first big break. Otherwise he'd be stuck in another dead-end job like the one at the car parts store.

He got a beer from the fridge and popped off the cap. If he had stuck it out longer he could have gotten her to sign over the house as well as the hardware store. But the pathetic wench wasn't sober two days in a row in the four years he'd lived with her. And when the folks from Walmart showed up on his doorstep waving a bundle of cash, he took one look at her, grabbed the money and ran.

Eighty-four thousand was more than he'd ever seen at one time before, but not near enough for what he had in mind. He strolled into the dining room and picked up his new sunglasses lying on the china cabinet ledge. He put them on, ran his hands through his thick blond hair and studied his reflection in the glass. Everyone always said he could go anywhere with his looks; but so far, all they had bought him was four years of tedious gymnastics in the widow's bed.

He took a long swig of beer. *Anywhere* was going to be Granada off the coast of Argentina. The widow took him there once on vacation, and he promised himself that someday *he'd* be the one getting a tan on the deck of a gleaming white boat in that exotic port.

That was the one big lesson the widow had taught him. His quickest path to an easy life was working his looks for all they were worth. But he wasn't going anywhere until he squeezed the last dime out of the farm. Granny owed it to him the way she made him slave as a kid, to say nothing of all the beatings. A half-smile tugged at his mouth. Turning the tables on her had felt good.

He reached over and shuffled through the stack of brochures he'd picked up at a boat dealership in Charlotte. He pulled out a glossy booklet, leaned way back in his chair and imagined himself as the Adonis in the white crewneck sweater behind the helm of the sailboat slicing through the blue sea. He could smell the salt air and feel the gulf breeze on his face.

He threw the brochure across the table. Where in the hell is that dealer!

The dogs began barking. He rose and started through the living room when Bubba Barnhill barged through the door. He was short and portly with the unlikely swagger of someone who believed he was doing the world a favor merely by existing. One of his workers hovered behind and gawked moronically as he looked around. Bubba stopped abruptly to look at a rocker, and the man nearly walked over him.

Bubba shoved him aside in annoyance and got back to what mattered: his next deal. "After what I got for the bedroom set, you finally decided to let everything go, did ya?" A self-satisfied grin spread across his face.

Travis responded with a nod.

Bubba crept into the dining room like someone who hoped there'd be a surprise around the corner. He ran his chubby hand across the table. "This could go for as much as a thousand." He pulled out a chair and examined the rush seat. "They need some work, but you don't come by a set of eight very often." He pulled his inventory book out of his back pocket and flipped past all the carbon copies to a blank form and wrote, "Eight chestnut chairs with rush seats, plus table." He looked up at Travis. "The same commission?"

Travis nodded again.

Bubba got right down to business. He went over and threw open the glass-faced cupboards, picked up a Depression Ware cup and studied it. "Hmm... Hocking's Open Rose pattern." He turned to Travis. "Are these the only pieces?"

Travis went over and opened a large cabinet in the corner. "I counted a hundred and twenty-seven in all. Complete place settings and glassware for twelve, plus a bunch of serving dishes."

Bubba raced out of the house and shouted to a woman sitting in the front seat of a big white Cadillac DeVille. "Honey, get a bunch of boxes and newspapers out of the truck and get in here, quick." He returned, forcing a smile on his face in an attempt to appear at ease, but his expression came out looking greedy instead. "My wife will pack them."

Last week, Travis had invited two other dealers over to look through the house and was keenly aware of what he had and what it would bring. They both had offered to buy everything outright, but he decided to take his chances with one of Bubba Barnhill's auctions.

He had settled on Bubba, even though his auction house was at the other end of the state, instead of someone from Asheville, because he didn't want any of the locals to know what he was up to and blab to Amy. When he took Granny's bedroom set to Bubba's place in Wilson he was impressed with the operation.

"What do you think this will go for?" Travis asked as they climbed the stairs, stopping at the grandfather clock.

Bubba looked it over. "Umm... maybe four hundred... maybe less." He labored up the stairs saying, "All depends on who comes. If the Raleigh-Durham crowd shows up, we could get more."

He reached the top step, went over to the door to Granny's room and bent down, exposing the crack in his buttocks. He picked up a wrought iron door stop. "These bring in a hundred bucks."

The remark made Travis uneasy. Bubba's wife was alone downstairs, and there were all kinds of wrought iron trivets sitting on the counters. By now, Bubba was in the bedroom pointing to the bookshelf that held all of Granny's diaries.

Travis was anxious to check on Bubba's wife. "Go on. Take the bookshelf. Just dump the books on the floor." As Travis raced down the stairs to the kitchen, the thought crossed his mind that with all the diaries lying in a pile he was going to have a time looking for the latest. But he wasn't worried. By the time he got finished with the old crow she was so broken she could barely sign her name, to say nothing of writing anything legible in one of her notebooks.

Travis let Bubba load up whatever he was willing to take, with the exception of the three fireplace mantles. One was walnut and two were chestnut, and would be a good selling feature when he went to unload the house. Hopefully, that would be in the near future. His lawyer had said he could stall Karen's lawsuit for months, giving him plenty of time to sell the place and get out of there.

Travis hung around as the two helpers finished wrapping and packing the furniture into a huge truck with what must have been Bubba's likeness painted on its side, just forty pounds lighter and twenty years younger. Bubba and his wife scurried in and out of the house loading the trunk and back seat of the DeVille with the glassware like they were running from the law.

After waiting a good hour for the caravan to get on the road, Travis got himself another beer and sank into the only piece of furniture left, a beat-up chair sitting in front of the dining room fireplace. He took a big gulp and let the beer slosh around in his mouth as he teetered on the chair's rear legs and gathered his thoughts. Someone was coming tomorrow to take the old machinery and tractors that were stored in the barn to Shelby for their next farm auction. Hopefully, no one from Fairview would find out what was going on and tip Karen off.

All the risks he was taking suddenly filled him with exhilaration, but he had to hurry and liquidate everything before the State started nosing around. The nursing home had Granny registered as an indigent, and there was no telling how long it would be before the Medicaid officials started checking to see if any of her assets had been transferred just before her eligibility kicked in, especially if Karen started making a fuss.

He mulled over that possibility. No, his sister was too high and mighty to do that. But if she dared, he could always threaten to tell the police on her. He finished off the beer and threw the bottle across the floor and watched it ricochet around the room. Boy, it sure would give the old farts in Fairview something to talk about if they found out what Goody Two-Shoes had done.

He rocked on the chair's back legs and folded his arms across his chest. The past four years had taught him that it only took one chance meeting... one lucky break to change the course of his life. He reached over to the counter and picked up the brochure and put himself in the picture. There were a lot of chance meetings left for someone with his looks, and he intended to be ready when they came.

HALI LAY ON her back on her bed listening to her mother order around the two boys the contractor had sent over to help her. The last time she went downstairs, they actually looked frightened. Yesterday when the movers showed up and shuffled along at the same dogged pace no matter how her mother urged them to hurry, it was plain they had seen it before. But the two teens downstairs had a way to go before they would let urgent demands from a distressed woman roll off them like water from a duck's back.

Hali's eyes roamed around her room. The ceiling was just a few inches taller than her mother, and it seemed odd to have a fireplace in a bedroom; but now that the mantle was painted a bright blue and lined with a row of her stuffed animals, she liked it.

The room across the hall was smaller and totally encased in dark pine boards. She thought it strange when her mother had the carpenter nail it shut. When she told her aunt, she just shrugged. "That was Travis's room when we were kids," was all she had to say.

The pounding from downstairs stopped and the house became quiet. Something had to be wrong. She got up and started down the steep, narrow staircase that led to the living room. One boy was sitting hunched over on a stool fiddling with a hammer and the other leaning against the wall with his arms crossed. Most of the paintings had been hung and the room looked nice. Especially the walls that had been painted a delicate yellow. The painter had put sand in the paint so the grain in the logs wouldn't be so noticeable.

Her mother was pacing back and forth holding the phone and saying something about the photo of her husband at three years of age standing in front of a Chevy convertible with his dog. Hali instantly knew who she was talking to and ran back upstairs into her mother's bedroom and picked up the phone.

"Oh, that," Monique was saying. "I knew how much it

meant to you, so I tucked it in the box with the blankets."

Karen thanked her and asked about the realtor. How many times had she shown the co-op and what did the people look like?

"I don't know if I'll ever get used to these New Yorkers," said Monique. "They'll stop at nothing. Yesterday, the vacuum had been running in your apartment for a while, so I went down the hall and opened the door, and there was your realtor going over all the floors in her slip. She was frantic, so I asked her if she needed any help. She shoved a rag in my hand and told me to dust all the windowsills while she finished vacuuming. Thank God, she got dressed before her clients showed up. I will admit, once she put her suit back on and combed her hair, she looked quite professional."

Karen interrupted her and told the boys to find something to drink in the refrigerator and take a break outside.

"Go on," she told Monique.

"She asked to take a look at my place. Evidently, it passed her inspection because she wanted to know if I'd be willing to let her show it to her clients to give them an idea of how your apartment might look furnished."

This was exactly what Karen had heard about the realtor. She had a reputation for stopping at nothing to sell a property. But mostly, she signed with her because she was the one who found Joel the place to begin with.

"She got my phone number, but didn't bring them over. I guess they just weren't interested."

HALI BLINKED BACK tears and slipped the phone back in the cradle. She could feel Monique's soft hands on her face and smell her Chanel No. 5, and yearned to be breezing down Fifth Avenue with her, looking in all the windows. She closed her eyes, curled up and withdrew to the same place she kept her father.

That night, she went upstairs to sleep in her room for the first time, and got an eerie feeling in spite of the cheery bedspreads and familiar furnishings. Moments after she was tucked in, she crept down the hall and slipped into bed with her mother. They were talking in the dark when Karen placed her finger on Hali's lips for her to hush. "Can you hear the whippoorwill?" she whispered softly.

Hali listened to the sweet melodic trill. She wanted to say that her father would have loved to hear it, too, but knew by the way her mother stroked her hair that she was thinking the same thing.

THE ELEVATOR DOOR opened to the floor that housed the offices of Smithfield, Rubinstein and Shirtz. The parquet floors and rich hardwoods showcasing the place made Tom glad he got all suited up for the meeting with Troy Shanahan, the real estate attorney who the bankruptcy court brought in to advise them. The bankrupt developer had properties all over the South in various stages of development, and they needed his kind of expertise.

As Tom was led into a mahogany-paneled conference room, he noticed his shirt was sticking to his back, sweaty after the hassle for a cab at the Orlando airport. He tugged on the back of his collar and pulled it free. Troy Shanahan greeted him with a firm handshake, asked the secretary to bring in coffee, and they both sat down. Tom took it as a good sign that Troy pulled out a chair directly across from him rather than at the head of the massive slab of mahogany.

"So you want to step into the Southern Blue Ridge Conservancy contract?" Troy asked.

"Well, not exactly. They're insisting we cut our own deal." Tom studied Troy's face. His brow was deeply furrowed for a man only in his mid-forties. Like Tom, his long, leathery cheeks were creased at the smile lines. Had to be a gift from the sunny south. But, in spite of thinning hair and a slight frame, Troy still had the intense aura of a high-priced legal eagle who wielded a lot of power.

Tom's biggest fear was that he might try to stir up a bidding war for the property instead of agreeing to switch conservancies. The deal was iffy enough already. The economy had his board pissing in their pants. One messy glitch and they'd shy away from the deal. His boss, Kevin, thought he might have someone to finance the purchase, and was counting on Tom to bring back a signed agreement at $1500 an acre.

The secretary arrived with the coffee. Tom reached for a cup saying, "I'm hoping to leave here today with a contract with the same terms you gave Southern Blue Ridge."

Troy seemed prepared for the statement. "What makes you think you can come up with the money?" he asked.

"Our director is in serious conversation with someone who has lent us this kind of money before, and we're pretty sure he'll come through again. But before we proceed any further, we need an agreement with you at the $1500-an-acre price."

The way Troy sat there stroking his chin, Tom was betting the guy was thinking Grassy Patch was one messy deal he thought he had put behind him, and was weighing whether or not to clean it up quickly rather than reopen it for bids.

Troy tapped an irregular beat on the table with his fingers. "I sold the bankruptcy trustee on that deal because the real estate market was in the tank, and there wasn't a chance we'd ever get another developer to take it off our hands. The down-and-dirty way to unload it was to go to someone who actually wanted it in a natural state."

He leaned back in his chair and fingered his cup. "I argued that, with that kind of buyer, everything becomes a lot easier... no roads would have to be built, no septic tests would have to be done... and that's why the court took it."

He reached for a pad lying on the table and fanned through the sheets with his thumb. "What kind of guarantee can you give me that you can come up with the money?"

Tom whipped out his BlackBerry and hoped Kevin would work his usual magic. "Let me put you on the phone with my boss." He tried to look confident while Troy sat sizing him up as they waited for Kevin to pick up.

Kevin had gotten a verbal pledge from the backer to cover the interest and principal on a loan for the property, but they had nothing in writing. Kevin was dealing mostly with the backer's lawyer, whose teaming up with this philanthropist had been a godsend for the state.

Kevin had expected the call, so after a few words, Tom handed Troy the phone. Troy kept nodding his head as he listened, until he finally said, "I was in law school with that guy." He laughed. "You know he represents the R.J. Reynolds Company and has fought all kinds of battles to protect them from the anti-smoking lobby… yet, he's an arch conservationist. I guess everyone has a right to equal protection of the law." He paused for a moment. Finally, he said, "We'll give you the commitment letter."

If Kevin was in the room, Tom would have hugged him.

Troy ended the call and handed the phone back to Tom. "We'll go for it, but you have to close in sixty days and provide a current survey."

Tom almost fell back in his chair. This guy was licensed in Florida and Mississippi where it was flat as a pancake. He evidently didn't know beans about what it took to survey land in the mountains. All they had to do in those two states was shoot their straight line on the flat surface.

"Troy, it's not the same in the mountains. There're no roads on that property. It's got sheer rock cliffs, rhododendron thickets. You can't compare it to surveying down here. It would take months."

"Well, that's the deal, and we're not going to budge on it. What are you worried about. The whole site, including the attached Graystone development, has already been surveyed. All you have to do is get them to survey the line that separates them."

"Troy, I already talked with the developer's surveyor for our own satisfaction. They figure they've got us over a barrel, and won't do it for less than the whole $40,000 the developer stuck them for."

"Then get another surveyor to separate the parcels."

"Troy, we're talking North Carolina here. A surveyor can't just take somebody else's lines for granted. North Carolina law requires the surveyor to survey all the lines himself, anew."

"That's your problem, pal. I'm telling you, we're not going to hand off that property without one."

Tom threw up his hands and fell back in his chair, purposely expressing his frustration. "Troy, if we're willing to buy that property without that strip surveyed, why should it make any difference to you?"

"When I walk away from this deal, I don't want to have to look back over my shoulder. The line that divides the property has *got* to be put down on paper."

Tom's mind raced. With money as tight as it was, the board would never go for the $40,000 survey, and to get moving on this, he had to show up at the office with a signed agreement. "All right. What if our surveyor goes out and gets points at the iron bars with his hand-held GPS device, and we come up with a description of metes and bounds from iron bar to iron bar instead of a full-fledged land survey?"

Tom clamped his jaw tight as Troy thought it over.

A slow grin finally surfaced on Troy's face. "That might work. I'll get it drawn up."

Tom turned down Troy's offer for lunch and said he would just wait for the commitment letter, then catch his flight back to Charlotte. While Troy was dictating the agreement in his office, Tom put in a call to Kevin.

"So far, so good," Kevin said. "Here's hoping nothing else comes up."

CHAPTER TEN

A LITTLE OF THE COOLNESS of the night lingered in the air. Cattle grazed languidly on the emerald hillsides in the distance, and endless acres of corn, washed over by the morning sun, stood upright across the road from the Flying Cloud Farm.

A car whizzed by, disrupting the serene remoteness of the place. The woman walked out of the woods and down the lane with a bucket. She wore the frayed jeans and rubber boots of a farmer. As she moved, the shirt hanging loosely over her tee swayed enough to reveal a lean yet feminine figure. A thick ash-blond braid hung down her back.

As she reached her roadside stand, Annie Louise looked up at the Blue Ridge Mountains fencing in the lush, green bottomland she'd known all her life. A dramatic cumulus drift moved across the sky and reminded her of how she and her siblings would lay in the grass and watch the white billows glide behind the mountains. No wonder the Sherills called the stagecoach they operated between Asheville and Rutherfordton the Flying Cloud. When her husband asked her what they should call their farm, she responded instantly with that same name.

Annie's husband, Isaiah, came from Pennsylvania and they met at school. Her last name was now Perkinson and before that, Hamilton. But her mother was a Clarke, and she'd always be considered a part of that clan. It wasn't so much that the family was proud; it was more like they were an institution.

It all started with her great grandparents, the McClures, who happened upon the valley in 1916 in their "Honeymoon Hudson." Coming from industrial Illinois wealth, they were a phenomenon from the moment the hard-scrabble mountaineers laid eyes on them. They bought the old Sherrill's Inn at the gap; and instead of it serving as a second home as they had planned, it sucked them into the valley's rural life and never let go.

Elizabeth McClure bore two children while Jim McClure gave birth to the Farmer's Federation, a consortium to bring modern farming and marketing techniques to the area. Their son died in WWII. Their daughter, Elspeth, married her first cousin, James McClure Clarke, who was destined to represent Buncombe County for three terms in the United States Congress.

Elspeth's and James's six children lived in two worlds. They knew what it was to work long and hard at farm chores alongside their parents, yet as they rambled around the historic drover's inn with oil portraits of their forebears staring down on them, their heritage never escaped them. Now, three of the six were still rooted in the agricultural life of Fairview, including Annie's mother, Susie, and her Aunt Annie who she was named after and who lived with her husband, John Ager, in Sherrill's Inn.

Turning back to the stand, Annie Louise erased the blackboard with her shirt sleeve and chalked up the prices for the fresh produce she'd set out in wire baskets earlier that morning. The four-by-eight-foot structure, with tin roof and weathered board and batten sides, sat on two recycled axles with the tires still attached so it could be hauled around. It resembled a gypsy caravan and served the folks who drove past the farm and wanted to buy fresh-picked, organically grown produce.

Annie bent down and unlocked the hasp securing the tube where people dropped in money for whatever they took from the self-serve stand. She folded the bills and stuffed them in her back pocket and put all the coins in a can hidden in the wagon. Then she flipped up the cover of the bin where they placed the more perishable items and poured in the ice from her bucket.

She walked through the dewy grass to take a look at the east field her husband had plowed in readiness for planting the fall harvest. The hoses had already been dragged out, and the team of summer interns would be setting up the irrigation system today; by the end of the week they'd have all the cauliflower and broccoli starts out of the greenhouse and into their good earth.

She noticed a silver SUV pull into the driveway and stop at the stand. She needed to hurry over to the row of flowers and get some cut before they left. For sure, they'd want some of her colorful zinnias. As she rushed across the lane toward the field, she eyed the mother and daughter spilling out of the vehicle and threw up her arms. "Karen!" she shouted as she rushed over and gave her a hug. She drew an arm's distance away and studied the face she hadn't seen in over fifteen years. "I heard you were back, but I've been so busy with the farm I haven't been able to catch up with you."

She stooped and looked Hali over. "I don't believe it. You're the spitting image of your Aunt Amy. My two girls can't wait to meet you. I understand you're signed up for my aunt's riding classes."

Hali nodded. "I'm starting this Saturday."

"I bet you're looking forward to it."

"Totally," responded Hali.

The two women laughed spontaneously, then hugged again, this time longer. Annie patted Karen's back and whispered in her ear. "It broke everyone's heart to hear about your husband. We all prayed for him, Karen."

After a few minutes of catching up, Karen started picking out some vegetables.

Annie took a bunch of beets from her and put them in a basket. "I hear you're doing a lot of work on the old house."

"It was quite a job. The contractors and I were like ships that passed in the night. I'd leave notes for them all over the place before I left for work, and the first thing I had to do every night when we got home was clean up after them. But it's all done now and I'm pleased."

"What are you doing out on a Wednesday? I thought you had a job."

"I worked last weekend, so I'm taking a couple days off. Our furniture arrived and we're still working on getting that in place, but I wanted to take some time to shop and make a few social calls."

Annie helped load everything into the SUV. "I hope you're going to drop in on Jason. He's working with his brother Jamie at the Hickory Nut Gap Farm. If you go over to the store, they'll find him for you. You know he just got back from serving his third tour in Iraq, don't you?"

Karen gave her a sidelong glance. "No, I hadn't heard." She hesitated for a moment before asking about Annie's cousin, "Is he all right?"

"He's just fine, but it's taking him a while to get back in circulation. He's still single, so he's living in The Big House with my aunt and uncle. You guys were so tight growing up, seeing you will be good for him."

"I bet your Aunt Annie's relieved he's back."

"Oh God, yeah. She worked herself to a frazzle to keep her mind off the war while he was gone." The way Karen changed the subject instead of asking more about her cousin, convinced Annie her friend was still hurting too much to reach out to anyone.

Karen walked over and stared out onto the field, and it gave Annie a moment to take her in. With her short summer skirt and lacey top, it was hard to believe this was the same person who came to school in overalls instead of a dress, so her underpants wouldn't show when she got into a fight.

Karen gazed out on the field. "Your crops look gorgeous."

"We grow everything sustainably."

Karen turned her head and gave her a questioning look.

"No synthetic pesticides, herbicides or fertilizers."

Karen nodded. "So how are things going for you?"

Annie was tempted to tell her not as well as things seemed to be going for her, but remembered Karen had lost her husband. "We're making out okay. We're doing four farmers' markets a week… we got this stand… and then there's our CSA."

"What's that?"

"Community Supported Agriculture. Every January we sell a hundred and fifty food contracts for five hundred dollars each. That's where we get the seed money for everything we'll need to get the ball rolling in the spring. And our members get a box of freshly harvested organic produce every week from May to October."

"What a good idea, Annie. We'll definitely sign up for next year."

Karen paid for the vegetables, and they all started back toward the SUV.

Annie held the door as Hali climbed in. "What do you think about coming over some time to play with my two little girls?"

"Way cool," answered Hali with a grin.

Annie Louise waved as the SUV backed up and headed toward the road, wondering what it had taken for the scruffy, combative mountain girl to transform herself into the poised, self-confident woman she had just met. Things had gone too bad too fast after Travis moved back in with Granny Whitfield, and everyone wondered what would happen next. But the minute Annie heard he had gotten his hands on the farm, she knew Karen would come back and put up a fight.

She stood for a moment mulling over the put-together woman her old friend had become and hoped the defiant tomboy who fought like a bobcat every time someone rubbed her nose in the family dirt was still lurking inside that polished package. Rumors were circulating that Travis was talking to a bunch of outsiders about selling off chunks of the Whitfield farm.

The zinnias needed to be deadheaded, so she picked up her scissors and made her way toward the long row of flowers, re-flecting on the beautiful woman Karen had become. That thought reminded her of the lady who stopped by the stand a week earlier. Statuesque like Karen, but blonde.

The woman had seemed too curious about everybody, almost nosey, asking about everyone in the valley, especially Pearl Whitfield. She thought it odd at the time. She reached the start of the row and began snipping off the paling flowers with her scissors. The next time she saw Karen, she would have to tell her about it.

"WELL, PUMPKIN, where do you want to go next? The tack and riding shop, or Bubba's in Chimney Rock?" asked Karen as she pulled out of the Flying Cloud's drive onto the stretch of Route 74 known to all the locals as the Charlotte Highway.

"Why not the Hickory Nut Gap store?"

"We'd have to take whatever we buy back home."

"Really, Mom. It's only down the road from us. And, don't you want to get something special for Cousin Bruce's dinner on Thursday?"

Karen gave a little shrug, turned onto Sugar Hollow Road and headed for the farm store. Now that Annie had piqued Hali's curiosity about the place, she'd come up with one excuse after another until she got there.

Remembering the keen interest Hali had shown in the man from the conservancy last week, Karen wondered if she just wanted to get a look at Jason Ager. The way her daughter was looking out for her like a mother hen, she was sure Joel had told his beloved little sidekick to take care of her.

He probably even told Hali he hoped someday she'd find another husband. She swallowed hard. How it must have hurt him to think of her with another man. The touching sentiment made her want to cry, and she reached over and squeezed Hali's hand. Oh, baby, if only it was that easy, she spoke in her head. Your mamma's got such a deep hurt, she's *never* gonna be able to look at anyone else.

About a mile up the road, she swung into a parking lot beside a clapboard building laid out in oddly attached segments as if it had been added onto over the years. They got out and took in the rolling meadows dotted with cattle that surrounded the farm. A big sign hung above the rustic door: Grass Fed Beef & Pastured

Pork. Another sign told of range-fed chicken.

The two scampered from the heat into the store section of the complex and welcomed its refreshing coolness. Sawdust was scattered on the floor and freezer cases encircled the room. Specialty food items sat temptingly on shelves in the center. Karen and Hali strolled along the cases perusing the assortment of organic meats. Handmade signs scribbled on card stock that were taped to the cases identified everything from Buncombe Brat to grass-fed lamb roasts.

Hali stopped, tugged at her mother and pointed to a sign listing heart, liver, sweetbreads, oxtail and stock bones. Karen gave her a wink, then picked up a package of sirloin steaks and started to examine it when out of the corner of her eye she spotted someone rushing in. She didn't know if it was the way he walked or his silhouette, but something made her eyes follow him to the counter where he started talking to the young man standing behind it. She stopped breathing at the sound of Jason's voice.

In spite of the soiled, loose-fitting tee shirt, she could see he still had the same solid, muscular frame. His shorts and scuffed high-top hiking boots were covered with red clay as if he had been wrestling in the dirt with a stubborn piece of farm equipment.

Jason turned to go out again, then caught sight of her and stopped. A slow smile spread across his face. He looked the same to her as he did just before she left for college, except now he was a man.

He took off his straw hat, ran his hand through his hair and walked over with the confident stride of a Marine. "Welcome home, stranger."

They stood taking each other in. Running through her head was the same kind of joy she felt when they were kids. They'd jump off the school bus and run up to his horse, Brownie, waiting at the fence at the bottom of the hill. They'd climb on, then yank Amy up and ride bareback up to his family's stables where they both worked after school.

Karen was embarrassed for gaping at him, and it made her

awkward about introducing Hali. She watched him make a big fuss over her little girl and laughed to herself when he asked Hali where she got her red hair, and she told him it was from eating too many beets.

Jason looked back at Karen and studied her face.

Her glance fell toward the floor while she searched for something to say. "How's your mom?"

"Pretty happy I'm home."

She looked up. "Did you know I'm back home, too?"

"Ooooh, yeah. In fact, I was planning to call and invite you to the square dance and covered dish dinner at The Big House next Sunday." He put a hand on Hali's shoulder. "And you, too, Miss Hali." He took the package of steaks from Karen and placed it back in the case. "First, how about you two girls riding around with me for a while, so we can do some catching up?"

Hali raced to the door. "Let's do it, Mom!"

As Jason led Karen out, he smiled the confident way she remembered. He went over and opened the passenger door of a Ford 250 pickup that had enough scars and dirt to prove it was used for everything from hauling cattle to pulling tractors out of the mud. Lying on the seat was a machete with a badly nicked blade that had seen its share of thicket. He tossed it on the floor, then helped them up. As he walked around the truck, Karen thought she heard a bugle playing reveille.

Hali nudged her. "It's his cell phone."

He opened the door and scooted onto the driver's seat with its edges worn through to foam rubber, while telling someone he was on his way to pick up a pump.

Karen pushed a pile of chain aside with her foot, then picked up a gritty pair of sheep shears off the dusty, tool laden dashboard and dropped them on the floor. Hali, sitting in the middle, picked a fluffy chicken feather out of the cup holder with more glee than necessary.

Karen put her hand on the dash and braced herself as Jason wrestled the truck out of the parking lot, one hand on the steering wheel and the other holding the phone to his ear.

"You won't believe who I've got here in the truck." He

listened for a moment. "News sure travels fast around here." He looked over at Karen with a big grin. "Yeah, I invited her."

Jason handled two more calls before they got to Fairview's business district, with Hali humming the reveille ring-tone with gusto every time the phone rang.

He swung onto a back road. "My brother's renting 350 acres from the family corporation, and I've been helping him out now for four months."

"What are you raising," shouted Karen over the clatter of the diesel engine. Air rushing through the open windows made her hair whip across her face. She gathered it in her hand and held it tight.

"Got red Angus and South Poll cattle. We're liking the South Poll. They were developed by Teddy Gentry. You know... the bass player for 'Alabama.' They're bred for the Southeast and thrive on grass and forage."

Karen gave Hali a little hug, hoping she was enjoying this jaunt through the countryside as much as she had when her grandpa carted her all over the county on errands. There had been something about bouncing around in an old workhorse truck with the wind rushing in through the windows and the pampered fields racing by that had given her the first genuine feelings of freedom.

"We got a bunch of pigs, and process a thousand chickens a year. Everything we raise is antibiotic free," said Jason, loud enough for her to hear.

"Did you learn all this at school?" Karen asked.

"Pretty much. At Warren-Wilson. But I keep up on sustainable agriculture all the time. Even when I was in Iraq. This movement is growing." He glanced over at Karen. "When I hear those cattle chomping away at the grass, I know this is how it's supposed to be. Heck, they graze right through the winter."

"What if it snows?" asked Hali.

"They just push it aside and find the grass."

The bugle call sounded for the umpteenth time, making Karen and Hali laugh.

Jason was talking on the phone with someone about chickens

that had to be slaughtered and dressed the next day as he pulled into a small engine repair establishment. He jumped out, and from the rearview mirror, Karen could see someone helping him hoist something into the truck.

"Need the pump for our drip irrigation system for the pumpkins," he said as he jumped back in and headed for the store.

He kept glancing over at Karen with a broad grin on his face. She was playing second fiddle to the farm business, but still felt important.

"Hey, on Friday I'm playing in a country band my brother put together. You wanna come?"

"You don't mean the Mountain Music Hoedown in Old Fort, do you!?"

"Yep."

"The mandolin?"

"Uh-huh."

"I wouldn't miss it for the world."

As they chatted, she was surprised at how much he knew about her. The truck screeched to a stop just before the store's parking lot. She and Hali got out, and he said he'd pick her up Friday at seven. Then just as he was about to take off, someone came running from the store waving and shouting, "The pigs are out!" and he floored the gas and disappeared down the road.

TOM SPOTTED THE SUV and suddenly felt foolish for driving all the way out to Karen's house to personally deliver his notes after she specifically told him to email them. He had been ready to send it off two days earlier, but changed his mind and printed it out instead. He'd caught himself thinking about her a lot lately. Barging in on them this late wasn't exactly professional, but he hadn't planned on staying at Josh and Josephine's place so long.

Every time he had gotten up to go, one of them dreamt up another question. He'd seen it before. He was the only link between their beloved homeplace and the irrevocable stack of papers that would be filed in the Buncombe County courthouse. The process virtually went against everything they'd ever been taught. The way mountain folk were raised to be staunchly independent, the last thing they would ever do was put a restriction on what was theirs.

He saw the house up ahead. No, this wasn't right. What was he thinking? She was too recently widowed. At any rate, she wouldn't be interested in him. By the looks of her, he pictured her more with one of the slick lawyers or businessmen from Asheville. He'd turn around at the driveway up the road and email the notes to her tomorrow.

Just as he was about to pass the house, Sweetie started barking at two figures walking on the road up ahead. Damn! It was them. There's no getting around this now. He slowed down, pulled in their driveway, then reached for his notes and got out.

Sweetie ran to Hali and danced around while Karen strode across the lawn. She came up to him and smiled. The sunset behind her had formed a golden red edge around her head. Her deep blue eyes were startling. Like a fool, he blushed, then quickly looked away and prayed the rosy glow of the setting sun washed the color from his face.

He figured he better start talking before he really made an ass of himself. "I brought you my notes," he said as he offered them to her.

She took the envelope and turned to Hali. "Should we reward Mr. Gibbons with a piece of blueberry pie for bringing his notes?"

"Just call me, Tom," he blurted out. A shock of his dark hair fell across his forehead.

When he told her he had to tie Sweetie up first, she insisted the dog come in. "I've got some scraps from dinner. Is it all right if I give them to her?"

Tom nodded. Heck, he wouldn't mind some himself, he thought as he stepped into the house. The change amazed him. The dark pine plank walls had been lightened up with paint and were now splashed with beautifully framed art work. There was just enough furniture to make the place cozy. Karen told him to sit down and disappeared into the kitchen with Sweetie and Hali.

He spotted a few framed photographs on the fireplace mantel

and quickly went over and examined the faces. He was ashamed to admit to himself that the one he was looking for was Karen's husband. There he was! In the photo with the two of them. He wasn't quite as tall as Karen and a little on the thin side, but he had an open-faced smile that made you want to like him.

Sweetie brushed up against his leg and startled him. His eyes darted over to Hali's penetrating gaze, and damn if he didn't blush again.

Hali solemnly announced, "That's my father."

They were both distracted by Karen entering the room with a tray. "Here's the blueberry pie, just like advertised."

He sat down and self-consciously dug in, careful not to drip any berries on the Persian Sarouk. Karen took everything out of the envelope, put it on the coffee table and said she'd be right back. Tom's eyes shot over to Hali. "I know. She's going to get the laptop." They both laughed.

He finished the pie while Karen diligently compared his notes with hers. Hali knelt on the rug and petted Sweetie. Feeling awkward just sitting there with Karen engrossed in the notes, he stood up. "Thanks for the pie. It's getting late and I… ah… better be going." He went to the door and slapped his leg. Sweetie looked up but didn't want to leave. That's loyalty for you, he thought. He slapped his leg again, this time hard enough for her to know he meant business. She got up and walked across the room hanging her head.

Karen put aside her laptop and rose. "Thanks for bringing me your notes. You really didn't have to trouble yourself with a personal trip, but I appreciate it."

Her comment made him feel like he had overstepped. His coming up there in the evening unannounced was definitely a mistake. He put his hands on his hips and looked around the room avoiding her eyes. He should open the door and leave, but that old persistence, a character trait he hated about himself, wouldn't let him. He shifted his weight from one foot to the other and looked at the ceiling trying to get up his nerve. He was in too deep to do anything but forge ahead no matter what the consequences.

Suddenly, Hali interrupted the embarrassing silence. "She'll go out with you."

His eyes darted around the room, and for a brief second, met Hali's. Finally, he looked Karen in the eye, and the kindness he saw there made him want to hug her.

"I'm not doing anything Saturday night," she said. "We can go out to dinner if you want."

He tried to keep a big smile from taking over, but couldn't. "I'll pick you up at six."

CHAPTER ELEVEN

T HE WOMAN CROSSED her long, shapely legs, and the swish of her silky dress broke the silence in the room. She was past fifty, but still exuded the kind of compelling beauty that could make one sad that it wasn't going to last very much longer. She picked up her purse and took out a pack of cigarettes, hesitated for a moment, and tossed them back in.

Wouldn't that be the last straw if the old woman lying flat and motionless on the bed woke up and caught her smoking? As a girl, she always had to smoke behind the barn where she wouldn't be seen. If she didn't, like sometimes at night when she snuck out on the porch, she'd get caught and the whole family drama would play out—Ma going at her with a belt, and Pa trying to get the damn strap away from Ma.

It had never ceased to amaze her how her parents could be totally in tune to each other, except when it came to her. Ma had never understood about her. She wasn't of Ma's bent, always keeping in mind how hard life had been and unable to get away from the old ways. All that endless planting, canning, and putting things up for the winter.

The woman on the bed had gotten satisfaction out of spending the afternoon picking vegetables in the unbearable heat; and then straight after dinner, the dicing, peeling, skinning and snapping. Then the sweaty, laborious task of boiling the jars, filling them up and boiling everything one more time. She could still see her the next morning carefully wiping each jar and then squirreling them away in the cupboard as if their whole existence depended on it. By fall, they'd have enough canned vegetables and fruits to last the winter, with plenty extra so no one paying them a visit would leave empty-handed.

Whenever she pictured her mother, instead of a smiling face, she saw her gnarled hands. They were always doing something. Pulling weeds, knitting, rolling out dough. It was as if the ten fingers had a life of their own and couldn't stop moving. The only time she saw her at rest was at night when she would rock and tell stories about the old times.

She could almost hear her yelling from the porch, *Angie turn down that blasted TV.* Lord, it took a lot of crying and begging to get that thing. She could hardly believe her eyes when Pa pulled in with a neighbor, and the two of them wrestled the giant Motorola out of the truck and into the living room, suddenly making everything else in the house look old and shabby.

Angie stood up, leaned against the bed and studied the eerie figure. If she hadn't read *Pearl Whitfield* on the chart at the foot of the bed, she wouldn't have believed it was her. What happened to the shoulder-length naturally wavy auburn hair she always pulled back with barrettes? On days she was so dog tired from work, the old woman would swear that she wasn't going to live long enough to turn gray; the now-cottony white folds around her head betrayed her.

Angie bent down and kissed the ashen forehead and tried to inhale her scent, but all she got was the same odor that hit her the minute she entered the nursing home—disinfectant mingled with a faint aroma of meatloaf. It saddened her. Most of the images of her mother were held together by the memory of the the familiar smells wafting from her clothes as she was rocked by her in front of the fireplace. Fels-Naptha soap from washing out

Pa's overalls, salty sweat from hoeing the potatoes just before dinner, fatback splattered on her apron. Clean, earnest scents that told the story of her day.

Over the years, when Angie got homesick, she would lie in bed and put herself back in the old homeplace and conjure up her parents. The two were always bigger than life. Especially Ma. To this day, she regretted how she never measured up to her. How she never measured up to the whole damn family. She knew it was because of the streak of stubbornness that drove her. And once that streak brought shame on the family, she had been driven to pile on even more to prove she didn't give a damn.

She pulled the bed sheet up a little and straightened her mother's gown. Why was she wearing that plain ole bleached-out institutional thing? She looked around the room, then searched frantically through the small cabinet for nightgowns and a robe, and when she found none, stood up disappointed. Tomorrow, she'd bring her some. Nice ones anyone would be proud to wear.

She sat down on the bed with slumping shoulders, remembering how ashamed she was of the plain hand-sewn frocks she and her mother always wore. The dull old things had just hung on her while all the other girls flounced around in frilly store-bought dresses.

No matter how much she begged to go shopping, Ma wouldn't hear of it. "We Whitfields don't live beyond our means," she would say as if it were a badge of honor. She'd never forget how she came home from a birthday party where everyone was dressed in their finest. She'd gone straight to the cupboard for the scissors, marched up to her room and cut up all her clothes. When her mother came in and cried in agony at all the shreds, it had made her want to do it even more, to hurt her for all the shame she'd felt having to wear them.

They barely said a word to each other the next day, until Pa came home with a bunch of packages. They were in the kitchen getting dinner ready, and he shepherded the both of them into the living room and told them to sit right down. First, he ceremoniously pulled three new dresses from a bag and held them up, one at a time. "These are for my pretty little girl," he said handing them to her. Then he pulled out a lady's dress. It was navy blue with little white flowers. "And this is for my Pearl."

Angie could still see him taking the dress over, kneeling down and gently draping it across her mother, then kissing her on the cheek. It was one of the only times she had seen him do something like that. He looked deep into her mother's eyes. "We're doin' right nice, now, Pearl." Then he reached behind for another bag and pulled out a navy blue straw hat with a ribbon and carefully adjusted it on her head. "In fact, good 'nough for my woman to have a fancy new hat with a doodad." For as long as she lived, Angie would never forget her mother hanging her head and clutching the first store-bought dress she'd ever owned.

She took a tissue from her purse and wiped the tears from her cheeks. Looking back, she could see that from the moment she cut up her clothes, the battle lines were drawn. She and her mother were two different people on two different paths, each afraid the other's would lead to disaster. She didn't know much back then, but she did know if she got dragged into her mother's world, it would have suffocated her. She was born at a time when the old ways were over and the new were dawning every day. Ten years earlier or ten years later, things might have worked out differently.

Angie looked down on the frail, almost lifeless figure and asked how much easier life would have been if she hadn't resented her mother from the time she was eight. Her voice rose just above a whisper. "Momma, why wouldn't you bend; why wouldn't you try to understand just a little. I know you were always doin' the right thing, but if you only let me have my way once... broken your rules *just once*... we might have had a chance."

CHAPTER TWELVE

K AREN LANGUIDLY WIPED off the dining room table and smiled contentedly as she listened to Bruce's voice drifting in through the screen door. It was surprising how interested Hali had become in hearing stories about the family, just like Joel had.

She blotted the sweat on her forehead with a paper towel, thankful it had cooled down a little. The air conditioning was turned off since she didn't want to sit through another one of Bruce's lectures on waste.

She got a rubber band from the drawer and wandered over to the doorway. The harmonic cadence of Bruce's voice and the familiar idiosyncratic mountain-speak brought back all the winter nights in front of the fireplace and summers on the front porch when they'd all sit around and listen to Granny tell stories.

She lifted her hair away from her neck, pulled it up and snapped on the rubber band, then went over and put away the last of the dishes. Deciding to give everyone time to digest their dinner before serving the dessert, she meandered out onto the porch. Hali had pulled her sandaled feet up on the wicker chair and was hugging her legs. She'd grown a lot in the past weeks, and freckles had taken over her face. Karen bent down and gave her a peck on the cheek, then sank into a comfortable wicker chair and listened to Bruce's mellow mountain voice.

"Hali, they didn't have radio and TV when I was a kid. Everyone would sit around at night... women would sew... men would shuck corn... and just talk about all this old stuff. So you grew up knowin' everything. You'd sit around and hear these stories thousands of times and you'd know every little memory. If someone cheated your grandpa, heck, you'd know about it and wouldn't have anything to do with the bastard. But with the coming of TV and radio, we kinda lost all that."

"What were mountain people like?" asked Hali.

Bruce thought for a moment as if it were important to get it right. "*Independent* would be the main word that would describe 'em. They didn't want nobody messin' with 'em at all. They didn't want nobody helpin' 'em at all. And they didn't want nobody stickin' their nose in their business. And they had no use for the government a'tall. Probably the first phrase a kid learned was, *None of your business.* And they'd sure enough tell you that."

Two cardinals Hali had been feeding landed on the porch railing but flew off once Bruce started up again. "We were brought up to hate the British. When the U.S. went to war on their side in World War I, local folks were likely to have a calf. Even preachers in the pulpit at the Baptist church would say *damn* in front of the word *English.* But see, after you had TV, radio, and the movies and stuff like that you lost all of that."

"What did they have against the British," asked Hali.

Karen closed her eyes, knowing what was coming next.

"They were rotten mean. Heck, during the Revolutionary War they cut Adam Cooper's thumbs off and hacked up his shoulders to make him handicapped... you know, so he wouldn't have the use of his arms. Then there were the Merrills from Thomasville outside Lexington on the Randolph County line. They raided their house and took old man Merrill, who was up in his 70s, out and beat him to death. His wife said something hateful to them and they took a knife and cut her tongue in half and walked off and left her. *And that was common.*

"And you wonder why all those mountain people hated the British. The British thought they were superior; that's why they did it. And two hundred years later we still hated their stinkin' guts. Now, you have the New Englanders that come here from up north... and the Floridians... they have that superior attitude and it ain't long before we hate their guts, too."

Hali rocked casually in her chair. "We read about the Civil War on a plaque over by Sherrill's Inn. Mom said people around here fought on both sides."

"A lot of folks in Fairview sympathized with the South, but for the most part they really didn't care. They got suckered into joining the Confederate Army and figured they'd go and kill some city boys and be back home in a couple of months. But that didn't happen. Lincoln had an endless supply of city boys, and they could kill 'em and kill 'em and kill 'em and he'd just replace them; but the South couldn't."

Hali thought about that for a while. "The plaque said the Sherrill's Inn was on a drover's road."

"The Charlotte Highway never compared to the big drovers' road that went from Kentucky, down from Newport, over to Hot Springs, Asheville, Saluda Mountain, to Augusta and into South Carolina to Savannah or Charleston. They would drive 15,000 ducks or 20,000 turkeys...hogs were the biggest thing... and they would stop every twenty miles. So, farmers living ten or twenty miles from there would grow food to feed these animals for the night. There was a big one in Alexander, between Asheville and Marshall. They would stop there and the next night make it down to Asheville near where the Biltmore is, then they might make it down to Fletcher the next night. That's where your great granny and grandpa would take their feed."

The screen door squeaked open and the cat stepped out onto the porch. Karen rose and put her hand on Hali's shoulder. "Honey, why don't you go in the house and play with Bonnie for a while. Mommy needs to talk with Bruce about something."

"Aw... Mom."

"Just for a while. I'll call you when I'm putting out the

dessert." Karen waited until Hali was out of sight before asking, "Did you get my message about the notary?"

"Yeah. I knew that was gonna be a dry gulch. Travis is too wily to use someone he knows."

She shrugged. "It was worth a try." She strolled over to the railing and looked out. The setting sun hidden behind the mountains made the sky glow a deep maroon. The rattle of the cicadas had started up, and off in the distance she heard a mocking bird's last song for the day. "The lawyer said we might as well kiss the money from the bank account and stocks goodbye. Travis cleaned everything out before he even knew about the easement. Once he moved in, he must have gone through Granny's mail."

She looked over at Bruce. "At any rate, with the information I got from Tom Gibbons at the conservancy, I can now prove that she signed the deed over to Travis only eight days after he found out she intended to put an easement on the property. I bet you anything, once he saw she wasn't going to allow more than ten houses on each of our plots, he knew the land value would drop and wanted to stop it from happening. Especially since the only other thing she was going to let the land be used for was farming."

She crossed her arms loosely and fell against one of the posts holding up the porch roof. "Granny wanted the place to stay just as it was when she and grandpa had it." She turned and faced Bruce. "I can't believe Travis could pull this much crap in just two or three months. Believe me, Bruce, if it's the last thing I do, I'm going to see that he doesn't get away with it."

"Now don't you go and set yourself up for a fall, Karen. The lawyer wasn't very encouraging."

"I don't need encouragement."

"You could be tied up in the courts for years. And remember, lawyers ain't cheap."

The thought of all the bills coming in took a lot of the steam out of Karen's resolve. If only she could sell the co-op. The comps the realtor sent showed things were selling for thirty percent less than a year ago. Monday she better call Joel's brother and see how their case against Madoff was coming. She strolled over to Bruce, her arms still folded. "Don't worry, I've got enough put aside to get me through this."

"I don't know about you, woman. On one hand, you still got the mountain ways about you, and on the other, you've picked up a lot of them nasty Yankee habits."

A snicker drew Karen's eyes to the corner of the porch that wrapped around the front. "Okay, Hali. I know you're there."

Hali jumped out and threw up her arms. "*Ta Dah!*"

Barefoot, in overalls and wearing a straw hat that she had insisted her mother buy when they went shopping in Chimney Rock, she had a bandana around her neck and a corncob pipe in her mouth. She pretended to puff on it as she strutted around.

Karen shook her head.

"Heck," said Bruce. "That getup's better than the one she was wearin' the first time I laid eyes on her."

Hali crept over to her chair with her shoulders all hunched up and settled down again, tacitly asking her mother to pretend she wasn't there.

Bruce stayed on the subject. "I mean it, gal. You're throwing a load of money at that lawyer... and you're gettin' in way too thick with them conservation fanatics like Granny did." He looked around. "And then there's all that fancy stuff you went and bought. The way this place is gussied up, you'd think it was the Taj Mahal. It's almost a good thing that Pearl's not here to see what you've gone and done to the place."

Now, he's going to drag out Uncle Clint, thought Karen.

"Your great-uncle Clint worked at the Beacon Mill for ten years before he married Maggie, and when she died fifty years later, he said, 'I guess I'll have to get some of my Beacon money and buy her a tombstone.' In all his years he never spent one dime of his Beacon money even though he had a dozen different types of linoleum on the floor and a patched-up roof. When you save your money, you preserve your independence."

"Wait a minute, Bruce. Aren't you the one with the big ole brick house filled with antique furniture and china?"

"That's a whole sight different, girl. I didn't hire on a bunch of high-priced outfits from Lake Lure to fix it up like you did. I practically built that place with my own two hands... and them antiques are gonna pay for keepin' up the family cemetery when I'm gone."

Hali sprang up. "I'll take care of it for you, Cousin Bruce."

Karen looked first at Hali, then Bruce, and shook her head again. "What am I going to do with you two?"

Bruce was like a dog with a bone. "We've always been independent where nobody could ever hold nothin' on us, gal. When my grandma died we found all her property receipts back to 1895 in her trunk. She never trusted any bastards in the court house to keep the records. They were that way. They made sure they weren't dependent upon anybody. And they could handle a dollar. I tell you they could. In the sixties, your great grandpa drawed $125 a month. Grandma got $35 of it; and with it bought all their food and clothes, and probably saved ten bucks.

"You hear about booms and busts in the economy. Actually, everybody here in these mountains always lived like they were in a bust... *permanently.* So a depression didn't make no difference. It just brought everybody down to their level. I hope you're not raisin' that child in the Yankee culture, where everyone goes in debt. That didn't exist anywhere around here until after the 40s."

Karen suddenly worried Hali might say something about their loss to Bernie Madoff. "Hali, come in the kitchen and help Mommy serve the dessert," she quickly ordered.

Hali jumped at it. She now considered herself a professional blueberry picker. When they were making the pie, she had gone on an endless dissertation on the art of picking them off the bushes. Karen had picked them her whole childhood and was impressed with the part about holding a grain scooper in one hand and dropping them in with the other.

Hali carefully put a piece on a plate while Karen loaded on the ice cream, then she took one out to the porch and held it just out of Bruce's reach. "I picked the berries at Aunt Amy's." She gave him a big wink. "In fact, I picked enough for Uncle Eddie to sell some at the flea market, too."

Bruce raised his eyebrows in approval, snatched his pie and

dug in as Karen announced she was making some coffee.

"Is that husband of Amy's still selling that used farm equipment of his?" he said over his shoulder loud enough for Karen to hear.

"Oh yeah. He's pretty busy with it. He's doing a good business with the small antique stuff like those hand-cranked corn huskers and things like that. People decorate their family rooms and porches with them."

"Hell, if he manages to fix all the junk he's got laying around, they'll be millionaires."

That crack got a big laugh from Hali. She liked her Uncle Eddie but knew the property's appearance bothered her Aunt Amy.

They had the coffee and chatted a little longer, then Bruce rose and told them he had to get along. They handed him a covered dish with a piece of blueberry pie for his breakfast and kissed him goodbye at the door. Hali was tired and went upstairs.

Karen gathered up what dishes were on the porch and took them into the kitchen. She knew Hali must already be asleep since Bonnie had come back downstairs mewing for something to eat. Karen got some table scraps she'd put aside, picked up the cat and fed her from her hand.

The glow from a small lamp in the dark room brought out the warmth in all the wood. The room had also served as the kitchen when she was a kid. One of Granny's workers was handy with carpentry tools, so she had let him turn the original attached one-room log cabin they used as a catchall into a kitchen, only he walled off the old fireplace that Karen planned one day to restore.

She'd been sitting with her chin in her hand staring mindlessly down at the floor, when suddenly she blinked and snapped out of it. Her painted toenails came into focus. She pulled her foot up onto the seat and rubbed her toes, remembering all those Saturday nights after she gave Amy and Travis their baths.

Afterward, she would sit at this very same table and soak her feet until the water was too cool to be of any further benefit. But no matter how hard she scrubbed, she couldn't get all the dirt out of her cracked heels. Granny always gave her mother money to buy them shoes for the summer, but most of the time her mother would spend it on something else. Joel always teased her about not going to bed without putting on lotion and socks, her ritual from the time Granny took them in.

The cicadas had quieted down for a moment and the expectation of their starting up again made her feel like she was teetering on the threshold of the rest of her life. She longed to turn around and run back in time.

The challenge of putting things right was beginning to get to her. The only way she was going to do it was to find the diary. And then, like Mailo said, it had to have a smoking gun. Granny's diary was like an old friend who she told all her secrets to. And no matter what it took, Karen was going to get them all. It meant more than getting the farm back. Hidden in their pages, alive and full of grit, was the dear woman who mended a childhood of hurt.

All Bruce's talk about money nagged at her. Except for the visits to Granny every week, for all the good she was doing, she could have handled everything from New York. She got up and went around checking the doors, then started upstairs. She reached the top and peeked in on Hali and wondered if her daughter were pretending to be asleep the way she used to when her mother checked on her and Amy after a night of running around.

The light from the hall cast a beam along the floor and shot up across the stuffed animals on the mantle. She went in and ran her hand along the mementos Joel brought Hali from assignments all over the world. He had built a bond Hali would never forget, and she felt good that since coming to the mountains, her bond with Hali was getting stronger. She was learning to read Hali's signals. The kind the girl never sent to her before. It reminded her of the way Amy could always say something with body language.

She looked around the shadowy room and felt at peace there

for the first time. It was true she wasn't funny and adorable like Joel. But she did have something special to share with her daughter: her heritage. It had been good to sit on the porch and listen to Bruce tell Hali the stories she'd heard all her life, and it satisfied something basic in her to think the chain wasn't broken.

She went into her bedroom and started to get undressed. She could make a good argument that coming to the mountains didn't make sense, but it didn't matter. Joel's yearning to be here was what really brought her back to stay. Only it was sad that he had to die to get her there. It was too late for her to do it for him, but she could still do it for his child.

CHAPTER THIRTEEN

M OM, ARE YOU SURE I'm invited to the hoedown, too," queried Hali as Karen helped her pull a pink and white striped sundress over her head.

"I wouldn't dream of going without you, pumpkin. Everybody brings their kids. Once you start your violin lessons in the fall, you're gonna want to learn how to play some of those ole timey country tunes."

A horn beeped outside and Karen ran to the window and hollered they'd be right down. She gave Hali's hair a quick brushing and put it up in a ponytail, and then they ran down the stairs. Jason leaned over and threw open the truck door and they scrambled in.

"Sorry I got to cart you girls around in this old farm truck, but I haven't had time to go out looking for a car yet...." He turned toward Karen and gave her a meaningful look. "...I guess I didn't need one 'til now."

Karen felt Hali's nudge. The windows were down and the warm air buffed Karen's face as she watched the lush green of the mountains whiz by. She turned and studied Jason. He looked sturdy and robust. Almost dauntless. She could picture him walking down a dangerous Fallujah alley holding an M14. Then she imagined him handing out candy to a flock of kids. That big handsome smile of his would have won anyone over. She gulped hard. God, thank you for bringing him home safe.

She rested her arm in the open window and let her hair fly in the wind, feeling like a kid again. Then she reached behind Hali and knuckled Jason. "Remember the last time you took me into Old Fort?" He laughed, and she remembered hearing the siren, and then him turning off his lights and swinging onto a muddy mountain road around a curve. They had sat there in the dark giggling until the cop passed. He had put an arm around her and reached under her blouse. Karen glanced over at him again, and when their eyes met, she was convinced he was remembering the same thing.

The truck wove up and around the back road chiseled out of the mountain; then down again until it hit the straightaway into Old Fort. They drove under the Route 40 overpass, over the railroad tracks and into the town square.

The town had started as a fort built by the colonial militia before independence was declared, and served for years as the western outpost of the early United States. Karen looked around at the buildings facing Main Street. They were frozen in the 1870s, a time when the Southern Railroad brought people and products to the foothills of the Blue Ridge. But progress passed over the prosperous little hamlet like it did a lot of places dotting the mountains. The last passenger train to stop there pulled away in 1975.

"What's that?" shouted Hali as she pointed to a huge monument in the middle of the town square.

"It's an arrowhead," responded Jason. "It's made of hand-chiseled granite and has to be over twelve feet tall. It was put up in 1930 to commemorate how well the pioneer settlers and the Native Americans got along."

"Honey, next spring I'll bring you to the town's Pioneer Days... and we can visit the museum in the old railroad depot," said Karen.

Suddenly Jason announced, "Okay, girls. What's it going to be? The Rail Restaurant... or the Whistle Stop Pizzeria?"

"Oh, Jason, we've already eaten," said Karen.

He pulled into a packed parking lot off Main Street and squeezed into the last space. "Okay. I'll grab a couple of slices at the pizza place." He reached behind and pulled out his mandolin case. "I was shoveling slop at the pig pen less than an hour ago, and only had time to take a shower and change before I picked you girls up."

Hali nudged him with her elbow. "That's nothing. I've been scooping poop out of thirty-four dog runs all day."

Jason rolled his eyes and threw a glance at Karen. "I can see we've got a real handful over here."

"You have no idea," responded Karen.

They walked onto the busy street and saw a crowd flowing into the pizza shop. "Oh, boy. Looks like I'm gonna have to skip that."

"What do you mean?" asked Karen.

"The boys have signed us up for eight o'clock performance tonight and they'll be looking for me."

"Then you go ahead and we'll bring it to you."

"Thanks. Look for us over in the corner up front." He threw her a salute from the tip of his baseball cap and took off. Music trailed out as he opened the door to the building up ahead and disappeared inside.

The Mountain Music Center was housed in the old Rockett Building on Main Street and had held a hoedown from 7 to 11 every Friday night since 1986. There was no admission charge and bands played for free for a half hour, then another country or bluegrass band took over. The concession stand didn't serve alcoholic beverages, but volunteers dished out homemade pies and cakes for fifty cents a slice, and soft drinks and coffee for a quarter. Most folks handed them more if they could.

Karen and Hali started to weave their way through the packed hall that must have been a general store at one time. There was seating of every kind for at least two hundred, consisting of everything from recycled old theater seats to church pews.

Karen found two thickly upholstered empty movie house chairs, pushed down the seats and told Hali to sit down and hold onto them, then she made her way to the corner where the bands were assembling. Jason was talking with a couple of men, so she tapped him on the back and handed him the large pizza she had bought in case any of the other guys hadn't eaten. She hollered over the sound of the band that she'd be sitting with Hali.

As she made her way back, the band's singer crooned, *Your cheatin' heart will make you weep. You'll cry and cry and try to sleep.* Before she sat down, she went to the concession stand and bought a brownie for Hali and a cup of coffee for herself and left a five dollar bill on the counter.

Karen wasn't concerned about Hali bothering anyone when she jumped up and waved her over, since half the crowd was either talking with someone or rubbernecking to see who all was there. The crowd was pure mountain, wearing everything from overalls to sequin-studded blue jeans. Some were engrossed in the music and others floated around in the back talking and laughing and just catching up. Kids were renewing friendships with each other all over the place.

Karen sank into the cushy seat and listened to the band made up of four elderly gentlemen dressed in mostly jeans and short-sleeve shirts. The vocalist played a portable keyboard, one man a guitar, another a harmonica, and a man with a long white beard and an oil-stained baseball cap with a John Deere logo strummed on a mandolin. Sound from the microphones streamed through speakers mounted around the room.

The song finished and the vocalist announced that their half-hour was almost up and they were going to close with a hymn. Karen, recognizing the notes of *In the Garden*, put her arm around Hali and pulled her close. By the time they came to the refrain, tears streamed down her cheeks. *And He walks with me, and He talks with me, and He tells me I am His own...* She noticed Hali looking up at her and quickly wiped away the tears. She started to say something when Hali said, "That's okay, Mom. It got to me, too."

The set ended and the woman who had sold the coffee stood

on the stage and introduced the Fairview Mountaineers. Jason and his brother quickly took their places, Jason with his mandolin and his brother with a bass. The other two band members had fiddles. Hali poked her mother with her elbow as a pretty girl in jeans and a sparkly tee shirt came up to a mike and threw the group a glance over her shoulder for the music to start.

Hali raised herself on her elbows and whispered in Karen's ear. "Don't worry, Mom. I saw her with her arm around one of the fiddlers before they came on."

Their half hour whizzed by, and when they finished, the audience gave out an audible moan of regret and a huge round of applause. Hali and Karen gave their seats to a couple standing behind them and made their way to the door to wait for Jason. It took two songs by the new band before he emerged from the crowd and led them out.

"You guys were good," said Karen.

Hali quickly added, "Awesome, dude! Especially the mandolin."

Jason patted Hali's head. "I'm warmin' up to this kid." He turned toward Karen. "My brother wants me to say hello for him. He needed to hang around for the next band. They need a bass for tonight. He'll catch up with you at the square dance. And everyone thanks you for the pizza."

They walked toward the lot where he had parked the truck. Lights coming from the two restaurants cast beams across the sidewalk. The street was quiet, except for every once in a while when someone would open the door to the music hall and let the sound of the band drift into the night. A family came out of the pizzeria, and a couple of teenagers sat at a table inside.

When they got to The Rail, where almost every table was taken, Jason asked, "You girls want to grab something to eat?"

"Thanks, Jason. But Hali's had a big day and I've got to get her to bed."

He gave Karen the kind of look that made her think he might have interpreted the remark to mean she wanted to be alone with him, and she hoped she hadn't sent the wrong message. It surprised her that Hali didn't make a fuss. Nights in New York after they all went out to a movie or something, wild horses wouldn't keep her and Joel from dropping into the restaurant on the corner afterward for something to eat. She wondered if this evening had made her miss her dad even more.

Hali rested her head against Karen's arm on the way home and Karen suspected she had fallen asleep. "It's funny, Jason. Sitting there tonight among all those mountain farmers, I felt like I never left."

"Yeah, I know what you mean. All I had to do in Iraq was strum something on my mandolin and it would bring me right back home." He was silent a while. "Times in Iraq when I'd see a farmer hoeing his small field, I'd really connect with him, and it brought our mission home to me. I'll never forget those times. It was surreal. You had to keep one-hundred-percent focused on killing the enemy if you wanted to survive, yet every once in a while something like a man in his field would hit you right in the gut.

"I met a lot of farmers in the Marines. Heck, they came from gigantic operations all over the U.S. Two hundred milkers and up. One kid told me his dad planted twelve hundred acres of corn every year. That's what makes us here in the mountains different. The 'get big or get out' model hasn't hit us yet, and I don't think it ever will. Sustainable agriculture is what we've got going for us. Hundreds of small family farms raising animals and crops the old fashioned way. No antibiotics, no synthetic fertilizers... none of that crud."

He looked over at her for an instant. "Have you been to any of our tailgate markets?" He didn't wait for an answer. "The selection is phenomenal. We're not growing fields and fields of the same damn thing. Instead of the standardized selection of vegetables, we're producing all kinds of exciting varieties... some you can't get anywhere else."

He was quiet for the rest of the ride, and she imagined his mind was stuck in Iraq. She reflected a while on some of the times they had growing up together, but then her thoughts landed on the man from the conservancy she was going out with the next night. She hardly knew him, but he had an intense passion for the land, too, and that appealed to her. She laughed to herself again, remembering how he had doggedly hung at the door until he got his date.

The truck pulled into her driveway and Jason jumped out offering to carry Hali in, but by the time he came around to their side she was awake. He helped them down and walked them to the door.

"That's okay, Mom. I can make it up to bed myself," Hali said groggily as Karen unlocked the door.

Hali went in and Jason quickly barred Karen from entering. She leaned back and crossed her arms. "Am I being detained, officer?"

He tossed his head back and laughed.

"Sunday after the square dance, you can come over and we can talk," she said.

He looked out in the distance and then back at her. "Can I at least have a kiss?"

She ducked under his arm and stepped into the house. "Absolutely not." She reached for the knob, pulled the door almost shut and grinned out at him. "I remember what you did the last time I let you kiss me."

CHAPTER FOURTEEN

I T WAS SATURDAY morning, but almost everyone had showed up at the office for one reason or another. The buoyant weekend mood was palpable, only this time Tom was getting caught up in it. Tonight he was taking Karen out. Even Kevin turned up with his two kids to get a copy of the agenda for the board meeting on Monday.

Kevin hadn't wanted to bring the Grassy Patch purchase to a vote until everyone's issues were fully addressed. By now, every member knew what was going on and had a chance to voice their concerns. This was Kevin's strong suit. Whether he agreed with a board member or not, each had a rock solid belief that he would hear them out and respond to any and all misgivings they might have.

The only thing missing for the Monday meeting was the letter from Graystone's home owners' association giving the conservancy access to the property; right now, going through the development was the only practical way to get to the site.

Kevin peeked in Tom's office, his two kids at his side. "Are you sure you'll have that agreement signed for the Monday meeting? Two board members made it clear they won't go for this deal without it, and if we don't get this thing passed soon, God only knows what else is gonna turn up."

Tom smiled at the two little faces that looked as if they were headed for fun. "I'm picking it up in Lake Lure at five. The homeowners' board is meeting at Rumbling Bald Resort, and they want it officially voted on and read into their minutes before they hand it over." Kevin tossed a wave and gleeful shouts from his two boys trailed down the hall.

By noon, the only other person still around was Rosemary who kept popping into his office with questions about the press release she was working on that would announce the Grassy Patch Mountain purchase. He wrote at his computer for a couple hours, but found it hard to concentrate. His eyes kept darting over to the time in the corner of the screen. Finally, Rosemary said she had to baby-sit for her sister, and Sweetie started dancing around like she needed to go. "Okay, girl. Let's get the heck out of here. *Daddy's steppin' out tonight.*"

By four, he was dressed and ready to leave for Lake Lure. He put on his jacket and patted it down to make sure he had the tickets for the play, then checked himself in the mirror. He liked the way the light blue seersucker jacket and white shirt looked with his tan, and he started to straighten his tie when he abruptly loosened it, pulled it over his head and unbuttoned his shirt at the neck.

That's more like it, he said as he ran his hand through his hair. The jacket would be enough for the dinner at the Kenmure Country Club, but just in case, he stuffed the tie in his pocket. He took off the jacket, slung it over his shoulder and started for his truck. With the play starting at eight, he and Karen would have a good hour to get comfortable with each other over dinner.

As usual, the weekend traffic was backed up from Chimney Rock to Lake Lure. He wound around the lake, took a left at the dam and made his way along the twisty road that hugged the side of the mountain, every once in a while glimpsing the lake below through the dense hardwood forest. All he had to do was run in and grab the signed agreement before heading over to

Fairview to pick Karen up.

Hopefully the meeting would be almost over and he wouldn't have to listen to depressing stories from people who felt they'd been cheated. What a dog and pony show the developer had put on, helicoptering folks from a meadow in Chimney Rock Park over the Round Top ridge to the Graystone property and letting them pick out their lot from the sky. With no roads, water or electricity, those parcels were now going for a quarter of what people paid for them.

The guard at the gate let him in the resort, but he had to hunt for a parking space. Shouts from people on the beach and at the pools filled the air as he made his way to the clubhouse.

He entered the building and could see the room ahead was packed, so he joined a group standing against the back wall. Tom looked around at the flushed, grim faces.

"Where in the hell is all the money?!" demanded a man standing in the middle of the audience.

The president of the home owners' association stood at a podium. "I'm afraid only Bob Ward knows the answer to that question, and he's sitting in the county jail in Orlando. Sadly, we're hearing that the reason he killed his wife was that she threatened to divulge where he stashed it."

One of the board members got up and leaned into the mike. "We've done the math. There's $79-million in lot sales registered in the county courthouse. His share of the HGTV dream house set him back a million, and with his marketing expenses and offices, and the front gate he put up... maybe... all together... he spent around $20-million. That left more than enough to pay off his loans and put in all the infrastructure he promised."

The president threw up his hands and shrugged his shoulders. "So where *is* that $60-million? So far nobody's been able to find it and a woman lost her life over it."

A man standing in the back yelled out, "We know all that. What's the board doing about it?"

A chorus of angry voices rose up, and the president looked over his shoulder, eyeing the board members as if he hadn't expected such a volatile reception.

Someone else in the crowd shouted, "And what's this about giving that conservancy a right of way through Graystone?"

Another board member stood up and said loud enough to be heard and stern enough to be listened to, "Because that's the only way they're gonna buy that parcel; and if we prefer a bunch of tree huggers for neighbors over some chiseling developer, we're gonna have to give it to 'em."

The man in the audience who had been voicing his concerns made eye contact with as many as he could. "Just think about it, folks. When a developer finally buys the 700 lots left in Graystone, sure as hell, we'll get hit with an assessment to help with the roads and amenities. Probably thirty thousand apiece, or even more. Why should we just hand over an easement for nothing?"

Suddenly, the president announced, "Tom Gibbons from the conservancy just walked in. I'm going to ask him to answer that question himself."

Tom felt his anger rising. The conservancy was doing everything in its power to save that ridge, and the effort was going to directly benefit these guys! They should be hailing this deal, not digging up objections. Damn. The stakes were too high to let a couple of overwrought owners derail the deal.

He had no choice but to lay everything out, plain and simple. "Our organization is dedicated to saving these mountains, but we can't buy this tract without being able to get to it... and other than going around Summit Mountain... which will be too costly, this is the only way in. The best possible use of that land... and the best possible benefit to you... is if it's kept in its natural state through a conservation easement. Otherwise, you're risking it being bought by some cut-rate developer who will treat it unkindly... or worse yet, a lumber company that will turn it into a moonscape before selling it off piecemeal."

Another man stood up. "He's right. This is our safest option."

Tom scanned the sea of faces. He was betting these people knew the value of conserving that mountain range, or they wouldn't have bought a lot in the middle of God's country in the first place. "Our option is good for another twenty-one days. And it's going to take that long to scrape up the money and finish up the paperwork. If we can't meet the trustee's deadline, he's going to be forced to let it go to the highest bidder... and believe me folks, you're going to like doing business with us a lot better than whoever's going to come after us."

A woman waved her hand and the president gave her a nod. "Is this a board decision?"

He cleared his throat. "Yes, but we've invited you all here to air everything. We have to move forward as a group. That's where our strength is."

Another man spoke up. "I'd like to see that land stay natural, but my lot borders that section and I'm worried about hikers and rock climbers traipsing all over our development if this place ever gets off the ground."

Tom could see this objection was getting a lot of traction. He caught a nervous glance from the president and hated like hell to do it, but quickly offered a compromise. "I understand your concerns. We can cut out a strip between our property and your development and create a forested buffer thick enough to create a barrier."

Tom held his breath as a motion was passed by the board to work out a license agreement to include the buffer zone.

Tom looked at his watch. Damn! It was already six. The crowd began to thin as the board laboriously ran through the rest of their agenda. He had to get out of there, but not until he set up an appointment for the next day to work out the details of the agreement and get it signed.

As he approached the table, the president looked up at him and said somewhat apologetically, "Several of our lot owners are quite litigious. That's one reason we like to be transparent."

"I understand, but we need to get this agreement done by Monday. Can we set up a meeting for tomorrow to finalize everything?"

When they all said they were leaving in the morning, except the president who would be there until Monday, Tom got a sickening feeling.

141

"That settles it, Tom. We either have to hash this out after we get through here, or we're going to have to put it off until we get another quorum."

"No. Let's get it done tonight."

He checked his watch. He was supposed to pick Karen up in five minutes. The information operator told him her number was unlisted, so he had no choice but to call Rosemary and see if she could go back to the office and get Karen's number from his file. He dialed and prayed she'd pick up. No answer.

Now he remembered. She was baby-sitting. Next, he tried Josh Freeman, who lived just a couple miles from Karen. If he didn't have her number, he'd go over and tell her himself. Again, no answer. Damn, he'd have to call Kevin. That didn't work either. *Where in the hell was everybody?!*

He went into the dining room bar and ordered a beer. By the time he finished the second one he had redialed every number two or three times and was resigned to the fact that instead of sitting next to Karen in a dark theater trying to make a move, he'd be wrestling with the board to forge an agreement that was going to stick to that mountain forever. Recalling how upset Karen got when he was only an hour late, he wondered how she was going to take being stood up?

CHAPTER FIFTEEN

THIS WAS THE FIRST time Jason felt really alive since he rolled out of the troop plane at Camp Lejeune. He raced through the switchbacks and pulled into The Big House's gravel driveway. He could see several cars had already arrived as he jumped out, grabbed the roll of meat-packing paper from the back and headed for the garden.

Giant trees and a wall of twelve-foot tall privets along the rugged stone path obscured the house. He ducked through an opening in the ancient garden. Half-dozen tables stood in a row and a box of supplies lay on the sloping lawn. He got busy spreading the paper, then made quick work of unfolding the chairs and placing them around the lawn in clusters.

Voices hollering orders back and forth drifted through the haze of wisteria and ivy draping the porches. He stood for a moment taking in the layers of veiled blue mountains circling the lush green valley below. Tater Knob Mountain sat off to his right, and Flat Top even farther in the distance. It was the very scene he had evoked a million times in Iraq.

Someone called his name from the porch. He tore his gaze

from the view and answered that he was coming, then raced along the stones on the path he knew by heart, taking the steps onto the east porch two at a time.

"Good. You brought the paper," said a volunteer.

He covered the tables, then moved on to the south porch. Mabel McGee, one of the founders of the Lord's Acre, spotted him from inside the house and came running out. She was wearing her Sunday best jeans and a billowy blouse designed to disguise the curves that had begun to turn into folds. Jason loved her. Running a farm on her own through thick and often thin for the thirty years since her husband died had made her hard and then soft again.

Jason wrapped his arms around her and felt the fierce connection to community he'd been raised with. It was just like her to resurrect that old project from the 30s where everyone banded together and donated produce from one acre of their crops to help feed others in need. Tough times had returned and she knew what it was like.

"Son, it sure is good to have you back. You nearly killed your ma with worry."

"I'm home to stay this time, Mabel."

Someone on the other porch yelled her name and she hollered back that she was on her way. Already breathless, she started to lift a box of donations for the raffle. Jason grabbed it up and followed her back around the corner, greeting the swarm of volunteers already at work on the east porch, then he went inside.

The house, built by the Sherrills in 1834, was bustling with volunteers busily arranging the higher priced auction items on the inn's colonial furniture. The room had been built large enough to seat all the peddlers, farmers, and stagecoach patrons traveling up and down the drover's road, plus prosperous gentry on their way to the cool mountains during the summer. Lying with other offerings on the heart pine floor in the dining room was a hand-carved poplar shovel he had his eye on.

Leaning against the chestnut paneling was a hand-made long rifle that someone had donated. Jason picked it up and ran a hand along the plain maple stock. He checked the aim, wondering about the frontiersman who had crafted it. Did he use it to hunt deer and bear to feed his family, or was he an Indian fighter. He wouldn't be surprised if the weapon had seen action against the English over at Kings Mountain during the Revolutionary War. He pictured his high-tech M14 and thought that after all these years, conflict was still a matter of a man and his weapon.

Mabel had come in and noticed his interest in the longarm. "You gonna make a bid on that, son?"

He shook his head. "I'm afraid it's too rich for my blood. I'd love to have it though."

"We got a bunch of offers from gun collectors and will sell it to one of 'em if it comes to that, but we're holding out hope that a local will beat them out and keep it in the valley." She shrugged her voluminous shoulders. "No matter, this gift's gonna underwrite the food bank for a mighty long time." She spotted someone coming in with another item and scooted off.

Before running up to his bedroom, Jason peeked in the music room. It was his favorite place in the house. Ever since he was a kid he would admire the delicate oil murals his great-grandmother had painted to depict scenes from the seventy-five years the old house served as an inn. It had welcomed guests of every kind and degree, including two U.S. presidents.

Out of the corner of his eye he spotted a woman coming into the house. She had wanted to fix him up with her sister. He quickly raced up the narrow stairs. Not only had that sister of hers been the school tattletale, he happened to be the one she told on. Besides, the bouncy lieutenant he'd had so much fun with whenever he got to Baghdad was coming in a couple of weeks, and he was interested to see how that might go. But most of all there was Karen.

TOM LOOKED AT his watch. Almost four. No one was in the office on a Sunday, and the only sound was an occasional *humph* from Sweetie as she got comfortable on the floor next to him. He emailed the agreement with the Graystone Home Owners' Association for Kevin to look over and turned off the computer. He'd make any changes in the morning before he took it to the resort for signing, and be back well before the conservancy's board meeting.

"Come on girl, let's vamoose," he said to Sweetie as he searched his desk for his keys. On the way out he snatched up the last of the candy from the bowl at the reception desk.

He let down the tailgate for Sweetie to hop in and slid into the truck. As he started to switch on the ignition, a piercing call from a mockingbird in a nearby tree made him look out the open window. An eerie quietude hung over the deserted business complex. He let go of the key and slumped back in his seat.

The problem with the Graystone association started to spill from his mind and the problem with Karen began to pour in. When he called her that morning to explain what happened, she was polite, but so ice cold he didn't dare ask her for another date. If he didn't have to come in and work up the agreement, he would have driven out and apologized in person.

In fact, if he didn't have to take two of their Americorps members to the fundraiser at Sherrill's Inn this afternoon, he'd go over there right now and tell her how sorry he was. If only he hadn't promised Tori and Nikki he'd take them! But this mess wasn't their fault. They were nice kids, and he owed them a good time, especially Tori. She'd been phoning around on her lunch hour for auction items for weeks now.

He could see why she was so loyal to The Lord's Acre. It was the reason she was brought on board at the conservancy in the first place. As an intern with the food bank during its first summer, she'd set up contacts and coordinated their efforts with pantries in three counties, proving her ability to interface with community groups, a talent the conservancy needed.

He turned onto a tree-lined street in one of Hendersonville's older neighborhoods a couple blocks from downtown and pulled up in front of his bungalow. A tricycle lay abandoned on the grass and plastic toys were scattered on the steps. He lived on the first floor and rented out the top to a nice couple. Newly married when he first let it to them, they now they had two kids.

Their occasional arguments were usually accompanied by slamming doors that shook the house. These spats told him they were having a tough time making ends meet, so he never had the heart to raise their rent, even though his taxes and insurance had skyrocketed in the four years they'd lived there.

Sweetie beat him to the door. He unlocked it, grabbed his mail and went in. The dog ran straight to her bowl in the kitchen. He looked around as though he were seeing the place for the first time. Every vestige of coziness was sucked out when Holly left.

A leather recliner sitting alone on the bare wood floor made the room look gloomy. At least when Holly was there she would artfully lay a throw over the rip down the center of the seat. Her mother had even stripped the windows of their curtains, leaving nothing but grim, water-stained roll-down shades. His giant flat-screen TV looked ridiculous above the ornate Victorian fireplace.

He went into the kitchen and beefed up Sweetie's bowl, gave her some fresh water and got a beer from the fridge. He took a long satisfying swig as he strolled into the bedroom. The legs of a chair were barely visible under a pile of clothes and the bed looked like it hadn't been made in weeks. He got undressed and hung his shirt and jeans on the bedpost. They were good for another wear.

Tomorrow he'd tell the lady upstairs to go ahead with cleaning his apartment. Last week when she came down to give him back his key after letting the plumber in, the place had been such a mess he had a hard time looking her in the eye. She made small talk for a while, but with the kids hollering for her upstairs, he knew she was just stalling. She finally came to the point and offered to do his housekeeping once a week for what sounded like a reasonable rate.

Showered and shaved, he put on a fresh pair of khakis and chose a light blue checked shirt Holly had given him for his birthday last summer. It looked good against his tan. He put Sweetie in her run in the back yard, then left to pick up the girls.

The minute he pulled up to their apartment house, Tori and Nikki came bouncing out, laughing and waving. Oh boy. He'd seen those two in high spirits before and hoped he could handle it. He reached over and threw open the door and they jumped in.

The pickup made its way to Route 64 and headed north through Hendersonville. Tori, sitting next to the window, held up the box she was carrying. "Wait 'til you try my double chocolate, double nutty brownies."

With no dinner last night and nothing to eat all day but coffee and a couple stale donuts he found in the office kitchen, Tom couldn't get his mind off the brownies. "You girls couldn't reach in that box of yours and wrestle one out for me, could you?"

"Should we?" Tori asked Nikki in a patronizing tone.

"Why don't you look and see if we have enough?" said Nikki.

Tom ignored their teasing sing-song voices and kept one eye on the traffic and the other on the box.

The lid off, Tori said, "Let me see. *One... twoooo... threeee...*"

Tom reached over and tried to grab one, but Nikki slapped his hand.

"All right... we'll give you one," said Tori. "But *just* one."

Tom downed it in two bites. Suddenly a car pulled in front of him. He slammed on the brakes and sent everything on the dashboard flying, including his BlackBerry. Nikki picked it up and started browsing. "Look! He's got all the restaurant carry-out numbers on automatic dial!"

Both of the girls howled.

"Oh my God! He's got two numbers for the Waffle House. I can just hear him ordering hash browns scattered, smothered and covered with eggs!"

With one hand on the wheel, Tom lunged for the phone, but Nikki held it beyond his grasp.

"Okay, Nikki, you've had your laughs, now let me have it."

Tori grabbed it out of her hand and handed it over, saying, "No wonder you're always scrounging for food. You can't live on stuff from those places. Someone told me all you have in your fridge is beer and milk, for Pete's sake."

Tom put his BlackBerry in his pocket wondering how these conscientious, devoted girls who worked tirelessly and brilliantly at their desks all day could turn into double nutty she-devils the minute they left the office?

He spent the drive through Apple Valley, and then the climb through the gorge, feigning interest in Tori's lecture on the nutritional value of fresh organic food while he thought about Karen.

The pickup pulled onto the inn's drive that jutted from one of the gap's hairpin curves, and was directed to a recently mowed upper hay meadow. Tom parked and they made their way to the house with a few other late-comers.

Tom followed the girls through an opening in the privet hedge. At least a hundred people were jammed into what seemed like the remnants of a formal terraced box garden. The tables were loaded with the kind of food he liked—home-made dishes brought to the gathering with pride.

Tori and Nikki ran off and he got in line and piled his plate high. Spying Josh and Josephine Freeman sitting by themselves, he joined them and ate while listening to Josh's friendly chatter. Then, still hungry, he excused himself and made his way back to the food. Just as he helped himself to a heaping portion of lasagna, he caught sight of Karen and Hali. Why didn't he think of it before? Of course they'd be there. Now he could get Karen aside and apologize properly.

Just then, a guy came up to her and put his arm around her waist. The way she slipped an arm around his shoulder made Tom wonder if he could be more than just a friend. Quickly, before she noticed him, he threw on some salad, grabbed a couple of rolls and made his way back to the Freemans.

"For someone as lean as yourself, you sure do put down the grub," said Josh as Tom ate with his back to the crowd. "Somethin' botherin' you, son?"

"No. I'm good." He hung around talking with the Freemans until the crowd thinned, then the three of them went up to the porch where everyone was looking over the auction items and writing in bids.

When Josephine got drawn into a conversation with two women, Josh nudged him. "Let's get the heck out of here. I'll show you the spring house."

They left the porch and made their way through the crowd to the side of the house where with the original log cabin stood and went in. It was paneled in hand-planed chestnut with chinks at the top for Indian fighting.

"This is the old Ashworth cabin built around 1806. That valley down there used to be all swampland, so the early settlers built up on the hills and mountains to avoid getting typhoid and malaria. Once the Sherrills bought the place and added on the inn, they used the cabin to put up the drovers, communally," said Josh.

The spring house, a small structure made of chestnut logs, was situated next to the cabin. Icy water gushed from a spring in the mountain and drained into a large cement tub big enough to hold at least a dozen buckets of milk and butter. Thick windowless walls trapped the coolness.

A country band sounded in the distance.

"Let's go up to the meadow and watch the dancin'," said Josh.

"Shouldn't we find Josephine first?"

"Nah. She'll find us. Haven't been able to shake that woman in over fifty years."

They fell in with the stragglers leaving the auction and climbed the wooded path toward the music. The lane opened to a peaceful meadow with a large wooden platform for dancing and a stage for the band: two fiddles, a bass and two guitars. Another fiddler was on the platform calling squares.

Tom surveyed the dancers and his eyes locked onto Karen, then the guy he'd seen her with in the garden. The music stopped and the man put his arm around her waist and led her away with more authority than Tom cared to see. The guy was definitely coming on strong.

Josh must have noticed his gaze. "That's the Whitfield gal home from up north. She's widowed with a child. That's Jason Ager she's with. He's one of Annie Clarke-Ager's boys."

They watched for a while and noticed Hali and a couple of kids running after a little rat terrier. It only had three legs but was still getting the better of them. After a while, Josh and Tom strolled casually through the crowd, stopping every once in a while to greet someone Josh knew or Tom had met through his his work in the valley.

Two conservancy board members were there with their spouses, and he wondered if they had gotten wind of his close call with the Grassy Patch homeowners' association. But they either didn't know about it, or weren't letting on.

Tom recognized Holly's lilting laugh the minute it rippled out of her mouth. She had to be just a few feet away. He stopped and folded his arms and looked out over the stage as if he were suddenly interested. Josh was fine with that and folded his arms and looked out, too.

What was Holly doing there? Now he remembered. One of the lawyers in her firm was a Clarke. He must have invited everyone in the company who was making enough to be looking for write-offs. Holly was hardly in that bracket. She was still paying off her student loans. She must have come with one of the senior partners.

He turned his head to get a quick look. Her long blonde hair had been bobbed and she was wearing a flowing summer dress… something expensive her mother must have talked her into. Boy, that woman was dead set on her daughter finding a rich husband. He sensed it the minute he first met her, with all her questions about what he did and why wasn't he with a big law firm.

He waited a few moments, then looked over again to see who she was with. Had to be the good looking one. The other guy was too old for her. He spotted the Rolex watch and the four-hundred-dollar alligator loafers. With the money everyone on the conservancy staff had given up to keep everybody on board, Tom was lucky to be meeting his mortgage payments.

Where in the hell were those two vixens, he asked himself. Probably at the house helping with the auction. With the mood they were in, there'd be no getting them away until they were good and ready.

He wished he wasn't wearing the shirt Holly bought him.

There was something about it that made him feel discarded.

Josh noticed he kept looking over to his left. "What's the big attraction?"

"My ex-fiancée."

Josh leaned forward to get a good look.

The music stopped and someone stepped in front of Tom. He nudged Josh to move over a little so he could keep Karen in sight.

It didn't take much for Josh to figure out what was going on. "Gee, son. You sure got your hands full."

Suddenly, a voice came over the PA system. "Okay, folks. Come on up for the next square."

Tom, keen to see if Karen was going to dance again, kept an eye on the stage. He was startled by someone clasping his hand. Hali stood in front of him with a solemn look on her face.

"Will you dance with me?"

Tom closed his eyes and rubbed his forehead with an expression of pain on his face.

She tugged at him. "Please."

He crouched down low enough to look her in the eye and whispered, "There's nothing I'd rather do than dance with you, Hali, but I just don't know how to do this type of thing. You don't want to see me make a fool of myself, do you?"

The speaker blared, "All right, everyone, we need one more couple."

Hali tugged harder and exclaimed loud enough to attract attention. "Don't worry. You won't make a fool out of yourself."

Nearby laughter made Tom's ears burn. He slowly turned and looked at Holly's party. Everyone had a friendly smile on their face, but hers looked forced. Then he glanced across the dance floor and caught Karen's stare.

"Go on. Dance with the lady," the man in front of him urged.

Two kids Hali had been playing with chimed in. "Go on. Do it."

Josh whispered, "You got no choice, son. You better get out on the floor with her before this crowd gets any rowdier."

Tom decided to take one more stab at talking Hali out of it, but when he looked into her eyes and saw they were teary, shook his head. "Okay, kiddo, here goes nothing." He grabbed her hand and led her onto the platform.

The music started up and the caller shouted, "Promenade left."

This wasn't difficult, thought Tom as he held Hali's hand and walked along behind the other couples. The only problem was he was at least a foot taller than the rest of the dancers and stuck out like a sore thumb. Hali's flaming hair and pink dress wasn't helping either. His eyes darted around and he could see everyone was watching them, including the wife of one their board members who gave him a timid wave.

Things went pretty well, other than the fact that they were always a couple of beats behind.

"Allemande!" the caller announced.

He made a quick turn right and ran smack into a buxom lady. A gleeful laugh rolled over the crowd. He apologized, then noticed everyone walking around their partners. Hali picked up on it and ran around him.

"Promenade right."

Flustered, they both turned in the wrong direction again and bumped into another couple. Tom heard the laughter and determined he wouldn't make another mistake if it killed him. He took Hali's hand and held it firm as they followed the couple in front of them. It wasn't helping matters that she was enjoying all the attention.

"Do-Si-Do, everyone."

Tom kept a grip on Hali and took a minute to study the next move. They were going to get this one right. Everyone had stopped and faced their partner. He took Hali by the shoulders and turned her so she was facing him. He watched for a moment and could see the dancers move around each other clockwise. He tried to steer Hali in the right direction, but she just twirled around. Someone laughed out loud, sending another ripple of laughter through the crowd.

He was concentrating so intensely he didn't dare look out at the crowd, but the one brief moment he did, all he saw was Josh and Josephine throwing up their hands and laughing. Somehow it took the sting out of his embarrassment. They didn't have a mean bone in their bodies.

By now, he was catching on. He held on tight to his little partner's hand and they bumbled their way through to the end. Walking off the platform they got a round of applause, followed by a curtsey from Hali.

Nikki and Tori ran up to them.

"She's so cute!" cooed Tori.

After all the mischief Hali had been up to, Tom felt the unconditional love she was getting from the two girls was a little unfair. Hali rocked on her toes and basked in the attention, while all he wanted was to talk the girls into leaving. He looked around. Josh and Josephine were chatting with someone and the crowd was thinning. Mercifully, Holly was nowhere in sight. It had grown dark enough that the lights were on and the mosquitoes starting to bite. A crowd had gathered around the band and was watching them pack.

While Nikki fawned over Hali, Tom pulled Tori aside. "Can we shove off?"

"Sure. It's pretty much over."

He turned to tell Nikki and saw Karen standing there with a warm smile. He broke into a big grin. "Hi."

"Hi to you, too."

Hali tugged at her mother and excitedly introduced her to her two new friends. Tom took advantage of the distraction and studied Karen. She had tied her hair back with a ribbon just like the first time he saw her. Soft dark curls peeked out along her hairline. Up ahead, Jason was talking to the caller. This was the first chance Tom had to get a good look at him. He was handsome, and handled an air of authority with ease.

Tom got a whiff of Karen's sweet scent as Jason finished with the caller and started toward them. Tom quickly raised his hand to interrupt Tori. "Karen..." He leaned toward her in an effort to shelter her from everyone's glare and whispered, "Can I have a rain check for next Saturday."

Her deep blue eyes fixed on him and their nearness almost overwhelmed him.

"Uh-huh."

"Six?"

"Yes."

Jason neared and Karen pulled him over to introduce him. Tom shook his hand and looked him square in the eye. After a few uncomfortable moments, Karen said they had to go, and the three of them walked off with Hali turning her back and waving impishly over her shoulder.

Tom said goodbye to the Freemans and walked the girls to the pickup, wondering what made Hali come over and ask him to dance. He had been sure she'd never forgive him for standing her mother up.

He replayed everything in his head. The evening had been a nightmare. No question about it. He'd been humiliated in front of Holly and her friend with the alligator loafers; it was pretty clear a handsome dog from a prominent local family was hot on Karen's trail; and now, to top it all off, he was going to have to endure merciless teasing from the girls on the way home. But it was worth it. She said yes.

JASON HAD STAYED to help load some of the heavier auction items, so they were late getting back from the square dance. "You've really fixed this place up nice," he said as Karen came down from putting Hali to sleep.

He followed her through the dining room and into the kitchen where she handed him a beer and opened one for herself. She leaned against the counter. "It was good to see your mom and dad tonight."

He went over and put his bottle on the counter, then took hers from her hand and put it down, too. She gazed at him, steadily. He braced himself against the counter and leaned toward her. "Boy, those eyes of yours are still as dark blue as ever. But you sure as heck ain't that skinny tomboy any more."

Karen reached for her beer and took a long drink. He took the bottle and put it down again, then surrounded her, leaning

155

with both hands on the counter. "Are you going to give me that kiss you promised?"

Karen folded her arms and raised an eyebrow. *"Kiss?* I never promised you a kiss."

Jason shook his head. "You mean I've got to wrestle you for it like the first time?"

Karen threw her head back and laughed. "Those were the days, weren't they? How old were we? Twelve?"

"I should have just left you there after you went and started that fight with Billy Hutchinson. When that whole damn clan came after us, I figured you got us killed. I never ran so fast in my life. I got one hell of a whippin' for losing my shoe."

"Heck, you got so many whippins', I bet you didn't even feel it."

He came nearer and slowly rubbed his cheek against hers, then brushed his lips along her ear. "You sure have filled out a lot since then."

She felt the heat from his body and his hand tracing her breast. She gently put her hand on his chest for him to stop.

He turned and stomped around in a circle with his hands on his hips. "Damn it! I knew it... the way you were watching that guy tonight. I can't believe he had the balls to ask you for a date right in front of me."

"It's not him, Jason. I'm just..."

"You're just not interested is what you're not. I started to get that feeling Friday night, but figured all you needed was a little time to warm up."

She went over, extended her arms and rested her wrists on his shoulders. "Okay. If you want the kiss, you can have the kiss. I don't want you goin' home mad."

He put his hands on her waist. "Oh, no. You had your chance." He broke into a big grin and tossed his head to the side, "Heck, why not." He put his arms around her, drew her tight and kissed her.

She wrestled herself free and fanned her face with her hand. "Wow, you sure aren't the same kid who almost peed in his pants the first time you tried that."

He held her shoulders. "You know, Karen. In all these years, I've never been able to get you out of my head. When you took off for college, I waited like a damn fool every summer for you to show your face... then I heard you got married." He rubbed the back of his hand along her cheek. "I better be going."

She walked him to his truck, and he started to get in, then stopped and looked in her eye. "Karen, if things don't work out with that guy, give me a call. But don't wait too long. Life is short and I'm done waiting around for you."

CHAPTER SIXTEEN

K AREN PULLED UP to the brown brick box. It looked more like a factory than a nursing home. There were only a few parking spaces in the narrow guest lot, and as usual, they were empty. She picked up a small bundle of colorful zinnias she got from Annie Louise's farm stand and got out.

She entered the building, walked through the small sparsely furnished reception lounge and turned down the first hall. She told herself to keep focused on the far end and not look in any of the rooms, no matter what sounds she heard. She didn't want to go back to work depressed again.

She was familiar with most of the patients by now, and as she was getting ready to hurry by the first doorway she suddenly couldn't stand the thought of any one of these lonely souls being passed over and ignored. She made a point of looking in each and every room, then threw a wave and smiled broadly at everyone who looked up at her.

It was mid-afternoon with lunch over and all the meds dispensed, so there was little activity and no attendants around. The first two times she had come, she used every plea, every argument and eventually every single ugly little threat she could conjure up to get the director to answer her questions, but the woman just kept repeating that she should talk with her brother. When she tried the next level, all she got from the attendants and nurses were inane smirks or nervous disregard. She was now at a stalemate with the whole institution and had finally swallowed the fact that Travis was the only one they would talk to.

She could picture Travis charming the director and then giving her a wink and a nod after she promised that no one would say anything to his sister except: *Ask your brother. He has your grandmother's power of attorney.*

She reached the end of the hall and peeked in her grandmother's room with trepidation. A sigh of relief escaped when she saw her in the bed. She choked back angry tears thinking they'd never call her if anything happened; just Travis, and he probably wouldn't let her know.

She went over and kissed the small deeply wrinkled forehead and smoothed the wispy alabaster hair. She remembered the flowers, and reached for the vase she had left in the stand next to the bed and found a plastic shopping bag stuffed inside. She hadn't seen that before. She pulled the bag out and took a look inside. Two nightgowns. How strange, she thought. For sure, Travis didn't bring them. Had to be one of Granny's friends from church.

She went in the bathroom for water and set the vase on the table. If Granny opened her eyes when she wasn't there and saw the colorful zinnias, she'd know who had put them there. It was a special link between the two of them, forged the day she had gone with Granny to the feed store to pay their bill in full from money Pappa Joe had gotten from selling fifteen prize heifers at the cattle auction. Since she was the one who had raised and cared for the heifers, she felt she deserved a little something extra. So while Granny was settling up with the owner, she carefully studied all the pictures on the seed packages, picked one with zinnias and slipped it onto the counter next to some things Granny had put aside.

Granny abruptly stopped what she was saying to the owner,

picked up the seed packet and stormed over to the display, then jammed it back in its slot with the disgusted expression that surfaced whenever she thought time or money was being wasted on something frivolous. Humiliated, Karen remembered folding her arms across her chest and biting her lip so she wouldn't say anything she'd be sorry for.

She knew there was never anything "extra" at Granny's and every spare penny would be squirreled away, but she never asked for things the way Travis and Amy did, and always worked especially hard to earn their keep. Why couldn't they have pretty flowers at their doorstep like everyone else?

The ride back from town had been strained with her wishing she hadn't pouted in the store and embarrassed Granny in front of the manager. At fourteen, she was too old for that kind of stunt. It didn't matter that there was never money for penny candy, store-bought toys or hair ribbons. They always had plenty of good food, a warm, clean home and the peace of mind of getting into bed without the fear of someone bothering them in it.

Karen reached over to the small, heavily veined hands that were finally at rest after more than eighty years of endless toil. It didn't seem possible they had accomplished all they had. She could still see them busily fanning though the recycled envelopes she put all her vegetable seeds in, then taking some out and saying, "Tomorrow, we're going over to your aunt's. She lost all her tomatoes to blight last year, and will be needin' some seeds from me. I'm givin' her some from my heirloom tomatoes, too. They're gettin' downright popular again and nobody 'round here gots 'em 'cept me. Reckon she'll trade them for some of them pretty flower seeds of hers."

Karen sat in the stillness of the room and remembered that time and that place and felt grateful for it. It was a simple life, and a lot of times downright harsh, but it healed her wounds. A cry rose from her gut. This lifeless wisp of a woman had been waiting for her to come home, for it was her time to be kept safe. Tears rolled down Karen's cheeks. "Oh Granny, I'm here now." She lay her head on the bed and fell into quiet sobs. "I'm here, Granny. I'm here."

Thinking she felt one of Granny's hands move, she sat up and stared anxiously at the withered face. The old woman slowly opened her eyes and spoke her name on a labored breath. Thin, parched lips barely opened and a raspy *grandfather* followed like she was trying to say something.

"What is it, Granny?"

Granny strained to raise her head from the pillow. *Diary* came out in a long, hoarse moan.

Karen looked into the tired eyes swimming in dark hollows and whispered, "Nothing's going to happen to the farm, Granny. I promise you."

Granny thrashed for a brief moment, then sank back into unconsciousness.

Karen must have sat there for a half-hour with no movement from Granny except the slightest rise and fall of her chest. Noticing someone come in, Karen turned her head.

"Scusa me."

A woman stood in the doorway wearing a uniform that was too small for her bosoms and rubber gloves that were too big for her hands. She went over to the waste basket, took out the plastic trash bag and replaced it with a fresh one.

Karen had never seen her before and wondered if she could get her to call her if anything changed with Granny. She took a twenty dollar bill from her wallet and pulled out one of her business cards, then jotted down her home number on the back. She got up and tried to hand it to the woman.

The woman shook her head. "No. No. I have three children. No want trouble."

"Take it. Call me if anything happens to my grandma. *Please, I beg you.*"

The woman's face was cloaked in sympathy. "No worry. I call."

Karen pointed to the business card. "See. My home phone number's on the back." She flipped it over and pointed to the center's number. "During the day, you can get me here."

"Sí, sí. I call."

Karen stuffed the card and the money in the woman's apron,

then went over and kissed Granny on her forehead. She would be late getting back. She picked up her purse, and was about to say goodbye to the woman who was wiping down the sink in the bathroom when she heard her say, "Another nice lady come." Karen thought the remark odd. Maybe she was talking about the person who brought the nightgowns. She sauntered up to the bathroom doorway. "Who?"

The woman shrugged. "Nice. Tall like you."

"My age?"

"No. Older. Not too old. Just older. And pretty."

"How many times have you seen her?"

She raised two fingers. Her glance fell to the floor and she hung her head. "She give me money, too."

Karen left with her heart beating wildly and her imagination running at full speed. When she couldn't get Bruce on the phone on her way back to the office, she left a message for him to come over that night.

Driving home that evening, she was thankful the rest of the afternoon in the office had been too hectic to think about what happened at the nursing home. When she had picked up the flowers in the morning, she hadn't had any small bills to put in the farm stand's payment tube, so she pulled into the Flying Cloud's driveway, jumped out and stuffed in three dollars. She turned and started back to the SUV, when she saw Annie coming with a couple of college-aged youths.

Annie introduced the interns who smiled, then moved ahead to a stack of boxes half-way down the field. "They're picking for a tailgate market tomorrow," Annie said, still lingering as if she had something on her mind.

Karen studied her. "So how's everything?" she asked.

Annie kicked a pebble, then looked up, squinting against the sun in the western sky. "Have you heard the rumors about Travis?"

Karen bit her lip. "What are they saying?"

Annie eased into the mountain farmer stance: legs set firmly apart and arms folded across the chest. "He's been talking with the Fultons."

Karen scrunched up her forehead. "Don't they have that junkyard up on Route Twenty-five in Fletcher?"

"It's not exactly a junkyard. They run a truck towing service and operate all over the country."

"Then what are they doing with all those trailers?"

"They recover a lot that have been abandoned and sell 'em."

Karen reached into the SUV for her purse, wrote her home phone number on a piece of paper and gave it to Annie. "Thanks for the heads-up." She opened the door and got in. "If you hear anything else, I'd really appreciate it if you'd give me a ring."

Annie looked up at her. "If *you* find out anything, please let me know. My family's upset over this."

KAREN WAS DOWNSTAIRS meeting with the contractor about screening in the porch and installing some fans, while Hali played dress-up upstairs with her ballet tutus and tiaras. She soon got bored. It wasn't much fun with none of her friends around to admire her. She took off the big fluffy red boa she had wrapped around her neck and went into her mother's room. She picked up the phone, threw herself on the bed and dialed.

"Mamie... it's me."

"How's my favorite little girl doing?"

"I miss you."

"I miss you, too, sweetheart. Are you making any new friends?"

"A couple, but it's not the same."

"Well, are you talking with your friends here in New York?"

Hali lay tracing the paisley print on her mother's robe with her finger. "There's nothing to tell them that they really care about. They sure don't want to hear about me scooping poop all day... I don't think I want to call them any more."

There was a brief silence on the other end. "How do you like living in the mountains?"

"I'm starting to like it. It's... it's... interesting. My Cousin Bruce is like way cool. He's a walking encyclopedia. Every time I ask him something, he tells me wonderful stories. I'm trying hard to remember them so *I* can tell them some day."

"How about your mom?"

"She's a lot better. She doesn't cry any more. It's kinda like she belongs here. You should see her, Mamie. She knows everything that's outside. Every day she takes me for a walk after dinner and knows a million stories about everything that grows around here."

"So, your mama's happy?"

"Uh-huh. Happy enough. There are two nice guys who like her, but she doesn't have time for them. All she thinks about is her grandma's place." Hali lay on the bed, running the back of her hand gently across her cheek over and over again just like Monique always did when she sang her a lullaby.

Suddenly she heard her mother call.

Hali put her hand over the mouthpiece and yelled out that she was talking to Monique and would be right down. "I got to go now, Mamie. Mom wants me downstairs."

Karen had picked up the phone in the kitchen. "Hello, Monique. How are you?"

"Busy with book signings. Was in Virginia last week."

"How're things going with the realtor? Is she showing the place much?"

"She called me yesterday. Said she was bringing through another client. I guess that was to let me know she wanted my place in tip-top shape. She's actually told me to act as if I don't know her when she knocks on my door. As if she'd never done it before. Well, I heard her let someone in your place and braced for a visit. The couple was from somewhere in the Midwest, and the wife kept asking me about crime. She was so nervous and dressed so Sears, I wanted to tell her about the woman across the street who got murdered by a pizza delivery boy and my getting mugged last year by a midget; but, for you, I didn't."

HALI LAY ON the bed listening, gently rubbing the back of her hand across her cheek and wishing her father was still alive and everything was the way it had always been.

CHAPTER SEVENTEEN

"**H**ONEY PUT AN extra plate out. Bruce might be coming," Karen hollered over her shoulder as she put the chicken leg in the fryer.

"He just pulled in, Mom."

Karen listened to him tramp across the porch, then the screen door squeak open. "Where have you been, Bruce? I've been trying to reach you for a couple of days."

He dropped a paper bag on the table with a thump. "Here's some yellow squash from your Cousin Phyllis."

"Good. I'll put some on for dinner. You're staying, aren't you?"

Bruce nodded. "I brought you a copy of my book on the family's history."

"I'm dying to read it. Get yourself a beer... I could use one, too."

He got a bottle from the fridge and handed it to her, and she remembered he didn't drink.

"Sorry you couldn't get hold of me. I've been out of town at an auction. I'm guessin' you heard all the talk about Travis."

That wasn't the reason she called, but it was now paramount in her thoughts. She took a swig, then put on the water for the squash while she listened to Bruce.

"They're runnin' the Fultons out of Fletcher along with all their trailers and trucks. Evidently your brother's been talkin' with 'em about sellin' the two hundred acres on the east end that were supposed to go to Amy."

She swung around. "He wouldn't dare!"

"From what I hear, the Fultons got a thirty-day extension from the Fletcher town board and stated on their application that they were movin' to your grandma's property."

"Doesn't Fairview have the same zoning laws that got them kicked out of Fletcher?"

"Girl, this ain't Fletcher. You keep forgettin' you're in the mountains. People value their independence here. That's why you have such a war when you talk about zoning and things like that. It's unfathomable to people here. Everybody wants to live in their own world with nobody messin' with it."

Karen pulled out a chair and collapsed.

Bruce sat down across from her and took her hand. "You got to buck up, girl, because I'm aimin' to tell you somethin' that's bound to upset you even more."

Karen frowned.

"I heard it from the lawyer this morning and told him I wanted to tell you myself. He just got the report from the nursing home. They got Granny in there as a pauper." He slowly shook his head. "If she wasn't out of her head by now, she sure as hell would go straight there if she knew."

Karen looked as if something had hit her. She bolted up and started to pace. "That bastard! I can't believe he did it! *God damn him!*" Her arms thrashed. "It's unspeakable! I can't believe that after taking almost two-hundred thousand dollars of her money he would pull this kind of shit! *To Granny of all people!* If it wasn't for her, all three of us would have ended up in the gutter."

Karen stopped pacing and gripped the edge of the counter, her back to Bruce.

Hali came from the dining room where she had been

listening and grasped her mother's arm. "Don't worry. You'll find a way to fix this. I know you will."

Karen turned toward Bruce, her hand resting on Hali's shoulder. "What are we going to do? He's got us tied up in knots."

"Not exactly."

"What do you mean?" She waved her hand for him to stop. "Wait, Bruce. I want Hali to go up to her room."

Hali looked up at her, dolefully. "I won't tell anybody, Mom. I know how important this is to you."

"All right. All right. Just go sit down and promise me you won't repeat a word. Especially not to Amy."

"I won't, Mom."

She gave Bruce the nod to continue as Hali sank into a chair, transfixed.

"The lawyer said Travis can't take all Granny's money and property, then put her in a nursing home and stick the State with the bill. Sooner or later they'll be comin' after him."

"Has he already sold the property?"

"No. From what I hear, the sale's contingent on their place in Fletcher selling. Meanwhile, he's leasing it to them."

"How many days do the Fultons have to move their equipment?"

"That was five days ago, so I want to say... twenty-five days. But they could start hauling that stuff over any time now."

"How long do you think it'll be before the State comes after Travis?"

"Hell, with all the damn crooks out there, it could be a year. That's why the lawyer wants to go to them with this as soon as possible. If the State presses fraud charges against him, he thinks he can get the court to serve a temporary injunction on the Fultons. Otherwise, you'll never get them the hell out of there."

"Oh... Don't you worry. If I have to put a stick of dynamite under every single trailer, I'll get them out of there."

"Are you gonna tell the lawyer to go ahead, then?" asked Bruce.

She folded her arms and leaned against the counter. "What

did the lawyer think his chances were for keeping the Fultons off the property?"

"He didn't say."

Karen kept bobbing her head, slightly, as if she were deep in thought.

"I know what you're thinkin', girl, and I don't like it. Sometimes you've just gotta let the law handle things."

She threw out a bitter little laugh. "I can't believe I'm hearing this from you of all people."

"That brother of yours is a rotten customer. There's no tellin' what he did to Pearl."

Everyone's eyes were on Karen as she took the bag of squash to the sink and started rinsing them. "I need to think on this. I'll let you know by Monday. Nothing's going to change between now and then."

Karen was quiet during the dinner, just half-listening to Bruce talk with Hali. Afterwards, they went out on the porch while Karen did the dishes. She glanced through the screen and could see Bruce was talking away as Hali brushed Bonnie.

Dessert was a bowl of ice cream topped with juicy poached Spartanburg peaches. Once everyone scraped their bowls clean, Karen said, "Hali, I really mean it this time; Mama has to talk with Bruce and I don't want you listening. Go up, get your pajamas on and get in bed."

"Aww.."

"You're going to need your rest. You've got your riding lesson tomorrow and we've got to get the house cleaned."

"Oooo...kay." She gave Bruce a kiss and opened the screen door to go in.

"Hey! Didn't you forget something?" shot out Karen.

Hali ran over and gave her a kiss.

Once Hali left, Bruce made sure she was out of earshot. "You got somethin' on your mind, girl? I had that feeling through the whole dinner."

Karen sank back in the wicker rocker. "I went to see Granny the other day." Karen told Bruce the three words Granny had spoken, then about her visitor. "Bruce, I don't know why, but I think that woman's my mother."

All became quiet except for the creaking of the rocker and the rattling of the cicadas as they both sat alone with their thoughts.

"Bruce... have you ever heard from her?"

"Once she called from New Mexico and I wired her some money. Some place with a Spanish name. That was a year or so after she left. The guy she was runnin' with left her in a motel and took off. She called four or five times after that. Funny, it was always on your birthday. She always wanted to know how you were doing... and... the other kids, too. You know, she was partial to your father."

"Do you think that could be her?"

"No way of tellin'. It's been quite a few years now since I've heard from her."

"I think about her sometimes. I always worry about whether she's okay. She was so child-like, Bruce. A sort of free spirit. I'd like to know some day that she had a good life in the end." She fell silent for a while. "I know who Travis's father is... or at least what he looks like."

"Them looks of his finally got the bastard killed. Someone over in Rutherfordton walked in on him in bed with his wife and shot him dead."

Karen kept rocking. "How about my father?"

Bruce shook his head. "None of that matters now."

"It matters to me. It's always mattered to me. I want to know, Bruce. Who is it?"

"Aw... he lived over on Garren Creek Road. He and your mom were just kids. Granny was fixin' to have a shotgun weddin' but Angie wouldn't tell her who it was. Granny whipped her good, but she wouldn't budge. The boy's father was as mean as snot and she was afraid he'd kill him. I figured the same thing and kept my mouth shut, too. His family moved to Tennessee for a few years and when they came back your ma was already runnin' with Travis's father. By then it was too late to say nothin'."

"Is it Bo Sullivan?"

He looked up. "You knew?"

"Not for sure 'til just now. Once I was bicycling on Garren Creek Road and got into a fight with a kid who said something about Ma. He had me pinned down and was getting ready to sock me in the mouth when Bo suddenly stood over us. He grabbed him and threw him off. He picked me up, put my bike in the back of his truck and drove me home to Granny's. Every time after that, when I'd catch sight of him in his truck, he'd be looking back at me. Not anything weird. Just like he wanted to see me."

"Well it's nothin' to fuss over now. He passed on a while back."

Karen stood up and walked over to the railing and looked out into the night. "Bruce, all I got besides you, Hali, Amy and Granny, is Travis. ...and I've been down a long painful road with him." She swung around. "Let's hold off on having the lawyer call the State just yet. There's something terribly wrong with Travis... and a lot of it's not his fault. That's why Granny and I have always covered his tracks.

"I can still remember. Gosh... I had to be... maybe not quite five. He was still a baby. Mom was always either running around or shacked up in bed with someone. Travis was too heavy for me to lift so I used to feed him and change him on the floor. Once the diaper was so bad, I had to get a wash bowl and put him in it to soak before I could peel it off. I remember once sleeping with him on the floor and Grandma coming in and grabbing him up and dragging me into the hall. Grandpa was fighting with one of Ma's boyfriends. Tossed him right past us and down the stairs." She grimaced. "Then he went after Ma."

"I remember that," said Bruce. "The bastard went and sold a couple of Papa Joe's cattle. Pearl kept you for a good year after that. 'Til Angie sweet-talked your grandpa into lettin' y'all move back in this place. He was a sucker for her just like you are for Travis. Pearl lost three babies... some kind of heart trouble... and Angie was the only one they had that took, and your grandpa couldn't say no to her. That was what was wrong with your ma. Their house was a genuine war zone with your grandpa lettin' Angie get away with murder and your grandma always beatin' the tar outta her."

Karen ran her hand along a post. "Ma may have been child like, but she sure was an expert at setting those two at each other's throats every time Granny wanted to take us away from her. I hated lying to Papa Joe that everything was fine at the house. But every time they were in an uproar and Granny asked me to tell him how things were, the only choice I had was to betray Ma or Granny.

"When Granny came over to check on things, I'd get the kids and we'd hide in the closet so she wouldn't know we were left alone and start another rumpus. I remember standing at the window crying as I watched her car pull away."

They were quiet for a while until Bruce started up again. "That's why they both took to you. You were the opposite of your ma. Heck, you were the best farm hand they ever had."

A screech owl startled Karen and her mind jumped back to the problem at hand. "Bruce, I've got to think about everything."

"Well, if you wait much longer to sic the State on your brother, sure as hell, those 200 acres are gonna get gone. You and Granny put too much store in that boy gettin' better. He ain't right... and he ain't gonna get right... just like that rotten father of his. You got to come down hard on him or he's gonna get away with this."

She stood silent with her back to her cousin. There was a hint of nervousness in her voice. "He's not going to want us to go to the law. He won't last a week in jail and he knows it. I'll go see him Monday and see how far I get."

"Sooner or later you're gonna have to bring that lawyer into this deal. The Fultons believe their contract's lawful. Not only do you have to invalidate that deed, now you have to invalidate that damn contract."

Bruce scratched the back of his neck. "Where have we gotten to? These kinds of things used to be taken care of in church. If someone stole your hog, you wouldn't have to take a warrant out in Asheville or hire some high-priced lawyer. You'd go straight to the church. At the end of every service they would ask if there was an issue someone wanted to bring up. 'Was everyone in peace?' they would ask. That's when someone would mention about the stolen hog.

"Then the church would appoint a committee and go out and see that person. After the next service they would have a meeting where both sides would tell their story. Anyone in the congregation who wanted, could ask a question. There was no such thing as 'out of order.' If they wanted to call them a liar and thief, that was fine. They'd hash it out and then the church members would vote. If the one that was convicted asked for forgiveness and made good, it was all right. If he didn't, they kicked his ass out.

"And if he went to join another church, they'd write to the former church to see why he left. They kept tabs on folks. And if they didn't like what they heard, they wouldn't let him join. That way they settled things quickly. When you think about it, it's the best way really. In those days everybody knew you since you were a kid. They knew your parents and grandparents and you couldn't get away with nothin'.

"Nowadays, those twelve men on the jury don't know squat. You can tell any kind of lie, put on a show. The person who's better lookin' or speaks better can make a good impression; but when the church folks were runnin' things, they knew every bad thing you ever did in your life. So when you got up there, you had to be a damn good liar or they'd call you a lying son of a bitch."

He sat here shaking his head. "Damn. This thing we're in is a mess."

CHAPTER EIGHTEEN

RESTLESS, KAREN CAME downstairs in her pajamas and drifted out onto the porch. The song of the whippoorwill floated on the night air as she strolled along in the dark. A field of stars glittered through the blanket of trees. Looked like tomorrow would be sunny. She sighed and meandered back into the kitchen yearning for someone she could pour her heart out to.

Thank God, she had Bruce; but it wasn't the same. He was steeped in old feuds and deep wounds that got all tangled up in everything. Then there was Jason. He'd always been a good friend, but the way Annie Louise had said the family was worried, she didn't think it wise to let him in on what was going on. He owed his allegiance to the Clarke clan, and they were influential enough to bring the sky down on Travis.

She was going to win this battle with her brother, but not by destroying him. The truth was, every cruel thing he ever did made her feel that much sorrier for him. This mess was her fault. She knew how dangerous he was and should have been there to protect Granny.

She needed a friend who didn't have anything to lose, yet was more connected to the valley than her city lawyer. Someone who knew what the land meant to people. She'd been pushing it out of her head, but her thoughts finally settled on Tom and the way he had gone along with Hali at the square dance. Anyone who would suffer that humiliation for her little girl had to be kind. But she couldn't tell him everything. She'd never even told Joel everything.

She locked the door, and as usual, kept the lamp on in the kitchen. Bruce's book lay on the table. She picked it up, then climbed the darkened staircase guided by the dim light streaming down the hall from her bedroom.

The first night she'd slept there, an oppressive feeling gripped her until Hali ran down the hall and jumped in bed with her. The loving gesture dissolved the ugly memories of her mother lying with another drifter she'd have to keep away from Amy and Travis.

She got in bed, picked up Bruce's book and examined the spine. No title, only the last names of his four grandparents, including Whitfield. Wasn't that just like Bruce; all he figured that was needed to make a statement were those four names.

She read his introduction and could hear her second cousin's voice. "I began gathering my family history in March of 1973 when I was still in school. It was very fortunate that I began at such a young age for almost every person who I interviewed and from whom I gathered information is now dead. Some of them died within months of my visit, taking from us not only their memories but, upon their deaths, their records, letters and Bibles that relatives threw in the trash."

He went on to describe how he researched and catalogued the family members. She was touched when he wrote, "You will find an asterisk placed beside the names of many persons in this book. This means that the person was illegitimate. I decided on this symbol as a compromise in order to avoid hurting people's feelings by drawing major attention to the fact, and to avoid lying, which I would not do."

She hugged the book and whispered, "I love you, Cousin

Bruce." She continued flipping through the pages, tracing the Whitfield family's Quaker ties as they migrated from Lancashire, England, to Chester County, Pennsylvania, then to Rowan County, North Carolina, and finally Fairview. !

She stopped and read the will of the husband of one of the Whitfield women written in 1785 in Rowan. "In the name of God, Amen. February fourteenth, 1785, I, Hugh McCormack of the County of Rowan and the State of North Carolina, calling to mind that it is appointed for all men once to die, being very weak in body, but of perfect mind and memory, I do publish and pronounce this my last will and testament.

"First, I recommend my soul unto the hand of God that gave it, and my body to be buried in Christian like manner at the discretion of my Executor, nothing doubting but I shall receive the same again at the General Resurrection by the Almighty Power of God that gave it, and as touching such worldly estate wherewith it hath pleased God to help me with in this life, I give, will and bequeath in the following manner and form..."

She leaned way back against the pillow and stared out into the shadowy room, remembering the impersonal legal terms in Joel's will, utterly devoid of any reference to God or the hereafter. She picked the book up again and continued to read.

The will went on to divide his six hundred acres among his six children and his wife. "To my wife I bequeath all my stock of horses and cattle and the wagon and plantation tools and four negroes named Tony, Dinah, Sarah and Frank, all of which are to be to the use of my wife on the plantation to enable her to help pay my debts and raise the younger children." The notation of the slaves surprised her, since Quakers, for the most part, believed slavery was against the Golden Rule.

As she scanned the pages, the cast of characters she'd heard about all the years of her growing up came alive in Bruce's plainspoken prose. There were those who had fought in the Revolutionary War and the six Whitfields who joined the Confederate Army. They didn't do it because they supported its cause, but because they were given only two choices: volunteer or be drafted. "Jesse Whitfield did not have a great deal of use

175

for slavery. He believed that people had slaves because they were 'too lazy and no account' to do the work themselves. He, like most Whitfields, was highly independent, with no great loyalty to any group or cause." !

She ran across a description of James Whitfield whose grave in Fairview's Cane Creek Cemetery had been kept up by Granny. "When he returned from serving in the Confederate army his appearance had changed so much that when he reached his farm and walked up to his wife working outside, she didn't recognize him. He started talking and asking her questions until she finally asked what he wanted and what he was doing there. When he told her he had come to spend the night with her, she picked up a chunk of wood and was about to hit him, when he started to laugh and told her who he was."

Inspiration suddenly gripped Karen. She was going to study Bruce's book and learn the facts of every story well enough to retell them to Hali before she went to sleep. Some of the best storytellers in the mountains had come from the Whitfield clan, and she was going to make sure the tradition wasn't going to end with Granny and Bruce.

Comforted by this new dedication and the thought that she might find a comrade at dinner the next evening, she turned off the light and went to sleep.

TOM HAD BEEN reluctant to volunteer for the hike, but once Nikki's dad fell ill and she had to leave for Cleveland, he was the only one available to take her place. With the way his luck was running, he was a little worried about getting home in enough time to get ready for his date with Karen.

He was waiting for the bus at the end of the narrow gravel road three-quarters of the way up the 4,232-foot Bearwallow Mountain. The kids piled out, and by the edgy way they were dressed and the purple hair on two of the girls, he could tell they came from Asheville's inner city. He huddled with the five teacher-volunteers and told two to bring up the rear as tightly as possible, and then he assigned Tori the lead. He and the other three teachers would float in the middle.

Ten minutes up the trail, he spotted a drift of lady's slipper plants off to the side and stopped the trek. He crouched down and waited for everyone to gather. "The flowers are gone, but these are one of the rare species that grow here in the gorge. They're either pink or yellow lady's slippers." He looked around and was surprised at all the inquisitive expressions. "It's an orchid that American Indians used to call the moccasin flower because of a moccasin-like section in the bloom. They'd boil the roots and use the extract for calming the nerves. The early settlers used it as a sedative."

Someone said something about Daniel Boone, then snickered. Suddenly a boy ripped a handful out of the ground. "In that case, I'm going to take some home and boil it myself."

Tom rose and towered over him. "Oh no you're not. You're going to put them right back where they belong." He gave the kid a look of benevolent authority.

The boy looked around at all the solemn faces. "I was just fooling around." Then he put the plant back in the earth.

Tom couldn't help wondering if this climb would be of any benefit to these city kids, but as the trail erupted from the forest, a girl who he had noticed earlier with two rings in her nose ran past him to the summit.

"Wow!" she yelled "You guys gotta see this!"

Tom winked at Tori as the kids clambered to the top and spun around in awe. They excitedly recognized downtown Hendersonville and the Asheville skyline from the 360° view, but Tori had to point out Mt. Mitchell and the Black Mountains.

"Where's Shining Rock Ridge," asked one of the kids.

"Over there by the Pisgah National Forest to the right of Hendersonville. Can you see it?"

While Tori answered their questions, Tom took out a kerchief and wiped the sweat trickling down the back of his neck, then he pulled out his cell phone and checked to see if he had any calls. Half the time they got dropped when he was in the mountains. Just one. Recognizing the number of the woman who did all their title searches, he called her back.

"Hi, Debbie. You need something?"

"I came in the office this morning 'cause I knew you needed that search for your closing next Friday."

"No problems, I hope." He prayed there weren't any.

"Nothing really big... but... the guy who bought the Grassy Patch parcel in 1919 gave a ninety-nine-year lease for hunting rights to a Walter Ishmael Whiteside...*and his survivors.* My assistant found it filed in the courthouse late yesterday. It had to have shown up when the developer bought it, but he evidently didn't have it removed."

He wasn't going to be that lucky, thought Tom. He shifted his weight. "Debbie, we got to find these people. I'm going to get in touch with my boss, but..." He hesitated for a moment. "Could you do me a favor?"

"I'm already on it. My mom goes to church with a bunch of Whitesides. They descended from slaves off local plantations. She's making some calls for me."

"Thanks Debbie; you're my kind of girl." He could tell she was smiling by the chuckle in her goodbye. He liked that about her. Always finding something to be cheery about. She was sweet on him, and if she were about ten years younger he would have taken her up on it; and she knew it.

He dialed Kevin and hoped he and his family weren't out on his boat with his cell phone turned off. Kevin answered on the second ring. Tom told him about the hunting lease.

"You're kidding."

"No. It expires in eight years." He knew Kevin was running the numbers in his head.

"I don't know. This is going to affect the appraised value and screw up the numbers on the loan." Kevin was silent for a moment. "We can't close unless it gets wiped off."

"I figured that. Debbie's working on finding the heirs."

Tom ended the call telling Kevin he'd keep him in the loop. He had been hoping that if things went well tonight, maybe he could take Karen and Hali for a ride along the Blue Ridge tomorrow. Maybe even a picnic. Damn! Something told him his Sunday plans had just gone down the drain.

Someone nudged him. He looked up and saw everyone

staring at him. The kid who pulled out the plants stood with his arms crossed and a smirk on his face. "Hey, Abe Lincoln, you're supposed to take us back down."

None of the kids laughed.

Halfway down the mountain, Debbie called. "I got hold of Martha Whiteside. It's a good thing my mother knows her, or I don't think she'd be willing to talk to me. She says she's the widow of Walter Whiteside, and if you want to talk with her you'll have to go over right now 'cause she's fixin' to go to Georgia early tomorrow morning."

"Did she say when she was coming back?"

"Yeah. September."

He quickly glanced at his watch. Two-thirty. "Okay. Where does she live?"

Tom jotted down the Lake Lure address and phone number. "Can you call her and tell her I'll be there in an hour?"

"Sure."

"Deb... If I get her to sign off on the hunting rights, I'm gonna want to get it notarized... tonight."

"I figured. Call me and I'll get over there. But do me a favor, not at one o'clock in the morning like the last time. I gotta get my beauty sleep."

By the time they had the kids piling back in the bus and he was able to take off, it was past three. He could make it to Lake Lure in a half hour if he didn't get hung up in traffic. Hopefully, he could cut a deal with Martha and be out of there by five. If there was enough time, he'd stop in at Bubba's store in Chimney Rock and pick up a shirt before he got to Karen's; otherwise he'd have to take her to his place and get changed. He hated the thought of her seeing the dismal way his place looked, but thanks to the lady upstairs, at least it would be clean.

Vehicles were parked all along the winding road between Bat Cave and Chimney Rock. A horde of humanity was crawling all over the rocks in the river, swimming in the eddies, pulling picnic baskets and coolers out from open trunks. With dripping wet kids in bathing suits running barefoot along the shoulders of the road, he didn't dare drive over twenty miles an hour.

He pulled around a hairpin curve and spotted the chimney rock four-hundred feet above with the stars and stripes waving proudly against the cobalt sky. Even though he'd seen it a million times, it grabbed his heart. By the time he passed the Esmeralda Inn at the edge of town, the traffic was already bumper to bumper. The village of Chimney Rock was packed with folks out for a day in the mountains, slowing his truck to an agonizing crawl.

Lake Lure wasn't any better. A bridal party coming from a photo shoot on the lake stopped traffic as they crossed to go back to the Lake Lure Inn. And it wasn't more than a hundred yards before traffic stopped again for people streaming across the highway from the beach to a craft fair on the square. By the time he pulled onto Bills Creek Road, it was past four, and things weren't looking too good for more reasons than one.

He decided to call Karen and let her know he'd be late. The answering machine picked up and he had to think fast. There wouldn't be enough time to leave a decent explanation, so he just said he might be late and for her to call him as soon as she could.

He kept crouching down to read the mailboxes and wished he had found out from Debbie which side of the road the house was on. None of them had any numbers and he was beginning to worry that he might have passed the place. He had a sudden urge to turn around and say the hell with it and let the chips fall where they may. No. That was an insane idea. That ridge would be there for millions of years, and they were too close to saving it.

He told himself to calm down. He had the woman's number and if he didn't find the house by the time he got up around the next bend, he could call her. Suddenly he saw "Whiteside" scrawled on the side of a mailbox. He slammed on the brakes and backed in behind an old Ford Escort.

Someone had made a half-hearted attempt at trimming and weeding a yard that looked as if at one time it had been cared for with pride. The house was small but well-built with a brick face and tin roof. He approached along a narrow mildew-covered cement walkway. So many crickets sprang up, the entrance couldn't have been used very often.

He knocked. Since the woman had to be up there in years, he expected it might take her a while to come to the door. Finally the lock unlatched and it opened.

She was aged, but her height and ram-rod straight back made her imposing. "So you're the nice young man my friend's daughter said wants to talk to me?"

"Yes, Mrs. Whiteside. May I come in?" He'd learned a long time ago not to give out too much information before he got his foot in the door. He'd had a couple slammed in his face the minute he mentioned *conservancy.*

"Sho 'nough. Come right along."

The woman struggled to turn her walker, then slowly made her way through the crowded room to a rocker. Tom came to her side and helped her lower herself into the chair, then pulled up another for himself. The room was a mass of photographs, as if the elderly woman had wanted to create a world of memories to live within. An inhaler and a clutch of medicine bottles sat on the table next to her.

"You sho is one nice lookin' young man."

Tom smiled. "Thank you. It's good to know someone besides my mother thinks so."

"Well, son. What can I be doin' for you?"

He sketched out who he was and the facts around the Grassy Patch project, careful not to make his visit sound too urgent.

"We got papers to hunt bear up there," she said.

"That's why I'm here." He could see her eyes light up. "You see, we're purchasing that land and want to buy out the lease."

"Well, I don't know, son. My boy, Bobby, still goes up there, and as I recall we got quite a few years left." She wiped her hands on her apron with deliberation and picked up the phone lying on the table. "He be comin' straightaway."

"Where does he live?"

"Next door."

Tom listened to her boss her son around. "You and Maizy can get over to the church a little later. You get on over here *right now,* ya hear. We got business to do." She put the phone down and slapped her hands on her legs. "There now. He's comin'

181

right over."

She rocked for a moment and must have felt she had to tell him something prideful about the family. "I'm Walter's second wife. He was old enough to be my father but he was a good man... and they're hard to come by. The Whitesides been farmin' around these parts since Ishmael Whiteside. He was born a slave in Virginia and sold twice. Finally to a man in Rowan County, North Carolina. Earned his freedom for servin' in the Patriot Army in place of his master's son. Fought at Kings Mountain and settled here."

That done, she leaned forward and took hold of the bar of the walker and started to lift herself. Tom rose and helped her up.

"You wait right there, young man. I'm gonna fix you some ice tea."

"Oh, you don't have to bother yourself with that, ma'am."

"*Yes...ah... do.* I may not get visitors no more, but I still got my manners."

As she made her way to the kitchen, he glanced at his watch. It was almost five. There was no way he was going to be able to pick Karen up by six. In fact, there was no way he was going to get out of there for a couple more hours. Bobby was going to want to deal. And if Bobby wasn't up to it, he suspected Martha was. Then he'd have to get the agreement drawn up and Debbie over there to notarize Martha's signature. Whatever it was going to cost to erase the hunting rights would have to be added on to the mortgage amount. Kevin was going to love that.

He dialed Karen's number and felt his face start to sag as the loneliness he'd been feeling a lot lately washed over him. Again, nothing but the answering machine. "Karen, I got hung up on a real important project... and... it looks like I won't be out of here until real late. I can't tell you how badly I feel about this... but I won't be coming to get you tonight. I'm really sorry, Karen."

Tom spread his feet apart, sank forward with his forearms resting on his legs and waited for the inevitable negotiations to begin.

"SCOOT, BABY. Mommy's got to hurry home." Karen

waved to Amy who was waiting for Hali in her doorway. "Hali, don't drive your Uncle Eddie crazy," she yelled after her. "I'll pick you up early tomorrow and take you to Angelo's for breakfast."

Karen pulled out of the driveway and headed home. She had just enough time to take a shower and get ready. She was surprised she was so excited. With his tall, broad-shouldered physique and Gregory Peck looks, Tom was definitely appealing, but she didn't think she could conjure up any of those kinds of feelings right now, even though it was obvious that was what he had on his mind. What she needed was a friend. Yet, a nagging suspicion this friendship might lead somewhere kept worming its way into her thoughts.

Bonnie was waiting at the kitchen door. Karen went in and gave her a can of cat food, then rushed up to take a shower. Putting in a new bathroom upstairs was one luxury she hadn't been able to live without. She came out wearing a robe and a towel wrapped around her head and threw open her closet. Tired of her stale professional look, she pawed through the clothes, looking for something frivolous, and pulled out a gossamer sleeveless dress Hali had seen in a trendy Asheville shop window and insisted she buy.

She fluffed out her hair with the towel and decided to go downstairs and pour herself a glass of wine. It would help her mellow out. Bonnie jumped off the staircase as she came skipping down. She waltzed through the house, and when she came into the kitchen, the blinking light on the answering machine caught her eye. Her first thought was that something had happened at the Folk Art Center, then the possibility her realtor had called. She hit the *play* button and was informed she had two calls.

I might be late was all of the first message she really listened to before she snapped it off. Dreading what the second call might say, she took a glass from the cupboard, got an opened bottle of wine from the fridge and slowly poured herself a glass. She leaned back against the counter and took a lingering sip, then turned around and punched the *play* button.

CHAPTER NINETEEN

"**M**OM! COME AND SEE! I want to show you something!"

Karen looked up from the antique milking stool she was staining and spotted Hali over by the shed. "I can't right now, honey."

"Aw, Mom. You *gotta* see this."

Karen wiped off the last of the excess stain and took off her rubber gloves. She brushed the debris from her cut-off jean shorts as she strode across a large heavily shaded barren stretch where a pig pen used to be, relieved all traces of it were gone. She had wanted to ask the contractor to tear the shed down, but was worried they might think that peculiar. She was tempted to burn it to the ground herself one night, and now, wished she had.

"Look, Mom. Isn't it pretty?"

Hali was kneeling next to a large feathery red flower on a tall stem. "Isn't it beautiful?"

She crouched down next to Hali. "It's a spider lily. Kinda early for it to be out. Maybe it's because of all the rain."

Hali jumped up and ran around the shed. "Mom, wait 'til

you see what else I found!"

Karen felt the blood draining from her face as she rose and stepped around to the door that Hali had swung open. She was pointing inside.

"Look!"

Karen's breathing became shallow. She neared and reluctantly looked in.

"It's an old wooden wheelbarrow, Mom. The lady down the road has one on her lawn and she's put flowers in it."

Karen fell against the wall.

"Mom! What's the matter!? You look awful."

Karen steadied herself. "It's nothing, honey. I just need something to eat. Let's go in the house and have lunch."

They went in, and Karen stood buried in thought at the counter making sandwiches while Hali pressed two flowers in a book.

"Mom, do you think Tom knows the names of these?"

Karen continued fixing the sandwiches.

"Mom. You're doing it again."

Karen snapped out of her stupor. "Doing what again?"

"Nothing."

Hali put two more books on top of the one with the flowers to weigh it down. "Mom, please don't feel bad that he stood you up again."

"Hali, wash your hands and sit down. And he didn't stand me up again. He called and explained that he was taking care of an urgent matter that he had no control over."

"Well, it was his bad luck. That dress is *sooo* you, Mom."

"Hali, Mr. Gibbons is a very busy man with a lot of responsibility. And…"

"Amy says she met him once when she went over to see Granny and she thinks he's a hunk."

"Oh, really, Hali. That's the last thing your mother cares about right now."

"Maybe you should, Mom. You haven't gotten dressed up to go anywhere but work since Dad got really sick last summer."

Hali washed her hands in the sink while Karen put the plates on the table.

"Can we have some chips?" asked Hali.

Karen started to open the cupboard door when she stopped and listened. First she heard a car door slam, then a dog galloping across the porch, and finally panting at the screen door.

Hali jumped up and screamed, "He's here!"

"Okay, Hali. Let's not get excited." Karen bent down, pressed the tip of Hali's nose with her finger and whispered. "I lied. He *did* stand me up twice."

A tall figure suddenly loomed near the screen. She went over and opened the door. Tom was leaning against a post on one arm and looking out into the yard as if he couldn't face her.

"Hi," she said.

He turned and gave her a broad, engaging smile. His teeth were luminously white against his dark tan. Deep creases ran up both cheeks and his dark eyes glistened. "Hi."

"Have you had lunch yet?"

"No."

She tossed her head toward the kitchen. "Then come on in."

He crouched down and ruffled Sweetie's fur. "There. Didn't I tell you she wouldn't throw us out? You sit here and be a good girl."

Karen laughed. "She's welcome, too."

Sweetie ran to Hali, and Tom strode in with a little more swagger than she thought he had a right to. "Sit down and I'll get you a sandwich."

"I came over to apologize in person... and explain about last night."

Hali put her fists on her hips. "This better be good."

Karen could see that statement took a little wind out of his sails, but not enough to hide his pride. He dove into his explanation as if he were wrapping up a case in front of a jury. A couple of times he even had Hali on the edge of her seat. "Those two did their best to hornswoggle me, but in the end I got us a good deal. They released us from the lease, and we're going to give them a thousand dollars a year until their lease would have expired." He broke into a wide grin, then his words floated out in a mellow, yet cynical tone. "It's going to make the board happy, but sure as heck, one thousand dollars or no one thousand dollars, Bobby's gonna be up on that ridge huntin' every winter."

Karen put a sandwich in front of him and gave him a nod. "Sure as heck."

They ate with Hali trying to reenact her riding lesson with as much flourish as Tom did his deal. Finished, she ran out of the house with Sweetie.

Karen had gotten used to the air conditioning being off, but the humidity in the room became suddenly oppressive. "Let's go out on the porch. I've had two fans installed."

Tom stood up and put his plate on the counter. "I noticed you had it screened in."

They meandered onto the porch and sat down. "When Cousin Bruce gets wind of it, I'm gonna be in for another lecture on the virtues of thrift."

Tom looked around. "I wouldn't worry. It's a good investment. This is a nice spot you have here." He sat down, crossed his arms behind his head and leaned back in the comfortable wicker chair. "Boy, I never thought I'd ever get out of there last night. I got to hand it to those two, they wrangled every dime out of me they could. I even had to call someone in Mills River at ten o'clock last night to verify how much he gets for hunting rights."

Karen kicked off her sneakers, put her feet up on a stool and crossed her feet at the ankles. She rested her head on the back of the chair and looked up at the ceiling. "You're really into saving these mountains, aren't you?"

"Hey! If I could throw a pretty thing like you over for a date with wily ole Bobby and Martha, you *know* I'm committed."

She laughed. This was the first time she'd seen him so relaxed. But the way he could be so proud of himself and happy over last night's outcome after leaving her sitting at home, made her want to torment him a little. She sat up, looked him in the eye and said with as much solemnity as she could muster, "Tom, if you've come here to ask me out again, the answer is *no.*"

The comment caught him unaware and he jolted forward

and coughed.

She slapped her bare legs and leaned toward him. "I really don't think I can stand being stood up a third time... *soooo*... I'm inviting you to come over here next Friday for dinner." She clucked her tongue and gave him a big wink. "That way I'm sure I won't have to go to bed without dinner again."

He threw his head to the side. "You're gonna play rough, are ya?" He leaned back and examined his fingernails. "Well... it all depends on what you're cookin'."

She nudged his leg with her bare foot. "Watch out, Mister, or you're gonna talk yourself out of my world famous barbeque. I want you to know it was the rage of Manhattan."

His expression turned serious. "In that case, Karen, wild horses won't keep me away."

"Ha! I'll have Hali raise the flag on the front lawn if you actually show up."

"I'm serious, Karen. Nothing will keep me away."

She self-consciously took hold of her tee shirt at the chest and flapped it up and down. "It sure is turning out to be a sticky day."

Just then, Hali came on her bike from around the front of the house with Sweetie running alongside. Bonnie arched her back and puffed up her fur as they streamed by.

"Hali's been spending so much time at my sister's kennel, she wants to be a vet."

"How's she gettin' along here in the mountains? This place sure isn't Manhattan."

Karen laughed. "Well, *ain't* is starting to creep into her vocabulary, if that'll tell you anything." She looked down at her folded hands. "Her father had wanted to be here so badly and told her so much about the place, she's really trying hard to like it... but actually, she's not doing as well as I had hoped. My best friend, Monique, is like a grandmother to her and Hali calls her in New York a lot. Hali's been putting up a good front with me, but she's spilled her guts to Monique that she's homesick."

"What are you doing about it?"

"For starters, I've enrolled her in the day camp the Clarke

family runs here in Fairview. It's over before I can pick her up, so my brother-in-law brings her to the kennel until I get home. She started last week and seems to like it." She grimaced. "But I'll have to wait to see what she tells Monique."

"She's a great kid," said Tom.

Karen ran a hand up and down the arm of her chair, self-consciously. "You have no idea, Tom. She was so close to her father. The little sweetheart had to be hurting, but all she did was take care of me." She shook her head. "The first weeks after he died, we sort of... reversed roles. She'd wake me up in the morning with coffee and coax me into getting dressed. Then, the minute she came home from school, she'd come in my room and dream up all kinds of things that had to be done just to get me back out of bed."

She threw out a bitter little laugh. "I'll never forget the time she insisted we get some groceries from the store down the street. Joel was crazy about the place. A Greek owned it. It was filled with exotic foods Joel had fallen in love with on all his travels. I hadn't been out of the house since the funeral, and the minute I walked into that place, the thought that Joel couldn't have those things any more... I started crying and couldn't stop.

"I got to hand it to Hali; she ignored all the eyes staring at us and kept rolling that damn cart up and down the isles, chattering away as if nothing was wrong. When she dug the money out of my purse to pay, two horrified women in the checkout line tried to comfort me." Karen dropped her head in her hand, then peeked up at him. "Hali got them to stop by making up an insane story about me winning the lottery and being so happy that I couldn't stop crying."

Tom chuckled. "That sounds like her all right."

Karen sighed. "Sometimes when I look at her, the song my mother used to sing runs through my head. She would always hum, *I won't last a day without you,* in my ear when she held me in her lap." She looked into his eyes. "It's a song Karen Carpenter used to sing. Do you know it?"

He nodded.

"It's funny how just a few words can mean so much. Sometimes when I hum them to Hali, I feel they're connecting the two of us to my mother."

She felt at ease telling him these things. It was as if he were a kindly blotter that she couldn't stop pouring herself into. "Her dad used to take her to all those ethnic events they're always throwing in New York. They'd eat all that strange food and then dance... no matter if it was a polka or a hora." She swallowed hard. "Tom, you don't know what it meant to me when you didn't turn her down at the square dance."

Karen sat quietly as she pulled herself together. They listened to the crickets and waved at Hali every time she rolled around.

Finally, Tom broke the silence. "Speaking of the square dance... what's Jason Ager to you?"

Her eyes opened wide in disbelief and her mouth fell slightly open. He certainly believed in coming to the point. She felt he had it coming to be tormented again, but he looked so earnest she didn't have the heart. "We're just friends, Tom. That's all I can handle right now..." She lowered her lids. "...with anyone."

He laid back and tapped his fingers on the arms of the chair as if he were considering what she said. He pulled up his foot, rested an ankle on his knee and flicked a piece of grass off his shoe. "All right. I guess we can talk about your grandmother's farm, then."

She could tell he was hurt, but this is where she wanted to be with him and she knew he'd appreciate her honesty.

"I heard the rumor about the Fultons and plan to look into it for you," he said.

The way he so easily switched gears and slid into his land protector's role hurt a little. "Cousin Bruce already did it. They have a contract for Amy's two hundred acres, contingent on their selling their place in Fletcher."

"A fat chance that's gonna happen any time soon with the market the way it is."

"Yeah, but meanwhile he's going to let them haul in all their junk."

He leaned forward with his elbows on his legs and rubbed his hands. "The Grassy Patch closing is Friday morning, so I've got to tie up all the loose ends before I leave for Florida on Thursday. But I'll try to look into the zoning laws for you. They're on my computer. Heck, you can pull them off the internet yourself."

"Tom, I've got another plan."

He raised his brows.

"Everything I'm telling you has to be absolutely confidential... even if it's something the law might be interested in."

There was a pause and she knew he was thinking his answer over carefully.

"Don't worry. It'll be safe with me. We'll consider it attorney-client privilege."

Karen studied his face and hoped his obvious feelings for her weren't putting him in a compromising position. "My brother Travis... is a problem. ...In fact he's been a problem for a long time now."

Tom's answer was measured. "I know. Josh Freeman... told me about him."

Karen made a face. *"I bet he did."* Her words came out harsh enough to leave a silence hanging in the air. He was watching her and she turned and gave him an apologetic smile.

He reached over and squeezed her hand. "Go on."

She leaned back in her chair. "I'm worried about what Travis might have done to Granny... and there's other things, too." She looked at him and hesitated for a moment, but she needed to tell it. "He cashed in her bank account and stocks, and put her in the nursing home as an indigent."

The raised eyebrow and wry smile she was getting used to appeared on Tom's face.

"Sooner or later, the State's gonna come after that guy."

"I know. My brother's in over his head. I'm going to take the afternoon off tomorrow and confront him with the facts and see if I can't straighten everything out."

"I wouldn't do that, Karen. Especially after... what might have happened to Pearl. I'll try to get over there sometime in the next couple of days and lay down the law. It wouldn't hurt for him to hear it from an attorney."

She studied his face. He had no idea of the world of hurt she shared with Travis, but it struck her that some day he would. "Tom, this is something I have to take care of myself. There's a lot of things I wish I could tell you... but I... I can't right now."

She wrung her hands. "My brother has always had extraordinary good looks... since he was a baby. But mostly, he has this... sort of exotic appeal... the kind a beautiful wild predatory animal has. Because of it, he's always attracted a certain type of person—mostly women drawn to this dangerous aura of his. And he knows it, too. He knows he's got this power over them." She shook her head in disgust. "They always end up as victims. I'm ashamed to admit it, but when I was a kid, sometimes he was so evil I wished he was dead." She looked up at Tom, pleadingly. "But, I was the only mother he ever had and I had to protect him." She covered her face with her hands. "God! I can't believe I'm saying all these things!"

She looked away. "Once when Amy was around five, she would have let him drown if I hadn't saved him. Thankfully, after most people get to know him, they figure he's too charming, too accommodating to be real and they avoid him."

"Yeah! Everybody but me." Tom reached over and took her hand. "I wish I had been more suspicious when I couldn't get in to see your grandmother."

She rose and got a couple of napkins from the kitchen and came back wiping her nose, but something drove her to expose herself even more. She'd gotten a pass with Joel about being illegitimate, but there were no secrets in Fairview. She dropped into her chair. "I suppose Josh told you about the three of us being bastards, too."

Tom took her hand again. "Hey, you're not the only one with a skeleton in their closet. Josh and Josephine... and probably everyone else in this town... have a lot of respect for you." He threw his head back and tried to make light of the situation. "But there's something I can't quite picture."

Her eyes darted over to him. "What?"

He tossed his hand. "Nah! It's not possible."

She blew her nose. "Are you gonna tell me or not?"

"No matter how hard I try... I can't quite picture you in overalls rolling around in the dirt fighting with boys."

She let out a bitter little laugh. "I want you to know I gave them a good run for their money."

Outside, Hali came around the corner, slammed on her brakes and skidded to a stop. "Mom! Annie and her girls are here!" She took off again.

Karen blew her nose once more, fluffed out her hair and stood up. "Annie Louise Perkinson is dropping off her two girls to play with Hali. I've got to go out and say hello."

He stood up. "I guess I better be going, too." He put a hand on her shoulder. "Karen, please don't go see your brother. Wait until I get back; and if you want, we can go over there together."

With the new information about the nursing home, Karen was confident she could handle Travis. "I'm sure I'll settle everything tomorrow, and when you come for dinner on Friday, we'll make it a victory celebration... for the both of us."

He still had his hand on her shoulder. She could read in his eyes that everything seemed simple to him. He liked her and longed to get on with it. If only she were as she appeared to be, it might be that simple. But it wasn't. She wondered if she could ever tell him the ugly truth she'd been hiding these past twenty-two years. She reached across and laid her hand on his. "We better go."

They went out to welcome the visitors. Tom stopped long enough to say hello to Annie and her girls, then goodbye to Hali, before putting Sweetie in the back and taking off.

After he left, Karen stood on the driveway and watched Annie pull out as the girls ran giggling into the house. She watched Annie's truck disappear in a cloud of dust and remembered the perfect life she'd had with Joel in New York. She'd gotten away with it. She'd shucked off all the shame of her childhood and it had been smooth sailing from the moment she met him. She kicked a stone across the road and started back to the house thinking life had a nasty habit of pulling the rug out from under you.

CHAPTER TWENTY

BIOGRAPHIES OF THE two ceramicists Karen was meeting with at two o'clock lay on her desk. The man specialized in stoneware and the woman in porcelain, and both had graduated from Penland School of Crafts the same year she finished Salem. She glanced at her watch. They wouldn't arrive for another fifteen minutes. Enough time to fish out the basket she wanted to use on the cover of her new volunteer brochure.

Before she ventured into the storeroom, she told the ladies tending the upstairs gallery, if the two showed up, to have them wait in her office. Both of the women gave her an odd look, and after she disappeared into the storeroom, she wasn't surprised to see one of them follow her in.

"Is anything wrong?" Karen asked as she pulled out a small stepladder.

The woman fidgeted with her necklace. "There's something you should know."

Karen raised an eyebrow. "Yes?"

"Those two you're meeting with... used to be married."

Karen closed her eyes and let out a faint sigh. She'd seen

similar situations get ugly at the Met.

"And, I'm afraid it wasn't a very amicable divorce," the woman added.

"How *un...amicable* was it?"

"Well... Beth Kensington's from a very wealthy family and her father got the best attorney in Asheville. Need I say more?" She shrugged. "With child support and alimony, Jack lives like a church mouse even though the ladies in the gift shop do their best to sell his work."

Karen reeled and threw up her hands. "Why didn't one of them say something when I invited them to have the show?!"

"Probably because he really needs the exposure and she didn't want to let an opportunity to make his life miserable slip by."

Karen thanked the woman, then found the basket. On the way to her office, she tried to decide if she should talk one of them into withdrawing. Beth Kensington was sitting there when she arrived. Karen shook her hand, thinking it felt like a warm rag.

Instead of the typical flamboyant jewelry and unique one-of-a-kind outfit artists usually wore, Beth had on a plain light blue sleeveless dress and a string of pearls. Karen put the basket on her worktable and sat down at her desk, wondering how such an undemonstrative woman could have created all the sensual looking vases in her collection.

The woman had made a generally favorable impression until she opened her mouth. She had an odd way of over-enunciating her words and contorting her mouth in an unattractive manner. So much so, Karen had a difficult time concentrating on what she was saying.

Just then, Jack Fellows appeared at the door. His face was flushed and his wiry blond hair was in need of a cut. He wore rumpled shorts, a navy tee shirt with dark patches of sweat under the arms and a belly pack.

He threw Karen a timid wave and introduced himself. Beth sat there, not acknowledging his presence, causing an awkward pall to settle on the room.

Jack sat down and ran a hand through his hair. "I'm sorry I'm so sweaty…" He abruptly turned toward Beth and spit out, "… but I had to come here on my *bike!*"

Beth stared ahead, coolly. Karen searched their faces for further signs of anger, then handed them both a floor plan of the exhibit room. "Beth, I've marked your pottery locations in red." She smiled at Jack. "Yours are in green."

She gave them a moment to look it over. "Now this is not set in stone. It's a guide for our preparator and we could have adjustments. But it will give you both an idea of how many pieces we're going to need. Keep in mind we do like to have a few extras to choose from."

They discussed the logistics of getting all the pieces to the gallery, with Beth doing most of the talking. Karen couldn't decide what was more annoying, her facial gyrations or the way she kept writhing her upper torso in a coquettish manner as she spoke.

"Beth, do you think you're going to have enough work by November to fill the spaces indicated on the chart?" asked Karen. As she listened to Beth enumerate her collection, she could see Jack grotesquely aping her facial expressions. Thankfully, his chair was too far back for Beth to see.

Afraid she might laugh, Karen put her elbows on the desk and covered her mouth with her hands to make it look as if she were hanging on to Beth's every word. She knew enough not to let her eyes stray over to Jack, but on the periphery of her vision she could still see he was acting out.

Finally, she couldn't resist a quick peek.

Noticing her glance at him, Jack crossed his legs, stuck a pinkie in the air and swiveled his chest around, then twisted his mouth in a hideous exaggeration. Karen dropped her head in her hand. She managed to keep silent but her body shook with laughter, until a resounding slap made her look up.

Beth's handprint was imprinted on Jack's face. His eyes bulged as he savagely leaned toward Karen. "That was just one of her *love taps!*" He swung toward Beth again. "Or at least… that's what she told the *judge!*"

Karen feared *judge* had been heard throughout the offices, and when the bookkeeper peered in, she gave her the slightest wink, and the lady kindly closed the door. Karen pictured the two in the gallery throwing pottery at each other and made up her mind to nip this in the bud. Careful not to appear to be taking sides, she told them she was putting another ceramicist with Beth, and Jack with a well known sculptor in a later show.

She walked Beth to the elevator while Jack took the stairs, then slipped into the bookkeeper's office, closed the door and the two of them roared.

She went back to her office thinking about the contentious family brawl and decided she better call Travis before going over there, especially since he'd been served with her lawsuit.

"I don't know what the hell you want to talk to me about," bellowed Travis.

"Believe me. You're going to want to hear what I've got to say."

"I don't want you haulin' your ass over here. I'm going to an auction in Shelby, and I'll hit your place on my way back... around six."

Karen hung up and didn't like what she had heard. With the way he had let Granny's two workers go and let the land go fallow, there was only one thing he could be doing at a farm auction. And why didn't he want her coming over? She remembered Granny's missing bedroom set and dialed Amy.

"Bruce told me you were going to see Travis. Are you out of your mind?" Amy screamed the minute she heard Karen's voice.

Karen sank into her chair. Amy's mood made her worry Bruce might have told her about Granny's status at the nursing home. Somehow she knew Hali never would have. If Bruce did, it wouldn't take Amy long to run to the authorities. "Amy... did... Bruce tell you anything else?"

"Isn't that enough!"

Karen was relieved. "He's coming to my house around six. Can you keep Hali for dinner? I don't want him around her."

"If you had any sense, you wouldn't want him around you either. What good is that lawyer of yours if he can't take care of

Travis? If it was me..."

Karen interrupted. "Amy... I want to ask you something. Has Granny given you her East Lake bedroom set yet?"

Amy's scream gave her the answer.

"If that bastard did anything with that set, I swear I'll kill him! Damn you, Karen! I could have gotten rid of him years ago if you had let me! Bruce is right. You're a sucker just like grandpa! Always lookin' for the good in people when there ain't none!"

"Calm down, Amy. I was just asking a question. I'm sure nothing's happened to it." She hated herself for lying.

The more Amy carried on about Granny promising her the bedroom set and dishware in her will, the more concerned Karen became. She had to get over to Granny's while Travis was in Shelby and see what was going on.

It was three-thirty before she could take off for Fairview. She sailed past the town's business district, and the four-lane highway narrowed to a winding two-lane road that swooped into the valley. She could see the tall irrigation pipes spraying water on the Flying Cloud's east field. As she looked on the peaceful scene of rolling green hills and orderly cornfields, she imagined tractor-trailers lined up across Granny's road frontage and winced.

She swung off the highway and drove slowly through the woods to the house. She could see Granny's car was in the same place as before. Good. Travis's truck is gone. She made the turn around the big hickory and got out. Oddly, the dogs were nowhere to be seen. She wondered what could have happened to them.

Other than that, everything seemed normal as she climbed the steps. The screen door was unlocked and the inside door open, and she went in. Suddenly, it was as if someone had kicked her in the stomach. Her eyes ricocheted around the barren space. Piles of old throws, books, papers... remnants from seventy-five years... lay sprawled on the floor. She bent down and picked up a photo that had been torn out of a frame. Granny, Papa Joe and her mother stood unsmiling in their church clothes in front of the house. She wiped away a tear that dropped on it, then looked around at the chaos.

Sobbing took hold of her. She spotted a box filled with magazines and flung them out on the floor screaming, then she feverishly sifted through the mess for photos and mementos and piled them in. She had to get what she could before everything was dragged out and set on fire.

She kicked off her heels and rushed from pile to pile. Never would she have believed that her grandparent's beloved homeplace would end up like this. She clutched the box and approached the dining room with faltering steps. Back when she assumed Granny would give the place to Amy and Eddie, she'd fantasized about her little family visiting them for Christmas. In her mind's eye she would see the chestnut table covered with a hand-woven linen runner and the chairs with checkered cushions fastened with bows of the same material, the fireplace aglow. Now, the empty trash-strewn room jarred her. The cabinet doors hanging open told her all the dishware was gone.

The old mechanism she used to keep sane as a child switched on, and she went to the sink and rinsed her face, then blew her nose on some napkins. That's right, she told herself, pull yourself together and stop crying over spilt milk. As far as the furniture was concerned, what was done, was done. Tonight she would settle the issue of the land once and for all; but right now, she had better get Granny's diaries before Travis tossed them on a roaring fire.

She started up the staircase with trepidation, and seeing the clock gone, recalled Granny struggling to blurt out *grandfather* and remembered she always hid money in it. That must have been what she was trying to tell her. She made the turn on the stairs. Now at eye level with the upstairs floor, her eyes darted around at the same disarray. Travis's room appeared intact, but the bare floors in her old bedroom told her the iron beds were gone.

She reached the top step and a cry escaped as she saw the diaries scattered across Granny's bedroom floor. She ran in and frantically started scooping them up. She could replace all Amy's dishware and find her another bedroom set, but these were irreplaceable. Thank God, she got there in time! First, she stacked the older ones with their pretty pink moiré covers, then the spiral bound kind that would lie open flat that Granny started using as her arthritis advanced. She was dying to know if she had this year's book, but couldn't waste time checking.

She ran back and forth to the SUV until she had them all, then picked up the box with the pictures and went back upstairs. At least, now she was getting somewhere. She checked her watch. Not yet five. She still had time. She went into Travis's room. Nothing on the dresser but a stack of brochures. She picked one up, and the instant she saw the boat, it dawned on her that Travis was selling everything and going south. *Of course.* He always hated the farm. Fear that he might have already sold the rest of the property suddenly gripped her. Bruce was right. She should have called the lawyer and sicced the State on him sooner.

A screen door slammed. She dropped the brochure and froze. It had to be Travis. She pictured Granny lying comatose in the nursing home, and for the first time in her life she was afraid of him. Her heart thumped in her throat. She could open the window in her old room, creep down the porch roof and climb down the trellis like she'd done a hundred times as a kid.

She felt a sudden cloud of shame descend on her. What was she thinking? Amy's hateful words were coloring her judgment. She searched her brain for an endearing memory of the beautiful little boy with the same piercing blue eyes as hers. *I'm hungry,* he had told her. She had made a game of picking up the last of the apples fallen to the ground and made some apple crisp with a few lumps of sugar she had squirreled away in her room. *You're nice, Karen,* he had said. *You're my real mother.*

She ran her fingers through her hair and examined herself in the mirror. That's it, Karen. Go down and do what you have to do. That darling little boy has got to be buried somewhere inside him. And once he knows you found out about the nursing home, he'll cooperate.

She took the steps while balancing the carton on her hip. A tall, menacing figure waited in the shadows. She struggled to sound unconcerned. "Well, I see you've sold everything and are planning on going south," she said as she strolled by him and into the living room.

She waded through the trash in her bare feet. "Travis, I hate to tell you this, but you're going to have to change your plans." She turned and looked at him. "My lawyer found out you've got Granny in that nursing home as an indigent, and he's waiting for a word from me to bring the law down on you." She looked steadily into his eyes. "You know you can go to jail for what you've done, don't you?"

She didn't like the way he appeared undisturbed, but she knew he was cagey enough to keep from showing surprise. "You're going to have to go down to my lawyer's office with me tomorrow and put all that money you stole from Granny in escrow to pay for her expenses so she can die in dignity. Then you're going to have to sign the farm back over to her. Everything can be divided according to her will when the time comes." She came close enough to give him a penetrating glare. "You won't like it in prison, Travis."

He whirled around laughing, then suddenly stopped. "Karen, how can you be so stupid? I've been screwing the whore who runs that dump for months. She called me the minute she got the notice to surrender her records. The slut was scared shitless. I gave her the money and she's already reimbursed the State... and to save her ass, she's willing to testify that it was nothing but a clerical error. As for handing any money over to anyone, you just try and prove it's not mine."

He leaned back against the wall and folded his arms. "I knew you'd come runnin' back home as mad as a wet hen the minute you heard I got rid of the old bat. That's why I was so careful. I'm afraid, big sister, this is one fight you're gonna lose."

Karen racked her brain for some way to reach him. "How could you do this to Grandma? You know how proud she is."

He went over and gazed out the window. "I did it because I could. I knew all that damn religion she pumped into us would come in handy some day. I told her I found Jesus and wanted a second chance." He threw out a nasty little chuckle. "I even got on my knees. Once I moved in, like a good Christian, I offered to go after the mail. That's how I found out how much money she had. Then I figured out how to get it.

"I had to get her manageable enough to haul her sorry ass down to the notary and get my name on all her accounts. I didn't let her have anything to eat for a couple days and slapped her around a little, but the stubborn bitch wouldn't budge. She kept saying I could kill her before she'd sign anything."

His head swiveled around. "You know what finally broke her? I'll tell ya. I told her I was going to kill you if she wouldn't... and she knew I would, and that I'd find a way to get away with it, too."

He looked out the window again. "I didn't take any chances at the bank though. I pulled her close enough to feel the gun in my belt when I walked her in. With what I got from her and the store in Morganton, I finally had enough to get the hell outta here. I figured once she passed, I could come back and sell my share of the farm."

Stunned, Karen stared at him for a long moment. Travis was no longer a mystifying little boy with no apparent sense of guilt; he was a grown man with no sense of honor—that thread of self-esteem that makes you feel good about yourself when you look in the mirror. But worse yet, it was suddenly clear to her that the reason this monster standing a few feet in front of her had no conscience was that he was incapable of feeling love.

"Don't look so shocked, Karen. You're the last person who's got a right to judge me." He dropped against the window frame and gazed outside. "Then when that guy came over with those papers, and I found out the wench was planning on putting enough goddamned restrictions on the place to make it worthless, I had to get her ass over to the notary one more time and get that deed signed over."

Karen had always feared his reckless risk-taking, but listening to him, she finally understood that all his conniving and manipulating was nothing but a game.

"By that point I had complete control over her. But I had to wait until her mind was clear enough for her to walk into the bank and sign her name."

Shivers went down Karen's spine as the beautiful little boy with the pleading eyes mutated into a dangerously insidious schemer, remorselessly describing how he'd gone about brutalizing an eighty-nine year old woman and methodically stripping her of her life savings and her home.

"After that, she went downhill so fast I had to force-feed her. The old hag had so many bruises, if she died on me, for sure, someone would see them and I'd be found out. That's when I decided to dump her in some nursing home.

"Every time I went out, I had to tie her up, tape her mouth and drag her in the pantry in case someone came snooping around the house. By the time I talked to a couple nursing home administrators in Charlotte, I knew the score enough to start looking real careful in Asheville. The minute that hussy brushed her boobs against me in the doorway of her office and flashed a big smile I knew that was the place."

Karen was seized with the kind of rage she hadn't felt since she was a child, and her expression went from a shocked stare to tight-jawed determination. She couldn't let Travis get away with doing this to Granny!

He wasn't the only one who could lie. "My lawyer told me if we could prove you coerced Granny into signing over the farm, he could get that deed overturned. And guess what, little brother? I've got a tape with her telling how you forced her into signing. I don't want to use it, Travis. There's already enough shame on this family; but if I have to, I will." She glared at him. "I'm not just talking fraud here. I'm talking assault on an eighty-nine-year-old woman. Your grandmother! What do you think a judge is going to do to you for something like that!?"

His upper lip barely quivered.

Thank you, God! She finally had him. She turned and strolled around even though her knees were starting to wobble. "I go see her twice a week and I always take my tape recorder."

"Don't hand me that shit. The old crow's totally out of her head."

Karen turned and went up to him. "Yes, most of the time she

is... But this *one time* she was as sharp as ever. ... and... as clear as a bell... I've got her saying she only did it because you threatened her."

Travis grabbed her arm and drew her close, his face savage.

She gave back the same intense look. "Don't you dare lay a hand on me."

His face was close enough for her to feel his breath. He raised an eyebrow. "What are you goin' to do? Kill me like you did that drifter?"

The room fell silent as they stared into each other's eyes. "If they come after me, I'm gonna tell them everything. You might have forgotten it ever happened, but I never will." He drew her even closer. "That little brat of yours is gonna jus *love* hearin' that nasty little story over and over again. Just like we did about our slut of a ma the whole time we were growin' up. Remember the little ditty they chanted on the bus?" His words came slow and deliberate. "Angie... Angie... who's in her pangies."

He twisted her arm. "You can gussy yourself up all you want, but you're still nothin' but a sorry-assed hillbilly trying to be someone she ain't. I can remember when you didn't own a pair of shoes." He suddenly thrust Karen across the room. "Get the hell out of here and keep your mouth shut or there's no tellin' what I'll do. No one's gonna get in my way."

Karen slowly rose, gasping for air. Every trace of Karen Godwell had disappeared and that wretched little girl stood clutching the box of photos. She backed out of the living room, then turned and ran in her bare feet over the rocks and roots to the SUV, feeling nothing. Her hand shook so much she could barely get the key in the ignition.

Her SUV careened down the driveway and onto the highway, almost hitting a car coming from the opposite direction. The sound of the angry horn faded as Karen sped down the road.

CHAPTER TWENTY-ONE

Almost to Amy's house, Karen pulled off the road and checked her hair in the mirror. Her hands were trembling uncontrollably. She kept pounding her head on the steering wheel trying to shake off the dark memories clawing at her brain. That pitiful little girl didn't exist any more. She'd seen to that. But the ugly images kept coming.

She sat upright and pressed her fingers to her temples. She had to get home. She turned the key in the ignition and drove, seeing nothing but blurred scenery whizz by. She pulled up in front of the kennel and kept the heel of her palm pressed against the horn. The blaring seemed to be coming from far off in the distance. Suddenly, the sight of Hali snapped her out of her fog, but the questioning look on Amy's face brought back the sickening dread.

Hali got in, and Amy sauntered over and tapped on the window. Karen lowered it a few inches.

"Well, are ya gonna keep me in suspense, or are ya gonna tell me why you got here so early?"

Karen stared blankly ahead. "Travis isn't coming tonight."

She zoomed the window closed, backed up and took off, sending a flock of squawking chickens scattering to both sides of the drive.

"Mom, what's wrong? You look terrible! Geez! Where are your shoes?!"

Karen didn't trust herself to look at Hali. She might fall apart. She just focused on the road until she got home. Then she went through the motions of making dinner like a zombie, while downing half a bottle of wine. Hali quietly set the table and said nothing. Later, as Karen washed the dishes and put everything away, she couldn't remember eating, remember driving home.

Hali busied herself bringing in the diaries and sorting them by year, finally announcing the one they wanted wasn't there. She kept stepping out on the porch as if she were expecting someone, until finally that someone showed up. When Karen saw Hali whisper in Bruce's ear, she knew she had called him.

"Mom, I'm going upstairs and getting ready for bed. Can I watch TV in your bedroom?"

Karen figured that was Hali's way of helping. She drew her close and brushed the curls sticking to the sweaty face looking up at her. "Sure, baby."

"Mommy, I had to call him."

"I know. Go on up."

Bruce went over to the counter and lifted the wine bottle. "This ain't gonna fix nothin'." He put an arm around Karen's shoulder. "Come on. Let's set a while on the porch. Amy called me, too. You sure did get everyone riled up." He watched her sit down with a weariness that startled him.

She put an elbow on the arm of the chair and dropped her head in her hand as if it ached.

"Tell me what happened, girl."

She looked up, ran her hands through her hair and sighed resignedly. "I called Travis this afternoon, and he said he'd come by here after he got back from an auction in Shelby, and... it made me suspicious. So I went over there as soon as I could get away." She looked up with glazed eyes. "I don't know how we're ever going to tell Amy her East Lake bedroom set is gone.

She's been counting on that since she was five. If she finds out, she'll run right over there and kill him."

"How about the rest?"

"Everything's gone. I didn't go in the barn, but I imagine that all got sold today at the auction. It's a shame. There were all kinds of old tools and things in there. I had told myself that once I got the farm back, I was going to give it all to Eddie."

She looked up at Bruce, and for the first time that evening seemed like herself. "But I did get all the diaries… except the one I need. Funny, but those little books with Granny's flowery script are worth more than all the rest put together." She reached over and squeezed his hand. "You're the family historian, Bruce. I want you to have them. I want you to write a book about Granny and her life here in the hollow."

"No. You keep 'em. I'm all wrote out."

"I'll do it, Mommy!"

Karen looked up. Hali's nose was pressed against the screen. "Come here, baby." Hali came out and Karen put her arm around her and pulled her close. "Bruce, I don't know what I'd do without this little girl of mine."

"Well, that little girl of yours has got to go upstairs, right now," said Bruce.

"*Oh, darrn!*" pouted Hali. "When am I going to be old enough to get in on everything?"

"Heck. Your Aunt Amy *still* ain't there." Bruce's expression turned serious. "Now, don't you be tellin' her about the furniture, ya hear. Or, just like her, you'll never be old enough to get in on anythin'. Now, git." He waited a few moments after Hali left, then got up and closed the kitchen door. "There."

He sat down again and listened to the rocker creak as Karen went back and forth.

"Hali said you lost your shoes… and I can see your dress looks a little done in. I hope you didn't pick a fight with that bastard." He leaned toward her, and looked as if he knew darn well that she had. "Well, after all the roughin' up, did you get him to agree to anything or not?"

"Uh-uh."

"Then are you gonna let the lawyer do what you're payin' him to do?"

She slowly shook her head.

"Why in the hell not?"

She stood up, hugged herself and shuffled over to the railing as if she were drained. "It won't do any good. Travis has been sleeping with the woman who owns the nursing home. She told him about having to release her records, so he gave her the money and she's gone ahead and reimbursed the State. They had enough time to alter all the documents and make it look like a clerical error."

"You waited too damn long to go after him. Gave 'em time to cover their tracks."

She appeared transfixed. "You're right. The way they were stonewalling me, I should have guessed something like this was going on." She looked out at the night and hugged herself even tighter. Lightning streaked across the sky and a breeze made the screen billow, a sure sign rain was on the way.

"He'd of been too cocksure of himself to rough you up over just that. What else happened?"

"I tried bluffing him. Told him I had a recording of Granny saying he forced her to sign. Told him he'd go to jail. But... it didn't work." She came back and sat down, then continued rocking back and forth. "Our only hope is the diary, and the one we need isn't in that pile in the kitchen. I went through the whole house. It's not there either."

"How did he respond to that bluff of yours?"

A gentle rain started and Karen was suddenly cold. She wanted to let herself drift away.

"Tell me, Karen. What on God's earth does he have on you?"

"Nothing." She was tired of fighting the nightmare clawing to come out all evening, and finally let herself slip into the cave of terror locked inside her. "He just has something on the pathetic little girl that used to be me," she answered. "Funny... I was sure she was gone forever." She tapped the floor with her foot just enough to barely move the chair back and forth, and remembered stacking the split wood as if it were yesterday.

"I can see her in the side yard next to the house. That girl's only thirteen but she's already wise to the ways of the world. There's a man. He's splitting a log." She rocked and gazed mindlessly ahead. "He's not the girl's father. There is no father. The girl's mother brought him home.

"I can see the door open and the mother come out. She's beautiful and will never do right by the girl. The girl knows this. The mother is taking a child with red curls into the car. The girl and the fair-haired beautiful boy are to stay and help the man until she comes back.

"The man wants the boy to hand him the logs even though the girl is stronger. The girl is waiting for his next move because there is always a next move at this house. He lays the axe against the chopping block and tells the girl to go into the house. He will finish up with the boy.

"She goes in and peeks out from the rip in the closed curtains. No one will see the round blue eye behind the ragged linen threads. The man puts a hand on the boy's shoulder and leads him across the yard past the pig pen. The girl watches as he opens the door to the shack and leads the beautiful boy in.

"She opens her door and listens. *Please mister. Please, don't.* The girl has heard the boy cry before and rocked him and held him and promised she would never let it happen to him again. *Never.* She picks up the axe.

"The shack is dark, but the light from the door falls over the man's back. His pants are dropped to the floor. The boy's cries pierce the air. The girl screams for the man to stop, but he won't. She lifts the axe and the man screams too, but only for an instant. The girl knows he's not going to scream any more. She's seen it all her life. Pigs... chickens... goats... rabbits...

"The beautiful boy is now sobbing. She tells him to pull up his pants and help. No one should know what has happened at this house, for that is the way of the mountains.

"The man is too heavy to lift onto the wheelbarrow. She picks up the axe again. Blood splatters on her face, in her eyes, in her mouth. The floor is slippery. The boy screams and she shakes him until he stops.

"The boy and the girl load the wheelbarrow and empty it into the pig pen and wheel it back into the shack. She makes the boy help her load the rest, for it is too heavy for her. This load they must take far into the woods for the other animals."

THE LIGHT FROM the kitchen window reflected eerily on the tears streaming down Karen's cheeks as she rocked back and forth. Bruce rose, went in the kitchen and came out with a wet cloth and what was left of the wine. He took a long swallow, pulled up a stool and put the glass in Karen's hand before wiping her face. He made her finish the wine, then held her in his arms and ran his hand gently down her hair. God, he asked, how could you have let this happen to this child?

CHAPTER TWENTY-TWO

E DDIE BACKED UP the van, got out and opened the rear door. He made his way up the narrow path zigzagging through the jumble of old parts and appliances and opened the door to his tool shed. Small but surprisingly well-organized, its shelves were neatly stocked with everything he needed to repair and restore the treasures he'd collected from dumps, old trash heaps and off the side of the road.

Lying on the counter were the four small enamelware wall bins he'd dug out of the heap left from the fire at the old Taylor Building in Rutherfordton. It had taken some doing to get them straightened out again. On the floor was an old farm table he'd found in a garage sale. The red paint had faded but the top hadn't warped. Bubba Barnhill was sure to give him a Franklin for it.

Next to the table was a weather-beaten cupboard that had to have been left outside at one time. It had an odd little door fastened shut with a rusted hook and eye. The brown paint was chipped enough to show what must have been its original robin's egg blue. A faded flower peeked out from underneath the crackled paint. He had a hunch he'd get more for this one.

He'd waited all summer to meet up with Bubba who was going to be buying wholesale today at Smiley's Flea Market in Fletcher. He had promised Bubba he'd bring his things before eight that morning. He carefully loaded his trove and wrapped everything in blankets for the forty-five minute drive. He had been careful not to slam the van's rear door so Amy wouldn't know he was about to leave, but just as he started to get in the front seat, she came out of the kennel.

She stood on the porch with her hands on her hips. "You gonna just take off without givin' me a kiss goodbye?"

He shifted his weight and tossed his head to the side as she came toward him.

"You got your inventory book?"

"Yeah, I got my inventory book."

She was now facing him. "I want you to put every single penny you get today down in that there book. I don't want any tax man comin' after us. Ya hear me?"

"Yeah, I hear ya."

"You gonna put your mileage down, too?"

"Yeah."

She shook her finger at him. "Now, don't you let Bubba take advantage of you like he did the last time."

"Nope."

She gave his huge belly a push, making him step back. "Why are you wearing that dirty ole shirt?"

"It was clean when I put it on."

"You wait right here while I go get you another one. We don't need folks sayin' I don't keep a good home. It's bad enough the way this place looks."

Eddie watched until the door slammed behind her, then jumped in the van and drove out slow enough for the chickens to get out of the way, yet fast enough to reach the road before she returned. Unlike his shed, the front of the van was littered with old swap sheets, candy wrappers, empty soda cans. A wicked laugh filled the van when he hit the asphalt.

Eddie wasn't clever, but all the abuse he'd suffered for being a little slow had made him crafty. He fabricated the figures in his inventory book so he didn't have to give all the money to Amy, always making sure he had at least five-hundred dollars squirreled away in his workshop. That way, he could cover up any mistakes he made, and Amy wouldn't yap at him like those dogs of hers.

There wasn't as much traffic as he expected, so he made good time getting to the market on the Hendersonville Road. Bubba's truck sat on the outside edge of the parking lot. He pulled up next to it and got out.

"Well, you showed up nice and early like you said you would." Bubba came over and shook his hand.

Good, thought Eddie, he was in a friendly mood.

Bubba thrust a box toward him and offered him an apple fritter. "They just came out of the fryer at the food booth. Still warm."

Eddie grabbed one up and took a big bite as Bubba went to the back of the van. "You got the key for this lock?!" he yelled.

Eddie rushed over and held the fritter between his teeth until he got the chain off the door and swung it open.

Bubba shouted for one of his workers to get everything unloaded, then he prowled around the items like a cat. "I'll give you two hundred for the lot."

Eddie rubbed his jaw. "Well... I..."

"Okay, Eddie. You got me. Two-fifty. And that's my top offer. Take it or leave it." Bubba took out a wad and started peeling off the bills.

Eddie stuffed the rest of the fritter in his mouth and rubbed his hands on his belly until they weren't sticky any more and took the greenbacks from Bubba. Just then another truck pulled up and Bubba went over. Eddie climbed into his van and started to leave, when Bubba came back and yelled for him to stop.

"Eddie, you're related to that Travis fella in Fairview, aren't you?"

"Yep. My wife's brother."

Bubba looked up at him. "We've got something of his. My wife was cleaning out a clock he sold us and found a notebook.

Can you get it over to him?"

Eddie said he would.

"Good. Now I don't have to drag my ass over there. My wife keeps one herself and made me promise I'd take it back or we'd get jinxed." Bubba scratched his head. "I think I stuck it in the big tool box." He left for a minute, then returned with the diary and handed it up to Eddie. "You take it over there, you hear. Don't want any bad luck on us."

Eddie tossed it on the seat and took off, thinking it a little odd that Travis sold the clock. He better tell Amy. On second thought, it might just get her all upset, and there was no tellin' how nasty she would be to Bubba. He didn't want to go and do that. Bubba was the only dealer that treated him with any respect. Plus, life would be hell 'til she calmed down again.

That family of Amy's was a complete mystery to him. Why she never shared anything about them with him was a vexation. She'd been upset ever since Travis moved in with Granny, and was always whispering on the phone to that sister of hers. He wished to hell someone would tell him what was going on. Every time he asked Amy, she'd just tell him to mind his own business.

He stopped for gas up the road, went in to pay and came out with a pizza. He ate sitting in the truck. After finishing off the last piece, he wiped his hands on his tee shirt and fished around for a pen and his inventory book, knocking the diary and pizza carton onto the floor.

The items he gave Bubba were scrawled in the book, then he looked up at the sky and calculated. He jotted down one hundred and fifty dollars in the received column. Amy was going to get that, and he was keeping the rest.

"YOU DIDN'T HAVE to sleep on the couch, Cousin Bruce. I have an extra bed in my room." Hali looked up and saw him drying the breakfast dishes. "You look cute in that apron."

He finished at the sink and hung the dish cloth on the rack. He wished he could think of something to say so they wouldn't have to keep pretending nothing was wrong. Hali had to have heard Karen crying last night and figured out that was why he spent the night at their house.

He studied Hali's face and was surprised all over again at how well she was holding up. Anyone would know the poor kid was having a time of it losing her father, then being uprooted from a big city and taken to God's country; and now her mother was in such a state...

Yet, there she was, artfully making it appear as if she were handling everything just fine. If it weren't for what she told him when she phoned yesterday, he wouldn't have known how well she grasped the situation. She sure was a self-contained little package. He studied her as she fanned through the pages of one of the diaries. Except for Amy's hair, in no way did she resemble any of the Whitfield clan he knew of. Karen was right; she took after her father.

"I'm glad you came over, Cousin Bruce."

"Any time your ma feels poorly, you just call on me."

Hali was kneeling on a chair by the table with a diary opened in front of her. "On this page, Granny says she loves this house the most. Why, Cousin Bruce? From what Mom says, it's not as big as hers."

Good, thought Bruce. She's trying to focus on something other than last night. "Papa Joe was born in it. That's why. The original log cabin—it's your kitchen now—was built in 1807 by the first Whitfield to settle in Fairview. They got along in it for a long time and didn't add on this here house 'til 1897."

"Where did they come from?"

Her question convinced Bruce the child wanted to hear a story that would take her mind off her mother's heart wrenching crying the night before. "Lexington, North Carolina, is where they came from. Almost everyone who settled Fairview come from within ten miles of that town. It's between Salisbury and High Point. Even the German families came from the edge of Randolph County. Most all of them were run out of England for being Quakers. The German families got run out of Germany because they were Annabaptists. Virtually everybody got run out of somewhere for religious persecution."

"Were there ever any Indians here?"

"Up until the Revolutionary War, Old Fort, just up the road, was the boundary of the Cherokee land. Anyone who lived in here before that was a traitor that married an Indian squaw or somebody who was runnin' from the law. The Cherokee were the dominant tribe... you could say the neighborhood bully back then, and if you got over that line you were subject to be killed at any time."

Bruce studied Hali. She was listening with wide open eyes, almost pleadingly. "During the Revolutionary War the Cherokee got talked into signing with the British, who'd send soldiers into the Cherokee Nation and burn settler's farms in the fall. That would pretty much put 'em out of business and they'd have to worry about starvation. Whites didn't start to get in here strong until after the war when the Cherokee retreated all the way to Waynesville. There had to be a buffer zone between them and the Catawba because they hated each other's guts."

They both looked up as Karen shuffled in. Her hair was twisted up and held with a clip. The whole thing flopped over the top of her head. Her pajamas were buttoned out of order, adding to her disheveled appearance. She went to the coffee maker and poured herself a cup.

Bruce took off the apron and hung it up. "I called that art place. Told 'em you're sick and won't be in today. Called Amy, too." He gave her a direct look. "Called the fire department. Told 'em we'd be burnin' somethin' here today."

The remark didn't get a rise out of Karen even though it was meant to. She opened the fridge, looked inside and closed the door again. She went over and gave Hali a kiss, then folded a leg underneath her as she slipped onto a chair and began sipping her coffee.

Hali, still kneeling on her chair, leaned over the table and rested her head in her hands. "I read about one of Granny's days when she was first married. She sure did work hard, Mom." Hali, flipped the page. "Says here we were originally Quakers. Did you know that, Mom?"

Attagirl, Hali, Bruce said to himself. The sooner we get Karen's mind off last night the better.

Karen drew her knee up and put her foot on her chair. She looked over at Bruce who was now sitting down with his coffee. "I always wondered how we went from being Quakers to being Baptists."

Bruce fingered his cup. "The folks that came here from Lexington were Quakers. The ones who had slaves eventually became Methodist, because they were the church of slavery. They'd get mad if anybody said that, but it was true. The rest became Baptists because the Baptist church never did have any central authority. They had a certain creed that they believed, and they'd kick anyone out if they didn't adhere to their basic beliefs, but they weren't dictatorial."

He patted the stack of diaries in front of him. "That was the big reason Quaker churches fell out, 'cus the Quaker Church is very controlling. No one could move to a new place without getting a certificate of removal. Stuff like that. On the other hand, the Baptists would run their church themselves, they'd hire their own preacher, and they'd make all their own decisions. That appealed more to folks who'd been persecuted in Europe.

"But the people who owned slaves... the Methodists... had a hierarchy that ran the church, so it was kinda like they ran things on the plantation. There was a master and everyone was under 'em... and there was a national church that was over everybody and even owned the property. Whereas the Baptist churches owned their own property and nobody else had anything to do with it. The Scots-Irish were mostly Presbyterian with names like Morrison."

Karen got up and poured more coffee, then took the pot over and topped off Bruce's. "I'm glad you're here, Bruce. There's something about hearing these stories that settles my mind."

"Me too!" Hali piped up.

Karen smiled at her. "Are you ready for camp, pumpkin?"

Hali said she was, and Bruce offered to take her over to Annie's mother's house where she ran her day camp. When he returned, Karen was sitting in the kitchen reading one of the diaries.

Bruce came in off the porch. "That's an improvement."

"Believe me; I look much better than I feel." She turned a page and glanced up. "Granny and Papa Joe spent their entire lives making that farm what it is."

Bruce nodded. "They worked their butts off to buy that land bit by bit over the years."

She brought both feet up onto her chair and hugged her legs. "I wonder why they picked this valley of all places."

"They all came to Fairview because they knew somebody. Your great, great grandpa, Jay Whitfield came by wagon train in the fall of 1800, after that, his mother and the rest of them moved up here. They settled these here mountains because they hated the government. They thought America would be what it said it was—a bunch of united states where every little state was its own country. But by the 1780s they realized these united states were gonna become one big country with the federal government in Washington runnin' things. They were fed up, so they started movin' this way.

"This place wasn't a good place to live, it wasn't a good place to farm. Hell, these mountains are a harsh environment, and if they weren't anti-government, they never would have moved here in the first place. There had been some asshole in England or Germany that gave them a hard time for generations, and they wanted to move here so they'd be left the hell alone. That was the draw. Basically, that happened for a long time."

He could tell Karen was thinking about Granny's place and reached over and squeezed her hand. "It's just as well, girl. What were you gonna do with another house?"

She tapped her nails on the table. "That diary has to be somewhere... and I'm going to find it. And when I do, I'm going to make sure Travis gets what's coming to him. I don't want to see him hurt, but he needs to be put away where he can't do the hurting."

"You don't want to be muddying the waters. He's mean enough to be tellin' everythin' like he said he would."

"If he does, so be it. If that's the price I've got to pay to put him away, that's the price I've got to pay." Karen got up and started making sandwiches. "I was up all night thinking about it.

The hardest part was admitting to myself that it all happened." She turned to him. "It is what it is, Bruce, and I'm just going to have to handle it."

She got lettuce out of the fridge and plopped it on the counter. "I'm not thirteen any more. If I can make it through watching the dearest man I've ever known waste away in front of me, I can make it through this." There was a thump on the cutting board as the knife sliced through the lettuce. "What are they going to do to me? I was just a kid." Still holding the knife, she brushed a strand of hair from her face with the back of her hand. "As far as the gossip is concerned... hell, there's been so much scandal in these mountains, what's another killing."

They both sat through lunch thinking over the things that haunted them, Bruce, the way life had changed in the mountains, and Karen, what had happened in that shack. The strangest thing of all was that the evil nightmare that had haunted her, that took so much effort to smother, that appeared bigger than life itself, had, once she faced it, shrunk overnight to the category of an unfortunate incident.

It struck her as odd how easily one could rationalize something away once they got too worn out to hide it any more. All you had to do was give it the right spin. A simple attitude adjustment. People did it all the time. When they didn't like the way something turned out, they'd toss a hand in the air and say *It's all for the best...* or *It'll make a better person of me.* Unfortunately, neither of these sayings worked for her situation. The only one that did was, *It is what it is. Let's move on.*

After thinking things over for a while, Bruce slapped his legs and said, "Let's go do what we got to do, girl." He looked around. "Where are the matches?"

CHAPTER TWENTY-THREE

B Y THE TIME Bruce raked the last of the shed's embers into the ground and left Karen's place, it was four-thirty. He pulled into his driveway that lay on the downward slope of the mountain. His house was a traditional brick, two-story, center hall affair he built mostly as a gallery for his collection of glassware. Every room was set up to display them; and he had all the Victorian oak furniture to go along with it. The kitchen was rarely used for anything but cleaning his new acquisitions or packing the ones he was going to sell.

He peeled off his smoky clothes and took a shower, then came out of his bedroom wearing a tee shirt and shorts. He strolled through the rooms and adjusted some of the glass pieces left out on trays, dusting where needed.

A beam of sunlight reflected off a vehicle and drew him to the window to look out. A car had turned into his driveway, and moments later a figure passed by the living room windows. The image was hazy as seen through the lace, but Bruce knew who it was. He went over and swung the door open, surprised that after all these years she was still beautiful.

"Come on in, Angie," he said.

Her silky print dress draped her trim figure and swayed to the rhythm of her gait as she crossed the living room. A flood of emotion washed over him—mostly joy that she appeared to be doing well.

She looked at him, amused. "You look like you've seen a ghost."

After what he'd been through with Karen in the past twenty-four hours, he wanted to hate her but couldn't. She must have known what he was thinking for her face suddenly took on a sad expression.

"I know it's nervy of me just showin' up here after all these years." She went over to the window, pulled aside the curtain and looked out. "I didn't come to cause any trouble. I just wanted to see my kids is all." She turned and looked at him. "I want you to help me see Karen."

"Well, you can go over there right now and say hello, for God's sake."

She looked out the window again. "No, I can't. I'm too ashamed." She went to an easy chair and sat down, crossing her long shapely legs as she broke into a slow smile. "You look good, Bruce. Gettin' a little gray... but still good." She seemed lost in thought for a moment. "I saw Ma. Couldn't believe it was her. Never thought the old battleaxe could look so fragile."

He sank into an easy chair across from her. "How'd you know where she was?"

"Gossip's all over town."

"Do you know about the farm?"

Angie nodded. "I guess Travis turned out to be a bastard just like his father. Looks just like him, too. I parked at that farm stand on the Clarke Family property one afternoon when no one was around and waited for him to come out in his truck. Then I followed him to a restaurant and watched him for a while. Got a look at Amy the same way. Followed her around the grocery store. She reminded me of Ma. Strong. Quick. Even talked to her. Asked her where the popcorn was and she took me right over there, nice and polite like. She had no idea who I was. I know Karen will, though."

Why not, thought Bruce. It would be like looking in a mirror. "She's always asking about you. In fact, just the other day..." He stopped himself. It wouldn't do any good to drag Angie into Karen's fight. Things were murky enough. With any luck, though, he might get the two of them together.

She had picked up her purse, and was rifling through it, not listening to what he was saying. "Do you mind if I smoke?"

He did, but he knew it had taken a lot for her to show up at his doorstep and didn't want to say anything that would break her spirit. "No, that's okay." He rose to get a dish from the kitchen. She was taking a drag when he returned, and he could see her hands shake. He placed the dish on the table next to her and took her hand. "Angie, how've you been all these years?"

She patted his hand then slipped hers from his, leaned way back in her chair and looked up at the ceiling. "Once the guy I ran off with found out I was pregnant, he walked out and left me in a motel. It was in this hick town off Route 60 in New Mexico's high country. Magdalena. I lived there on the money you sent me for a while. That's where I met Art. He owned the motel." She took another deep drag, hung her arm over the side and slowly blew it out. "He was retired from the army, and he and his wife ran the place along with a gas station. When I ran out of money, they didn't have the heart to throw me out; and she wasn't doing well, so they hired me on to keep up the rooms and gave me a place to live."

She swallowed hard. "Bruce, do you have some water?"

He went in the kitchen and got her a glassful and returned to find her wiping her eyes with a hankie. "You don't have to tell me any more, Angie. Have some water and lie down in the bedroom for a while."

She took a swallow. "No, I'm all right. I want to." She picked up the cigarette, flicked the ashes in the dish and took another drag. "I don't know what was wrong with me, Bruce. I was wild crazy. They had a lot of folks comin' around there to hunt elk, and like a fool, I left my boy and ran off with one of 'em. He was good to me at first. Then after a couple of months he started beatin' on me. One night he went after me real bad, and the folks next door took me in and sent me back to Magdalena on a bus the next day. By then, Art's wife's heart had given out and he was takin' care of the motel, the gas station, the baby… pretty much all by himself.

"I had a couple of broken ribs and two black eyes, but he took me in again and never said a thing. Never ever made me feel ashamed or nothin'. He was twenty years older, but we raised the boy as if he was his and eventually got married. It broke his heart when little Freddy ran after a ball in the parking lot and got hit. He was the cutest five year old you ever did see. It broke my heart, too, but I figured it was God's way of punishing me for runnin' out on my kids the way I did. It happened almost twenty years ago, but it still hurts as if was yesterday. Havin' all those kids when I was so young, I never appreciated what a gift it was 'til I lost that boy."

She cried softly in her hanky, then wiped her eyes. "Art sold the motel to the highway department this past winter, and we were fixin' to come east to see if I could get a peek at the kids. Then one night after dinner, he got up and started for the kitchen and his heart plumb gave out. He was a good man. More of a father to me than a husband, but I loved him."

She reached over and squeezed Bruce's hand. "I came over to ask you if I could do anything for the three of them. I'm too ashamed to ask myself."

"They're doin' all right, Angie. Keep what you have for yourself." Bruce felt good seeing her motherly instincts had finally kicked in. He scratched the back of his neck. "It might do Karen some good to see you, though."

"I can't, Bruce. I can't face her. I just want to get a look at her and that little girl of hers. I hear Karen's done well in spite of her upbringin'."

"She's picked up some ornery Yankee habits like spendin' too much, but she sure did make somethin' of herself. That little Hali of hers is right nice, too. She doesn't have the nasty temper both your girls do. She's thoughtful and even-natured."

Angie blew her nose. "I can't bear for Karen to see me. I

heaped a world of grief on that kid."

"She told me."

Angie's brow wrinkled. "You mean about the..." She saw him nod and she grasped the hanky to her mouth and let out a pathetic cry. "Oh, Bruce, that's why I left. I'll never forget the way she looked when I got home. All covered with blood and shakin'... yet iron-willed the way she was since she was a baby. As much as I hated Ma, I knew I had to give her the kids and get out of their lives." She looked up at him with a twisted smile, "So I stole all the money she'd stashed in the grandfather clock, left the kids and took off with that bastard."

Bruce could see that life had finally taught her enough lessons to make a real woman of her. "So what are you gonna do now?" he asked.

"I'm fixed good and just came to see the kids and tell you to let me know if there's anything I can do for 'em." She looked deep into Bruce's eyes. "That's all I deserve." She pulled out a piece of paper. "Here's my address and phone number in New Mexico. I've been stayin' in a motel in Asheville for three weeks now, but I still got the gas station and need to be gettin' home." She looked up at him, pleading. "Bruce, I haven't been able to get close to Karen, and I gotta get goin'. I need you to set something up so I can see her up close before I leave... see the little girl up close, too."

"She's gonna know who you are the minute she sets eyes on you."

"I got a blonde wig and I'll put on some sunglasses."

Bruce shook his head. "This whole thing is nuts. She needs you, Angie."

She tugged at his arm. "Please, Bruce. Do this for me. Fix this and I promise some day I'll come back... I just can't do it now. I gotta write her a letter and tell her how much I love her. Amy, too."

"Okay, Angie. Give me your number and I'll call you when I come up with somethin'."

"No. I'll call you tomorrow around three. I need to know then."

KAREN PULLED ONTO Route 74 and her stomach dropped when she drove past the farm and saw the trailer being towed down Granny's lane. She watched until it disappeared into the woods. Thank God, they weren't parking them right on the road. Hali had watched too, and didn't say a word as Karen pulled into the next driveway where Annie's mother ran her day camp. When Hali gave her a hug goodbye, Karen couldn't let go.

"It's okay, Mom. We still got our place. Next spring we can put in some vegetables and get a couple of goats."

Karen laughed and rocked her in her arms as the song streamed through her head. "I won't last a day without you, sweetheart," she said as she kissed the top of her head. A couple of girls were clustered at their door, and when Hali got out, ran with her to the craft shack on the side of the house.

On the drive to the Folk Art Center, Karen remembered the show that was going up that day in the permanent collection gallery and was surprised she actually felt some happiness. Maybe it was because her nerves were rubbed raw, but she filled with love thinking about the flood of talent that was going to flow into that gallery.

She'd gone into their collection and put together a show that would speak to people in the language of art… unsophisticated art from the hearts and minds of people whose hardships couldn't dampen their yearnings to express the simple beauty they saw around them.

She pulled off the parkway and went upstairs as fast as she could. Their preparator was already at work. She was placing one of Karen's favorite pieces in a glass case. It was only six inches tall but had the power to capture anyone's heart: a horse fashioned with braids of cornhusk. The animal looked as if it had paused a moment to let its two riders, a mother and child, take a last look at their cabin before setting off. The horse held his head with pride and showed off his mane of cornsilk.

The mother's dress, made of a single cornhusk, looked like a long skirt of muslin flowing down across her body as she sat sidesaddle on the horse. The child's arms were wrapped around her and her face pressed against her back. Their faces were drawn with delicate strokes, and a now faded rosy bloom had been dabbed on their cheeks. There was something about the simple square, denoting the horse's eye, and the slack in the cornstalk reins that said there was trust between them as they set upon a journey.

The woman suddenly turned to ask Karen a question. "Karen? You're crying."

Karen waved her away and choked out. "I'm okay. It's just so… poignant."

Karen went back to her office and buried herself in work, but every once in a while couldn't resist strolling over and watching the exhibit take shape. She slipped out at noon for lunch, then went back to her paperwork. The phone rang and Bruce was on the other end. How dear of him, she thought. He'd never called her at work before and had to be worried about her.

"You said somethin' about goin' over to that Hickory Nut Gap Farm and gettin' a brisket for your barbeque on Friday."

"You're coming, aren't you?"

"Yeah, sure. I just wanted to pick out the meat with you so I know what to buy when I make barbeque. You can give me your recipe on Friday."

How strange, she thought. He never seemed interested in cooking before. "All right, but you've got to promise not to share my secret recipe with anyone." He didn't laugh and she was a little embarrassed at her failed attempt at humor. "I'll meet you there around five-thirty. Don't be late; they close at six."

Around four, Karen walked through the exhibit and felt a surge of wonder; and later, as she drove home, its aura was still with her. She may have failed in getting the farm back and would have to see it scarred and debased, but still, she had done the right thing coming back to the mountains and taking this job. She'd turned her back on religion years ago, but felt that either Joel was in heaven and had guided her move, or he had left such an indelible mark on their lives, that they were being pulled in the direction he had wanted them to go.

She called ahead to Amy so Hali would be out waiting, then picked her up and drove over to the store. Hali pointed out

Bruce's red Malibu sitting next to a big white Cadillac. They got out and ran in. No one was there except Bruce, the guy behind the counter and a woman checking out the condiments and nick-nacks in the center aisle.

"Okay, Bruce. It's important to get the right size brisket for your crock pot. You do have a crock pot, don't you?" She waved her hand. "Don't worry, if you don't have one you can borrow mine." She found the section with the briskets and beckoned Bruce with a curled finger. "I always make beef barbeque with a nice brisket. Four pounds is perfect for my pot."

She started picking through the meat and noticed Bruce looking over at Hali who was talking with the woman. They were examining a set of shakers in the shape of bears. Karen was a little annoyed that Bruce was taking more notice of them than he was of her instructions. "Pay attention, now," she admonished as she flipped through the packages. She pulled one out and showed it to him. "See. This is a good piece." She pointed to the marbling. "The more of this, the better."

Someone touched her arm and she turned to see the woman smiling at her. She was blonde and wearing sunglasses. Karen thought that odd since the store was so dark. She was holding a set of salt and pepper shakers in the shape of black bears.

"I'd like to buy these for your daughter, if it's all right with you?"

"Well, that's very nice of you. I hope she didn't press you for them."

"Oh, no! She's just so darlin', I wanted to buy her a present."

"All right, then. Thank you." Karen turned back to the meat and started to say something when Bruce nudged her and motioned toward the woman who was now walking to the counter with Hali. Karen shrugged her shoulders a little and whispered in annoyance, "I already thanked her."

Bruce wasn't paying much attention to the meat so she gave up on him and decided she'd write all the instructions down and give them to him on Friday. She carried the brisket to the center aisle, looked over the barbeque sauces and chose one with honey and hickory-smoked seasoning, then headed for the counter.

The woman had finished paying for the shakers and was bending down and handing them to Hali.

"Thank you. I'll love them forever," said Hali.

The woman stood up, adjusted her glasses and abruptly said goodbye. Karen watched her leave and for a moment her thoughts slid away.

Hali shook her arm. "Hurry up and pay, Mom. I want to get home."

Karen let the packages slip onto the counter and slowly walked to the door and went out. She watched the woman get in the Cadillac and look up at her for a moment before backing up and pulling out. Karen walked out onto the lot, and as the car passed by, read the New Mexico license plates.

Bruce was now behind her. Karen swung around and fell into his arms shrieking "It was her. It was my mother!"

He held her tight and patted her head as she sobbed uncontrollably. "She's coming back, honey. She just couldn't do it this time." Bruce held on to her with one arm and took a kerchief from his back pocket. "Damn, if this ain't makin' me cry too." Hali stood with her arms around both of them.

Bruce waited for Karen to settle down, then walked her over to her SUV and helped her in. "I'll take care of the meat and bring it right over," he told her, then looked at Hali and could see she was thinking hard. He led her around to the other door and helped her up. He wasn't prone to showing affection, but he looked at her owl-like expression and gave her a big hug. "You go on along with your ma. I'll be right over."

CHAPTER TWENTY-FOUR

"**G**ET ME TO the airport as fast as you can," Tom told the cabbie as he threw his bag on the seat. He grinned at the dark-skinned man. *"I got a date."*

That morning when he walked into the offices of Smithfield, Rubenstein and Shirtz, Troy's assistant told him her boss had been called onto another case and the closing had been put off until eleven. Luckily, she found him another flight back to Charlotte at three. It was cutting it close, but he could go directly to Karen's from the airport. He smiled to himself thinking it wouldn't hurt to let her see him in his new suit.

Troy was a few minutes late for the closing and rushed through the paperwork as if he had more important business waiting elsewhere. Finished, he apologized for not taking him to lunch and took off again. Tom put the copies of the precious documents in his briefcase and caught a cab for the airport.

There was something about a terminal that energized him. This was the "going somewhere" crowd with a glimmer of expectation on their faces. He moved through the security check, then bought a paper and found a restaurant. He ordered a sandwich and opened the *Orlando Sentinel.* Bob Ward stared at him from the front page, only this time in a business suit instead of a rumpled jail jumpsuit.

Tom studied the picture. Ward looked surprisingly like any typical middle-aged businessman. He was probably twenty pounds over his ideal weight, but still fit enough to give someone an idea of what he might have looked like in his youth. No more than a snapshot of an instant in the man's life, yet the photo still captured the animal cunning in his eyes.

Tom read with interest. "Orange County Circuit Judge Walter Komanski denied a defense motion to keep crucial statements made by developer James Robert "Bob" Ward out of his upcoming murder trial. Tuesday's ruling means statements Ward made to a deputy at his Isleworth residence soon after his wife's shooting death will be allowed at his trial. Other statements permitted include those Ward made to a deputy in a patrol car after his arrest; those he later made to law enforcement in an interview room at the sheriff's office headquarters; and recorded comments he uttered while making calls on his cell phone inside the interview room. Ward is accused of shooting his wife, Diane, in the bedroom of their Isleworth mansion. He is charged with second-degree murder. He has said that she was trying to kill herself and that the shooting was an accident."

Tom knew it was silly but couldn't help hoping any bad karma on Grassy Patch Mountain would disappear now that the conservancy owned it. He spent the next two hours answering emails and checking in with his boss.

No sooner had he glanced at his watch and noticed the plane hadn't yet rolled up to the gate, when the announcement came over the PA that the flight had encountered severe turbulence coming from Chicago and would be a half-hour late. Tom nervously thought through a timeline and concluded if he went straight to Karen's, he'd make it in time.

The plane finally arrived and started loading passengers. Tom made his way down the aisle and discovered he was sharing a seat with a young woman and her baby. She didn't look more than sixteen, but the baby, who was somewhere around one, was obviously well cared for. They got settled in, with Tom sitting in the aisle seat.

Tom leaned around and gave the boy a big smile. The child's face started to pucker and his lips began quivering, then he let loose a blood-curdling scream. When the girl whipped out a bottle and stuck it in his mouth, the baby grasped it with his chubby fingers and sucked as if this were the last bottle he'd ever see.

"We live with my mother and he's not used to men," she told him.

He gave her a wink. "It's good to know I'm not that scary." She fidgeted with her hands and he could see she wasn't wearing a wedding band.

One hour out of Orlando, Tom was cradling a cup of coffee when the captain's voice came over the speaker. "They're experiencing severe wind shear in Charlotte, so our flight has been diverted to Atlanta. We'll wait on the tarmac until we get clearance to continue the flight. It shouldn't be more than an hour."

He pulled out his BlackBerry to call Karen. It made him smile when the receptionist at the Folk Art Center said she had gone home early; she was evidently making a big effort for tonight. His mood changed the minute he thought of telling her he might not get there until late.

There was no answer at the house and he decided against leaving a message. He didn't want to take a chance of getting her angry. He'd call her again once they landed in Atlanta and smooth everything over.

SINCE SHE HAD to put in a few hours at the center on Saturday, Karen didn't feel badly about taking off a couple hours early. On the drive home, she wished she hadn't invited Bruce, and made plans instead to leave Hali at Amy's. She would have liked to be alone to talk with Tom. She found herself anxious to get to know him.

Camp ended at two on Fridays, so she headed for Amy's to pick up Hali. She started to feel confident that Bruce would know enough to find an excuse to go home before it got too late and Hali would leave her alone with Tom. She smiled to herself; of course Hali would. When she looked back, she could see that Hali's plans were evident from the first time Tom came over. The sound of the two laughing had stayed in her head ever since that night.

She yearned to be with him, but she had to tell him the whole story before things went too far. She wanted him to know who she was and where she came from before he committed. Now that she had aired her story to Bruce, she believed she could face it. Even if Tom were repulsed, he'd never give her away. No more keeping secrets as she had with Joel. She had grown up. Any man who was willing to push his life to the sideline so he could save the land deserved the truth.

If she had bared her soul to Joel, she might have come back a long time ago. She drove home tracing the journey she took reinventing herself. It had taken her the whole four years at Salem College to scrub away every trace of the mountains, never going home summers for fear of slipping back into mountain-speak. Instead, she got jobs in the Catskills, close to her ultimate destination: New York City. When she landed the internship at the Met after graduation, she figured she had finally made herself into the person who had led the kind of life she wished she had.

She didn't keep that pathetic mountain girl hidden from Joel because she was afraid he'd stop loving her. That was impossible. She did it because, by keeping her locked away, she could go on pretending she was someone else, just like the beautiful lady in the painting. Maybe this whole mess with Travis was God's way of forcing her to make peace with the past instead of pretending it never happened.

She remembered the night in Joel's arms after they were married when she finally agreed to bring him home to meet her family. The words sounded so much like a death sentence that she wanted to tell him everything before they got there so he'd understand; but curled up in his gentle, loving arms, she couldn't do it. He was too innocent to hear her story. Too kind to understand how life can happen to an innocent child.

After Joel's visit to the mountains and seeing the backwoods world they lived in, she waited for him to ask her how she had gotten so polished and sophisticated. Or why, for that matter. But he never confronted her with those questions. He just waited patiently for thirteen years for her to tell him her story; and she would always regret that she let him leave this world without giving her whole self to him. It had needed to be done, but she hadn't been able to do it.

She reached Amy's driveway and braced for the inevitable rant about their mother. She was sure Bruce had kept in touch with Amy over the past two days and fed her as much information as he figured she could handle. Amy had to be in a snit over missing an opportunity to rail on their mother for leaving them the way she did. Poor Hali must have had a job calming her down. She smiled inwardly. Just like Joel, Hali was better at that than she was.

That was the biggest gift her husband had given her. He had started to draw her out of her isolationist mountain character and made her see things in a broader light. She had even surprised herself over the years as she saw how she was becoming more tolerant. Less frequently, she found herself judging people out of suspicion and fear and being rewarded with a reciprocal generosity of spirit that made life a whole lot nicer.

She learned from him to accept people for what they are and roll with it. Especially some of the people at the museum. If it weren't for Joel, she might have killed a couple of them. Reflecting on it, she came to the conclusion that tolerance was a characteristic of New Yorkers in general, the only way eight million people packed into five crowded boroughs with hundreds of different languages and religions could co-exist.

She pulled onto Amy's lot and the dogs in the fenced pens started barking. No one being around, she went into the building, and for a moment was keenly aware of the pungent smell. She peeked in one room and a bird screaming "Stop it! Stop it!" startled her, and she quickly slammed the door shut. Hali wasn't exaggerating when she told her about the parrot. The door at the far end of the hall burst open and the two came out with Hali holding a puppy.

"Look, Mom! It's a dachshund. Amy said I could have it! Can I?"

Amy put her hands on her hips, leaned her head to the side, and glared at her. Karen had first seen this stance years ago when she told her sister she couldn't bring her cat to bed. It was no use to argue. "Sure, honey. What's his name?"

"Her name, Mommy. It's a *her.* "

"Well?"

"Angie! Aunt Amy thought of it!"

Amy flashed her wide toothy grin, raised an eyebrow and projected her head forward like a chicken, as if to say, "I gotcha."

"What are we going to do with it when you're at camp?"

"Oh, during the week she can stay here until she's potty trained and I'll play with her when Uncle Eddie gets me."

Amy lifted a plastic bag of wood shavings she was toting. "Here. You'll need these. There's enough for the weekend."

On the way home, Karen laughed at Amy's little dig and figured she got off easy. "How was your aunt today?" she asked.

Hali was busy playing with the pup's ears. "Oh, you know what your sister's like, Mom."

"No, darling. Tell me. What *is* she like?"

"Well, one thing for sure, she likes animals. She gets to know them just like they're people. Yesterday a man brought in his wife's little dachshund for us to take care of while she was in the hospital. The poor little thing was shaking something awful. So Aunt Amy dug through her storeroom and got out a fuzzy pink cat bed and put it in his cage with him, and he curled right up and went to sleep. She said it took her a dozen tries to hit on that bed the last time he was there. Think of it, Mom, of all the dogs she boards, she remembered the exact bed that exact dog liked."

She lifted the pup in the air and rubbed noses with it. "But, she never talks about people the same way she does animals. It kinda gives me the impression she doesn't like them all that much. And she doesn't have any friends like... you know... you and Monique. Poor Uncle Eddie. Every time he tries to hug her or something, she tells him to scat. They sure aren't lovey dovey like you and Dad were. But I know she likes him, the way she's always fussing over him."

"Did she say anything about our mother?"

"Not really. Mostly that she can't wait until she shows her face in Fairview again." Hali said it with a half amused detachment.

"Honey, I don't think Angie's a good name for your puppy."

"Why not, Mom?"

"Someday, I'll tell you, honey." She glanced over at the dog. "She's a medium brown. Why not call her Ginger?"

"I like that."

Once home, Karen rushed into the house to check on the brisket. She had let it marinate all night and put it into the crock pot before she left for work. "Perfect!" she proclaimed as she took it out with a pair of tongs and placed in on a plate to cool down before she started pulling it apart. She checked the time. "Good. It's not even five. We'll have over two hours to get everything ready." She glanced at Hali who was playing with the dog. "You better get those wood shavings out of the car. I'll fix Ginger a place with a cardboard carton."

She rushed into the dining room and studied the table she had set the night before after Bruce left. Where should she seat Tom? By all standards, Bruce should be put across from her at the other end of the table. No. She was beyond pretending Tom was simply a guest. He wanted her and she wanted him and that was the way it was. She would seat him at the head of the table across from her, and they'd all know why. She straightened one of the tapered candles and decided to go outside with Hali and pick some flowers for a centerpiece.

A HALF-HOUR on the runway and Tom was on a first-name basis with Becky. She told him her baby's father was stationed at Fort Drum in Upstate New York and was going to meet them in Syracuse. "Don't worry," Tom said. "If you're late, when he gets to the airport, he'll be able to see your flight's been delayed. Why don't you show me your ticket." He could see she had a three-hour layover in Charlotte. "If we get out of here in a little while, you'll have no trouble catching your connecting flight."

Next, he called Karen. Again, no answer. He was starting to get nervous.

ONCE THEY CAME back in with the black-eyed Susans and got the puppy settled in, Karen put the baked beans in the oven, then went upstairs to take a bath before pulling the dinner together. She took out the dress she had worn last week and laid it on the bed.

For the first time since Joel died she felt like the future held a wonderful promise. She couldn't believe she could be so excited about what lie ahead after the nightmarish events of the past days. A line from a Pope essay ran through her head. It was true. Hope does spring eternal in the human breast.

The phone rang. She turned and looked at it as if it were a dangerous object. She let it ring two more times. Oh Lord, it can't be Tom telling her he wasn't coming. The prospect of seeing him tonight was the only thing that had held her together for the past two days.

She went over to the table and checked the clock. Six. What was she thinking? He had to be back from Orlando by now. She picked up the receiver and said hello.

"Hello, Karen. It's me."

She could tell by the tone in his voice he wasn't coming.

"I'm on the tarmac in Atlanta."

She screamed and slammed the phone down, then threw herself on the bed and sobbed for all the heartbreaks since that night Joel came home and told her he was sick.

TOM PUT HIS fingers to his forehead and pressed so hard he thought he was going to make his skin bleed. He threw his head back on the seat and looked up, only to have the stagnant air nozzle taunt him. He pressed his eyes shut and felt himself holding Karen in his arms, remembered the scent of her at the square dance.

She had dominated his thoughts for weeks, and he had

pictured himself married to her as if it were inevitable. He remembered laughing with glee when Josh told him Jason had been seen around town with a pretty blonde who folks said had been in the Marines with him. There was no way Jason would have given up on Karen unless she had made it clear to him he wasn't in the running.

Finding a life partner hadn't happened for Tom. When he thought back, he was the one who always got dumped. He knew now all those girls had made the right decision. Never had he felt about them the way he did about Karen. Like he would die without her.

Now, the thought that she might not forgive him started to panic him. He pressed his head against the back of the seat and stared at the top of the bald head in front of him. She was the one. Anyone who could leave a fabulous position at the Met and come back home to save the family farm knew the value of the land. That was important to him, because that would always be his life's work.

Okay, so she's mad. He could understand that. But he wasn't going to let her go to sleep mad. No matter how late he came in, he was going to go over and hold her in his arms. He dug into his pocket and pulled out the two bracelets he bought at a jewelry kiosk in the airport, one for Hali and the other for Karen. Nothing lavish. Corny, in fact. Slim gold chains, each with a single heart-shaped charm.

Suddenly the air-conditioning came on and the plane started to move. A voice came over the intercom. "Well, folks, we've been okayed for takeoff. We should be touching down in Charlotte around eight." A cheer rose and a big smile spread across Tom's face.

By now, the baby was done for the day and didn't stir during takeoff. The stewardess started announcing the gates for connecting flights and Tom calculated that Becky might make her flight. He leaned toward her. "I know the Charlotte airport. If we hurry, I can get you to your gate in time."

"You mean you're going to help me?"

He gave her a knowing wink and pulled his briefcase from

under the seat in front of him. "Not only am I going to help you, I'm going to beef you up for the big run." He put the case on his lap, unsnapped the latches and flipped it open with a flourish. He gave her another wink, then pulled aside a folder and exposed a trove of snacks. He tilted the case so she could see them. "Go on. Take a couple."

They both indulged and were grateful when the stewardess came around with drinks. "Do you want another one?" Tom asked before he snapped his briefcase closed.

"No thanks." She touched his arm. "Thanks for being so nice to me and Joey." She hesitated for a moment. "I'm really scared. Joey's dad and I aren't married. My mother thought if he saw Joey and all, he'd want... well... you know... to make everything legal."

Tom patted her hand. "That little boy of yours is something special... and so are you. I'll tell ya, if that fellow you're going to meet doesn't grab you and Joey right up, there's something wrong with him."

She blushed. "That's what my mother said." She gazed out the window for a moment. "Was that your wife who hung up on you?"

"No. Not my wife."

"She didn't give you much of a chance."

"It's not her fault. I've done this a couple times before."

She came close and whispered in his ear. "If *she* doesn't grab you up, there's something wrong with *her.*"

By the time the plane landed and he raced with Becky to the gate and saw her and Joey off, it was eight-fifteen. He wouldn't get to Sugar Hollow until around eleven. Hopefully, Karen would still be up. Maybe, if he was lucky, he'd even get some of that world famous barbeque of hers.

The slam of the phone still resounded in his ear, but she'd had plenty of time to cool off. He smiled to himself thinking she wouldn't have been so upset, unless she was really looking forward to seeing him. Not only was he in the running, he was pretty sure he was going to wrap this deal up.

Instead of going through the gorge, he took the longer but

faster lowland route to Fairview, then doubled back onto Sugar Hollow. He strained his eyes to see if there were any lights on in the house. One dim one in the kitchen. She must be waiting up, hoping I'll come, he thought.

He figured that going straight to the kitchen through the porch would be a little presumptuous, so he knocked on the front door. He waited a while, and when no one answered, he knocked loud enough for anyone who might be upstairs to hear.

A heavy stomping of footsteps sounded on the stairs; but then disappeared. Puzzled, he waited a few minutes, then raised his fist to knock again. Suddenly the door flew open and a plateful of barbeque came flying at him, then the door slammed in his face. He stood there with the whole hideous scene replaying in his brain.

He peeled the paper plate off his chest and put it on the porch. I guess she's not cooled off yet, he admitted to himself as he swiped some of the gooey sauce off. He walked back to his truck, first taking off his tie, then his shirt. As he started to get in the truck, he caught sight of Hali's silhouette in the window. Then the light in the hall behind her went off and the little girl vanished.

CHAPTER TWENTY-FIVE

K AREN KEPT GLANCING over at the phone as she slipped on her pajamas. Tom had called her a dozen times in the past two days, and if he phoned her again tonight she was going to have her number changed. She ran down the stairs determined to tackle an idea that had been rolling around in her head for the past two days. But first, she needed to talk with Bruce, so she picked up the phone in the living room and dialed.

"How's life treatin' ya, gal?"

"Don't ask. I need a favor from you." She went over and curled up in an easy chair. "I want you to find out how much the Fultons are paying Travis for Amy's two hundred acres."

"You're not thinkin' what I think you're thinkin', are ya?"

"Uh-huh. They don't have any emotional attachment to that land. They're just looking for something cheap," said Karen. She pictured Bruce scratching his head while he thought.

"I wouldn't be surprised if you offer to buy it for... let's say ten percent more than what they're paying... they just might go along. Especially since nothin's changed hands yet. I reckon they'll want to get paid for movin' everything. Can you come up with the money?"

"It depends on how much. I'm going through all my holdings tonight." She couldn't believe she was actually voicing an idea she had toyed with ever since her last encounter with Travis. "Can you do me another favor? Call that appraiser friend of yours and ask him what the going price would be for the rest of the property."

"You're not aiming to buy that place from that bastard, are you?"

"Let's say I just want to know how much it would cost."

"It would stick in my craw to see you go and do that."

"This whole mess is sticking in my craw. I should have been here to take care of Granny like she did us. I don't know if I can pull it off, but I want to give it a try. Granny wanted the farm kept in the family, and if I lose it, I'll pine for it the rest of my life. But Bruce, no matter what, I want Amy's land back from the Fultons. I promised her I'd get it. And Bruce, please, don't breathe a word of this to her."

She hung up and went into the den to turn on her laptop, then ran into the kitchen for a glass of ice tea. She spotted Ginger cuddled up against a teddy bear in her box in the corner and felt a wave of gratitude to Annie Louise's mom for letting Hali bring the dog to camp with her. She knew they were getting a special pass and appreciated it.

Karen meandered out on the porch and listened to the gentle rain tap on the tin roof for a while before picking up her tea and reluctantly going back into the den.

First, she would catch up on the Madoff case and see if there might be any money coming in from that. She clicked the icon sitting on her desktop and "Madofftrustee.com" booted up.

When Joel's father died and left one million dollars to his wife, and five-hundred thousand to each son, it made sense to Joel to let his brother Marty give it to the same firm his wife's parents were heavily invested in since they were making a return of ten percent.

Marty was the older brother who had been on a steady, predictable path since he was twelve. He looked a lot like Joel and, even though he wasn't gifted with his charisma, his job as a CPA at one of the nation's largest accounting firms made him the family's authority on finances. Once Madoff went bust, Karen asked him to retain the same firm as his in-laws to represent them for a contingency fee of 25%.

She scanned the slew of lawsuits the trustee had slapped on Madoff, his family members, his employees and their relatives and the money managers who fed him the billions.

Joel had considered himself invincible, and the only life insurance he bought was accidental death since he traveled so much. Luckily, she had added him to her policy at work, but only for fifty thousand, all of which she put in Hali's college fund. Thankfully, her insurance covered every penny of his medical bills.

She pulled up her accounting and figured it was costing a little over three thousand a month to carry the co-op. She had enough saved to get through another eight or nine months before she had to start digging into her 401(k). She needed to get an idea of how long her co-op might be on the market, so she thumbed through her rolodex for her realtor's card and dialed.

SUSAN REYNOLDS HAD witnessed four recessions in the twenty-seven years she'd been selling real estate, but had never seen anything like this one. In 2005 she'd raked in a half-million in commissions, but four years later was barely making enough to keep her head above water. Luckily, she hadn't been one to throw her money around and could still hold on to her co-op and the house at the beach in the Hamptons; but the loft she was renovating was putting her in a pinch. If she'd only finished it before the bottom fell out of the market.

The phone rang and she glanced at the clock on the table. Ten-thirty. Probably one of her clients who couldn't get to sleep and needed some hand-holding. She picked up the receiver and put on her well-practiced smiley voice. "Hello."

"Hi Susan. It's Karen Godwell. Sorry to bother you so late, but I was wondering how things were going with my co-op."

Susan didn't believe in handing out false hope. "Karen, I ran some comps on your place for one of my clients last week and you're getting undercut by everything for sale in that area. I was going to call and suggest you think about lowering your price to stay in the game."

"Susan, I'll do what you think is best, but can you honestly tell me what my chances of selling the place are?"

Susan closed her eyes and for the hundredth time that day wished she could see the future. "Karen, people are feeling real insecure right now. And the ones that are secure are worried their kids might lose their jobs and need some help. All those financial types that were making sky-high bonuses are collecting severance pay and putting their places on the market for less than they paid for them. People are afraid to make a move, and the ones that aren't, are out trawling for bargains."

"Have you had *anyone* looking?"

"Several. But you keep losing out for one crazy reason or another. They liked the view from the other one better, or it was closer to their favorite restaurant... stuff like that."

"Do you think lowering the price will help?"

"Definitely. It will get us more lookers." Susan gauged by Karen's responses that she needed to sell. "Karen, one good thing is that in spite of the collapsing prices, inventory hasn't risen that much. So once the economy does turn around and things start to move again, prices should start to edge upward rather quickly. But for now, let's lower the price by twenty thousand and see what happens."

Susan ended the call promising to email Karen a price change form. She didn't tell her she had pulled every trick she knew to sell her co-op to the last client she took over there, including dragging the woman through a half dozen horrible units so she'd be ecstatic by the time she got to Karen's. She wanted to break the woman's neck when she picked something else because she liked where the hall closet was located. Both of the co-ops were her listings, but the Godwells held a special place in her heart. Mostly because of Joel.

The two weeks she'd spent showing him property were some of the most enjoyable in her career, not only because of his playful personality, but also because of the way he and Karen kissed after they'd signed the contract. She sighed. Tomorrow she'd change the price and whip up another brochure. Then she'd call a friend who owed her a favor for two staging jobs she threw her way. She'd take her over there tomorrow and see what she could do. Karen had already had the place painted and the floors refinished. It wouldn't take much.

KAREN WAS GLAD she called Susan. At least the part about there not being too much inventory was good news. She paid a few bills on-line before turning off the lights. If Susan could only sell the co-op, she could easily buy the farm. She started up the stairs and regretted pulling up the Madoff page. Reading about all his lavish homes and offshore accounts made her so upset, she was never going to fall asleep. A glass of wine might settle her down, so she turned around and went back downstairs. The bottle of Chablis in the fridge was barely good enough for cooking, but she poured herself some and went out on the porch.

There was something about looking out at the night and breathing in the sweet smells of the wet earth that always fed her spirit. It had stopped raining and the fragrant scent of the honeysuckle climbing the porch columns drifted in and out of the air. She listened for the whippoorwill and admitted to herself that her money problems weren't the only thing keeping her awake.

She shouldn't have let herself need Tom so much that night. She couldn't believe she was actually going to tell him everything. What in the world was she thinking! She had assumed too much. Had the whole damn mess made her lose her marbles? He would have just loved hearing about her hacking some drifter to pieces. She barely even knew the guy!

Tears welled in her eyes. A team of horses couldn't keep Joel away from her. She smiled remembering how she refused to go out with him because he had been dating her roommate who was crazy about him. Every night as she left the Met, he kept showing up with different ridiculous disguises and introducing himself as someone else until she finally caved in.

She went back into the house, locked up and started up the

stairs. It was a good thing Tom didn't show up on Friday after all, she concluded. What that guy needed was some nice unencumbered girl who was a natural-born caregiver. She felt her ire rise as she climbed the stairs. Someone who knew how to keep a meal warm... *for hours!* If he dared call her again, he was going to get the brush-off of his life!

CHAPTER TWENTY-SIX

"**Y**OU WANTED TO TALK to me?" asked Karen as she sat down in her boss's office. From the way he fumbled with the stainless steel clip he used for his notes, Karen could tell he was uneasy. He put the clip down and smoothed back his already smooth dark hair.

She'd never seen him like this before. In fact, his pleasant easy-going demeanor usually set the tone for the entire office staff. An administrator more than an arts advocate, his unemotional, business-like management style kept him out of the sometimes rancorous goings-on of the menagerie of artisans they catered to.

He cleared his throat. "You know, Karen, sometimes things happen in this business you can't do anything about, and you just have to live with it."

She'd heard the phrase, *and you just have to live with it,* enough times to know what he was about to say wasn't going to be pretty.

He fumbled with the clip again. "I got a call from Beth Kensington's father. He's quite a big deal in this town... and a big contributor of ours."

This was the last thing she ever thought would come up. "Jim, I did the best I could in that situation. I had to put them in separate shows or we were going to have a big problem on our hands."

His silence was difficult to interpret.

"I know that." He looked as if he were steeling himself. "What seemed to bother them the most is the way you laughed at Jack's antics."

Karen couldn't believe she was on the carpet for such chicken shit. "Jim, Beth set herself up for that scenario when she failed to tell me that she had been married to Jack. But that's beside the point. What do you want me to do? Apologize?"

"Twenty thousand dollars worth."

Karen rolled her eyes toward the ceiling. "No problem. I'll take her to lunch." She struggled to keep the edge off her voice. "In fact, I'll call her right now." She started to get up. "Is that all?"

He nodded. "Thanks for being a good sport about this, Karen, but maybe you should run these things by me first so I can let you know if I see any red flags. This isn't the Met, and we have to tiptoe a little lighter around here. The girls downstairs in the shop have had nothing but problems with that woman. It's to a point where it's simply easier to ask her where she wants her pieces located, and then work around it."

Karen went back to her office and could feel her face was feverish even though she tried to be as cool as she could. She couldn't blame Jim. She'd been in his position a couple of times and understood there was no other way to handle it. She didn't like the dig about the Met, however. She looked up the number and quickly dialed before she changed her mind. "Hello, Beth?"

"Yes."

"It's Karen Godwell. How are you?"

"Fine."

"I'd like to talk with you about your show. Can you do lunch today?"

"Is that *all* you want to talk about?"

247

So that's how it's going to be, thought Karen. She wants me to grovel. "Well, I did want to apologize about the other day… in person… over lunch."

"Good. I'll see you at Carmel's at one."

She phoned and told Jim, then fought off an urge to grab her purse and walk out. She picked up her pen and began proofing her newsletter. Unable to concentrate, she tapped the pen on the desk, searching for some rationalization. Finally she remembered the time when she was still an intern at the Met and Earl had inadvertently upset the wife of one of the museum's multi-million dollar contributors at a cocktail party.

He had offhandedly dismissed one of her suggestions, and when the director told him to apologize, he had called Karen into his office and asked her to write the letter for him. He said to make it good enough so he wouldn't have to revisit the incident; and that was what she did, even going so far as to "beg on his hands and knees for her forgiveness." He read the slavishly fawning document, pulled a sheet of his personal stationery out of a drawer, and without changing a word, asked her to get it typed up and bring it in for him to sign.

Hopefully, she wouldn't have to go that far with Beth this afternoon. No wonder Jack acted so insanely hateful. She must have made life hell for him. Karen started back on the proofs when she sensed someone was near. She looked up to see Tom filling the doorway. He was an eyeful, but not the one for her. She looked back down and pretended to read.

He crossed the room, pulled up a chair and took her hand. "I had to come see you, Karen. I couldn't stand to have you hang up on me one more time." She kept looking down at her papers. "Karen, if we get married, this kind of thing is gonna happen a lot."

Her eyes shot up at him. She didn't know whether to laugh at his audacity or cry. Didn't he know she was used to being adored! No! Worshipped was more like it. Uh-uh, buddy. I'm not going to play second-fiddle to your land saving business.

She slowly pulled her hand away and smiled at him. "Wait a minute, Tom. I'll be right back. I've got to do something." She rose and picked up her purse from her worktable and went out of the room, down the ramp to the first floor and out of the building. She spun out of the lot and onto the Blue Ridge Parkway and drove for over a half-hour, then turned around and came back.

She hurried to her office, picked up the red pen again and spotted a note on her desk. She recognized Tom's handwriting. The bookkeeper appeared in her doorway and watched her toss it in the wastebasket.

"He sat there for almost an hour," the woman said, somberly.

Karen picked up the pen again and looked down at the newsletter. "Did he?"

"I don't know about you, Karen, but he looks like a keeper to me."

Karen waited for her to leave, then picked the note out of the basket. *I won't last a day without you,* was all he had written. Her eyes pooled with tears and a pained whimper eked out. It took everything she had to force him out of her head and slip the note under her desk pad. She felt a sudden need to talk to someone who loved her or she would die. It had been a while since she chatted with Carrie. She picked up the phone and dialed the Met.

"Karen! I miss you!" squealed Carrie. "Wait. I've got to close my door."

Karen pictured her reaching over and thrusting the door of her closet-sized office closed.

"There, now we can really talk. How's everything with you and Hali?"

"Kinda good. Wish I could sell the co-op, though."

"You and everyone else in New York. The real estate market here is in the can."

"How are you and the Met?"

"Wait 'til you hear this," Carrie squealed. *"Earl is getting the directorship!* It's not official yet, but the director's secretary eats lunch with our Beatrice, and she says the big man's retiring and his job's going to Earl. The board's already approved it."

Karen couldn't help asking, "Who's getting Earl's job?"

"Why? Do you want it?"

"No. I'm not saying that. Just curious is all."

"Well... you better get a little bit more than curious. Someone read a memo that they're going to ask you to come back and take his job."

"Carrie, are you reading things on other people's desks again?"

"I wouldn't dream of it."

Karen suddenly missed the exhilaration of New York and dangerous waters of the Met. When you grovel in New York, you grovel for millions. The whole time Carrie gossiped, the fabulous salary she'd be making if she had Earl's job bounced around in her head. If she did it for five years, she'd have enough to retire comfortably in Fairview for the rest of her life, and that would be without having to deal with some small town bully's spoiled brat.

She hated to end the call to Carrie. It had given her a high she needed after the depressing past days. New York would be so easy to take right now. Nothing to worry about except being stabbed in the back by a bunch of cutthroat curators angling for her job. Child's play next to dealing with Travis.

THE SKY HAD turned gray, but it took more than Mother Nature to dampen the vitality of Asheville. Throngs of casually dressed tourists swarmed through the streets and meandered in and out of the jumble of unique specialty shops. Outdoor cafe tables overflowed with talkative diners, many with dogs lying obediently at their master's feet.

Karen welcomed the change. After her call to Carrie, her confidence had waned again. She even worried her status at the art center had plummeted from super star to washout, but she managed to shake it off. She parked in the garage across from the Grove Arcade and braced herself for the lunch with Beth.

As usual, Carmel's was packed and vibrating with energy. Beth sat at a table reading the menu in an outfit befitting an affluent matron about to witness the comeuppance of a disrespectful underling. Karen was sure Beth had seen her come in and ignored her as an added slight.

God, please don't let me lay a hand on her, she prayed as she waved away the hostess and made her way to the table. It irked her to think she was being considered for one of the most prestigious museum positions in the country, yet having to debase herself to soothe the hurt pride of a spurned spouse. If it was the last thing she did, she was going to land the center a couple of really big patrons and put that woman in her place.

Beth gave her an icy greeting, leaned back in her chair and folded her hands on the table, sending the message that she was refusing to say another word until the apology was delivered to her satisfaction.

"It was so very kind of you to meet me for lunch on such short notice," Karen said. Getting no response, she decided to just get it over with. "I wanted to tell you how very sorry I am for taking that outrageous slight from Jack so lightly. But, actually Beth, I was laughing *at him,* not *with him.* If in any way you thought I was amused by the *despicable* way he treated you, I want to beg you to forgive me."

Beth's lips curved up ever so slightly and she put her hands in her lap and savored the moment. Then she cheerfully picked up her purse and pulled something out. "I took the plans you gave me, painted everything out and made some copies. Here's how I want the show set up." She looked up at Karen. "But first, you've got to switch my show with Jack's so I can be with the sculptor."

Karen was incredulous at first, then her interest piqued. Just how far was Beth willing to go? "What do we do if Jack can't get enough pieces together for the earlier show?"

Beth looked at her with a feigned bewilderment. "Then you'll just have to find someone else. Won't you?"

Karen got a momentary reprieve when the waitress came to take their order. As Beth laboriously continued with the details of her layout, Karen saw that she had pushed the sculpture to the back. Beth had a manipulative way of reinforcing every demand. "Don't you agree," she kept saying, confident she wouldn't be challenged. Karen wondered why she even bothered.

The only reason Karen didn't step in and straighten her out was that, ironically, the woman's work was genuinely world class. Although, the only way the sculptor was going to get a fair deal was if she could convince him to bring his biggest pieces.

The food arrived and it eased Karen's mind that Beth was finally mollified. Hopefully she wouldn't order coffee and dessert and want to sit there all afternoon and bask in her triumph.

"I want to be friends with you, Karen." Beth was delicately cutting a sweet potato fry with her knife. "Especially since you're probably still smarting over what happened at the Met."

Karen's eyes shot up. "What do you mean?"

"Well, there's no way anyone would have left the position you had for *this* job... unless they were..." She looked up with a disingenuous smile on her face. "*...let go.*"

Karen sat there, her ears burning and her heart pounding in her throat. How could this insidious bitch think she could get away with terrorizing everyone she came in contact with? She suddenly realized that Jack's antics hadn't fazed the woman one bit. She simply seized the opportunity to pull Karen into her sphere of influence so she could torment her, too. The woman was sick.

Karen's cell phone rang. Before she picked it up she knew it was Hali with her two o'clock call. She flipped it open and started talking over Hali's words. "Oh my goodness! It's a good thing you called me." She checked her watch. "I'm downtown right now. I can be back there in twenty minutes." She listened to Hali laugh. This wasn't the first time her mother had gotten away from a luncheon this way.

She snapped the phone closed and took out enough money to pay for both lunches and placed it on the table. "Beth, something's come up at the center, and I've got to get over there right away. You know how it is: *business before pleasure.*" Beth's insipid smile made Karen wonder if she knew she was lying.

Karen stomped across Battery Park fuming. Jim owed her one for this. As she drove past the mass of people on the street, she wondered how much collective angst they all held in their hearts. How many were being cheated, or insulted, or running away from something. If all of it were turned into a sound would it be a roar, a scream, a whimper?

She arrived back at the center and had to park in the back since both lots were full. As she walked up the ramp to the second floor, she heard a visitor comment to her companion. *Those toys and dolls were made with such love, weren't they, honey?* Karen felt suddenly grounded. More than anything, she had wanted the exhibit to speak of the inherent human need to create beauty. She stood to the side and let the couple pass and felt at peace for the first time that day.

Back at her desk, she tried to concentrate on the newsletter, but stinging retorts to Beth's insinuation that she was fired from the Met kept popping into her head. That woman had no idea how close she came to having that vapid smile slapped off her face. Karen decided she needed a break, so she ran downstairs to the center's shop to pick up a couple more glass ladybugs to attach to their porch screen.

There was something about the way the ladies were so attentive and sympathetic even though they had nothing to be sympathetic about that made her suspect they knew she had been asked to apologize to Beth. She could read the concern on their faces and it was as if she were now another aggrieved member of their club. She hated herself for buying all the colorful glass ladybugs they had, but it was her way of telling them she had nothing to fear.

She returned to her office, disappointed that her effort to cheer herself up had backfired. The way gossip evidently flew around the place, Karen suddenly worried that Beth might spread rumors amongst the guild members that she had been fired. She pushed it out of her mind as absurd and continued editing the newsletter until the phone rang.

She recognized Earl's voice the minute he spoke her name. "Karen dear, how are you… and that precious child of yours?"

It took a moment to get her bearings. There was only one reason Earl would be calling. "We're good, Earl."

"Carrie told me you called this morning," he said.

"Yes. When I heard the rumor, I was thrilled for you Earl."

"It's not a rumor, Karen. It's finally happened. God knows I've waited long enough. They're going to make the official announcement at the same time they announce the director's retirement. In a couple weeks."

Karen closed her eyes tight and waited for the words she had dreamt about for years.

"Are you ready to take over as head of the American Wing?"

Her eyes swarmed with tears. All she could think of was *yes!* But she needed to consider it calmly. "How long can you give me to think about it, Earl?"

"The committee is prepared to launch a search with that headhunter out of Chicago, but as it stands right now, you're our first choice. We'll mail you a formal proposal tomorrow. After you get it, take a few days to think it over; but Karen, we can't give you much longer than that."

CHAPTER TWENTY-SEVEN

C HATTING WITH ANNIE Louise would be like old times, Karen was thinking as she headed for Annie's house. Hali was playing with her two girls after camp again. They lived just behind Annie's mother's place where most of the camp's activities occurred.

Afternoon rush-hour traffic swallowed up Karen's SUV, and she drove chalking up the past eight hours as another day she wished had never happened. That included the offer from Earl. In fact, except for seeing her mother, she wished the whole week never happened. She'd go through it all over again just for that. It had been vindicating that her mother had looked so good, as if she had finally straightened her life around. None of her missteps mattered any more. What counted was that she cared about her kids.

As Karen neared the Flying Cloud Farm, she spotted Annie Louise writing on the chalkboard at the stand. She pulled in next to it and zoomed down her window.

Annie looked over and wiped her sweaty forehead with the back of her hand. "Hi there. My aunt has taken the girls riding.

They're supposed to be back by now… but you know my aunt."

Karen pulled the SUV in far enough for someone to get around her and got out. She was happy the girls wouldn't be back for a while. She strolled over to Annie who had started busily snipping dead heads from an endless row of zinnias.

"If you've got another pair of scissors, I'll help you," said Karen.

Annie glanced at her feet. "In those shoes?"

Karen kicked off her heels, looked around, and not seeing any cars coming, quickly reached underneath her dress, pulled down her panty hose and stepped out of them. Annie got another pair of scissors from the stand and handed them to her. "I see you haven't changed any."

"Oh yes I have." She gave Annie a big wink. "I am now wise to the ways of the world." The words weren't out of her mouth before she was sorry she had said them. They both knew she had reached that stage before she was ten.

"So what have you been doing except breaking my cousin's heart?" Annie asked with a grin.

"From what I hear, he's had no trouble finding someone to soothe his grief." They both laughed. "I remember lying in bed and thinking a thousand times that I was going to marry that boy someday. I bet you anything, if I had stayed, I would have."

Karen had started clipping the flowers a dozen feet ahead of Annie, who had now caught up to her and jumped ahead. "It's a good thing you got out of here, or you wouldn't have accomplished as much as you have." She threw her a sidelong glance. "And you might have killed someone with that temper."

Karen kept on snipping at the flowers, leaving the remark hanging in the air.

Annie must have noticed Karen didn't laugh. "I didn't mean that, Karen. Your temper wasn't any worse than a lot of the other kids. You just got your nose rubbed in the dirt more than they did. Every time you got in a fight, you were just trying to prove you were as good as they were, is all."

That's just like Annie, thought Karen as she concentrated on finding the next spent flower. Always taking my side. She smiled to herself. Funny, she didn't care much any more about what people thought. The difference was she knew who Karen Godwell was and liked her. They reached the end of the zinnias. "Now what do we do?" she asked.

"The cosmos, dummy."

They both laughed again and continued in the same fashion, with Karen now moving almost as fast as Annie and enjoying the feel of the cool grass under her feet. "I got a big job offer from the Metropolitan Museum today," she said off-handedly.

"Nothing surprises me, Karen. You're a real winner."

"*Sure.* That's why I failed getting the farm back and those Fultons are stuffing it with those damn trailers."

"At least they're out of sight."

"For now. I feel like a damn fool. I uprooted my daughter, spent a fortune fixing up the creek house... thinking I could get the farm back. But I've come to the conclusion that the only way that's gonna happen is if I buy it. If I take this job, I should be able to swing it. The only other way is if we can prove my brother forced Granny to sign it over to him. I keep praying for her diary to show up, but I'm ready to give up hope for that to happen."

"That's what you kept saying about the scholarship. Remember?"

"Yeah, I remember." Karen ran a finger down the petal of a big pink bloom. "It's funny how one little piece of paper can change someone's whole life. I remember I couldn't wait to tell you." Karen looked at her old friend. She hadn't changed much since then. Her hair was still the same ash blond, the thick plait was still hanging down her narrow back and the chiseled Clarke profile was still sharp and clear. "I'm sorry we lost touch. I want you to know I never forgot all the really nice things your family did for me. Your aunt hiring me for the stable... the friendship when no one else wanted anything to do with me. Remember that going-away party your family threw for me?"

"Heck, yeah. Everyone was so glad to get rid of you, the whole town turned out."

Karen laughed and tossed a spent flower at her. "Damn. I

sure needed all that stuff. I still have the suitcase from your mom." They fell quiet for a while, the snipping scissors harmonizing with the chirping of the crickets.

Karen reached way over for a wilted flower in the back. "If I take the job, it means going back to New York."

"When?"

"I haven't made up my mind if I'm going to take it, yet. They're giving me a couple of days to think it over. The thing that's bothering me the most is, if I pass it up, it's never going to come my way again. It's a genuine once-in-a-lifetime opportunity." Running through her head were two other once-in-a-lifetime opportunities she blew. Joel and Granny.

"You don't seem to need the money."

"Actually, I do if I want to buy the farm. Right now, I've got a big mortgage on my co-op." Karen knew that statement would make an impact on her friend. In the past hundred years, there probably hadn't been one single lien against the more than two thousand acres the Clarkes owned.

They came to the end of the row and Annie started cutting long-stemmed flowers that Karen knew would be for her. "If I translate everything into numbers, there's no question I should jump at this job. And... it's not only the money." She looked off in the distance through squinted lids. "I can actually see my name on the door: *Karen Godwell, Director, The American Wing.*"

She turned to her friend. "God, Annie. I *deserve* this job. It wasn't just handed to me; I *earned* it. You can't imagine how hard I worked. All the hours... the goddamned weekends... I literally gave it fifteen years of my life." Karen suddenly laughed at herself when she saw the prideful grin on Annie's face. "I'm really getting carried away, aren't I?" Karen grasped the bundle of flowers Annie was handing her. "I have no idea how Hali's going to take it. What do you think?"

"It's hard to say. My girls said she had a hard time fitting in at the camp at first, and acted kinda dejected; but all that seems to have vanished. She's made a lot of friends, and just this afternoon I heard her talking to my aunt about taking English riding lessons all winter so she can compete in the spring."

258

Her aunt's beat-up Jeep pulled in, emitting gleeful shouts from the girls.

"We put the horses in the stable and gave them their feed before I brought the girls back," her aunt shouted. "Hope I didn't hold you up any."

Karen chatted with Annie's aunt for a while and, out of the corner of her eye, noticed the three girls draped on each other's shoulders, talking excitedly. The aunt took off, and Karen yelled over to Hali to find Ginger so they could get going. Once they were on the road, she announced they were going to drop Ginger off at the house and then go out to dinner.

"Mom, you look different tonight."

"You'd look different too if you had the kind of day I had." She recalled how happy Hali had looked playing with Annie's girls. "You had a lot of fun today, didn't you?"

"The ride was incredible, Mom. I didn't want to go to camp at first 'cause Aunt Amy kinda needed me." She picked up the pup and kissed it. "But me and my little baby just love going there."

If they went back to New York, thought Karen, Hali could be fifteen or sixteen by the time they came back. She hated to admit it, but there was Tom, too. The sudden thought that they may never return put her back on the emotional see-saw she'd been riding all day.

The rolling hills of the valley looked vividly green and rich as she drove along thinking about how she was going to tell Hali about the job offer. "Where do you want to eat tonight?" she asked.

"Let's go to that place I like where we can sit outside and look at the Chimney Rock."

"Okay. It's a deal. We're eating at Medina's!"

The towering forest swallowed the SUV as it started its climb into the gorge. Karen glanced over at Hali and saw that the monotonous swaying, as they took curve after curve, was mellowing her mood. Karen casually threw out, "I got a call from my old boss today." Silence followed. "It was good to hear from Earl," she added.

Hali looked out the window for a long moment, before finally asking, "What did he want?"

"He was pretty happy about landing the number one job at the museum." Karen knew that Hali would have figured it out by now. She had heard her tell Joel a thousand times how much she wanted Earl's job. Karen hesitated for a moment, then asked, "What do you think about going back to New York?"

Hali sat with her cheek against the window, staring out.

"It won't be forever, honey. Just long enough for Mommy to make enough money to set us up for life." The silence that followed worried Karen. She sailed around a switchback, and seeing a rest stop ahead, pulled in. She turned off the engine and stared at Hali. "Honey, if Mamma lets this opportunity go, it's never gonna come around again and it means a lot of money... a *real* lot of money. Ten times what I'm making now."

Hali's head shot around. Tears streamed down her face and her eyes had a wild look. "You don't have to explain it to me, Mom! I knew all this was too good to be true!" Her face was painted with bitterness. "It must have killed you to come home every night and take me for walks and tell me all those stories. Daddy wanted to live here more than anything in the world and *you wouldn't let him."* Her face twisted in anguish. *"And now you want to take me away, too!* Just so you can be a big shot!"

Karen was stunned. She reached over and tried to pull her close.

"No!" Hali screamed as she pushed her away and covered her face with her hands. "I want my Daddy."

Karen sat listening to Hali sob. Finally she started the car, backed up and headed home.

All through dinner Karen tried to talk to Hali, but each time the child burst into tears. Karen measured every word she spoke, for like those that came out of Hali's mouth in the car, anything she said would be remembered forever.

After dinner, Hali went out on the porch with Ginger while Karen cleaned up the kitchen. She turned on the small TV sitting on the counter to interrupt the oppressive silence, but after a couple of minutes listening to an inane commentator gush about some actor half her age, she flicked it off. When the last of the dishes were put away, Karen strode over to the screen door. "Hali, it's getting late. Why don't you go upstairs, take your shower and get in bed. I'll look after Ginger and then come up and tuck you in."

Hali took off the little dress she had put on the puppy and stuffed it into the small suitcase where she kept all her doll clothes. She picked Ginger up and came in through the door Karen was holding open. She handed the pup to her mother and padded out of the room in her stocking feet. Karen quickly settled the dog for the night and followed Hali up. She wanted to talk with her, but at the same time knew they were both too worn out to hold their emotions in check.

"You want me to draw you a bath?" she asked while Hali shed her clothes in the bathroom. Hali answered *yes* in a whisper and sat on the side of the tub as Karen poured some of her daughter's favorite bath beads into the water and swirled them around. While Hali soaked, Karen went in the bedroom and got on her pajamas and returned with Hali's. She helped her out of the tub and wrapped a towel around her, then got down on her knees and hugged her. "I love you so much, baby."

Hali rested her cheek on her mother's head. "I'm sorry, Mommy. I didn't mean those things I said."

Karen squeezed her tight. She held her whole world in her arms and couldn't make a mistake. She would get a good night's rest and think things through tomorrow.

CHAPTER TWENTY-EIGHT

THE KENNEL'S OFFICE looked like the kind of place no one wanted to be stuck in any longer than necessary. Every stick of furniture was second-hand before it was even hauled in there. Two of the desks were piled high with paraphernalia needed for the care and feeding of everything from birds to horses. Cartons were stacked along one wall, and a playpen sat in the middle of the room ready for puppies that needed special attention. Pictures of dogs covered every square inch of wallspace.

A typewriter that any antique dealer would jump at sat on the corner of a third desk where the actual business took place. A pencil holder in the shape of a curled up dog held a handful of pens—the free kind covered with advertising. Amy kept good account of her clients and paid every bill on time, but her heart lay with all the animals in her care.

Amy had believed from the time she was four that dogs were kinder than most people. She studied them her whole life, just as she had Travis. Her sister had bonded with their brother like a bitch with her pups, but she never could. He was an aberration like the dachshund she once owned that grew up to bite everyone who came near it, including her. The vet chalked it up to either a brain tumor or a genetic disorder and recommended it be put down.

Now that Karen had seen what Travis did to Granny, Amy wondered if she ever thought about that day he fell through the ice. She had, hundreds of times as they were growing up. Maybe because Granny and Karen covered up every rotten thing he ever did.

Eddie pulled in the lot with Hali, and Amy snapped out of her reverie. She missed having her niece around all day. Hali played mostly with Ginger when she came from camp, but Amy didn't mind. She had given her the best pup her finest bitch had ever produced.

The pup would have brought more than fifteen hundred dollars, but she couldn't let her go. In fact, if she hadn't given it to Hali, she'd of kept the dog to breed. She was hoping Karen would let Ginger have a litter before she was spayed. That way Hali could either discover if she had a real interest in taking care of animals, or get bored and move on to something else. At the same time, Amy would see the genes passed on.

She sent Eddie over to his brother's to pick up a van-load of hay. Hali helped her feed the goats until he returned, and then they all dragged the bales to the lean-to next to the corral. Amy noticed papers and trash fall out when Eddie opened his door, so when they finished, she walked over and peeked in the window.

"With all the junk you got in the front seat, Eddie, how on earth are you gonna keep your accounts straight? You get right in there and clean it up before you come in for dinner. And don't you be throwin' out any receipts."

EDDIE GRUDGINGLY PICKED OUT the receipts and slapped them on the dash while Amy and Hali went over to the dog pens and turned on the hose to fill up the dogs' water bowls. He began gathering the trash and taking it to the burning drum at the edge of the driveway. By the time he got to the floor on the passenger side, he was on his third trip to the drum. He stacked two pizza boxes and piled on the candy wrappers, napkins and papers until he could see the floor, then he reached under the seat and felt a spiral binding. He pulled it out and recognized the diary Bubba gave him to take to Travis.

He tossed it on the heap. His brother-in-law didn't give a rat's ass about any diary, and he wasn't going to haul himself over there to give it to him either. He took everything out and stuffed it in the burning can.

I'M REALLY GETTIN' so I'm lookin' forward to seein' ya every afternoon," Amy said to Hali as she turned off the hose. "You got a way of gettin' under someone's skin." She wrapped her arms around her and rocked back and forth.

Hali looked up. "I'm hungry."

"Well you come on in the house and I'll fix you a little somethin' while I start dinner. We're pretty much done for the day."

Amy fixed Hali a peanut butter and jelly sandwich and watched her devour it, then started rinsing lettuce from her garden. "I'm just gonna make chicken salad tonight with leftovers." After a few minutes, she glanced over at Hali. Her elbows were on the table, and her chin had sunk onto a fist. "You look a little put out, Miss Hali. Didn't things go so good at that camp today?"

Hali abruptly folded her arms across her chest and threw herself back in her chair. "Mom's thinking about going back to New York."

Amy gave her one of her expressive questioning looks. "What do you mean?"

"The museum offered her a big job with lots of money."

Except for the dog slurping water from her dish in the corner, the room fell quiet.

Amy wiped her hands on a towel and came to the table and sat down. She bit her thumb and looked off in space through squinted lids. Finally, she slapped her hand on the table. "Nope. She ain't gonna go." She raised an eyebrow into her signature arch and looked at Hali. "People are like animals. They got characteristics. Now sometimes they waver from side to side away from these characteristics, but in the end that's what controls 'em.

"Now there's two characteristics your ma's got. Number one—she's ornery. When she sets her mind to somethin', you can kill her but she ain't gonna be taken off it. And number two—when she promises you somethin' she stands by it. She promised me she wasn't gonna let Travis get away with what he's done, and there's no way she can do that if she ups and leaves again. Nope. She ain't goin'."

Then she studied Hali's face. "Somethin' tells me you're hopin' to stay. I'd a thought you'd want to go back to the big city."

"Maybe… a while ago… but I'm beginning to see what my dad liked about this place. Especially the belonging part. It's like I'm connected to something."

Amy reached over and squeezed Hali's hand. "Oh, darlin'. That's for sure. You're connected to my heart."

THE TRASH BARREL was getting full, so Eddie thought he better set it on fire before Amy got on him about it. He lit a match and ignited some papers to get it going good, then picked up the diary and lay it like a tent over the flame.

Eddie's devious nature started to tickle his imagination. What if Granny hid some money somewhere and wrote about it in that book of hers. He heard about those things all the time. He quickly snatched the diary off the fire and slapped it shut to put out a flame crawling along a page. He'd take it in and read it tonight while Amy watched her shows.

He swiped away the ashes and lifted his tee shirt, then stuffed the book under his arm so she wouldn't see it when he went into the house. If he found any of the old woman's money, she'd just take it from him. He entered the house warily, and seeing Amy and Hali busy in the kitchen, headed for the stack of magazines next to his recliner at the far end of the living room.

Amy suddenly screeched, "Eddie! Get in here!" and he almost dropped the book. It was barely in place in his armpit as he lumbered over to the kitchen.

Amy thrust a bottle of mayonnaise at him. "Don't just stand there. Open it!"

He grabbed hold of the jar with his left hand and twisted the lid with his right, careful to keep the book secure by pressing the inside of his arm against it. He twisted until the skin on his hand burned, but it wouldn't budge. "I'll run it under some hot water," he mumbled as he trudged to the sink. He turned on the water and let it splash on the jar as he put his hand under his shirt and readjusted the book. Suddenly he sensed Amy standing next to him. He fixed his head straight ahead, slowly rolled his eyes to the side and saw her leaning around and peering at him.

"What do you got there?"

He ignored the question and looked ahead stubbornly.

"Come on. Show it to me."

She reached under his shirt. He pulled away and knocked over a chair as he made a clumsy dash for the living room. She caught up with him and patted him down, but there was nothing there.

"Okay. Where did you put it?" She studied the cagey expression on his face and followed his gaze toward the kitchen where Hali stood with a book in her hand.

"Aunt Amy! This is it! This is the diary Mommy's been looking for!"

Amy rushed over and examined the cover, then turned angrily to Eddie. "You big oaf. We've been lookin' all over tarnation for this diary and you had it all the time!"

She pounded him with it, and he scrunched his shoulders and put up his hands in defense. "How should I know you were lookin' for it?"

"Because that's all I've been talkin' to my sister about for weeks. That's why!" She hit him again. "That's for not bringin' it to me!" She flipped through the pages to make sure they were filled with Granny's handwriting. "Where'd you get it?"

Eddie was wily enough to know the less he told Amy, the better. If he let her know it was from Bubba she'd get right on the phone to him and start asking questions. And if she found out he got paid a lot more for the antiques than he had given her, she'd blow her top. "Granny gave it to me."

EXCITED ABOUT FINDING the diary, Hali anxiously dialed her mother. "Karen Godwell, please." A shadow of disappointment fell across her face as she listened. She put the phone down, discouraged. "I remember now. She's at a conference at the Civic Center. She told me not to bother to call her because she'd have her phone turned off. I bet we're not going to be able to talk to her 'til she comes to pick me up."

Amy wiped her hands on her shorts. "Well, it's probably for the best we can't reach her just yet. Let's see if Granny says anything about Travis. No sense in gettin' her all worked up if there ain't nothin' in it."

Amy went over to the table and leafed through the book. "First, let's find the last entry." She found the page before the first blank sheet. "My God, I can barely read it." She wrinkled her forehead and squinted at the page. "I can barely make out the words."

Hali was hanging on her shoulder. She pointed to something on the page. "Look, there's a K. That's got to be my mother's name."

Amy flipped the pages back until the writing appeared more legible and skimmed it over. Finally, she read aloud. "He's pounding on me to give 'em the homeplace but I keep tellin' him he got to kill me first."

Amy slowly pulled out a chair and sat down, heavily. Her hands trembled and tears rolled down her cheeks as she read. Her shoulders slumped and her jaw fell slack. "That rotten son of a bitch. I knew Granny went downhill too fast. He needs to go to jail for this."

Hali had never seen Amy like this. She grasped her shoulders and searched her eyes. "Don't worry, Aunt Amy, Cousin Bruce will get the cops after him for what he did to Granny. Just think, now you can get your land back."

Amy eyed Hali for a long moment, thoughtfully, as if she were thinking everything through. She suddenly snapped out of her ire and slapped her hands on her face and hollered, "Thank you, Lord!" She jumped up shouting, "We got to call Bruce!" She reached for the phone shouting "Hallelujah!"

"Can you make me a sandwich with that chicken," asked Eddie as she dialed.

"Do it yourself, you big lug. You'll be lucky if I ever feed you again."

Hali got up. "I'll make it for you, Uncle Eddie."

Amy slammed her hand on the counter. "Damn if he ain't there either!" She left a message saying they found the diary and for him to come straight over.

"Let's throw ourselves a little celebration party," she said. "I'll make a pineapple upside-down cake. It's your ma's favorite."

Hali recalled one that Monique had made, and couldn't picture it being her mother's favorite. She marveled at Amy's high spirits as she practically danced around the kitchen.

Amy got out the Bisquick and started mixing the batter. She let Hali line the pan with the pineapple slices, then the cherries, before sprinkling on butter and brown sugar and pouring on the batter. "There!" she proclaimed as she popped it in the oven.

Amy threw up her hands and wiggled her hips making Hali laugh. "Listen up everyone. I've got a plan. We're not gonna tell that big sister of mine a darn thing. When she pulls in here tonight and starts beeping that horn of hers and gettin' everyone all riled up, I'm gonna insist she come in for dinner and a piece of the upside-down cake I made especially for her." Amy fell against the fridge and folded her arms with a big satisfied grin on her face. "She's gonna try to beg off, but we're gonna coax her in." She went over and put an arm around Hali and squeezed. "Then we're gonna pretend like nothin's happened."

She kept adjusting the diary's position on the table and draping a dishtowel over it so just part was showing. "She's gonna eat her salad and then take itty bitty bites of the cake, then be wantin' to get along. But we're not gonna budge one little inch 'til she notices the book. And when she does, we're gonna say somethin' like... *Oh that. That's just somethin' Granny gave to*

Eddie..." She stooped to Hali's level and went forehead to forehead with her. "And she's gonna find them pages herself, just like us!"

She paced and sang out, "Oh Lordy, I can barely stand all this." She swung around and faced Eddie. "I got plans, Eddie. Big plans!" She went behind him, slid her arms down his barrel chest and snuggled up to him. This was the first intimate show of affection Hali had ever seen between them.

"Eddie, honey, some day we're gonna sell this place, and build on my 200 acres." She ran into the living room and returned anxiously thumbing through a magazine. "Here it is!" She thrust the magazine in Eddie's face, then dropped it on the table. "My dream house!"

Hali picked it up. A rambling ranch sat on a green hill with mountains in the background. A horse that looked exactly like Amy's grazed in a picturesque corral.

"Oh, I got so many dreams!" she sang as she hugged Hali. "Wait 'til you see that house when I'm finished."

Hali was swept up in the spirit of her aunt's excitement and quickly threw out, "And don't you worry, Aunt Amy, my mom says she can find you another bedroom set just like Granny's."

Eddie's eyes shot open like saucers and Hali put her hand over her mouth.

"That bastard! That goddamned bastard!" screamed Amy. She swung around and came at Eddie. "Granny never gave you that diary, did she?"

He slowly shoved back his chair with terror in his eyes as she came toward him.

"Did she!?"

Eddie rose, trembling. "Travis sold Bubba the grandfather clock and it was in there."

Next she stuck her face in Hali's. "Did your mother say anything about my dishes?"

Hali closed her eyes, crunched up her face and started bawling out loud.

Amy rushed out of the kitchen and into the living room where she took the shotgun from the rack over the fireplace. She flung open the china cabinet drawer, got out the box of ammunition and methodically loaded the gun. Eddie cautiously approached her with Hali dissolving in tears beside him.

"Put that down, Amy."

She pointed it at him. "Nobody's going to stop me from taking care of that varmint once and for all." She spotted the keys to his van lying on the desk and reached for them, then she backed up to her purse and grabbed hers. "You two stay put and don't call anyone. I'm gonna handle this my way."

Hali buried her face in Eddie's side. "It's my fault!" she howled. "I broke my promise!"

CHAPTER TWENTY-NINE

A N AUDIENCE OF two hundred hung onto every word the speaker from the North Carolina Arts Council uttered, for they were eager to learn anything that would help them in their application for a grant.

Karen Godwell, however, wasn't listening. She sat in the Civic Center's huge convention room immersed in a self-induced out-of-body state. She could imagine herself running a hand across the surface of Earl's antique desk that was now hers. She could see herself strolling to the window and looking down on the museum's courtyard below, feeling as if she were encased in an aura of the elite. She squeezed her eyes shut. After all the humiliation and defeats in the past days, she couldn't stop feeding on the delicious taste of success.

Suddenly a folder with fund applications was dropped in front of her. She shook off the hypnotic state and thumbed through her packet like everyone else at her table. Now that she had what she came for, she was tempted to sneak out early and rush home to get the mail so she could study Earl's proposal. But she knew it would be generous.

It was pouring rain when the conference ended at four-thirty, and instead of driving to the office to check her phone messages, she headed straight to Amy's to pick up Hali. Once they got home, she'd have to make a cake or something for when Bruce came over. He had called and said he had information on what the Fultons were paying for the property and what the rest of the land was worth, but couldn't get over until after eight. What he had to say would have a bearing on her going back to New York.

By the time she got onto Route 74, the wipers were slapping across the windows at full speed. Their angry thumping back and forth reminded her of Granny shaking a finger at her after one of her fights saying, *No! No! No!* It unsettled her.

Now that she had one foot in the mountains and one in New York, she found it easier to sift through all that had happened since Joel died, but the only thing that stuck in her head was the betrayed look in Hali's eyes last night. She had failed Joel and Granny, and it suddenly became clear to her that she was now about to fail Hali. But, then again, was she really going to fail Hali, or did she just want to bask for a couple of days in the intoxicating glory of achieving a dream she'd clung to for fifteen years.

She swung into a grocery store parking lot and pulled out her phone. She had to do this before she changed her mind. If she thought about Earl's offer one more day, one more hour, she'd be totally seduced and wouldn't be able to turn it down. He wasn't in, so she left a message. "Earl, I am so very honored by your offer, but I've decided to remain in Asheville. Thanks for thinking of me. I love you for it."

She got back on the road, hoping she hadn't just made the biggest mistake of her life. By the time she reached Amy's turn-off, all her elation over the fabulous job offer was replaced with anxiety over the same old irksome pile of woes. She was already starting to regret the phone message, and dreaded reading the museum's offer.

Something struck her as amiss as she drove up the gravel lane that twisted through the woods. Where were all the bothersome chickens? She cleared the woods. Eddie was in the lot waving wildly. He looked as if he were calling to Hali who shot from the house. Karen slammed on the brakes and jumped out. Hali came running toward her and flew into her arms.

"Mom! I'm so sorry!" Hali looked up, her face swollen and blotchy. "Aunt Amy's gonna kill Travis!"

Karen put her arms around her, then looked over to Eddie.

He stood wringing his hands. "We found Granny's diary."

"Mamma, it says your brother forced her to sign!"

Karen struggled to figure out what was going on.

"Mamma... I'm so sorry." Hali collapsed in tears. She heaved a couple of times before getting everything out. "I told Amy... about her bedroom set... and she went crazy."

Karen quickly scanned the lot for her sister's truck. "Where is she?"

"She's gone over there and taken the shotgun with her."

"How long ago?!"

Hali barely eked out, "Ten... minutes."

Karen tore herself from Hali and raced back to the SUV shouting, "Call Bruce. You two stay here."

AMY PULLED UP next to Travis's truck, grabbed the gun and stomped up the steps. She threw open the screen door with enough force to rip it from one of its rusty hinges. She went in with her finger on the trigger. Travis was chewing on a toothpick and watching her from the dining room entranceway, trying to size up the situation.

Amy pointed the gun at him and approached slowly but deliberately. "You goddamned bastard. I'm gonna kill you."

"And what do you think's gonna happen to you if you do?"

"I don't give a shit. You broke your promise."

"What promise?"

"You know what promise, you filthy pig. Now you've gone and sold it!"

Travis tossed the toothpick. "Relax, Amy. If you're that upset over that bedroom set, I'll go get it and bring it right over to your house."

"Do you think I'm stupid enough to believe you!?"

273

"It's in Bubba Barnhill's warehouse. He's saving it for a big auction next month." He turned to go into the dining room. "Here, let me show you his brochure. There's a picture of it." He nonchalantly strolled over to the stack on the counter and picked up a boating pamphlet. "Here. Take a look yourself."

It took Amy a second to calculate what to do, then she crept toward him like a primitive animal stalking prey. Cautiously, she reached for the brochure, and in the one split second she took her eyes off Travis, he grabbed the gun and slammed her against the wall.

KAREN FLEW DOWN the lane with her head hammering the roof every time she hit a big rock, but she kept her foot on the gas pedal. She wanted to will herself out of her body and fly. An old familiar fear seized her. Something horrible was going to happen if she didn't get there in time. The vision of the bloated jacket floating to the surface of the pond and the desperate girl pulling her little brother out kept flashing in her brain. Her heart pounded and she screamed for God's help.

An ugly, unwelcomed thought suddenly gnawed at her consciousness. What if she hadn't had that premonition that day, and instead, took her time bringing them back their cookies. What a world of grief and pain it would have spared every one of them. She shook her head clear and forced the shameful thought out of her mind.

Route 74 was straight ahead. She craned her neck to see if anyone was coming from either direction, then swung onto it. Annie Louise was in her field and looked up when she heard the tires screech. Karen spotted her and started to brake. Maybe she could help. No! That was insane. Every second counted. She flew past, then slowed at Granny's drive. She gauged the speed of a car coming from the other direction, floored the gas and cut out in front of it. The car's horn blared behind her as she sped onto the lane.

Her ears focused keenly on listening for a gunshot. She hit the woods and slowed to a cautious crawl. Amy's red truck sat just beyond the far end of the thicket. God, please don't let

Travis be home! Her eyes traveled along the driveway as she came around the circle. If he wasn't in, she could calm Amy down and get the gun away. The hair on the back of her neck rose as she spotted Travis's truck beside Amy's.

She pulled up, slid out and closed the door, noiselessly. The front screen door hung awry as if it had been thrown back in a fury. She crept up the stairs, clamping her jaw tight and listening. A Carolina wren sang in a nearby tree and a slight breeze whished through the woods as if the world were at peace. She snuck to the side of the door and peeked in. She could see clear through to the kitchen. No one. Not a sound. The same fear that had struck her at the pond that day when she saw Amy's hat balled up on the ice came over her again. She wanted to puke. They both might be dead.

A scream made her flinch. She saw Amy crawl across the dining room floor and look back, eyes fixed on someone. Travis came from behind the wall and moved toward Amy. He seemed to be holding something. He turned slightly, giving Karen a glimpse of the shotgun barrel.

The stealthy way Travis moved toward Amy terrified Karen. Like he didn't want her to get up and leave. He was cornering her like a stalking animal does just before it pounces on its victim. It dawned on her how easily Travis could get away with killing Amy. It was his home and her gun, and everyone in the valley knew what a hothead she was. But he'd never get away with shooting the both of them.

She rushed in shouting, "Let her go, Travis!"

He swung around. "Well, if it isn't the other banshee." Blood oozed from scratches criss-crossing his face. A grotesque bite mark on his arm had swollen and was turning colors.

Karen ignored the gun pointed at her, walked over and reached for Amy. Her sister's bloodied swollen face shocked her. "Let's get out of here."

Amy and Karen started past Travis when Amy swung around with her hands on her hips and a defiant expression etched on her face. "Travis, this time you ain't gettin' away with it!"

Karen grabbed her arm and tugged. "Amy. Let's go!"

Amy tore her arm away and flounced toward Travis. "We found Granny's diary, and you're in big trouble with the law. She says how you beat her and forced her to sign this place over." She thrust her bizarrely disfigured face toward him and sneered. "We're gettin' everything back, Travis, and puttin' you in jail where you belong. Those men in there are gonna have a lot of fun with a pretty boy like you, just like you did with me."

Amy turned toward Karen, and the hatred on her face sent a chill through her. "Yes, Karen. That's our dirty little secret. I was only five. What he did to me hurt, Karen, but I let him, else he was gonna go over to Granny's and gouge up my bedroom set."

A big smile fanned across Travis's face. "She's making this up, Karen."

Amy wiped the blood dripping from her lip with the back of her hand as she looked directly at Travis. "Am I? How come I've never been right down there since you did all those things to me." She turned to Karen. "Just talk to Dr. Bennett. He'll tell you why I can't have kids."

Karen studied Travis's face, searching for an ounce of remorse.

"Karen, get that stupid look off your face," Amy spit out. "He had you conned all these years, just like everyone else. Granny knew what a pig he was. When I found out I couldn't have babies, I told her everything. But in the end, that bastard used her faith in the Lord to con her, too." She swung around and faced Travis. "But you ain't gonna con the police. We got what you did to Granny in black and white, and you're goin' to prison. Just think about it, Travis. You're gonna be their pretty little toy... just like I was."

"Stop it!" screamed Karen. "For God's sake, Amy, stop it!" She pressed her fingers to her forehead and tried to think. Amy's words echoed in her brain, and she wanted to fall on her knees and cry out to God. No. She had to keep her head. She had to shut Amy up before Travis pulled the trigger.

"Amy, we don't have to go to the police. Travis is going to give us back everything he stole from Granny and I'm going to get your bedroom set back." She quickly shot a glance over to Travis. "Tell her, Travis. For God's sake, *Tell her!*"

A weird smile spread across Amy's face. "Oh no. That ain't enough for what he's done to me. I ain't ever gonna have a dar- lin' little girl to tuck in every night. I want to see him locked up. And I want to go visit him, and ask him how he's gettin' along with all his boyfriends."

Rage surfaced on Travis's face. He picked up his foot and rammed it in her stomach. Her face crumpled in pain. She dou- bled over, staggered backward and fell to her knees. He raised the gun and aimed.

Karen lunged for it. Desperate screams and grunts filled the air while the two struggled. Amy dragged herself over, grabbed Travis's leg with two hands and bit. He kicked his leg free, loos- ening his grip on the gun just long enough for Karen to wrench it away. She quickly jumped back and aimed. Her hands trembled, making the weapon quiver. The sound of her heaving filled the room. She feared her knees were about to buckle.

"Amy! Get up!" she screamed. There was no response. Her body shook all over as Travis stepped toward her, speaking in the soft, soothing voice he used every time he lied.

"Karen, if she turns me in, you know I'll have to tell everyone what you did to that drifter. I don't want to, Karen, but I'll have to make them understand that none of this was my fault. You can see how you makin' me throw all those horrible bloody chunks to the pigs messed me up, can't you?" His pleading tone slid into overtones of a threat. "But you don't want everyone to know what you did to that drifter, do you Karen?"

He gave his words a moment to sink in. "Don't worry. I can fix everything, Karen. Just give me the gun, get out of here and I'll take care of the rest. It'll end up nothin' but a simple case of self-defense, and I'll split everything with you, fifty-fifty. Whatever you want."

Karen was incredulous. *God above, help me!* He's talking about killing our Amy like it's nothing! That day long ago shot into her head. She had heard something as she reached in the cupboard for the cookies, and in that one moment of compassion and love, ran down to the pond and saved this creature's life. "You're through taking care of things, Travis. I don't give a damn if the whole world knows what I did." She was suddenly overcome with sorrow and her eyes flooded with tears. Oh God, is Amy finally going to get her way.

Travis was cunning enough to know what she was thinking. "You'll never forgive yourself if you pull that trigger, Karen. You're the only mother I've ever had. Just give me the gun."

She backed up and lost her grip for a second as she hit the wall. "Don't come any closer, Travis, or I swear to God I'll shoot."

Karen's mouth was dry and her tongue swollen. Sweat poured down her face and back. She knew what a risktaker Travis was. Something unthinkable was going to happen unless she broke him down. She steadied her voice. "In spite of everything you've done, Travis, I feel sorry for you. You're sick and you need help. I may never forgive you for what you did to Amy and Granny, but I promise I won't let anyone hurt you.

"Didn't I promise you that once before, Travis? Didn't I take care of that drifter just like I said I would? Now pick Amy up and put her in my car." She locked onto the blue eyes that mirrored hers, and started to sob out loud. She could see he was willing to gamble that she'd never pull the trigger. Her hysterical sobs grew louder. She couldn't fix this. There was no one to axe, no pulling him out of the pond. He came one step closer.

The explosion seemed to come from far off in the distance. She wondered if her arm had been ripped off as her head banged against the wall. The beautiful face in front of her had an odd, frozen look of surprise as the long beautiful arms floated into the air in slow motion. She slowly slid down the wall onto the floor and stared ahead as the scene replayed over and over again in her head and the sound of exploding gunpowder sounded endlessly in her ears.

THE BRAKES SCREECHED and Bruce jumped out before the Malibu came to a full stop. He shouted for Hali to stay in the car and ran inside. The smell of spent gunpowder permeated the air.

Two sets of legs were visible on the floor up ahead. Amy was curled up in a heap. *Good God! Are they all dead?!*

He rushed in and spotted Karen sitting propped up against the wall like a doll someone had placed there. The shotgun lay at her side. She was staring mindlessly ahead, but he could see she was alive.

He slowly turned and saw Travis lying with his chest blown apart and his eyes wide open staring up at the ceiling. All the scratches on his face made Bruce reluctant to let his glance travel to Amy. He gasped for air. Her face was a bloody pulp. He rushed to her side and checked her pulse. She was alive but needed a doctor.

He heard Hali talking to Karen and turned to see her kneeling next to her mother. He stood up, went over and grabbed her arm. "Didn't I tell you to stay in the car!" He started to yank her up, when her penetrating stare made him stop.

"Is Aunt Amy going to be okay?"

"Yes. And so is your mother."

Hali turned to the man on the floor. "Is that Travis?"

"Yes. He's dead."

She looked up at him. "Do we have to chop him up, too, Cousin Bruce?"

Bruce was momentarily stunned as he realized Hali had been listening when Karen told him about the drifter. "Where were you that night?"

"Around the corner of the porch. I snuck out through the front door."

"No, Hali, we're not going to chop him up. Your mother's a big girl now. We're going to call the sheriff. He looked her square in the eyes. "I want you to promise me you'll never talk about what you heard to anyone, *ever,* especially not to your mother."

"I won't, Cousin Bruce."

For some reason, he believed her. He took out his cell phone and dialed 911 as Hali knelt back down and took her mother's hand. "There's been a shooting at Pearl Whitfield's place on the Charlotte Highway in Fairview. There's one dead and two that need emergency care." He looked down at Hali. "Now, go sit in the car until I come for you. I'll take care of your ma."

"I'm not leaving her."

He went over to the fireplace and put the phone on the mantle, then yanked the throw off the chair next to it and covered Travis's upper torso. "Keep talkin' to her, then." He picked up the phone and interrupted the man's questions. "I've got somebody here in shock. What do I do?" He listened for a moment, then swiftly went into the kitchen and found a cardboard box. He knelt down next to Karen, laid her flat and used the box to raise her legs. Her color didn't look good and her breathing was shallow. He told the man on the phone, "You better hurry."

He heard Amy groan and went to her side and held her hand. "Where do you hurt?" he asked.

"My gut."

He reached for a cushion lying in the clutter on the floor and gently lifted her head and put it under. "You hang in there. Help is on the way."

He rose and noticed Karen had come out of it. The sooner he got her where she couldn't see Travis, the better. He went over and helped her up, then put his arm around her waist to steady her.

"I'm okay, Bruce. Take care of Amy."

"She shouldn't be moved 'til the EMTs get here. Once I get you out of here, I'll go sit with her." He started walking her out.

"Wait!" Karen turned and her eyes locked on the draped body on the floor. She stood lost in thought for a moment, then she looked back at Bruce, tears streaming down her cheeks. "He was the most beautiful baby boy you ever did see."

CHAPTER THIRTY

T OM LOOSENED HIS TIE and couldn't make up his mind which city was muggier, DC or Hendersonville. He pulled up in front of his house and sat there until the truck became unbearably hot, then reluctantly reached over for his jacket and briefcase and got out. What he really wanted was to go see Karen, but the last time he went over there Hali came out and solemnly announced he better leave or her mother was going to call the sheriff.

With the heat and being the middle of the afternoon, the street looked like a ghost town. Sweetie's bark sounded from inside the house even before he climbed the steps to the porch. *Damn, if she doesn't know I'm home!*

He unlocked the door and made his way to the kitchen with the dog prancing around and begging for attention. He tossed everything on the table. "Okay, girl. Daddy's home." He crouched down and gave her a vigorous rub.

The dog trailed him out of the house and back to the truck for his suitcase. He came into the kitchen and smiled as he looked around. The lady upstairs had neatly lined up his newspapers and mail on the counter next to the phone and put a plastic placemat on the floor for Sweetie's dishes. It wasn't that much, but still, he told himself, there was something about a woman's touch.

Sweetie sat looking at him with her large, wide-set dark brown eyes. "Oh, boy, has she ever been spoiling you." He gathered the papers and mail that had accumulated for the ten days he had been gone, and tossed them on the table, then took a beer from the fridge and sat down. Half the bottle was gulped before he finished skimming through the mail. He rose and found a bag of chips in the cupboard, slumped back down in the chair and picked up a paper. Sweetie was sitting upright trying to stare a hole through him. "Okay, girl. Just a couple."

He put the paper down and reached inside the bag. The dog gobbled down the offering and dropped to the floor. He spilled a pile of chips on the table and took up the paper again. He started to take a drink when from the corner of his eye he spotted Karen on the front page of the Hendersonville *Times-News*. It was the typical kind of PR shot everyone used for press releases. Next to it was a photo of Travis.

He read the headline, but it took him a moment to grasp the meaning. *Curator kills brother in Fairview.* He slammed the bottle down and stared in amazement. He raced through the copy and didn't blink until he read, *The Sheriff deemed the incident self defense.* The article went on to say her sister Amy was taken to the hospital with a ruptured spleen.

Damn it! He should have known something was wrong when Tori kept stalling on the phone every time she called him in DC, as if she couldn't make up her mind whether or not to add something. His eyes darted around the room and his mind raced. Tori knew he was teaching two courses at the symposium and must have judged it would be better if he didn't find out until he could do something about it. He checked his watch. Three. He jumped up and grabbed his keys. Sweetie knew what the sound meant and beat him to the door.

On the drive to Fairview, he replayed every moment he'd spent with Travis, and hated himself for being taken in. If only he had reacted on his first hunch that something was wrong. He reached for his phone and dialed Josh.

"If anybody ever deserved to get gone, it was that bastard," said Josh. "We haven't had a justifiable killin' like this one in a long time."

"How's Karen?"

"Good, I reckon. Everyone around here thinks she's a genuine hero. There's no tellin' what Travis would have done to Amy if she hadn't gotten there."

"How's Amy doing?"

"They didn't have to remove her spleen, but she's still in the hospital."

"Have you seen Karen since it happened?"

"No, son. Why don't you go over there and take a look for yourself."

"I'm almost there now."

He finished the call and tried to recall the facts in the newspaper article. There was something about a family argument that turned violent. Pearl's name was mentioned along with a bit about the family living in the valley for generations.

He swung onto Sugar Hollow Road and cautiously approached Karen's house. No vehicle. Where could she be? He couldn't imagine she'd gone to work. He pulled to the side and called Josh again. "Do you think she might be staying at her Cousin Bruce's house?"

"Why in the heck would she be over there?"

"I thought with all the publicity…"

"Nah! I bet you anything she's gone to work. She's not the first person who's shot their kin in this town."

Tom knew the number by heart.

"No. Mrs. Godwell isn't in today," said the operator.

It never occurred to him that the woman might have been told to give that answer after the Folk Art Center had been deluged with calls from the press. He phoned Josh again.

"Well, son, if I didn't know better I'd think you were sweet on me."

Tom tried to hide his frustration. "Josh, she's not at work.

Where does Bruce live?"

"You don't give up easy, do you. Something tells me you're really stuck on that gal." He gave Tom the directions and ended with, "I don't blame you, son."

Tom raced to Whitfield Road and hoped like hell he could find the place without having to call Josh again. There it is—a two-story brick house on the downward side of the mountain. He pulled in the driveway and was surprised to see a man standing in the doorway as if he were expecting him. He'd bet anything Josh had given him a call.

He checked his watch and looked around for Karen's SUV. No sign of her. He was tempted to pull out and keep looking, but it was too late. Bruce was walking toward him.

Tom got out and extended his hand. "Hello, I'm Tom Gibbons, a friend of Karen's."

"I know. Josh just called."

They stood there for a while with Bruce sizing him up. "So, where're you from?"

"Tennessee."

Bruce thought about it for a moment. "There's nothin' wrong with that. Tennessee used to be part of North Carolina."

The comment brought a trace of a smile to Tom's face. "I went over to Karen's house and when she wasn't there, I thought I'd look for her here."

"Did you ever stop to think she might have gone to work?"

"I called. She's not there." Tom gazed across the valley beyond. "This is a nice place you've got here." Unwilling to waste any more time on small talk, he put a hand on his hip and shifted his weight as he looked down on the ground and then back up again. "How do I get to Amy's place?"

Bruce laughed. "It looks like you're on some kind of a scavenger hunt, boy. I called already. She ain't there."

Tom took a kerchief from his back pocket and wiped the sweat rolling down his face. He wondered if Bruce had any idea how desperate he was. "I've been out of town. I just got back today and read about everything in the paper." He ran a hand through his hair. "How's Karen doing?"

"She's had a hard time. But not hard enough to break her. She'll be all right. She started feeling a whole sight better after we had a service for her brother and got Pearl outta that home she was in. Granny's off those drugs they had her on, and when I was over there this morning, her eyes were open. I'm guessin' she knew who I was."

Another wave of regret rolled over Tom. Something about the way Bruce brought up the drugs made him fear Pearl might have been mistreated at the nursing home.

Bruce put a hand on Tom's shoulder. "Son, Karen should be home any time now. Why don't you just take it easy and go over there and wait."

On the drive back to Karen's, Tom figured by now everyone in her circle of friends knew he was chasing after her, if not everyone in Fairview. He got the distinct impression that Josh and Bruce were rooting for him. Hali had been in his corner since that first night when he took Karen his notes.

He rounded the curve and saw they still weren't home. He pulled in the shady driveway and let Sweetie out, then leaned against the truck and thought everything through. He was in the business of negotiating deals, and had learned a long time ago that the first thing you had to do is establish what both parties wanted, then deal with the impediments standing in the way of their getting it.

There was no question what he wanted, and he was pretty sure Karen wanted the same thing. After all, didn't she say yes to him twice? Every woman knows the fastest way to a man's heart is through his stomach; and didn't she make him her world famous barbeque? And there was no question she preferred him over that handsome dog from the Clarke clan. Her temper was the only impediment he could see. He picked up a stick and threw it for Sweetie. Yep, this was going to be the toughest deal he ever closed.

Tired of strolling around, he got back in the truck and let the door hang open. The longer he sat there, the more his confidence drained away. He checked his watch for the umpteenth time, and when he saw it was six-thirty, began to wonder if they were ever going to show up. Tired of checking out every vehicle that went by, he was caught off guard when the silver SUV suddenly pulled in.

Hali jumped out clutching a small dachshund with a pink rhinestone-studded collar and matching leash. "Tom! See my new puppy," she shouted as she ran over and showed it to him.

He stepped from the truck and wanted to hug her, but he didn't have the right yet. Instead, he crouched down and took the puppy. Sweetie romped over and almost knocked them both over.

"I go to camp every day and they let me bring my baby," said Hali. "Her name is Ginger…"

The way Hali suddenly stopped talking and looked up over his shoulder, Tom could tell Karen was standing behind him. He handed the puppy back and stood up. He was overcome with emotion and couldn't turn and look at her or he would blush scarlet. Leaning against the truck on one arm, he tried to summon his courage. After a moment, Hali tugged at his shirt and whispered, "Go help her with the groceries."

Karen had gone over to the vehicle's back gate, opened it and was about to lift out a large case of bottled water. Tom reached over and picked it up, careful not to make eye contact. It might give her an opportunity to tell him to leave. Neither spoke.

Hali grabbed a bag and led her dog to the house with Tom and Sweetie trailing close behind as if they were in her custody. They waited for Karen to unlock the door. He studied her and thanked God when he realized she wasn't hurt. Her skin looked firm and smooth and he had to glance away to get hold of himself.

The door opened and they all streamed in and trooped through the house to the kitchen. Karen dropped her bags on the counter and stood with her back to them. An awkward silence filled the room. Finally, Karen said, "Hali, put the dogs on the porch and get them some water."

We're in! Tom shouted to himself.

Hali went to let the dogs out and quickly signaled for him to put the water in the fridge. He opened the refrigerator door and could see they kept it on the bottom shelf, so he crouched down and began putting the bottles in one at a time. Karen came over and started repositioning the contents so she could stuff in some groceries. Her calf pressed against his back, but neither of them moved. He closed his eyes and forced himself into a calm state until she left.

Finished putting the water away, he stood up. Hali was leaning against the wall looking from one to the other watching to see what would happen next.

"Set the table, sweetheart."

Tom felt the sweat trickle down his face as he watched Hali go to the cupboard and get out the dishes. He looked away until he counted three thumps on the tablecloth. His eyes darted over to Hali who gave him a devilish wink.

Karen put a bag of fresh-picked corn in the sink, then turned to take the apron from the hook and faced him. Tom summoned all his nerve and went over to her. He put a hand on her shoulder, looked her in the eye, and said, "Karen, I came to take you and Hali out for dinner."

She turned her back to him, picked an ear of corn from the bag and started husking it over the sink. He gently gripped her shoulders from behind and buried his face in her hair. "Please, Karen."

She turned to face him and they stood with their bodies touching. He brushed back a shock of hair that had fallen across her face and the glistening blue eyes reached into his soul.

SHE LOOKED UP into the trusting brown eyes. He loved the earth and everything in it, and that was good, for she was of the earth. He would come to know her heartaches, yet he would still want her because he would understand how evil sometimes visits a family and begets evil upon evil until it finally turns on itself.

And she would begin to understand that the young girl who picked up the axe was just trying to survive, and she would come to forgive her. But, she would never understand the devil that came to live in the little boy she loved like her own.

She reached up and touched Tom's face. There was no

decision to love him, just an acceptance of what was destined to be. She ran her hand down his face and spoke in a sweet, warm Western North Carolina cadence. "I'll fix dinner tonight. You can take us for breakfast in the morning."

ACKNOWLEDGEMENTS

I want to begin by thanking C. Bruce Whitaker, Fairview's town historian and columnist for the Fairview *Town Crier,* who generously shared his vast knowledge of the town and inspired one of the main characters in *Render Unto the Valley.*

Bruce has authored a book about the families of his two parents: Whitaker, Reed, Harper and Wright. It contains the carefully researched history of these families and includes charming and interesting stories of the town's early settlers. Titled: The Whitaker Family of Buncombe County, NC, and Geneologies of the Reed, Harper and Wright Families, it is available by writing to: C. Bruce Whitaker, P.O.B. 162, Fairview, NC 28730.

I thank my dear friends, Carolyn and Gary Bleeker of Fairview who introduced me to many of the characters you meet in this novel. Members of the Clarke family clan at the Hickory Nut Gap were also generous with interviews and tours of their farms and the historic Sherrill's Inn, known to the locals as The Big House. They include Annie Louis Perkinson, John and Annie Ager, Jamie Ager, and Will and Susie Hamilton.

History buffs might find John Ager's biography of James

G.K. McClure interesting. In *We Plow God's Fields,* Ager recounts the life and work of the first two members of that family to settle at Sherrill's Inn: James and Elizabeth McClure. They had a daughter, Elspeth, and son, Jamie, who died while in the U.S. Navy. Elspeth married her first cousin, Jamie Clarke and they had six children, many who are still active in the Hickory Nut Gap community. John Ager is married to Annie Clarke and they have four sons. In this novel, I have given them a fifth son and named him Jason.

Tom Fanslow, the land protection director, and Kieran Roe, the director of the Carolina Mountain Land Conservancy, again, were of great assistance in tracing some of the many challenges encountered in their work to save the mountains and farm lands of the Southern Blue Ridge.

The book's plot loosely parallels the conservancy's dauntless efforts to secure the 1600-acre Weed Patch Mountain tract owned by the bankrupt Land Resource's Development in Lake Lure, NC. The chief executive officer of that firm, James Robert Ward, has been charged in Orlando, Florida, with second-degree murder in the death of his wife, Diane.

I am very grateful to Elaine Watkins of Fairview who kindly gave me a tour of her family's historic Pinkerton House that she lovingly restored with the help of her husband. I used it to create the creek house where my heroine lived. Ridgeway Lynch graciously recounted the history of the house his father built on the Charlotte Highway in Fairview that I fashioned into Granny's homeplace. Susie Hamilton, the current owner, kindly showed me through.

Attorney Richard Maita of Asheville was most helpful with information related to deed transfers.

The Fairview Oral History Project of the Friends of the Fairview Library, in association with the Buncombe County Public Libraries and the Pack Memorial Library Special Collections, was also an excellent resource.

I am grateful to the friendly folks at the Mountains Branch Library in Lake Lure who were always helpful in securing the books and data I needed for my research.

Ever since my first visit to the mountains of Western North Carolina, I have been in love with the Folk Art Center on the Blue Ridge Parkway. I am grateful to Nikki Joseph, their curator, who gave me an insight into her daily routine.

I can't thank my editors, Paula Jordan and Sandy Horton, enough for all their advice, diligence and insight on behalf of this manuscript. Linda Ketron, Joanne Goldy, Deborah Chalk, Margie Warwick, Cari Morningstar, Jim Gordon, Elizabeth Pilbeam, Danny Holland and Tammy Owens all deserve my heartfelt thanks for their help and camaraderie during this year-long project.

Carolyn Sakowski and Angela Harwood of John F. Blair have unstintingly supported my efforts to bring this book to publication, and I will be eternally grateful for their astute input and suggestions. I am especially grateful to Debbie Hampton who transformed a picture of the valley into a beautiful cover and did an excellent job of designing the entire outside of the book.

Fred Chappell, a beloved teacher, mentor and friend to writers and poets, kindly read this novel, and I thank him for the wonderful endorsement that appears on the back cover.

Last but not least, I want to thank all my friends in the charming village of Chimney Rock. After hours writing at my computer, I found it refreshing and heartwarming to stroll across the bridge over the Rocky Broad into town and chat with the wonderful people who make up the fabric of this iconic mountain Main Street: Postmaster Elizabeth Dalton, the gang at Bubba O'Leary's General Store, including Peter and Ann O'Leary, Steve Gale of Gales, Pam and Bob Mendenhall of Pam's Place and the crew at The Old Rock Café, to name just a few of the many friendly faces that greeted me and my dog, Lucky, on our daily jaunts.

PLACES MENTIONED in this Book

Other Novels by Rose Senehi

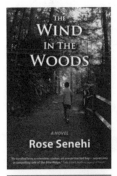

The Wind in the Woods. A romantic thriller that reveals a man's devotion to North Carolina's Green River Valley and the camp he built to share its wonders; his daughter's determination to hike the Blue Ridge—unaware that a serial killer is stalking her; and nine-year-old Alvin Magee's heart-warming discovery of freedom and responsibility in a place apart from his adult world.

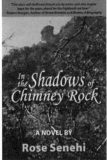

In the Shadows of Chimney Rock. A touching tale of Family and Place. A Southern heiress reaches out to her mountain roots for solace after suffering a life-shattering blow, only to be drawn into a fight to save the beauty of the mountain her father loved. Hayden Taylor starts to heal in the womb of the gorge as she struggles to redeem her father's legacy, never suspecting the man who killed him is stalking her.

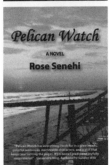

Pelican Watch. Laced with the flavor of South Carolina's low country, this love story is told against a backdrop of murder and suspense. Nicky Sullivan always nurses injured animals, but this time she's going to heal herself. She flees to a SC barrier island and discovers a kindred spirit in Mac Moultrie, a salty retired fisherman. From the moment she meets Trippett Alston, she's smitten, but the dark forces swirling around the island threaten to keep them apart.

Windfall . Lisa Barron, a savvy marketing executive with a kid and a crazy career in the mall business, keeps one step ahead of the FBI.

Shadows in the Grass. Widow, Lynn Richardson, has to make a go of her heritage seed business if she wants to hang on to the farm for her son.

ABOUT THE AUTHOR

" All my life I have loved hearing people's stories, and during the writing of my Blue Ridge Series, I was enthralled with the rich history and tales of the Southern Blue Ridge.

"Researching *Render Unto the Valley,* I found that the challenges the early settlers faced in this often harsh, hard-scrabble environment forged a unique American character that exists to this day in these mountains, hamlets and farms.

"*Render Unto the Valley* takes place in Fairview, NC, where the Hickory Nut Gorge spills through the gap onto a beautiful valley surrounded by layers of hazy blue mountains. In fact, the photograph on the cover of this book was taken from Route 74 looking onto this valley from the gap.

"I wrote this story to express my empathy with the universal desire to hold onto one's land and heritage against the forces that are changing the places we love.

"*Render Unto the Valley* is the third novel in my Blue Ridge series, *The Wind in the Woods,* the second, and *In the Shadows of Chimney Rock,* the first. They are all stand-alone stories that can be read in any order, but readers will start to recognize many of the characters I've created as well as actual places in the Hickory Nut Gorge, Asheville, Fairview, Hendersonville, Chimney Rock and the Lake Lure area.

"Part family saga, part mystery, part love story, the books in my Blue Ridge series tell of the rich history and lore of this historic area as well as the heroic efforts of the people who are working to preserve the beauty of these mountains by staving off unplanned overdevelopment."

"Throughout these books, I have strived to portray historical events as accurately as possible. I do hope you enjoy them."

ROSE SENEHI is known for her contemporary fiction told against a backdrop of environmental concerns.

Senehi moved to Murrells Inlet, SC, in 1996 from Upstate New York where she was active in the shopping center industry while raising her two children, Jessica and David, on the family's hundred-acre farm outside Cazenovia, NY.

She started her first novel, *Shadows in the Grass,* shortly after arriving in South Carolina. "This novel expresses my deep reverence for the way of life of the farmers in the uplands of Central New York and tells the story of the 'seed saving' movement, which is helping to abate the shrinking genetic diversity of plant life on our planet. *Windfall,* my second novel, is a love story woven into the mall development mania that swept the country in the seventies."

While she was actively engaged in real estate, specializing in beach property in Pawleys Island, she wrote *Pelican Watch.* "This novel reflects my warm feelings for the South and the wonderful people I've come to know and love in Pawleys Island and Murrells Inlet—especially those who are working to preserve the beauty and habitat of the lowcountry."

"Part family saga, part mystery, part love story, the books in my Blue Ridge series tell of the rich history and lore of this historic area as well as the heroic efforts of the people who are working to preserve the beauty of these mountains..."

Visit Rose Senehi

www.rosesenehi.com
www.hickorynut-gorge.com
www.rose-senehi.blogspot.com
or email at:
rsenehi@earthlink.net